good girl's guide to love

Guide to Love
Book Four

chelle sloan

Cover Design: Chelsea Kemp Art

Editing: Kiezha Smith Ferrell, Librum Artis Editorial Services

Proofreading: Michele Ficht

To the good girls. The ones who always do the right thing for fear of disappointing others. The ones who sacrifice their happiness to make sure others are taken care of. The ones who are the shoulders to cry on, but never want to bother anyone to return the favor. This one's for you (and your praise kink).

guide to love rule #51

When you meet a hot-as-sin professional athlete, make sure you know your name. Or remember how to speak in general.

1
ainsley

I fling myself back into my chair at the nurse's station as Mia, my best friend and the only reason I'm working today, stares ahead as she bites on the tip of a pen cap.

"Correct me if I'm wrong, but do you ever have anything *appropriate* to say?"

The answer is no, but she doesn't respond, which is strange. Mia's always one for a witty comeback or some sort of playful dig. She's a lot like my sister Quinn in that regard.

Instead she's just staring ahead, pen dangling from her lips as a touch of drool escapes her mouth.

"Earth to Mia!" I say as I snap my fingers in front of her face. "What is with you?"

She nods toward the doors at the end of the hallway of our unit and then tells me everything I need to know. "It's Fury day."

I look toward the direction, and frankly, I'm disappointed in myself for not realizing that it's a group of huge, attractive men who are making my best friend catatonic. This is what happens to Mia every time the Nashville Fury comes for a visit to Nashville Children's Hospital. The pro football team comes in fairly regularly to spread good will and to brighten the spirits of our patients. You'd think Mia would be used to it by now. But my football obsessed best friend always ends up with a dry mouth and bulging eyes.

As for me, sure, I can appreciate a good-looking man. I'm a red-blooded female in my late twenties. But the muscular, athletic guys aren't my type. No, give me a straight-laced, trim build any day of the week.

"They're just men," I say as I sit back down, knowing I have a ton of charting to do before shift change in twenty minutes.

"If they're just men, then the Mona Lisa is just a painting." Mia pulls me up from the back of my scrubs, making sure that every inch of my five-foot-four self can see over the nurses' station. "Look at them. Tall. Handsome. Strong. Like, you just know they can hold you against a wall like it's nothing while murmuring you're a good girl and you can take it."

I look back to her because, frankly, that sounds dangerous. And a little threatening. "You want a man to pin and hold you against a wall?"

She slowly nods, and I'm pretty sure she licks her lips. "Like I need air to breathe."

I shake my head, but not before really trying to see what she's literally drooling over. Maybe I'm missing something.

Walking down the hall is a group of about eight football players, all carrying stuffed animals, balloons, and signed paraphernalia as they start popping into different patient's rooms. Yes, it's sweet and all, and while they are very attractive, I've seen this dozens of times. And heck, I don't even normally work on this floor anymore. I'm now in labor and delivery, but since I used to work here, I'm used to this kind of circus. And while it's amazing for the morale of the patients and families, and I'm sure great PR for the players, it's just another day.

And despite what my best friend says, they're just men.

"I'm loving this for you, but I need to finish up," I say as I sit back down. "If you recall, per our agreement of me picking up this shift, I have to leave by five. Not a minute later."

Mia waves me off as she angles her neck to better see the players making their rounds. "Yeah, yeah. Gotta leave. Family stuff, blah blah. You go finish those charts; I'm going to watch a linebacker read to a seven-year-old."

All I can do is shake my head and laugh as Mia walks away. Now, most days I would watch with her. But not because I want to drool over one of her many football player crushes. No, it's because days like today are the reason I originally wanted to become a pediatric nurse. Because days like today give hope and joy.

I'm settled back into my patient charts when a bump at the back of my chair nearly sends me into the floor, scaring the bejesus out of me. "Ainsley, you need to come with me. Now."

I scowl at her and rub my chest, where my heart is pounding. "Were you running? Wait, where did you come from? Is it a kid?" I'm already halfway out of the chair, thinking the worst.

Mia grabs my shoulders and turns me to face the hallway where the football players disappeared. "No, no. Nothing like that. But really, you need to come with me for thirty seconds to see what I just saw."

I quickly check the time on the computer. Fifteen minutes until I have to get on the road to my hometown of Rolling Hills. And I can't be late. I have important papers I need to deliver to help take down my sister Quinn's boyfriend's mother, who's trying to extort him.

How my family gets wrapped up in these things, I have no idea...

I tug out of her grasp and drop back into my chair. "I really can't."

"Ugh, you're no fun," Mia groans. "You really don't want to see a six-foot-five, tattooed football player taking selfies with your favorite patient?"

Now that gets my attention. Not the tattoos—those have

never really done it for me. But seeing Marcus, a sweet ten-year-old who's been in and out of this unit for most of his life, smile? That I'll stop my paperwork for.

"You play dirty," I say with a sigh as I stand.

"One minute isn't going to kill you," Mia says as she grabs my arm, hustling me down the hall toward Marcus's room. "And this view is worth being a few minutes late for."

"I swear if I'm even one minute late, I'm going to—"

I don't know what the last part of my threat was going to be. It doesn't matter, because at this moment, I know I'm going to be late. And the worst part? I don't even care.

I stand in the hallway, peeking in the room to see Marcus's megawatt smile. He's talking and laughing and handing his phone to the man who currently has my jaw on the floor.

Because holy mother of molasses, this man is hotter than a sidewalk on a July Tennessee day.

"That's what I thought," Mia whispers, apparently reading my mind. "Now aren't you glad you came over?"

I nod and force my jaw back into place. "Who is he?"

"That, my friend, is Linc Kincaid, the Fury's newest tight end. And boy does he live up to his position. I mean, look at that ass…that's Nashville's ass."

I rack my brain, going through the few Fury players I know. Which is just a few, and one of them has been retired. I'm not a football die hard by any means, but when you grow up in a house where football—specifically the Nashville Fury and the Tennessee Volunteers—rule, you learn a thing or two just for survival purposes.

I also learned over the years that big games come with parties and snacks. And I never turned down snacks.

"I've never heard of him," I whisper as I watch him sign autographs for Marcus.

"He got signed midway through last season," Mia says, who knows more football than my brother. And that says a lot. "He wasn't even on a team. Had a ton of potential coming out of college, but got into it with some players at the draft combine. It was a nasty fight that he started. Killed his draft stock. He's been on a few practice squads over the years, but has a bad reputation because he apparently has a hell of a temper. Always getting in fights and shit."

"Really?" I ask, only understanding a little bit of what she said. And what do combines have to do with football? "But look at him. He doesn't seem like the type."

"Oh sweet, sweet, Ainsley. Always wanting to see the good in people. What I'd give to have a day wearing your rose-colored glasses."

I turn my head away from my gawking to glare at Mia. "What's that supposed to mean?"

"It means that I love you, and I love that your heart is so big it overflows from your soul. But with that comes you always wanting to see the good in people, even if it's not really there."

"I don't always do that." Keyword in that statement is always. "I knew my sister's ex-fiancé was a pile of garbage long before she did."

Mia gives me a slow clap. "Congrats! You're now a proper cynic."

"Listen, you can be your glass-half-empty self all you want. I'm going to continue believing that everyone is good until they prove me otherwise. And right now? I'm going to think that about Linc. Because all I see is a professional football player making a kid's day."

"And that's where we differ." Mia pulls me in closer, like somehow that's going to give me a better view of the room. "What I see is the newest bad boy of the Fury, who needs a new start. So he goes with the team on a public relations visit to the children's hospital. That smile? Fake and forced."

I look a little closer at their interaction, and while what she's saying makes sense as a possibility, I'm just not getting that vibe from him.

The smile he's giving Marcus is big and bright. I don't know what they're talking about, but whatever it is, both of their faces are animated. I know I should be watching Marcus—he doesn't have a lot of good days anymore—but I can't. Linc Kincaid is by far the most attractive man I've ever seen in real life.

His dark brown hair is perfectly styled, his locks just long enough to be swept back off his handsome face. The corners of his eyes are crinkled from the smile and laugh he's sharing with Marcus. His jawline is defined, so sharp it could cut glass. My eyes travel down, landing on biceps that are threatening to bust through the fabric of his T-shirt. His skin is tanned, but you can still see every drop of ink on his left arm. It looks like a full sleeve, and even though I've never understood the big deal about tattoos, I can't help but want to get a closer look at the details.

"Oh my!" I don't mean to audibly gasp, but I can't help it when Linc stands from Marcus's bedside. Holy smokes, he's tall. At least six-foot-five. I didn't know men could be that built and also be that tall.

How would that even work...logistically...

"Damn..." Mia says, breaking me from my not-pediatric-floor-appropriate thoughts. "Is our resident good girl having some naughty thoughts right now?"

I shake my head, needing to get a hold of myself. "I was just observing. That's it. No thoughts what-so-ever."

"So you don't think he's hot. He's here because he wants to be. I'm sure it's all true."

I roll my eyes. "You know, if you think this whole thing is fake, why pull me over to watch?"

"Fake can still be hot."

I shake my head at her. "You're ridiculous. And it's time for me to leave."

"Fine. But remember, we're going out Friday night. I know you need multiple business days to prepare."

"Got it!" I yell back as I jog backwards away from her and return to my manic charting.

There's chatter all around me as the players go from room to room, but I block all of them out to finish my paperwork. As I finish up the last of my documentation, I feel a buzzing from my cell phone on the desk.

QUINN

T-minus forty-five minutes! It's go time!

"Shitake mushrooms!" I yell as I scramble up from the chair. "I'm late! I've got to go."

I frantically grab my two tumblers from the station and scramble to slip my phone back into my pocket. "All the charts are caught up. I left notes for the next shift. Can you hand them off?"

"Yes! Go," Mia directs and waves me out of here. "Thanks for covering!"

I know it's rude to not say "you're welcome," but I literally don't have time. I'm supposed to be in Rolling Hills before six o'clock and it's already five fifteen. No way in rush-hour traffic am I going to make it in time.

I dodge and weave through the crowds of people as I scan my card to let me into the nurse's locker room. There are a few others in here, but I don't stop to make small talk, which I'd normally do. Instead, I grab everything—my empty third tumbler, which I had this morning for my juice, my lunchbox, and my purse—before sprinting back toward the exit.

I rush through the door and turn left, because that's how I leave every day. I'm two steps into my power walk when I realize that I'm not on my normal floor, and I should've turned right.

"Darn it," I let out, pivoting to go the other direction.

Next thing I know I'm tumbling backward after bouncing off of someone, and there is no recovering my footing. I go down in a racket of insulated metal tumblers and a squeak.

"Oh, shit! Sweetheart, are you okay?"

I blink a few times, flat on the hospital floor, as the male voice registers in my brain. What the heck just happened? One minute I'm turning around, next minute I'm falling and now.... Well, now I'm looking up at the most beautiful set of green eyes I've ever seen.

"God, I'm so sorry," Linc says as he kneels down to bring us to eye level. "Are you okay?"

I nod—because what are words?—as I assess pain levels.

Butt? A little sore since that's where I landed. Luckily I was blessed with some extra cushion back there so I'm good.

Rest of body? Fine.

Inner self? Mortified. Though that might be more because I realize I've forgotten every word in the English language.

Seriously though? How can a man's eyes be *that* green?

"You turned on a dime. One minute you were marching down the hall, next thing you're running into me like it's Sunday night football."

"I..." Look at me with a word! I try again. "Leave. Car. Go."

My eyes go wide as I realize what just came out of my mouth. Linc is struggling between concern and amusement, but it's a losing battle.

Leave, go, car? What the heck, Ainsley? Full sentences would help right now. He probably thinks I'm some sort of idiot, which I'm not. Or worse, he probably assumes I'm one of those wanna-be football player groupies I've heard Mia talk about.

Joke's on him. I'd probably be acting like this if he were an accountant. Or a professional stamp collector. That's how beautiful this man is. And if he keeps smiling at me the way he is right now— big, bright, and with a hint of mischief—I don't know if I'll ever speak in full sentences again.

"Well, far be it from me to stop any of those things."

He holds out his hand, which completely engulfs mine, as he helps me up from the floor. I lost a hold of my lunch box and one of the tumblers I was carrying, but before I can reach down for them, Linc already has them scooped up.

"Here," he says, his voice a little lower. "You'll probably need these before you leave, car, go."

My cheeks are suddenly on fire, which means that sensation has caught up to my body.

"Thank you," I whisper. It might not be a big sentence, or a loud one, but at least it makes sense. I'm unreasonably proud.

"No need for thanks. I've never been so happy to run into someone in my life."

I think my eyes jump out of my head when his words hit me. I mean, I'm still trying to gain my balance, but still. Who says things like that? No men that I know. Then again, the men I'm normally attracted to don't have a full sleeve of tattoos and could probably be bench-pressed by this man.

I know I should say something, even if it's my one-word sentences, but before I can, a beautiful blonde woman bounces up next to Linc, cell phone in hand, interrupting our moment.

"Hey, Linc, you need to get going," she turns to me, a smile as wide as can be. And it's as fake as the fullness of her lips. I might wear rose-colored glasses, and I always want to see the good in people, but I was also in a southern sorority. I can spot a fake smile a mile away. "I'm so sorry. We need to get going. You know, visit the patients and all. But if you want an autograph, I'm sure I can get you one."

"No, that's fine. Sorry to hold you up." I return the smile, maybe not as fake as hers, but it's close.

I turn to walk away, making sure I check my surroundings before I take a step. But just as I take a step, I feel Linc's hand on my elbow, stopping me in my tracks.

No, actually, his touch literally shocked me into place and now I'm feeling tingles.

"Are you sure you're okay?"

I nod. "Yeah. Sorry again for running into you. But thank you for coming to visit these kids. You're making their day."

The tingles are just about gone, and then Linc smiles. Just a small one. But enough to send the tingles straight to my stomach.

"That's funny. Because you just made mine."

My jaw drops slightly as he sends a wink my way before walking off. I watch him go, really unsure if that all just actually happened.

But if it didn't, and this is some sort of dream, then I never want to wake up.

2

linc

"HOLY CRAP! YOU'RE LINC KINCAID!"

I laugh as I step into the hospital room of a teenaged boy. Maybe thirteen, if I had to guess? He's not as young as some of the patients I visited earlier, but he still has something youthful about him, despite the wires and machines that are surrounding him.

"In the flesh. But since you know my name, wanna tell me yours?"

"Caden."

"Nice to meet you, Caden. You a Nashville Fury fan?"

He nods as he grabs a Fury snapback hat from a bedside table and waves it at me. "Hell yeah, I am! I never miss a game."

I laugh at his language, but only because it sounds like me at his age when I started pushing the boundaries of what I could say and get away with. My poor grandmother didn't know what to do with me.

"That's awesome. Can I see that hat? I don't know if I've seen one of those before."

I have. I think I might even have it. But if I've learned one thing about kids in visits like this is that they love telling people about stuff. And if this boy wants to talk to me about hats, well then, I'm all ears.

"My parents got it for me for Christmas a few years ago," he says. "I wore it every game of the playoffs. And they won the whole thing!"

"Then it's a good luck charm," I say with a smile as I take a seat next to him.

"I don't know about that," he says, his excitement fading. "I think the luck wore off last year. I was wearing it when Brad Rockwell got hurt."

Don't smile, don't smile, don't smile…

"Injuries happen, my man," I say, trying to give a baseline answer. Even though Brad's injury is the reason I'm sitting here today. *And* I fucking hate the guy. "Believe me, you and your hat had nothing to do with it."

In my years of playing football, I've never wanted a player to get hurt. I'm not a superstitious guy, never have been, but even I know it's bad juju to do that. Plus, I wouldn't wish an ACL tear on my worst enemy.

But Brad Rockwell is a shitty fucking human who would be rising up about twenty spots on my people ranking if he was given the title of my worst enemy. We've hated each other since college, when I transferred into the same conference and dethroned him as the best in the league. It didn't help that he went to my rival school.

I'd never met him off the field, so I thought our rivalry was just that. Then I got signed to the Fury to replace him after his injury. Since then, he's made it his mission to make my life miserable.

"I know that," Caden says. "And it wasn't all bad luck. I wore it when you started playing, and the luck came back. Do you remember that one catch you had? It was against Cincinnati when you…"

Do I remember? I could be on my death bed at ninety-eight years old and still remember that catch.

Seventy-five yards. One handed. Leaping over a defensive back who was on my ass the entire time I was running down field. It was a beauty. Play of the year on every sports network. But it was more than a highlight-reel catch. It was the kickoff to my tear through the league. I was shattering numbers. Guaranteed a touchdown a game. I was a fantasy football player's dream come true if they picked me up.

In the blink of an eye, I went from the guy no one would sign because of my problematic past to the guy everyone wished they had taken a chance on. And all during that, the man who hates me most in this world had to sit on the sidelines and watch it happen.

But I can't let him get to me. I have to block out his dirty looks, and his goading words. And more so, keep my "famous temper" in check. Because I've been given a second—hell, my millionth—chance with the Fury, and I'm not about to fuck it up.

Which is why I'm here today. A little good will goes a long way. Plus, I like talking to kids. I know what it was like to be given a hand you should've never been dealt. If I can make them forget about that for even an hour, it's worth it.

And if I run into a cute nurse while doing that, then that's just a bonus.

"So Caden, have you ever been to a game?"

His eyes turn sad, and I immediately realize that may have been the dumbest question I could've asked him. "No. I'm...I'm in here a lot. And the medical bills, it doesn't leave a lot of room for things like football games or extra things. But it's okay. I get to watch every Sunday. And maybe watch with an autographed hat?"

I make a mental note to make sure I get this kid's information so I can get him and his family to a game this year. *And* the name of the nurse with the gorgeous blue eyes and body that had me biting my bottom lip.

Two birds. One stone.

"Damn straight an autographed hat," I say, sending him a

wink as he hands me the flat brim hat back to me. "You know, there are some of the other guys here today. I bet you can fill this up if you want."

His eyes light back up. "Seriously?"

"Absolutely. I'll make sure everyone comes and visits. And if they don't sign it, you let me know. I'll rough 'em up."

His smile punches me in the heart. "You're the best Linc!"

"This is nothing," I say as I hand the hat back to him. "But I need you to do something for me."

"Anything."

"I'm going to need you to get better to make sure you can watch every single game this season. I'm not a guy who believes in things like luck, but you do, so I'm going to need to lean on you for that this year."

"You got it!" he says as we exchange a handshake we somehow make up on the fly. I take a few selfies with him before Katie is standing outside my door, pointing to her watch.

"I gotta get going," I tell him. "But I'm going to be checking up on you this year. Now that I know who our good luck charm is, I have a vested interest in your recovery."

The smile this kid gives me chokes me up. Fuck. He didn't ask for this. Wires and tubes and living in a hospital. And he could be so fucking angry right now—I don't know if I believe in God, but I don't know how a god could make innocent kids like this have to fight for their fucking lives against diseases that they didn't ask for—but he's not. He's a fighter. The good kind. Not like me.

When I was his age, I was mad at the world. Pissed that I was becoming an orphan at thirteen. Having to move school districts because my grandmother was the only one who could take care of me. I was always getting in trouble, fights specifically, a few shoplifting and vandalization charges along the way. But mostly my anger was taken out with my fists. Hell, up until a few years ago, they still were.

But not now. I can't. Not if I want this chance with the Fury to go right.

"Linc, I know you probably hear this a lot, but you're one of my heroes."

I shake my head as I grab Caden's hand. Mostly because I'm trying not to fucking cry.

"Nah, you're mine," I say. "When I was your age, I...let's just say I know what it's like to be in a situation you didn't ask for. And you're handling it much better than I did. So while I'm flattered, how about we be each other's?"

Caden nods and we do our handshake one more time.

"I mean it, you get better," I say as I stand up. "We're going to need you at a game this year."

"Hell yeah!"

I laugh and give Caden one more goodbye before making my way to the nurse's desk. On my way, I pass two of our defensive linemen and ask them to stop into Caden's room. There are about ten of us here today, so I fill them in and ask them to pass the word along to the other guys. But I have another important thing to do before my time is up.

Katie seems to have left me alone, so I try to nonchalantly look for my new favorite nurse. I have a feeling she was on her way out, judging by her words of "leave, car, go," and the cup collection and tote bag she was carrying, but it never hurts to look.

I hate that I didn't get her name. Now I have to go ask her coworkers who the beautiful blonde was with rose-colored cheeks and eyes I could get lost in.

Rookie move, Kincaid. Rookie move.

I've normally gravitated to brunettes, but I couldn't take my eyes off of her. Being a professional football player, I'm around beautiful women more than most. But never in my twenty-eight years have I seen a woman more naturally beautiful. I don't think she had on an ounce of makeup. Her hair was in a long braid that looked like it had been through it, strands poking out everywhere. But her eyes. Holy shit those eyes were a color of blue I've never seen before. I've never seen the ocean, but I have to think that's what it would look like. I caught myself staring at her a few times, which I only got away with because she was just as frazzled as I was, only hers manifested into the cutest way.

And I don't even know her fucking name.

I start heading to the desk where I see a few other nurses, but before I can get there, I see a familiar head of blonde hair step in front of me.

"Ding-ding, Linc. Time's up. We gotta go."

"Come on Katie." Do I sound like a toddler having a tantrum? A little. And I know I pay her to keep me out of the news and to run my schedule, but today she's even more Type-A than usual. "I'm done visiting rooms, but I need to make one more stop. It'll take five minutes."

"I really wish I could let you, because I know how much you love things like this, but we can't today." I stand with my arms crossed, full pout, as she pulls out her tablet, also known as my life schedule. I hate that fucking thing. "We have an hour to get you across town for a podcast interview, and you know traffic is just going to be horrendous. And, something's come up that I need to talk to you about. We need to go. I have a car ready downstairs."

"What happened?"

She shakes her head and tries to give me a reassuring smile. "Let's talk about it in the car."

Feeling like I'm in trouble—because usually I am—I hang my head as we walk down the hall and step into the empty elevator. Katie doesn't say another word, instead spends the entire elevator ride typing something on her phone. But that's not unusual, the woman's job as a publicist is to be chronically online. But I can't be in too much trouble, because she's not swearing at me. Katie's more on the prim and proper side. Hair always in a bun or off her face. Doesn't swear unless I'm really,

really, in trouble. And is always smiling. Like always. Sometimes I wonder if her mouth hurts.

"Good job today," she says, finally making eye contact with me as we drive away. "And as it turns out, we can use all the extra good press we can get."

The good mood I was in just twenty minutes ago is now completely gone. "What does that mean?"

She lets out a sigh and places her hand on my leg, like she's trying to comfort me, before handing me her iPad. "This came out while you were at the hospital. And before you say anything else, I'm already taking care of it."

I grab it out of her hand and stare at the massive headline in a bold font:

***HONEYMOON OVER?** Nashville Fury's Linc Kincaid might be back to his old ways.*

"What the fuck!"

I scroll past the first few sentences of the article—I'm just going to assume that whatever it says is bullshit—before stopping at the first picture I see.

There I am, fist cocked back. I take a closer look, trying to remember where I was, or what I was doing. My teammates are all around me, and not just the few I hang out with on a regular basis, but the entire team.

Then it hits me. This was our last night of training camp. Coach told us to go have fun, so the captains arranged for us to go to one of those adult arcades.

An arcade that had a boxing game.

I remember it vividly now. A bunch of us were trying to get the high score, but our punter wanted it more than anyone. Something about getting his girlfriend a rare Pokémon plush from the prize counter. And since I'm the guy in the locker room who is known more for fighting than football, I took it upon myself to show him how to pull back for a proper—and powerful—punch.

He got the high score.

I got a misleading photo on the internet that could fuck up my world.

"This is fucking ridiculous," I say, tossing the iPad back to Katie. "It's so out of context it's almost funny."

Except it's not. Because the Fury made one thing clear to me when they picked me up last year—and doubled down on it when they signed me to a one-year deal in the offseason—no fights. Not one. If I do, I'm done. Contract void. I'll be back home in Detroit, delivering pizzas and praying that some schmuck will start a semi-pro football team that I can join to make a few bucks.

"I know you didn't do it," Katie says softly. "If you'd fought any of your teammates, I'd have heard about it immediately. And I know you've changed, Linc. I see you doing it every day."

I appreciate her faith in me, but then again, I do pay her to say things and think like that. As my publicist, it's literally her job to keep me on the good side of the news, and if I do get in trouble, to make sure I'm in good graces sooner rather than later.

It was a smart suggestion by my agent to bring her on board. I've never been in a place in my career where I actually have something to lose, so knowing that Katie has my back is reassuring. Because I guarantee you, if this photo got out and she wasn't on my team, I don't know if I'd be handling it as calmly as I am.

"You're taking care of it?"

She nods and pats my leg for emphasis. "It's already handled. I'm trying to dig into who took the picture and who gave it to the gossip blog, but this isn't anything. Coach McAvoy knows nothing happened. Your teammates have vouched for you. I just wanted you to know in case it comes up during the podcast interview.

"Thanks. I appreciate it."

"Just doing my job," she says, with a shrug, like she doesn't know how invaluable she is right now. "You just relax. Let me take care of everything. And luckily, in this case, it wasn't anything we couldn't put out in five seconds. Plus, today was a good day. If anyone reads this garbage of an article, they'll forget about it in three seconds when pictures from today start rolling out. And judging by the notifications I'm already getting, that ball has already started rolling."

"I know," I say. "It's just…things have been so good. No trouble or anything. I just…every time I think I'm getting past the 'bad boy Linc Kincaid' persona, some shit like this pops back up."

She shakes her head and reaches over, grabbing my hand. Sometimes I forget how touchy feely she is. "It was a few photos, Linc. Please don't worry about it. That's what you pay me to do. And I'm happy to do it."

I nod as I move my hand away from Katie's, letting my head fall back against the window.

She's right. It's just one picture. And I've kept my nose clean since I arrived in Nashville last season. This was just a blip. A fake one at that.

But even as much as I try to convince myself, there's that little worm in my brain telling me that nothing has changed. I'm still Linc Kincaid. The troublemaker. The rule breaker. The bad boy of whatever team I've ever played on. And no matter how many hospitals I visit, or how much time passes, that title will never leave me for as long as I live.

guide to love rule #140

There's nothing worse than being the odd man out. Well, that and wet socks, blue cheese dressing, and bad sex.

3
ainsley

"Dɪᴅ ᴛʜᴀᴛ ᴀʟʟ ᴊᴜsᴛ ʜᴀᴘᴘᴇɴ?"

I look over to Quinn, and I can't blame her for asking the question. The last hour would be unbelievable if I just didn't witness it for myself.

But here at The Joint—the hometown bar where each of us have spent our twenty-first birthdays, countless family nights out, and some very not-family-friendly nights too—we as the Banks family helped Porter—the owner of said bar and my sister's former situationship turned roommate turned love of her life—run off his mother, who was trying to extort money from him in exchange for custody of his niece, whom he's been raising.

I can't imagine saying all of that out loud. Just thinking about that insane run-on sentence is hard to wrap my head around. Then again, we're the Banks family. Chaos seems to follow us. But in the end, we always seem to come out on top.

And take those down who've done us, and the ones we love, wrong.

"I still can't believe all of that actually worked," Porter says as he sets down a round of drinks for everyone at the long table in the middle of the bar. Except me. I don't drink. I tried a few times in college, the first being on my twenty-first birthday.

I puked for two days. Just hearing the word Jägermeister makes my body shake.

I tried again, but I just don't think alcohol agrees with me. And why would you do something that's not working for you? If it's not broke, don't fix it. That's my motto. Which is why I stick with cranberry and club soda with a lime. It's quite refreshing.

"Everyone, I'd like to propose a toast." My brother Simon stands up and holds his glass of bourbon in the air. "To Quinn and Porter. May this be the worst thing your relationship will have to endure and from here on out it will be nothing but smooth waters. And to my family, can we please not do this again? I'm getting too old for this shit. Cheers!"

Everyone at the table laughs as we clink glasses and take sips of our drinks.

"I don't want it to be the last time," Stella, the baby of the family, says. "It's fun creating diabolical plans and making assholes realize that karma is, in fact, a bitch."

"Plus we're getting good at it," Quinn adds. "Why put this kind of talent to bed? Oh! Maybe we can start a vigilante business."

"Really, Quinn?" This is coming from Maeve, our oldest, and most practical, sister. "Who do you think we are? Some kind of small-town, southern Avengers?"

Everyone laughs as Logan, her husband and the reason she knows any Marvel references, kisses her temple. "That might've been the sexiest thing you've ever said."

"As much as I do fancy myself a modern-day Iron Man, I don't think that would fly," Simon says. "So unfortunately, our shenanigans are going to stop here. We've all had our fun and taken down our enemies. Ainsley's the only one left, and we know she doesn't need the help of our services."

Everyone nods and tips their glasses at my brother's statement. I chuckle, but it's more of the nervous variety. Is nervous even the right word? I'm not sure. I just know the words "only one left" are now running laps around my brain.

Because…I mean…

I quietly shrink back from the conversation as I look around the table. Every one of my siblings is laughing, smiling, and has love radiating from them. Porter has his arm around Quinn as Grace, his niece, sits on her lap. Logan has Maeve in an embrace as he kisses her forehead. Stella is whispering something into Emmett's ear that's making her normally stoic boyfriend smile. Simon and his wife Charlie aren't having such an intimate moment—Charlie is currently checking my niece's diaper—but the way he looks at her, even during something so mundane and pretty stinky—is inspiring.

And then there's me. Sitting at the end of the table because that's where the extra seat would fit. No one is holding my hand. No one is kissing my cheek after a day that will go down in Banks family history. No one's talking to me low, sharing a secret or whispering something only meant for us.

It's just me.

The ninth wheel.

The reason we need an extra chair at a table, because I make the numbers uneven.

I'm the cheese. And I'm standing alone.

I pick up my drink, slowly sipping it as the realization overwhelms me. I mean, I knew this. It's not brand-new information. Once Quinn finally admitted that Porter was much more than her roommate—and former situationship—I did the mental math. So I don't know why it's hitting me now? Maybe Simon's phrasing? Maybe seeing everyone together in one space? Maybe both?

But whatever the reason is, I'm very, *very*, aware of my singleness.

"Ainsley, I love you. We're perfect together. Come back to me and come with me."

I physically shake myself out of that train of thought. Dang… I really must be headed for Depression City: Population, Ainsley, if I'm even entertaining any thoughts about Dr. Jonathan Ainsworth.

Jonathan moved away almost three years ago now, and I think that was the last time I even thought of him. I remember it distinctly because it was a hot fall day when he was literally on his hands and knees begging me to come back to him. That he'd been crying for five days because of the heartache, and that he had to move to San Antonio to get away from me. Unless, of course, I wanted to come with him.

It was very dramatic. And I'm saying that as a member of the Banks family.

He was everything I thought I wanted. A mild-mannered pediatric surgical resident. Came from a good family. Clean cut. Polite. Ambitious. Wanted to spend every second of every day with me when we weren't working.

No doubt he would've been here with me today. Sure, he might not've joined in on the antics of helping take down Porter's mother, but he'd have come for the celebratory drinks. Though he probably would've asked to drive separately, because he'd have to be in bed by nine. But he would've been here. And I wouldn't have been alone.

As much as I'd love to have someone next to me, I need to remind myself why I'd rather be here alone. That Jonathan wasn't right for me. We weren't right together. That being together all the time is great, until it isn't. I don't know what true love is supposed to feel like, but I know what I had with Jonathan wasn't it. Even in the beginning, I never had the butter-flies. Couldn't tell you what tingles feel like.

I definitely didn't have the orgasms. I still think those are a myth.

So yes, I'm alone now. And that stinks. But if my options are being the ninth wheel or being Mrs. Jonathan Ainsworth, then I'll be the odd man out any day of the week.

Plus Ainsley Ainsworth? Absolutely not.

"Yo! Earth to Ainsley!"

I jump a little in my seat at Quinn's outburst. "I'm sorry. Did you say something?"

"What were you daydreaming about?"

"That wasn't daydreaming," Maeve says, giving me a skeptical look. "She smiles when she daydreams. There was no smile. Is everything okay?"

I never lie to my family, or anyone really, but there's a first for everything. Because I'm not about to bring down the mood of the day because I'm feeling a little lonely. I'm surely not going to bring up the subject of Jonathan—that would send Simon into a rage, and now he has brothers-in-law to help him bury bodies.

And Quinn.

Plus, today isn't about me. It's about Porter, Quinn, and Grace, who's currently giving Simon the side-eye as he tries, and fails, to make her smile.

"Nothing important. Sorry, though. Did you ask me something?"

I notice that all my sisters are now thoroughly examining me, but luckily, none of them press me on my clear deflection.

"What I was asking was how the Fury visit to the hospital was?" Quinn asks. "I figured it had to be a big one if it made you late today."

"What!" Maeve yells, who arrived after I did. "Ainsley was late?"

"By like five minutes," I protest.

Maeve shakes her head in disbelief. "Damn. Even after everything that happened, I think that might be the biggest news of the day."

"Right?" Stella says. "For the first time in history, Ainsley Banks didn't follow specific directions and *was late*."

"I mean, what's next?" Quinn asks. "Porter! Go check behind the bar. I bet she stole a few bottles of liquor."

I narrow my eyes at my sister as the rest of the table snickers. "You're being dramatic."

"I'm not the one headed for a life of debauchery."

I add in my own dramatics with an eye roll, which gets a snicker from the rest of the table. "Yes. I was late. I picked up a shift today on Mia's unit. A few Nashville Fury players came for a visit. Time got away from me. That's it."

As I'm not going to mention where my traitorous brain was taking me a few moments ago, I'm *also* not going to be bringing up the six-foot-five football player who is the entire reason I was late. If I tell them that I literally ran into one of the Fury's biggest stars, I'll never hear the end of it, I just know it.

"Who was there?" Simon asks, suddenly in fan-boy mode. "Was Bryce the quarterback there? I doubt Cole Campbell was there. He and his wife just had a baby. Oh! What about Linc Kincaid? Dude is a fucking beast. Won me a shit-ton of money last year."

I feel my cheeks heat at the mention of Linc's name. Or maybe it's because I'm remembering the smile he gave me that I could feel across every inch of my body. All I know is I need to fix my face immediately and not give anything away.

"I don't know? Maybe?" God, I'm such a bad liar. I can't see myself, but no way am I believable right now. "There were a lot of them there. And you know I don't know football."

"Do you mean to tell me you don't know the name of the man whose eyes you were staring into a couple of hours ago?"

My neck whips to Stella, and if I was blushing before, I'm sure it's as red as a tomato right now. "Excuse me?"

Stella turns her phone to me. "Is this not you and said football player? My, my…Ainsley's had quite the day."

I grab her phone to study it closer. The actual picture is of a patient posing with one of the other players I didn't meet. But in the background, through the glass wall of his hospital room, is Linc and I, having a moment that I'm going to remember forever.

My mind replays the interaction. I'm going to guess, based on that I'm actually looking down and not into his hypnotizing eyes, that I was probably apologizing for the tenth time about running into him. I can tell I'm blushing, so maybe it's when he said I made his day. Which I'm sure I didn't, but it was nice of him to say it nonetheless.

"Let me see!" Quinn grabs the phone out of my hands, and Maeve runs around the table to get a look for herself. "Damn, sis. That's more than a moment. That's a *look!*"

"Are you serious?" Simon jumps from his seat, coming to look at the phone, because despite being the only male sibling, he loves gossip maybe more than we do. "Ainsley! What is going on, and why is one of my favorite football players giving you a fuck-me smirk?"

I let out a deep sigh, because despite not wanting to admit all of this, it looks like what I want is not a consideration here. "I ran into him. Literally. And whatever you think, it's not an eff-me smirk. He was just being polite and making me feel better because it was an awkward situation."

"Wait," Quinn says as she sits back down. "Do you mean actually literally, like you physically ran into him? Or like how Stella likes to say literally but she means figuratively?"

I hold up a number one to the question. "The first. I was running out of the nurse's locker room because I was running a little late to get here—which *was* because of the Fury visit, so I didn't technically lie—and I wasn't looking where I was going. So yes, ran right into him. Fell on my butt and everything."

"Holy shit," Porter says, a little laughter in his voice. "I had an idea what I was getting into with this family, but every time y'all tell a story, I'm amazed a little more that these kinds of things happen to the Bankses."

"We are one of a kind," Quinn says. "And now my sister is going to get with a hot football player!" She raises her hands like she just scored a touchdown personally.

"That's not happening," I say definitively. "I ran into him. I fell on my butt. I apologized. He didn't make me feel bad about it. The end. We didn't even actually exchange names."

"Neither did Emmett or I at first," Stella said. "And look where that got us."

"You two are different," I say. "You did it because you were running from a wedding. I did it because I was panicking that I was late. It's not like I'm ever going to see him again."

"But you want to," Quinn sing-songs as she wags her eyebrows.

I narrow my eyes at my sister, because she knows I can't lie to her. They all do. It's not in my blood. I've always been a rule follower, and telling the truth is my number-one rule.

But Linc isn't my type. I might not've met my match with Jonathan, but that's what I'm looking for. He's my speed. Not a six-foot-five, larger than life, tattooed football player who gives smirks and winks to embarrassed nurses. Sure, he might be hot, but that doesn't mean anything. Plus, if what Mia said is true about his past, then he's *definitely* not my type. I'm the good girl of the Banks bunch and bad boys are not my scene.

"No, I don't," I say as confidently as possibly. "You know he isn't my type."

"Oh, and Jonathan was?" Quinn says sarcastically. "I love you, but if you honestly tell me that a five-foot-seven, balding, clingy twerp is your type and not this guy? Then damn…we as sisters didn't do our job."

"Jesus Christ, Quinn," Maeve says, shaking her head. "You need a fucking filter."

"Did I tell a lie? Tell me the lie, and I'll take it back. And I didn't even mention his weird weather fascination. Who logs daily humidity levels?"

"I still don't get that one," Simon says. "I asked him to go golfing once and for the entire round he told me about the dew points and barometric pressure. It was horrible."

I almost forgot about his weird weather-tracking hobby. Though the information I learned involuntarily via being around him has come in handy when I'm trying to decide if I need to bring my rain boots to work.

"Y'all, we're missing the bigger picture," Stella says. "You ran into him, Ainsley. Literally bounced off of him. How is that not the movie meet-cute that you've been dreaming about since you were a little girl? How is our soulmate-believing sister *not* saying this is fate?"

She's right. I do believe in that. Soul mates. The invisible string. If it has even the smallest hints of a happily ever after, I'm the champion of it. But this wasn't it.

Right? No. My moment isn't coming at the hospital with me on the floor and a bruised butt.

"I'm just saying, if you run into him again—literally or figuratively—I'd maybe drop your name." Stella sets down her phone on the table, the picture now taking up her whole screen. "Because if any man ever looked at one of us like that, you'd be telling us to marry him on the spot."

I don't say anything in response to Stella, and thankfully, the conversation flows to another topic, and within the hour, everyone is saying their goodbyes and heading home.

When I slip into my sensible hybrid sedan, I turn it on but don't go anywhere. After the conversation turned away from me, I thought I was over my sad single blues. That's until I watch as Emmett helps boost Stella into his massive truck. And look on as Logan kisses Maeve's forehead before closing the door behind her. Quinn and Porter stand hand-in-hand at the door of The Joint, waving goodbye, Grace opening and closing her small hand too.

They're all going to go home and fall asleep next to their people. Someone that isn't blood related is going to say "I love you."

Then there's me. I'm going to climb in bed and curl up with my Kindle and read about an epic love that might one day find me. No one is going to kiss me goodnight. No one's going to hold me in their arms as we fall asleep together. I could've had it...but I sent it away.

"No, Ainsley," I whisper to myself as I turn on the car. "You're better off single. He wasn't it. So as lonely as you are, you are not, under any circumstance to call him. Or text him. Don't like a social media post. Don't go look up his hospital profile. Just drive."

I let out a breath and put my phone on the dock when I notice a text come through. And thank God I wasn't driving, because when I see who it's from, I would've no doubt driven into a concrete road divider.

JONATHAN

Hey you. Can we talk?

I quickly close out of the text and throw my car into drive. I know I won't text him back if I'm on the road, and maybe after my drive back to Nashville I'll conveniently forget he messaged me.

Or by the time I get home I'll convince myself that it's a sign and message him back.

Only time will tell.

4

line

"Lincoln Kincaid! Get your ass up! We're going out!"

I groan from my couch as I hear Wyatt, my best friend, teammate, and annoying neighbor, barge through my door. I say this to myself about once a week, but I really regret giving him a key.

I don't move as I watch him help himself to a beer from my refrigerator.

"Make yourself at home."

Wyatt tips the bottle to me as he takes a seat. "I will. At least, for the next thirty minutes, as we wait for you to get ready."

I don't move an inch. "You're going to be waiting a hell of a lot longer than thirty minutes, because my ass is staying right here."

"Wrong. You're getting up, and you're coming with us to karaoke. It's Maddox's birthday so you have no choice."

That makes me snort laugh. "Actually, you're wrong. I do have a choice, because this is America. And I'm absolutely the fuck *not* going to karaoke."

Normally I love celebrating birthdays. Maddox is a good dude—a safety who's a few years younger than me who's going to be a fucking stud in this league when he hits his peak. But a night out with my team, singing bad songs from our youth badly, sounds like the worst night ever. Especially when I had a night of pizza and a binge watch of *The Sopranos* on deck.

"Why would I want to do that?" I ask. "We just spent the last month together every fucking day at training camp. We should be sick of each other and wanting some space before the season starts."

"Oh, but that's where you're wrong," Wyatt says. "We need more time together. Team bonding and shit."

My groan echoes off the walls. "Well, then call me a bad teammate, because I'm going to sit this one out."

I'm all for team bonding, especially because I was thrown into the fire last year so I really was learning my teammates on the fly. Well, everyone except Wyatt. We played together in college. But other than him? I was lining up around a bunch of strangers.

So yes, in theory, getting to hang out with my teammates would be a good thing. But considering the last time I went out I ended up on a gossip blog—and that was an organized team outing by our coaches and somehow I was still painted the bad guy—I really don't think a night of karaoke is a good decision.

"Oh, come on," Wyatt says. "Is this about that picture? The bullshit one?"

"Partly," I admit. "Listen, the season hasn't even started. I don't need any fuckery happening. It's safer to stay at home where I know nothing can be leaked or taken out of context."

"So you're going to stay home the whole season?" Wyatt asks. "Here, on this ugly-ass couch, is where I'll find Linc Kincaid when he's not on a football field?"

I pat the cushion next to me. "Exactly. It's quite comfy."

Do I like this decision I just made for myself? Not at all. I'm a social guy. Always have been. Which is probably why I've always found myself getting into trouble.

When I was in grade school, I was just the loud kid who liked to cause commotion. A little bit of a prankster. A bit of an actor.

And sure, I got in trouble more than a few times, but it wasn't anything to worry about.

Then that fateful day happened when I was thirteen. The day my life changed.

The day my parents died.

That's when the innocent little pranks became near crimes. Fights were regular. I was hanging with a crowd who skipped school and did drugs. During those years, I spent more time in in-school suspension than anywhere else and teetering on the brink of a stint in juvenile detention.

Then I met my high school football coach. Coach Henry saw something in me no one else did. He saw an angry kid who needed an outlet. So he gave me a football helmet and told me to start hitting shit.

It was the day that changed my life. And only once since then have I let that anger get the best of me—and it nearly ruined my life.

So I'm taking lessons of the past and putting them into practice today. Diving head first into football. No distractions. Eye on the prize. If I'm not tempted by trouble, I won't get into any.

"I get what you're doing," Wyatt says. And if anyone does, it's him. He's the only one who knows my whole story. So if anyone could understand this, it should be him. "But I actually think hiding is the worst thing you can do."

I quirk an eyebrow. "Explain."

"For starters, humans aren't meant to be kept inside. You need to go out. Be among the people."

Okay, this doesn't sound like my best friend at all. "Says the man who owns a cabin in the mountains because every few months he needs to get away from humanity.'"

"But that's just a break. You don't see me staying in tonight." Wyatt stands up and does his best to physically pull me up from the couch. He might be a lineman who I know for a fact can bench-press my body weight, but his efforts are futile as I go boneless against his hold.

"Get your ass up, Kincaid. Get out of this house and come have some fun!"

"Get off of me," I say, pushing him away as I finally sit up. "Why do you want me to go so bad? There's going to be plenty of other teammates out. You don't need me to hold your hand."

Wyatt was my first true friend when I transferred to Mississippi State, but we didn't start out that way. Like most of the guys there, he was recruited out of high school. I, on the other hand, went the junior college route first, since I didn't start playing football until my sophomore year of high school and didn't have the best grades.

We were both on offense—he's on the line, and me being a tight end, I'm in enough of their plays that we got to know each other pretty well.

Unfortunately, my old habits came back the second I stepped foot in Starkville. Instead of hanging out with Wyatt and the players who kept their noses clean, I started cozying up to the guys who thought they were untouchable. The ones who smoked weed behind the scenes and paid for tests to keep their grades up. I know the saying is that insanity is doing the same thing over and over and expecting a different outcome, and that's probably what I was—insane for hanging out with guys who were exactly like the ones I grew up with and expecting that I wasn't going to get in trouble.

And I did. Busted cheating on a test. And it wasn't even a hard one. Your basic economics class. But of course I was given the easy way out, so I had to take it. I was put on academic probation and suspended a few games. I felt like I had blown my chance at having a solid college career and maybe making it to the pros.

That's until Wyatt stepped in. He invited me to study with him and some of the other linemen that night. Before I knew it, we got into a routine where it was morning lifts and night-time study sessions. Hell, we ended up moving in together during our last season. He's the one who kept me out of trouble. The one who kept an eye on me and made sure I didn't make any bone-headed moves.

Until the big screwup. But neither Wyatt, nor God himself, could've stopped me that day.

Needless to say, I owe this man more than I'll ever be able to repay him.

But not enough to go to karaoke tonight.

"Can't a guy just want to hang out with his best friend?"

I raise an eyebrow to that. "He can. But in the entire time I've known you, Wyatt Atkins, hanging out has been you sitting on this couch with me and grabbing a beer. Not going to a loud bar and hearing bad singing amplified by a microphone."

"Come on, Linc. I need a wing man."

Now I know he's serving me a line of bullshit. If there's one thing that man doesn't need, it's a wing man. He's not a manwhore or anything, but if he sets his sights on a woman, whether it's for a night or for longer, he has no problems approaching her and taking matters into his own hands. So, if he's forcing me to go out, there has to be another reason behind it.

"Bullshit. Try again."

Wyatt lets out a sigh like he really thought that was going to work. "Okay, fine. I lost a bet to Maddox, and I have to sing an embarrassing song of his choice."

I spit out a laugh. "And how does this involve me?"

"Because you're my duet partner."

I look around the room to see if anyone else has suddenly entered. "Me? Since the fuck when?"

"Since always."

"We've literally never sang karaoke together before."

"Yes, we have."

"In the locker room or in your truck doesn't count." Wyatt starts to say something, but I cut him off with a raised finger. "And neither does us being drunk at a house party."

Wyatt's eyes narrow. "Come on. If I have to sing fucking

"Islands in the Stream," I need a duet partner. I need my best friend. Come on, Linc…I'll owe you."

Shit, this is serious. Wyatt doesn't throw out potential IOUs often. He doesn't like feeling indebted, whether that's something silly like a karaoke night or something to the extent of borrowing money. If he throws that out, he means business.

"Really? This is worthy of a coveted Wyatt Atkins marker?"

He nods. "If I don't do this, I have to let Maddox and the rest of the defensive backs use my cabin during the bye week."

"Oh, shit," I say. Wyatt's cabin is sacred. No one's been there, not even me. "Yeah, I get why karaoke wins."

"Which is why I need you," he says. "I know why you want to stay in. This seems safe. Believe me, I get it. But you can't hide. Plus, I'll be there. So will Maddox and the rest of your teammates. We'll make sure, beyond a shadow of a doubt, that nothing will happen that will even remotely make people think you're trying to get into a fight."

I feel my walls starting to crack and slump back on the couch. "I hate that I trust you."

A slow smile forms on his face. "No, you don't."

I don't, but I do need to make one thing abundantly clear before I actually commit. "I'll go. I'll sing. But this needs to be a low-key night. Katie just put out the fire with that picture. I can't be starting shit all over again."

Wyatt nods in understanding. Luckily for me, he knew that photo was bullshit from the minute it came out on the internet. Apparently, he was one of the loudest advocates for me to our coaches and gave a full description of what actually happened.

Yet again, Wyatt coming to my rescue. I guess the least I can do is sing some Dolly and Kenny.

"I understand," Wyatt says. "Did Katie ever figure out how that photo got out?"

"She has no idea," I say as I make my way back to my room. "I'm just glad it blew over as quick as it did."

The hospital visit I did earlier this week helped a ton in that department. The photos that Katie took and posted on my social media, along with the others that families posted on their own, made any headline of the not-fight fade away. I also jumped on a few podcasts and radio interviews where I talked about the season, wanting to repeat what I, and in turn the Fury, did last season, and when they asked me about troubles from my past, I made sure to say that those days were far behind me.

And I mean that.

For my entire football career, I've been this guy with nine lives. I've survived suspensions and punishments. Not being drafted and living off of practice squads. Every time I think I've had my break, I do something stupid to ruin it. I might not be the guy who graduated at the top of his class, but even I know I can't have that many lives left.

Which is why I know I can't fuck this up with the Fury. Brad is still injured, so I'm walking into the season as the starting tight end. But he's on the mend and is set to come back sometime during the year. I'm not sure what's going to happen when their ten-million-dollar-a-year player comes back, but I do know that if I'm playing my best ball, it's going to be hard to bench me. And even if they do decide to go with Brad, if I put together good enough film and make myself an asset on offense, then another team will sign me.

But that's only if I put the bad decisions of my past behind me.

Which is why tonight I have to make sure that I can have fun with no trouble. No bad decisions. Minimal drinks. Certainly no women. I don't have time—or spare lives—to have distractions leading me down paths I don't know if I can navigate. I want to say that I'm at a point in my life when I can make good decisions and stay on the right path, but I also know I've said that before and failed miserably.

I can't fuck this up. I have too much riding on this season.

And I have a feeling I'm on my last life.

guide to love rule #92

Be careful what you manifest. Sometimes it can be a winning lottery ticket. Sometimes it's your horrible ex.

5
ainsley

Dear world, what did I do to tick you off?

All I wanted was a night out with my bestie. When Mia and I made plans, it was because we had the same night off for the first time in months, with a corresponding day off tomorrow to recover. I might not drink, but that doesn't mean I don't like to sleep in after a late night out.

But as the week's gone on, and the more into my "Ainsley is super-duper single" depression that I've got, the more I was looking forward to this. I don't know if it was the talk with my siblings, or the still-unanswered text I received from Jonathan, but it felt like every day the cloud above me got bigger and bigger.

Which is why I wanted a nice, quiet night out with my best friend where I could enjoy her company, forget that I'm extremely single, have no prospects, that my ex texted me, and the most action I've gotten from a man in a really long time is when I ran into a football player this week.

Is that too much to ask for?

Apparently that answer is yes. Because we're sitting at my favorite bar, and everywhere I look, I'm smacked across the face in my aloneness. Couples as far as the eye can see. Bachelorette parties in droves—even more than the usual for a Nashville Friday night in August. Even my favorite bartender is now sporting a wedding ring.

Sometimes I wish I did drink, because I don't think the song "Crying in the Club" meant crying into your club soda.

"Okay, what gives?"

I pick my eyes up from my sad mocktail and look to Mia. " What do you mean?"

The look she shoots me clearly says that she's not buying my fake confusion. "We've been here for a half-hour, and you haven't smiled once. That in itself is very un-Ainsley-like."

I start to defend myself, but she holds a finger in the air, signaling that she isn't done. "Now, if it was just that, I wouldn't be panicking. But you've barely said two words. The ones you *have* said were asking about me and giving me one-word answers when I ask you anything in return. And while I love that you're the best listener I know, tonight I feel like you're purposefully not talking."

She knows me too well.

"So," she continues. "You're going to tell me what has my best friend in the biggest funk I've ever seen her in, or I'm going to go into great detail about Cleopatra's sister and her role with—"

"Please no!" I moan. I love Mia, but I really don't understand her fascination with this portion of history. "You wouldn't."

"Bet. Now spill."

I start to say what I'm feeling, but I immediately swallow it down. Because I'm single. So what? Is that worth a vent session? It feels selfish to bring down the mood because I'm in a rut. "It's nothing. It already sounds silly just thinking about it."

"Nope. We're not doing this," Mia says, leaning across the table and tipping my chin up so I can't look away. "Whatever you want to get off your chest, we're going to do it. And if it takes five shots of whiskey to get there, well then goddamn it, that's what we're going to do."

"Did I start drinking and you didn't tell me?"

She shakes her head. "Those are for me. Because if something has you this down, I know it has to be something big."

I shrug again, knowing that it *is* big to me. And I know that Mia would listen to every word and return the ear and shoulder to cry on that I've given her so many times. But when you've gone your whole life being the listener... Well, it's hard to flip that switch and sit on the other side of the conversation.

"Actually, I've changed my mind. I choose a thirty-slide power point on Julius Caesar."

"For the only time ever, I'm going to deny that request. Now spill."

All I can do is groan and send her an angry look. Which knowing me probably isn't that threatening. "Fine. But you play dirty."

She smiles and sips on her espresso martini as I try and figure out how I want to start this conversation. I don't know why this is so hard. Mia's my best friend. I know she's going to listen to me and be the girl's girl that she is. It's just...saying this all out loud makes all of these feelings very real. And very vulnerable.

"I almost called Jonathan a couple days ago. And then, out of nowhere, he texted me."

Saying the name of my ex-boyfriend makes Mia sit directly up in my chair. I also watch as she does her best to swallow her drink and not spit it in my face.

"Hold, please."

I look on in curiosity as Mia starts digging in her purse. "What are you doing?"

"Because the night you finally realized you can do better and left that jackass, I kept a list of reasons why you ended it, in case you ever felt bad for him or had a moment of weakness. I was never going to let you forget all the reasons why being single is better than being with Dr. Stalker. And it's finally coming into play."

"His last name is Ainsworth."

"Could've fooled me."

I always tried to defend Jonathan, which now I know was my kindness blinding me to his red flags. Even now, I feel bad that Mia calls him Dr. Stalker, even though she's probably right.

When we were a couple, if we weren't working, we were together. And again, at the beginning it was great. I had dated a few guys in college, and I always felt bad that I wanted to be around them seemingly more than they wanted to be around me. So finding a guy like Jonathan was perfect.

Or so I thought.

When I broke up with him, I thought he'd be sad, which he was. And I was too. It sucks realizing after spending more than a year together that you just aren't the right fit. But better to end it when you know then to keep trying to find magic that isn't there, right?

That's how I felt. Jonathan felt another way. He'd leave letters on my car. Send flowers constantly at home and work, with notes begging me to take him back. It was…a lot. Overwhelming in the worst kind of way. Mia, along with my siblings, all suggested that I needed to do something to stop it, but I felt like a restraining order was a bit excessive. Especially because nothing was threatening. Luckily, it didn't come to that because within a week of me breaking up with him he declared that he couldn't live in Nashville without me and took the job in Texas.

"I'm glad you kept that list, but I don't need it," I say, half believing the words coming out of my mouth. "I don't know, this week just felt…for the first time in a long time, I felt really alone. I've never minded being single. I knew breaking up with Jonathan was right for me because *he* wasn't right for me. But something about this week, on top of his out-of-nowhere text, just got me really acknowledging how alone I truly feel."

I go on to tell Mia about this past week: helping out my family, coming together for the greater good. Then me sitting at a table, the extra chair needing pulled up at the end, and feeling more alone than ever.

"There I was, sitting around my family during this happy occasion, and all I wanted to do was sneak out and cry in a corner somewhere. Then I felt selfish for feeling bad about me. Rinse, repeat, and then a text received, and that's been my week."

"Wow," Mia says, taking a healthy swig of her martini before continuing. "First, I want to say that I'm glad you didn't text him. That would've required a whole other intervention."

I laugh. "I know. It was a true moment of weakness. But kudos to me for leaving him on read."

"You're right, I tip my glass to you," she says. "Also, it's okay to feel alone and sad. Even when you're happy for others. You've been single for a long time, and it's a natural feeling. Are you trying to date? You haven't said anything, but I also didn't want to push."

All I can do is shrug at her question. "I downloaded a dating app a few months ago. I deleted it in two days. One man asked me if I liked horseback riding, and if so, then I could ride him. Another sent me a picture of his…" I visibly shiver. Because who says penis pictures? "That was too much for me. How do men just do that?"

"It's too much for anyone. But I'm proud that you tried."

"Thanks, I guess." I slump in my chair. "I just felt like I had to try something. I've also seen videos about looking confused at a grocery store? Maybe that's where I'll meet my soulmate."

"Nah, girl. The hardware store. That's where you look confused," Mia says. "That's where I plan into find my lumberjack."

"Lumberjack? After the way you drooled over the football players this week, I figured you were on a football player kick."

"I'm *never* not looking for a lumberjack," she says. "Now, don't get me wrong, if I ran into a Fury guy tonight, I wouldn't say no to a night of fun. But end game? A six-foot-five man of the woods with a cabin and a healthy 401K."

"That's oddly specific."

"I like what I like. What can I say?"

I laugh at my best friend, who's always marched to the beat of her own drum. I knew she was going to be a special one the first day we met at orientation at Nashville Children's. I had my notebook out, ready to take detailed notes on everything our guide was about to tell us. I even had color-coded pens to make sure I could keep my notes organized. I came equipped with two water bottles because I didn't know when we'd get a break, along with pretzels and a granola bar in case I got hungry. All Mia brought was a can of Monster Energy and her cell phone. Later I found out her phone died ten minutes into training and that the Monster was her second of the day.

It was nine in the morning.

I asked specific questions that took me ten minutes to piece together. She at one point blurted out a question about what the acceptable reactions were if someone stole your lunch.

On paper, we shouldn't have become friends. We have nothing in common. But when you work enough traumas together, and need to literally pick your person up from the floor after they lose a tiny patient, you're bonded forever.

That, and I always have gum.

"Okay, so let's recap," Mia says. "You're lonely and don't want to be single anymore, and your best option, which isn't an option, is your ex who randomly texted you this week?"

"Yes."

"Dating apps suck."

"Big time."

"And despite you wearing a neon sign at the grocery store announcing that you're single, no one is randomly approaching to ask you out."

I shake my head. "I even made sure to put on makeup and change out of my scrubs before I went."

Mia takes a deep breath and reaches over to hold my hand. "Well, my friend, I hate to be the one to tell you this."

My heart sinks. "What?"

"I think it's time we shake things up a bit."

That doesn't sound fun. "What's that mean?"

"It means you're in a slump. You work with the same people and see them every day, and there are no prospects there. Unless you haven't told me a huge secret, there's not a former love of your life pining for you back in Rolling Hills. You see the same people day in and day out, which means you're never going to meet someone new."

I groan, but only because she's right. My days blur together for the most part where I can't tell one from the other. Dating apps aren't my jam, and I'm not the kind of extrovert that would ask someone out if I saw them in the wild, and clearly, no one is asking me for my phone number. Even when I literally run into them. "So what do you suggest we do? Because if you're making me do this, I'm not doing it alone."

The grin that forms on her face is worthy of the Cheshire Cat. A frisson of alarm runs down my spine. "Mia...why are you smiling like that?"

I was concerned before. But now that she's wagging her eyebrows, I'm down right petrified.

"Let's go do karaoke."

Thank goodness I wasn't having a sip of my drink, because I would've spit it in her face. "That's your idea of mixing it up? Can't we just go to another bar? Or line dancing? That doesn't sound so bad, and I can dance much better than I can sing."

She shakes her head. "I love you. You're my sister from another mister. But you play it safe. In every aspect of your life. We come to the same bar because it's comfortable. You play by every rule in the book. You don't swear. You don't drink. You're the most non-risk taker in the world."

"Exactly," I say. "And you'd have to get me to drink a whole bottle of something if you think I'm going to stand in front of a bunch of strangers and sing."

I was a competitive dancer my entire childhood, so being on a stage doesn't scare me. But all those people staring at you?

Likely laughing at you, especially when you're me and can't carry a tune? No, thank you. That sounds horrible.

"How about this? Baby steps," she says. "Let's just go to the bar. See what it's about. You don't have to sing. But at least by doing this, mixing it up in this small way, you're going to at least break the monotony. What can it hurt?"

"Oh, I don't know," I say, grasping for straws because I really don't want to go to a karaoke bar. "What if tonight is the night? What if I've been coming here for years, and the one night I'm not here is when my future husband walks through the door? Would you ever be able to forgive yourself, Mia? Huh?"

I know that's a stretch. And by the loft of Mia's right eyebrow, she agrees. But I really, really, don't want to go to karaoke. "I doubt that tonight of all nights, after we've been to this bar countless times over the years, that this is the one where your future husband is going to suddenly appear. And if he does, then it's proof that God is a man. Because no woman would ever do you dirty like that."

"Let's see. Let's look at the door right now and see if my future husband is about to walk in."

Mia groans but indulges me as we both turn toward the entrance. From where we're sitting in the middle of the bar, we have a straight shot.

Which is how we don't miss the man walking through.

The blast from my past.

"What the frick…"

I rub my eyes. No way am I seeing what I think I'm seeing. Because walking through the door, with a confidence I didn't know he had, is Jonathan Ainsworth.

A coy smile.

Sharply dressed.

And with hair?

"Is that who I think it is?"

Okay, if Mia's seeing him too, then it's not just me. I hunch over, terrified he'll see me. "Yes. What the heck is he doing here?"

"I don't know." Mia does a horrible job of hiding her stares in his direction. Me, on the other hand? I'm trying to somehow hide under the table. "Did he always look like a slime ball? The hair makes him look like he's about to be the next murderer featured on a true crime doc."

"What is happening?" I ask, not expecting an answer. "First I think about him for the first time in years. Then he texts me. Now this. Wait! Do you think I summoned him? Did I say his name three times and then 'Poof!' he's here?"

"I mean, maybe? He is giving *Beetlejuice* vibes. I'm all for men enhancing their hair, but not like he did," Mia says before averting her eyes back to me. "This is your call. What do you want to do? Stay? Leave? And don't tell me to pick, because what I want to do will get me kicked out of this bar."

I don't want to look at him, but I can't help myself. He's here. *Here.* In Nashville. Last I knew he was in San Antonio. Is he visiting? Is that why he called me? I have so many questions.

When we make eye contact, I feel a cold chill go up my spine. Maybe it's because he hasn't looked away from me. He hasn't approached, but his stare isn't wavering.

It's unsettling. And as much as I want answers, I'm not *that* curious.

"The polite person in me wants to go over and say hello. See what he's doing in town. Apologize for not texting back. But…"

Mia's smile reactivates as my word trail off. "I don't know what's going through that head of yours, but I feel like this is the beginning of a night we're never going to forget."

I look over to Jonathan one more time, and if I hadn't made my decision before this, I would now. And all it took was him tipping his glass to me and giving me a creepy wink.

Which is when I jump up from my seat and say words I never in a million years thought I'd ever say.

"Let's go sing some karaoke."

guide to love rule #78

Fairytales say that the princess will be saved by a prince. They didn't say anything about the prince having tattoos.

6
ainsley

"HOLY SMOKES, THAT WAS CLOSE."

Mia and I both let out a big sigh of relief as we walk into the karaoke bar in downtown Nashville that I didn't even know existed.

"Girl, I hate your ex. Like despise him. But if he's the reason I got you down here, then maybe I need to buy him a drink." She pauses as she looks for a table. "Actually, no. I can't even do that. Maybe I won't key his car. Yeah, that feels fair."

I want to laugh at her joke, but I can't because my eyes are wide as we walk through the bar. People are everywhere, cheering and singing along with a bad rendition of an ABBA classic by a bachelorette party. Mia tries to go snag a table in the front, but I immediately grab her arm and pull her back.

"We can't be that close," I say, looking around for another table. "Oh! There's one."

The table I pull her toward is closer to the bar, surrounded by people, and most importantly, away from the stage. I'm not even mad that there aren't any chairs at it.

"I know it's going to take a miracle to get you on stage tonight, and one already happened to even get you here, but you won't even sit near the stage?"

"No! What if they're not good, and I make a face and they see? I'd feel bad."

Mia laughs under her breath. "Only you, Ainsley. Only you."

My best friend heads to the bar to grab our drinks and I let out a breath as a new song comes on.

Why is Jonathan in Nashville? He's not originally from the area, but he went to med school at Vanderbilt before his residency at Nashville Children's. He does have some friends here, but where were they? On their way? Jonathan didn't go anywhere alone, let alone a bar, so that doesn't seem right. And even if that was the choice, why was he at that bar? He had to know he might run into me there. It's been my regular bar for years.

Was he there for me? No, that's silly. He can't be. We broke up more than three years ago. Sure, he was sad then, but he has to be over it, right?

I feel my eyes get big and stop blinking. Because my mind is officially racing.

What if he *is* back? Would that mean he still wants me back? If that's true, then he's not going to stop hounding me until I finally give in. Which I will. I know who I am as a person. I'll feel bad, and he'll catch me in a moment of weakness—much like the one I was in this week—and just give in. And then, I'll feel bad breaking up with him again, so I'll have a lifetime of cloud classifications to look forward to.

Or, on the other hand, if I say no, is he going to go all creepy stalker on me? I've never been a dark romance girlie, let alone in real life.

"Oh no. What happened? Where is he? Do I have to kill him?"

I take a breath and give myself a little shake. "I'm fine. I just let my mind wander for a minute."

"I get it," Mia says, handing me my club soda. "It's like seeing a ghost."

I take a sip as my heart rate comes down. "It's just...what are the odds of all this happening this week? And why was he at the bar? That had to be because of me, right? He only went there with me. Or am I being conceited?"

Mia shakes her head and picks up one of the three shots she brought back to the table. "No, you aren't. He found you the second he walked in. That was on purpose. Which is why it's best that we came here. Because unless he followed us, no way would he ever expect you here."

She's right about that. And Jonathan is a lot of things, but actual stalker isn't one.

Hopefully. Except I did make him watch that one Netflix show...

"Hey, ladies, I noticed you just came in. Welcome." Mia and I look over to a waitress who hands us a piece of paper. "These are the instructions for how you can put your name in the queue to sing. If you have any questions, just give me a shout."

I slide the paper to Mia. "Oh, that's for her. I don't sing."

"Famous last words," she says. "One thing to know about karaoke is that no matter how bad you are, there's always someone worse. Believe me on that one."

"And we can't wait to hear them," Mia jokes as she walks away. "Now let's see...what should I start out with?"

"You're going to sing?"

Mia shoots me a "duh" look. "Why wouldn't I? I didn't spend days on end in my misspent youth learning words to very specific rap verses to just sit here."

"You could sing in your shower. Or your car."

"Oh I do that anyway," Mia starts typing on her phone, which is how I'm guessing you put your name in. "And I don't want to push you too far. I know getting here was enough. And I guess thanks to Jonathan for that. But, maybe if I show you it's not that bad, maybe I can convince you to a duet? Maybe we could tell everyone why Earl had to die?"

I laugh at that prospect. "I'd have to start drinking again for that to happen. And I might've slightly crashed out earlier, and I also saw my ex for the first time in years, but even those put together is not enough to get me to try liquor again."

"Wait! Again? Meaning you've done it before?" Mia grabs the second shot off the table and throws it back before slamming her hands on the table. "How did I not know this? I just always thought it was a no-no because it's semi-rebellious and you are, well, not…"

I laugh at the dramatics of my best friend. But then again, I do understand why for her this would be very much breaking news. "Yes, again. I've drank once. Well, one and a half."

"Forget Jonathan. Forget karaoke. This is the story I need to hear."

"It was my twenty-first birthday," I begin.

"Of course, because it was against the rules to drink before you were legal."

"Exactly," I say. "Anyway, being that I had never drank, my whole family was excited. My birthday was on a Wednesday, and I was planning on going home that weekend to celebrate with my family, but my sorority sisters were bound and determined to take me out. Actually, we were cliche Nashville and went to Tootsies."

"That tracks."

"Yes. And things were going fine. I was having a good time. Taking shots, making sure I drank water between, because I knew I needed to stay hydrated."

"We love a responsible queen."

I was. Until I wasn't. "Well, the responsibility went right out of the door when someone handed me a shot of Jägermeister."

I watch as Mia visibly shivers. "Are you meaning to tell me that your aversion to alcohol is because of the dark liquor of death?"

"Pretty much," I say with nod. "I puked for two days. I barely made it back to Rolling Hills for my birthday. I tried to take a drink, but the smell of alcohol made me gag. I convinced the lovely bar owner to substitute my shots of vodka for water.

The club soda and cranberry? It was the drink he gave me to make it look like I had some sort of fruity drink. I've drank it ever since."

"Damn," she says. "Many of us say that we're never drinking again after visiting the Porcelain Princess then go back within a week. Your willpower is amazing."

"What can I say? When I commit, I don't waver."

Mia laughs as the song and performer changes. The two guys who get up on stage look familiar as they start rapping a boy band classic, but I can't put my finger on it so I turn back to Mia.

"Now, I don't want this to come out as peer pressure-y," she says. "But have you ever wanted to take a drink again?"

"Sometimes," I admit. "But it's more out of FOMO. Take tonight, for example, pre-Jonathan. Your martini looked good, and I felt like my being depressed over my singlehood didn't hit the same with club soda. And there have been times I've wondered what the wine my sisters shared was like. But never enough to take my chances again."

"That's fair. It also tracks. Knowing how you are with actual rules, it makes sense you'd be like that with self-imposed ones."

"Exactly," I say. "Rule follower to the core."

"One day I'm going to get you to be a little bad," she says with a wink. "And it's going to be the best day of my life."

I laugh. "Many have tried. All have failed. Remember, my sister is Quinn Banks. If she can't get me to act up, I don't know if it's possible."

And believe me, growing up, she tried. I'm the next born sibling to her, so I think she felt it was her duty to try to get me in trouble. Or at least, an accomplice to her crimes. Even at a young age, I wanted nothing to do with it. It only took me going to time-out once to know I never wanted to be in that corner again.

Once I hit middle school, I realized I needed to put my good-girl ways into overdrive. When teachers look at you and mutter, "Are you Quinn's sister?", you do everything you can to make sure you break any sort of preconceived notion they have about you.

Because of course they couldn't remember that Maeve was a prized student. Or that Simon might've caused some trouble, but teachers loved him too much to care. No, all they remembered was the most recent. Though in their defense, Quinn was a memorable student, and not for positive reasons. Which is why it's hilarious that she went into education.

However, what I didn't realize was that going out of my way to be the good girl of the Banks bunch triggered what I'd learn later was a people-pleasing mentality. I loved it when teachers praised me for a good job. Or for being the only one to follow directions. And not only did I want their approval, I was fueled by it. I still am. I live for when a doctor compliments my work. Or when a new mama thanks me for everything I did for her. Of course, I love my job, and bringing new babies into the world is the best feeling I can imagine. But a patient telling you that you made their experience better? It's a close second.

"Well, your self-control, and your rule following ways, astound me," Mia says as she holds up her drink. "Though, I need you to know that if you ever want to try again, not all alcohol tastes like ass. Which is what Jäger tastes like."

"If I ever decide to take the plunge again, I'll make sure you give me your top recommendation."

Mia taps on her nose before excusing herself to use the restroom. I offer to stay here, since the bar is filling up and we don't want to lose our table. With her being gone, I turn to the stage and listen to a singer who's way too good to be at karaoke. Then again, this is Nashville. Finding a good singer is easier than finding a worm at an apple orchard.

I start to get lost in the melody and lyrics of the bluesy song that I'd honestly forgotten about. I feel my eyes close, which is what I do whenever I hear a good song. I think every girl who once danced competitively does this. We hear a song, and just like we used to do in our bedrooms, we start seeing movements.

Or think about what trick we'd do during a strong accent of a song. I haven't danced in more than ten years, but I don't think this ever goes away. Especially when I need to take my mind off something. To me, there's no better way to forget about your problems then just dancing it out.

"You always did look beautiful when you danced."

My eyes fly open and my blood turns cold. How did Jonathan find me here? Maybe he is Dr. Stalker.

"What the heck, Jonathan! You scared me."

He laughs and stands way too close for my liking. "I'm sorry, Ainsley. But you ran out of the bar so quickly earlier. I didn't want to take the chance you'd leave again."

Well, that's not creepy at all.

"Jonathan, what are you—"

I can't finish my question before Mia comes speedwalking back to the table.

"Holy shit, Ainsley! You're never going to believe who I just saw!" Before Mia can finish that thought, she realizes who's at our table. "Oh, absolutely the fuck not! Get your bad fucking toupee and your creepy ass out of here."

Jonathan turns to my best friend, each of them shooting daggers to the other. "Always one with words, weren't you?"

"Listen, I know you've never been great with picking up on context clues, but when women literally run from you, that's not a sign to follow them."

"Good to see you, Mia."

"The feeling is not mutual."

"Oh, that's too bad," Jonathan says. "Especially because we're going to be seeing so much of each other here soon."

Mia's spine stiffens, and my eyes bulge out of my head as my blood goes cold. "What do you mean?"

He turns to me, a smile on his face that at one time I thought was handsome, but now it's just eerie. "That's why I'm back in town. And why I reached out. There was an opening at Nash-ville Children's. I'm back. I start Monday."

I don't say anything. Neither does Mia. In fact, if we weren't in a bar full of people, and a group of guys weren't singing a very loud version about feeling the rain on your skin, you could hear a pin drop.

Before I can say anything in response, Jonathan grabs my arms and turns me to face him. And he doesn't let go. "I want to try again, Ainsley."

Be strong. Being single is better than daily talks about the UV levels.

"Jonathan, we didn't work. And that's okay." I do my best to use a gentle voice as I shrug out of his hold, without sounding fake. I don't know though if it's working. "I'm happy for you, career wise. I know how much you loved Nashville Children's. But nothing has changed for me. We're better off apart."

Jonathan lets out a maniacal laugh. I've never heard him sound like that before. "Exactly, Ainsley. Nothing has changed for you. You're still hanging out at the same bar. Still drinking the same nonalcoholic drink. I'm going to guess you've been down to whatever the name of your hometown was at least once this week to see your parents and your sisters. Nothing's changed. And that's okay. I love you exactly the way you are. And I know if you look deep down, you still love me too."

Oh my, this man is delusional. Also, did he really just insult me and then try to make it about him in the same sentence? What did I ever see in this man?

"But Ainsley, I have changed," he says, his eyes pleading. "Please, let's just get out of here so we can talk."

I shake my head, proud of myself for not wavering. "Jonathan, no. That's not a good idea. I think you should go."

His eyes turn crazed, and before I know it, his hands are squeezing my biceps. Hard.

"No, Ainsley. You're going to leave with me. Now."

I start twisting to get out of his grip, but it's useless. And not because of his strength, but because before I can, Jonathan is pulled back from me and nearly thrown across the bar.

"Whoa! What the fuck?" Jonathan yells as he stumbles back. "Who the hell are you?"

I watch in awe as Linc Kincaid steps between me and Jonathan, making him shrink with every step.

Holy freak, that was hot...

"Her fucking boyfriend, you dipshit. Now get your hands off my girl."

7

linc

"You? You're her boyfriend?"

"I am. And you are?"

Obviously I'm not. I don't even know my supposed girl-friend's name. But from the second I saw the cute nurse from the children's hospital while I was standing on stage with my team-mates, I couldn't stop looking at her.

I don't know how I saw her. It's not like the karaoke stage has the bright lights of the Grand Ole Opry, but there is a spotlight, meaning that when me and my boys were making asses of ourselves, I could only see a little bit of the audience.

But I could see her clear as day.

When I saw that smarmy jackass approach her, and her reaction to him, my feet were already marching toward their table. Where I came up with the idea of saying I'm her boyfriend? That I'm not sure.

Dipshit puffs out his chest, which doesn't do much considering I'm close to a foot taller than him. "Dr. Jonathan Ainsworth. Her boyfriend."

"Ex," my new girlfriend says quickly. "He's my *ex*-boyfriend."

Oh, this is going to be good...

"Huh. You never mentioned him, babe. Must not've been that important." I lay it on thick as I step in front of her, blocking out Dr. Dipshit. I lean down, making it look like I'm kissing her cheek. "Are you okay?"

I'm so close I can feel her skin against mine as she squints and tips her head side to side. I push down the warmness I feel, simply because we have a bigger task at hand.

"Do you trust me?"

The question is a lot to ask of a stranger. She doesn't know me from Adam. I'm sure by now she knows my name, and depending on if she's a football fan, she probably knows my reputation. Which means she might just say no.

That's why I feel a new rush of heat surge through me when I simply hear one word.

"Yes."

I smile and give her a small kiss on her cheek, one that lingers a little longer than it probably should, but hey, I'm her boyfriend, aren't I? "Then follow my lead."

I turn back around and pull—fuck, I forgot to ask her name, again—girlfriend into me, throwing my arm over her shoulder for a little extra emphasis. "Sorry, Jimmy. I hadn't seen my girl here all day. I'm sure you remember what that's like."

"It's Jonathan."

"What's Jonathan?"

"My name."

I almost have to bite my lip to keep from laughing. It's so easy to get under this guy's skin. "Apologies. But anyway, I hadn't seen her all day. That's what happens when it's almost football season. You a Fury fan? I'm Linc Kincaid by the way, starting tight end. Anyway… Babe? You want to come over to our section? The guys can't wait to see you."

I start to pull her away when dipshit steps in front of us.

"Why are you calling her that?"

I'm confused for only a second before recalling the few names I've used for her. "Well, I call her my girl, you know, because she is. And babe? I don't know. It's just always felt right. Wait. What did you call her? Did I repeat? God, James, I'm sorry. I hate being unoriginal."

Girlfriend's face lights up and dipshit's becomes as red the lights coming from the stage.

"I didn't. She hates nicknames."

"Huh. Weird," I say, pulling her in closer so I can kiss her temple. You know, for emphasis. "She's never had a problem with me using it. Must've been a you problem."

To say that I've been an antagonizer my entire life would be an understatement. From a young age, I knew how to get under people's skin. Over the years it's served me well—and gotten me into trouble. In football, it allows me to get into the head of whoever's covering me, throwing them off their game before I go out to pull in a pass.

Who knew I could use this power for good, piss off a dipshit, and save a beautiful woman? All without raising a fist. Look at me, evolving.

"I don't know who you are," Dipshit says, stepping up to face me. It's comical, really. I have to literally look down on him, which is also why I can see that whoever glued his toupee on did a horrible fucking job. "But you aren't Ainsley's boyfriend. She doesn't date tattooed thugs like you."

Ainsley...what a beautiful name. I don't know what I expected it to be, but it wasn't that. But I like it. It's so...her.

As for the name Dipshit called me, I've been called much worse by men who have the height and weight to turn me into a greasy spot on the field, so I don't know why dipshit's little dig is making me see red right now. I ball my fists, doing my best to temper my anger, when I see my six-foot-four, three-hundred-and-fifty-pound best friend step up next to me. "Everything okay here?"

"We're just fine," I say. "I didn't realize my girl here had come in with her sidekick, so I thought I'd bring them over to our section, if that's okay?"

I level a look to Wyatt, who hopefully picked up on my use of the words "my girl." Luckily, this man knows me well enough to know that something's up, and now he's just along for the ride.

"Absolutely," Wyatt says as he walks over to her friend. "Come on. We've got drinks waiting and a queue full of karaoke songs."

Wyatt holds out his arm for Ainsley's friend, and I keep my hand on the small of her back as she grabs her purse off the table. Dr. Dipshit looks on in disbelief.

"See ya, Jimothy," I say, giving him a slap on the shoulder. "Actually. No. I don't want to see you. Because you're the ex. I'm the now. And neither of us want to live in the past."

———

"Holy Moses, what was that!"

I laugh at Ainsley's choice of words. "Holy Moses?"

"She doesn't swear," the sidekick explains, extending her hand to me. "That one is in her regular rotation. I'm Mia, by the way."

"Linc," I say, shaking her hand back. "And this guy who came in as my backup is Wyatt."

"Oh, I know," Mia says as she turns to Wyatt, a smile on her face that says she knows exactly what, and who, she wants. "Offensive guard. Played on the left in college but transitioned to the right side as a pro. Played with Linc at Mississippi State."

Wyatt's eyes light up. The man is a sucker for a woman who can throw some stats his way. "You know your football."

Mia shrugs. "I dabble."

I smirk as the two of them fall into a conversation, which I'm sure is going to lead to things that will end tomorrow morning. I know how Wyatt operates, and judging by Mia's boldness, he's about to have a fun night.

Which is fine by me. With him distracted, I can concentrate exactly where I want: on my, at least tonight, fake girlfriend.

"I need to thank you," Ainsley says. "I don't know where you came from, or how you knew to come in and intervene, but I don't know if I'll ever be able to thank you enough."

"You don't need to thank me at all," I say. "But are you okay? I could tell that you were shaken up, and then it seemed like he was getting rough."

Ainsley nods, her crystal blue eyes looking down for a second before meeting mine again. "Jonathan. I haven't seen him in a few years. Since we broke up. He moved, and I didn't know he was back in town until he showed up out of nowhere. I was shocked when he said he was moving back to town and that he wanted to get back together. I froze. I don't know what would've happened if…"

She trails off, and I push back the anger that I thought had subsided. He looks like the kind of guy who can't take a hint, or thinks his title of doctor gets him things he hasn't earned. Now I'm even more glad I stepped in.

Though I do wish I wasn't on a strict no-fighting warning. It would've been satisfying to bust his nose open.

"No thanks needed," I say. "Well, except maybe one thing."

She looks almost relieved that I'm asking something of her. "Anything. Well, maybe not anything. Anything is a lot. But my brother knows a lot of people, so maybe anything is closer than I think?"

I laugh because this rambling is definitely different than the girl I first met who said all of three words. "I don't think we'll be needing him. I just think now that I've run you over, saved you, and at least for tonight, am your boyfriend, maybe we can have a proper introduction?"

Her cheeks turn rosy. Damn. She's fucking adorable.

"Yes. I'm Ainsley Banks."

"Well, it's nice to meet you, Ainsley. I'm Linc. Linc Kincaid."

Her blush deepens. "Yeah, I know."

I swallow the frog in my throat, hoping that it's not because she's a fan of sports gossip. "I hope I wasn't out of bounds before. It just looked like you needed help, and well, a lot of times I act without thinking."

She smiles and shakes her head. "That's how most of my family operates, so I'm used to it."

"Not how you operate?"

She shakes her head and sends me a bashful smile. "Oh no. I'm the oddball in that sense. I overthink everything and then usually don't do it because of the one thing that could go wrong, even if there's a million things that could go right."

"So you're not a risk taker?"

"Absolutely not," she says with a laugh that hits me square in the chest. It's light and a little shy. And right now, I'm not as mad as I was that Wyatt dragged me out tonight. "Coming here tonight was as big of a risk as I've taken in…well…longer than I care to admit."

"I mean, I get that," I say as I look up at the stage and see two people singing a duet that sounds more like cats dying. "Karaoke can be intimidating if you don't like putting yourself out there. Or, you know, risking your dignity."

"Oh I could never get on stage. I meant just physically coming here. I'll never actually sing. That's way too much."

I laugh and grab a beer out of one of the buckets in the VIP area the team secured for tonight. "Want one?"

She shakes her head. "No, thank you. I don't drink."

"Really?" I ask. "So you don't drink. You don't swear. And coming here was a risk?"

She nods, that blush coming back over her cheeks. Goddamn it, if she keeps doing that I'm going to keep wondering where else she's blushing…

"That's me. Your boring, good girl."

"I don't know about boring," I say. "You did almost have two men fighting over you at a bar."

She shakes her head. "And if that had happened, that would've been the most exciting thing that's happened to me in, well, ever."

Ainsley takes a sip of her drink, I'm guessing something with cranberry in it, as she starts looking around the bar. Which is fine. This gives me a chance to really look at her. Because if I thought she was beautiful when I ran into her in her scrubs and hair a little messy from a day's work, she's radiant tonight.

Her long blonde hair is slightly wavy and draping over both of her shoulders. She's wearing a thin-strapped sundress—a garment that should be illegal—and sandals that have some lift to them.

Am I having thoughts of those legs and those sandals wrapped around my hips as I fuck her in that dress? Yes. But in my defense, I'm a man, and sundresses were made to drive us fucking crazy.

But I quickly push that thought out of my head. If Ainsley is the good girl she says she is, then she's definitely out of my league.

She might be too good for me, but I can't get over how effortlessly beautiful she is. I have a feeling she doesn't realize how stunning she looks, and I bet you dollars to donuts she doesn't even try. Her makeup is light, her lipstick is subtle, and her scent is sweet and addicting.

It's probably a good thing I know this is just for tonight. Because I have a feeling that this good girl would ruin me.

Or worse, I'd ruin her.

My eyes roam off of Ainsley for a second, which is when I see Dr. Dipshit staring at us from the bar, a look of anger covering his punchable face.

"Hey," I say, leaning in to her. "We're being watched. I'm going to hold your hand, but it would probably be good if you were looking at me. You know, since you're my girlfriend and all."

She nods and does her best to be nonchalant as she turns to face me. I take her hand in mine, threading our fingers through each other's as I inch in a little closer to her.

"I'm sorry, because I know this is awkward as hell, putting on a show like this, but he can't take his eyes off us."

"I don't understand him," she says. "We've been broken up for three years. We haven't talked since he moved. And now he's stalker-staring. I just don't get why."

"I do."

Her look clearly says she doesn't believe me. "And why is that?"

"Well, for starters, he fumbled you. And he knows it." I lean in a little closer. You know, for effect. "And I'm going to go out on a limb and say that he can't stop staring because you're the most beautiful woman in this bar, and I'm the lucky bastard who gets to hold your hand."

Ainsley's jaw drops a little—probably because what I said likely sounded like the biggest line ever. But it can't be a line when it's the truth.

"Can I be honest, Linc?"

"Of course."

"I have no idea how to do this."

"Do what?"

She takes a big breath before worry floods her face. "I don't really date, let alone have fake boyfriends. I for sure have never done anything like this in front of an ex. Oh my gosh! Is this now a thing? Do I have to keep this up when we're at work? Are you my fake boyfriend forever? Oh gosh…maybe this wasn't such a good idea."

I know she's worried, but her panic is cute. "Do you always ramble like this when you're worried?"

"Yes. Rambling when I'm panicked. Speechless when I'm taken off guard. Worrying when…well…always." Ainsley takes a sip of her drink, and I notice that she looks over to Dr. Dipshit. "Maybe we should stop while we're ahead. No harm, no foul, and I don't have to answer questions when I see him at work next week."

Well, that's not going to happen. Actually, that sounds like a fucking terrible idea, if I do say so myself.

"Or, and this is just a suggestion, we double down."

She raises her eyebrows as her eyes widen. "Double down?"

This is about to be the best or worst idea I've ever had. "Exactly. Rub it in his face that his ex-girlfriend is with a professional football player until he storms out in a rage. That way, he won't even come around you when he sees you at work."

"What if he still does?"

"I guess then I'll have to make another visit to Nashville Children's. Only this time, with flowers in my hand."

Ainsley doesn't immediately shut down the idea, which I take for a win. And I wouldn't mind going back to the hospital. I really do enjoy doing visits like that. And if I can see my temporary fake girlfriend in the process of pissing off a man who can't take no for an answer? Well, that sounds like a fun day.

"I don't know," she says, worry all through her voice. "It seems like a lot could go wrong."

She wasn't lying when she said she wasn't a risk taker. Which means I'm going to need to step up and help her out.

I bring our joined hands to my lips, placing a small kiss to her knuckles. "Or, it could go exactly to plan."

I stay there for a second, begging her with my eyes to go with my plan. But the way she's looking at me right now? A little scared, a lot nervous, but all the trust in the world? I've never wanted to come through for someone so much in my life.

"Come on, Ainsley. Do something a little scary. And let's make your ex-boyfriend jealous as fuck."

guide to love rule #88

There's something to be said about liquid courage. It makes you do all sorts of crazy things.

8

ainsley

I wasn't lying to Linc earlier when I said that I freeze when I'm not sure what to do. Which is why I haven't blinked, let alone said anything, in what feels like hours, but is more like seconds.

Do something scary…

How is this the second time that phrase has been said to me tonight? And tonight of all nights. The night that my ex is back in town. The night I was already wondering why I feel like my life is in this constant state of neutral.

Do something scary…

"I don't know," I say, because I don't. But also, I wouldn't even know where to begin. Yet, something in me is wanting this more than practical Ainsley wants to play it safe. "I wouldn't even know where to begin."

"Easy," Linc says with an easy smile. "I have the perfect starting place."

"And what's that?"

"You need to get out of your head."

"Ha!" Suddenly Mia is back in the conversation. "Good luck with that. I've been her best friend for years, and I've continuously failed to accomplish that. You're talking to the queen of overthinking."

"You shush," I say to Mia, who gives me a wink before returning to her conversation with Wyatt. "And you, Mr. Know It All. How do you propose that I get out of my head?"

Linc doesn't say anything at first, just giving me a devilish smile as he leans over to the table in front of us that has an array of liquor bottles scattered on it. He picks up one that says Fireball, and as someone who takes fire safety very seriously, I already know this isn't a good idea. "We're going to take a shot."

"Oh no," I say, remembering the feeling in my stomach the last time I took shots. "I'm not a shot girl. Or even a drinks girl."

"This isn't very strong," he says, pulling up four plastic shot glasses. "Plus, it tastes like cinnamon gum."

Well that sounds better than the black licorice demon water. "I understand what you're thinking, Linc. And I'm sure it would help loosen me up, but I haven't drank since—"

Just as I'm about to explain to Linc about my aversion to alcohol, I get an eyeful of Jonathan across the bar. Linc was right, he *is* staring. And not in a covert way. The man isn't blinking. It's unsettling.

And to think I was going to reach out to him this week because I was lonely. Maybe I need to do shots just as punishment for that moment of weakness.

But as a chill goes down my spine from Jonathan's gaze, I can't help but think about what he said to me before Linc saved me.

I am drinking the same mocktail. I did go to the same bar with the same friend. I visited my family this week—twice. Jonathan's right: I am predictable. Boring. The only exciting things that happen to me are through my siblings. And, most importantly—and depressing—is that I'm the same person I was when Jonathan and I broke up.

Not that I'm a bad person then or now. I love myself and who I am. But clearly *that* Ainsley isn't going anywhere. She's not dating or married. She's not fulfilling her dream of having a family and a career. She's not traveling or living it up.

She's scared and waiting.

Well, not anymore.

"Frick it," I say to try to pump myself up. "Give me the shot."

"Excuse me!"

Mia flies from the chair she was sitting in next to Wyatt and nearly throws herself on my lap. "Did I hear what I think I just heard?"

"You did," I say, suddenly growing confidence I didn't know I had. "Pour me the shot, Linc."

"That's my girl," he says, giving me a wink before signaling Wyatt to come over to join us.

I start to feel a little out of body as I watch Linc pour four shots into glasses, and then I feel a tug on my arm. "Are you sure? You know you don't have to do this."

I love Mia, and this is why she's my best friend. She knows this is *very* out of the norm for me. She might be excited, but at the same time, she'd be remiss if she didn't triple-check to make sure that an alien didn't possess me in the last ten minutes.

"I'm more than sure," I say, unable to stop myself from looking back at Jonathan. Mia follows my eyes, and because she's my work wife who knows everything about me, she knows exactly what I'm thinking. "I don't want to be the same girl from three years ago. And nothing changing means nothing will change. So let's change it up."

She smiles and brings me in for a side hug. "I like that mentality. But just one. Two, tops. You're still Ainsley Banks, and I feel like baby steps are the best option."

"Agreed," I say as Linc passes the filled glasses. As soon as I have it in my hand, the strong smell of cinnamon hits my nostrils.

"Oh mylanta!" I say, shaking a bit just from the smell.

"That's about right," Wyatt says. "Send it! To douchebags and bad singing!"

I watch as the three of them somehow know to tap the glasses on the table before throwing them back. I don't do that. Instead, I hold it up in front of my face, looking at it like it might grow legs and attack me.

"You can do it," Linc says softly, his hand resting on the small of my back. "And if it helps you right now, Dr. Dipshit looks like he wants to murder me because I'm touching you. And I don't blame him. If I fumbled you, and you moved on? I'd hate the man touching you, too."

I look to Linc, wondering if this man is just pouring it on thick for the audience of one. But I don't think so. The look he's giving me right now is…I don't know if I've *ever* been looked at like this. He's not looking at me like I'm delicate Ainsley, the nice girl who always done everything right. The one no one would ever suggest do something that would go against my good-girl reputation.

No, he's looking at me with…more. Fire? I don't know why that's the word coming to my mind right now. Probably because my body is heating from his gaze.

"I can do this," I say.

He taps his forehead to mine. "Send it, babe."

I smile at the use of his nickname from earlier. "Okay. Here I go. Bottoms up!"

I sling back the shot, hoping if I take it quick, I won't taste it as much.

Unfortunately, I do.

"Snap, crackle, pop!" I yell as the shot burns down my throat. I let out a cough and shake my head a little as it settles in my stomach.

"How was it?" Mia asks.

I take in a deep breath, which has remnants of cinnamon to it. "Woo, that burned! Not too bad now, though!"

And it's not. Actually…it was pretty good…

"And how do you feel?"

I know I can't be drunk yet—I took the shot thirty seconds ago—but I do feel different.

Confident. A little bold. A little reckless.

A little *bad*.

"I feel like I want another."

———

I throw back the shot because I'm a pro now, slamming it down on the table before turning to Linc. "Thank you."

"For what?"

I don't think I'm drunk yet, but I'm pretty darn close. I feel loose. The room is swaying a little, but that also could be because the karaoke choices tonight are amazing, so I've found myself dancing more than normal. But the biggest giveaway is that I'm holding Linc's hand because I took it. I even put my hand on his thigh.

I'm downright scandalous.

"Everything."

The part of the bar we're in is dark, but I can swear that I see his cheeks turn a little red. "All I did was suggest getting drunk."

I shake my head and move a little closer to him. "Um, was that not you who came over and saved the day?"

"Well, it was," he says, looking away in mock humility. "But I didn't want to rub it in."

"Oh, rub away," I say, and as soon as the words leave my mouth, I slap my hand over it. "That didn't come out right. And neither did that! Is drunk me a dirty talker?"

Linc laughs. "Do you not know how you act drunk?"

I shake my head. "Only got drunk once. And it was really, *really* bad."

His laughter comes to a screeching stop. "That was serious? I thought you were joking!"

He puts the bottle down, but I immediately grab his arm. "No. Don't."

When he turns back to face me, the look of guilt is all over his face. And maybe because I'm drunk, or maybe because I feel bad, but I lean in and kiss his cheek. The short hairs of his beard tickle my lips. And I think I've been hanging out with Mia and my sisters a little too much—and that the Fireball is kicking in—because I'm wondering how that beard would feel in other places.

Not that I know what that's like, either. Jonathan never did that. He said it was gross.

I think *he's* gross.

"Linc, listen to me." I lean in, close enough so it looks like a couple is just having a private conversation. "You're the first person maybe ever who hasn't treated me with kid gloves. Tonight you told me to do the scary thing, and I am. But I can't do it without you. Because tonight I don't want to be the good girl. Tonight I need you to forget what I just said and treat me exactly how you have all night. Can you do that? Please."

I do my best to plead with my eyes, but considering the room is starting to spin a bit, I'm not sure how that's going. He must get it, though, because he nods and adds a kiss to my forehead for good measure.

Oh, this guy is a great fake boyfriend…

"What can I do to help?"

I smile and lean over, grabbing the bottle of Fireball.

"How about another shot?"

———

"Linc! Dance with me!"

At some point after the fifth shot, I decided that mocktails weren't enough. Also, why didn't anyone tell me that vodka cranberries were delicious? They basically taste like my cranberry with lime but with bonus fun!

My hips are swaying, and my drink is in the air. I'm getting lost in the beat, because bless the heart of the singer who decided to sing a classic R&B song, when I feel Linc's hands on each of my hips.

"How about I just stand here and make sure you don't fall?"

I shake my head, and good thing he's holding me, because I stumble a bit as I turn around. Luckily, I don't spill my drink.

Look at me go. I'm even wearing wedge sandals. I feel like this is some sort of accomplishment.

"Why not?" I'm still dancing in his hold, and the smirk on his face is enough to make me want to do this all night.

"I'm not much of a dancer," he says. "I feel like this is a safer bet."

I swat away his words, and sway a little myself with the motion. "You don't even have to move your feet. It's all in the hips."

He laughs. "I'll take your word for it."

Out of nowhere, Mia grabs my free hand and pulls me from Linc. "Well, if you aren't going to dance with her, I am!"

He sends me a wink. "Please do. I'm going to head to the bathroom. You okay? If you need anything, just grab Wyatt or any of the guys."

"I'm fine," I say with a smile as Mia and I make a dance floor in the roped-off area of the VIP section. We're right by the entrance, so this is as close to the other bar-goers as we can get.

"I had a feeling this night was going to be epic, but I had no idea it was going to be like this."

"Right?" I yell, probably a little too loudly, but because I'm drunk I don't care. "Thank you for making me come here!"

"Believe me, if I knew that bringing you here would mean partying with Fury players and lead you to drinking, I would've dragged you here sooner."

I realize I've been in such a Linc bubble I have no idea what she's been up to. "Oh! Is something happening with Wyatt?"

Mia shrugs in that nonchalant way she does. "He's going to be fun for tonight. But that's it."

I swear she's the most hard-headed woman on the planet. I think he's perfect for her, at least from the five minutes I've talked to him. "Oh! I love this song!"

We start jumping and singing, and even some of the other Fury players and guests inside our VIP area join us. I'm so in the moment, and not paying a lick of attention to my surroundings, when I lose my footing and stumble back.

Oh no! I'm falling. Backward. Between the tight area, and the fact that I'm pretty drunk, I can't get my balance. Though I do take a second to congratulate myself that I haven't dropped my drink.

God, I'm good.

My side thought doesn't last long when I feel me starting to go down. I have no idea what to do except just brace myself for the fall and hope I'm drunk enough to bounce. Just as I'm sure I'm about to hit the floor, I feel arms underneath me, bracing me from my fall.

"I told you I'd always be here for you."

The voice sends shivers down my spine as I scramble to stand up and break out of Jonathan's hold.

"What were you doing so close? Just waiting for me to fall? Freaking creep!"

His eyes narrow. "Well your *boyfriend* wasn't here, so someone had to."

I might have double vision right now, but I did notice that he said boyfriend with air quotes. But in between the two versions of Jonathan standing in front of me, I see my fake boyfriend standing behind him.

Not just standing. Looking murderous.

And I have a feeling if I don't do something right now, Linc is going to do something really, really stupid.

"Baby!" I yell, pushing past Jonathan, and without thinking, I jump into Linc's arms. He catches me, and I mask his shocked face by kissing him.

Holy molasses, I'm kissing Linc.

And I kissed him *first*.

And he's kissing me back.

The heat I just felt coming from his look? It's now being channeled into what is, without a doubt, the best kiss of my life.

Linc adjusts his arms, holding me underneath my butt, as if I weigh nothing. I'm not plus size, but I'm not tiny either. But the way I feel at ease in his arms as I wrap my legs around his waist, I have a feeling he's not even breaking a sweat.

But I am. I'm sweating. Because this kiss is hot. I don't know if it's because it's in public, or because I know it has to be making Jonathan angry. Or that Linc's tongue is the perfect combination of giving and taking. But I do know that I could kiss him all night.

And maybe even other things.

Oh damn, I am drunk…

I don't know how long we stand here like this, and I'm going to bet my booty that everyone is watching us.

The best part? I don't care.

And that feels good. Darn good.

Eventually we pull back from each other, and Linc slowly puts me down. I wobble a little when my feet hit the floor, but my eyes stay trained on his to make sure that the murder-y looks have gone away.

He gives my hands a squeeze, letting me know he's okay.

I think. Again, drunk.

"Thanks for catching her man," he says as he brings me into his side. "But as you can tell, our time here is coming to a close. I need to get this girl home. But you remember what that's like, right?"

Jonathan doesn't—in the years we were together, never once did we kiss in public, let alone be so into each other that we needed to leave the bar immediately.

"Whatever," Jonathan huffs before training his eyes on me. "Hope you had fun tonight, Ainsley. When you're done playing pretend with this guy, let me know."

"I won't!" I yell as Jonathan walks off. When he's far enough away, I spin back to Linc and jump into his arms again. But no kiss this time.

Drat.

"We did it!"

"Damn right we did," he says, and I don't know if he's doing it for good measure, but his words come with a kiss to the cheek. I'm not going to complain about it. "But we should get you home. I think you've had enough for tonight."

I shake my head, because I want to do one more thing. If I don't do it now, I'm never going to have the courage, or liquor level, to do again.

"Ainsley…"

"Linc…please? Just one more thing. Pretty-pleeeeeeese…"

The tiny grin on his face is freaking adorable. Kissable. Oh! I just kissed him, so I can kiss him again!

And I do. I kiss at the corner of his mouth, where the tiniest dimple is peeking out. I let my lips linger for a second, and I can't see, but I could swear that this man—my hero for the night—is now in a full-wattage grin.

And when I pull back? That theory is confirmed.

"Well, if you're going to keep kissing me, I don't know how I can say no."

"Good," I say with a wink. "Because I want to sing."

guide to love rule #44

When you wake up hungover in a stranger's bed, first thing you do is make sure you're wearing clothes. Second is to see if he is.

9
ainsley

I was an active member of the "Free Britney" movement. She's an icon. But I can promise you that I never, and I mean never, have woken up with *Womanizer* in my head.

Then again, I've never woke up with this kind of raging headache, either, so I guess two things can be true.

I can't bear to open my eyes yet, so I keep them closed as I pull up the cooler-than-I-remember sheets. Also, when did my pillow become so supportive and somehow also soft? I'm not sure on either of those things, but I'm not going to complain.

The song refuses to leave my head as I do my best to fall back to sleep. I start to drift off again, but the lyrics aren't leaving me. And now, they're accompanied by images…

How was I opposed to karaoke before? This is amazing! I mean, it helps that I know every word to this song, thanks to my obsession with it when I was twelve years old. I even remember the dance moves I came up with for it. Hip curls and fierce marches. Dropping it low, which I don't know if I've ever done as an adult. But I am now, and I'm killing it.

Mia's behind me being the best backup singer ever. But what's really fueling this performance is that Linc can't stop looking at me. It's empowering. Like I'm putting on a show just for him.

Which is why I throw in a big booty roll for the end of this song. And if it makes Jonathan jealous, who for some reason is still freaking here, then oops, I did it again...

Oh fudge....

The dream is vivid. Too vivid. We're at the bar from last night. I'm wearing the same sundress. Mia, Linc, and everyone else I just saw were also in the same outfits. But I couldn't have sang karaoke. That's a hard limit for me.

Not unless I was really, really drunk...

Jonathan.

Linc.

Fireball.

Karaoke.

Oh fudge is right...

I slowly open my eyes, scared to what I might see. I don't think I'm in my bed—nothing about this feels familiar—but I can't tell where I am. The room is dark—nearly pitch black except for the small sliver of light peeking through one of the drawn curtains. I do my best to adjust my focus, but it's hard, between the dark room and the hangover that is suddenly pounding in my head.

Okay, seriously, where am I? My mind is now racing, which is a bad combination with the jackhammer that's currently going through my brain and my stomach that feels like it's about to stage a riot.

Where am I? How did I get here? Am I being held captive by a morally gray man who doesn't talk, only grunts, but is secretly in love with me?

Or worse...did I go home with Jonathan?

I don't know why this is the first thing I think to do, but I pull the covers up, checking to see what I'm wearing. I let out a sigh of relief to see that I'm wearing the same dress as last night. And you know what, while I'm here and successfully hiding from the world, I'm just going to bury myself under said covers and think about what the heck happened last night.

Why did I drink? Why did I think that I was the kind of girl who could handle that? I can't. I know who I am as a person, but apparently seeing my ex—and one sexy football player—is enough to make me forget that I'm not the person who does scary things.

Because scary things put you in a stranger's bed and make you want to chew a bottle of aspirin.

As much as I'd like to stay buried under this blanket for, let's say eternity, my bladder is telling me that possibility isn't on the table. I let out a groan as I sit up, doing my best to steady myself before going on this adventure. My head is spinning, so I take a second and close my eyes to get my bearings.

Which is when I almost pee my pants.

"Hold on. Let me help you."

"Ahhhh!"

I jump out of my skin, which because I have the balance of a toddler trying to walk for the first time, sends me falling back into the bed.

"Oh shit, I'm sorry."

I register that it's Linc's voice, and I try and calm down my racing heart. When I sit back up and see his shirtless self walking toward me, I'm lightheaded all over again. And it has nothing to do with the alcohol.

Holy tattoos…

They're everywhere. A full sleeve on his right arm. A large one on his chest that I can't make out. But the one I can't stop staring at is the one on his thigh, half covered by the tight shorts he apparently slept in.

Mia's talked about slutty thigh tattoos before, and I always had to nod like I knew what she meant.

Now I know.

Oh boy, do I now know…

"Here," he says as he sits next to me. "I'm sorry. I didn't realize you hadn't seen me."

I shake my head. "I…how…where—"

My inability to form a sentence, combined with Linc holding me up, is reminiscent of our first meeting. Frankly, I don't know which one is more embarrassing.

"You were pretty drunk," he says. "I didn't feel right about you going back to your apartment by yourself. And since Mia was going to be two floors up with Wyatt, doing God knows what, we all agreed it was best if you crashed here."

"Oh," I say, trying to piece together what happened last night. "Did…you…we…"

I don't know what I'm trying to ask him, but he gives me a small smile and shakes his head. "You passed out on the car ride here. I wanted to give you a T-shirt and shorts to sleep in, but you were out cold. I put you to bed and slept in the recliner in case you needed anything. Or, you know, to scare the hell out of you in the morning."

"Thank you," I say softly, hating that he needed to take care of me, but also kind of loving that he did. Also, how many ways can one man save me? "And I'm sorry you had to do that. I swear I didn't think I was that drunk."

This makes Linc laugh. "You weren't. Until you were."

———

"Touching you!"

This song is so fun! How did I forget this song was so fun! It's going to become my go-to karaoke song, because I think this is my new favorite thing to do.

It helps that we're singing this song with the whole gang, Linc and me and Mia and Wyatt and the other Fury football players that came out tonight. I've learned some of their names. But I don't remember them. I also don't remember how many drinks I've had.

But they were all delicious.

"Woo!" I scream into the microphone before we all exit the stage, smiles and laughs all around. "We'll be here all night!"

That gets another round of applause from the audience as Linc takes my mic away.

Rude.

"Have you drank any water lately?"

I shrug as I walk back to the VIP area. Well, Linc basically carries me, but my feet are moving. "I did."

His eyebrow goes up. "When was that?"

I look at my watch—I'm not wearing a watch—then back to him. "An hour ago."

He laughs and flags down the waitress for a few bottles of water. "Let's fix that."

I cross my arms in a huff and push out my bottom lip. "I thought you were fun."

He smiles and leans in. "I am. But I don't like my girlfriend being dehydrated."

This makes me smile. "I like being your girlfriend."

"I do too, Ainsley. I do too."

We fall into a comfortable silence—and I do my best to ignore the way the room is starting to spin—when I see a dust up happen just on the other side of the roped of area we're sitting in.

"I just want to talk to her!"

I turn and see that Jonathan is trying to push past a bouncer standing at the front of the section.

Why can't this man take a freaking hint?

"Ainsley! Please! Just talk to me!"

"Stay here," Linc says as he steps up to the rope, Wyatt and a teammate of his...I think his name is Maddox...quickly following behind. "What the fuck is your problem, man?"

"My problem is you!" he yells. "I don't know what the hell is going on here, but clearly this is fake. You don't know her. You're not dating her. You date supermodels and cleat chasers. Ainsley dates...well...not fucking roided-out football players!"

That's it. I'm tired of Jonathan and his Jonathan-ness. I stand up, and only stumble a little, as I approach the fracas.

"Go away! I don't want you here!"

Fracas…that's a fun word…

"Get the hint, Jonathan. You don't know me anymore! And I'm going to prove it."

Before anyone can stop me, I grab the bottle of Fireball off the table that's almost empty, tip it back, and polish it off. There was more in there than I thought, but I don't care.

I'm the new Ainsley. Drunk Ainsley. Bad-girl Ainsley.

As I take down the last few sips of the bottle, I wipe my mouth off with the back of my hand. Jonathan's jaw is hanging open, which is good. Because if it wasn't then, it's about to be.

I grab Linc in with my free hand, grabbing him by his T-shirt, and pull him in for a kiss. A big one. Sloppy. It's probably not super-hot or sexy looking, but it feels good.

He feels good.

The kiss doesn't last long, but when we pull away, I'm greeted by Linc's mischievous smile. It makes me want to kiss him again. But I can't. The plan that I developed two minutes ago to get Jonathan to leave me alone needs to continue.

"Here, hold this."

I give Linc the empty bottle before I ungracefully climb over the rope.

"Ainsley! What are you doing?"

I don't turn back to answer Jonathan, or anyone else who might be calling for me. Instead, I walk right up to Miguel, our lovely karaoke host who's now my new best friend, and request a song.

"For you, girl? Anything."

"Thanks!" I say, grabbing the microphone from his table as I walk on stage. I haven't heard this song in years. But for some reason it seems fitting right now.

And Miguel even turns the lights to red for added effect.

"This is dedicated to my boyfriend!" I point to Linc, who's waving

to the crowd like he's the grand marshal of a parade. Just then the sultry music begins to play, and my cue is up.

All right, Jonathan, you think I'm the same? That this is fake? Watch this…

"Take a good look at it…"

———

I feel my face turning red, but apparently not as red as the stage lights last night. "I did not…"

"Oh, you did. Not going to lie, it was pretty hot."

I let my head fall into my arms as Linc chuckles. "Here. Try and eat something. Let the grease soak up the booze."

I look up to see the ham, egg, and cheese sandwich on a bagel that I requested when he said that he was ordering breakfast delivery, along with the large, crispy Coke I asked for. I'm usually not a huge caffeine person, but today, it's warranted.

Also, as I sit here in Linc's kitchen, at his island, wearing a T-shirt and shorts he gave to me so I'm not still in my dress from last night, I hereby do declare that I'm never, and I mean never, drinking again.

"I'm mortified," I say.

"Don't be. Dr. Dipshit stormed away in the middle of your song. Which was rude, if you ask me. I guess he was just jealous that you were singing to me and not him."

The embarrassment I feel on my face isn't going away with Linc's teasing words. "I was singing to you?"

"Dedicated it to me and everything," he says as he unwraps a monstrosity of a sandwich that I can't even begin to imagine what's on it. I didn't know breakfast sandwiches even came in that size. "You pointed to me and swerved your hips. It was quite the show. Any farther and I would've had to tell the bar to avert their eyes."

I slam my head down again, my arms catching it before I hit the breakfast counter. "How does this keep getting worse?"

"Don't say that," Linc says as I feel his hand on my forearm. "It wasn't that bad. You were the bar's favorite performer after that. Probably something to do with the surprising rasp you have in your voice."

I pick my head up just enough to see if Linc's messing with me. "A rasp? Who do I think I am?"

"A true karaoke pro," Linc teases. "And I haven't even told you about our duet to 'Hey Mickey!'"

Now this makes me sit straight up. "We did *what*?"

I hate that song. Years of competition dance make you cringe anytime you hear a select few songs. That one is a top absolutely-not for me. How drunk was I?

Apparently the panic on my face is enough to make Linc break out in laughter. "Gotcha."

Excuse me? "Gotcha? You mean—"

He shakes his head. "We didn't. But good to know you would've believed it."

I sit up straight, needing Linc to rip off the rest of my humiliating Band-Aid. "Is there anything else I need to know?"

He shakes his head and sets down his sandwich. "Pretty soon after your red-light performance, you started to get sloppy. Which is what happens when you down probably four shots of Fireball straight from the bottle after quite a few drinks already. We knew it was time to go. And it was the right call, because you passed out in the ride share before we even got you here."

Okay, that's not too bad. "Thank you. So much."

He waves me off like it wasn't that big of a deal, even though it very much was. "You're my lady…what kind of fake boyfriend would I be if I didn't take care of you?"

His sentiment warms my body, but I need to temper it down. The key word in that sentence is fake. He was pretending to be my boyfriend last night to help get Jonathan away from me. Today is a new day. Today he's just a guy I hung out with at a bar and…

"Oh my God, we kissed! Like a lot!"

Devilish. That's the only word I can think of to describe the smile on Linc's face right now. It's just at one corner of his mouth. A mouth I apparently mauled last night, if my hazy memory serves me right.

"We did," he says. "Actually, you kissed me a few times. The highlight of my night."

Panic now starts racing through me. Embarrassing myself is one thing. Getting drunk is another. But kissing a guy in public—a guy who's personal life gets posted on the internet more than most—is something that I never, and I mean never, thought I'd have to deal with.

Especially with a raging headache. How much Advil does a girl need to take to make it stop?

I feel myself starting to breath heavier, but I start to calm the second I feel Linc's hand on the small of my back. His touch isn't much, just his thumb slowly rubbing up and down, is enough to do the trick.

"Hey," he says, leaning in close so his words are quiet. Comforting. Gone is the flirty smirk. Gone are the teasing eyes. No, right now is just Linc, the man who stepped in last night when he didn't have to. The man who I knew I could trust when I knew nothing about him beyond his immense kindness to a special little boy. "I know this is a little insane. And so was last night. I don't want to tell you how to feel, so I'm not going to tell you to not be embarrassed, but please know, last night was one of the best nights I've had in a very long time. And it's all because of you."

I want to believe that's a line. But I don't know…there's something in his look that's telling me he's serious.

"But, we should probably go over what comes next," he says with a soberness to his tone. "I'd bet my contract there are going to be pictures. Jonathan caused a few scenes last night, and frankly, so did we. And, I'm not sure if you know this, but I have a certain reputation."

"I've heard a thing of two," I say, trying to play it off without coming across like I was some sort of crazy internet stalker. I'm not. That's my sister Stella. "So what do we do?"

"I'll handle it," he says. "I pay people a lot of money to make sure things like this are handled appropriately. If pictures do come out, and depending on what the headlines are, we'll handle them as they come in."

"Do you think the whole boyfriend-slash-girlfriend thing is going to be a thing?" I ask.

He just shrugs. "Probably. But I'm not a fan of thinking about things that haven't happened yet. Waste of brain space. I prefer to only think about it when I have to."

That makes me laugh. "Oh, we are very different people, Linc Kincaid."

We share a smile, and just as I'm about to take a bite of my sandwich, I hear a phone starting to buzz somewhere nearby.

"That's you," he says, getting up and taking it off the charger. Wait…did he plug my phone in for me last night? He must've. That is so…thoughtful. "Says it's from 'The Siblings?'"

"Oh no," I say, snatching my phone and sliding the messages open. "Don't worry about gossip blogs or leaked pictures. I have a feeling what we *really* need to worry about is this group chat…"

QUINN

WHAT THE ACTUAL FUCK AINSLEY.

STELLA

I was JUST about to send the same text. What the hell were you doing out with Linc Kincaid? And he's your boyfriend? When the hell did that happen? Wait! Did he ask you out after the hospital visit?

MAEVE

Were you drinking? Ainsley Mae!

SIMON

Can we go back to the part where Ainsley is dating Linc Kincaid? What the fuck happened between you not knowing his name and being his squeeze?

QUINN

Fuck Linc. Wait…did you *fuck* Linc?

MAEVE

Jesus Christ Quinn…

QUINN

I'm just saying. She was drunk enough to sing karaoke; she could've been drunk enough to have sex with the man she's apparently dating. Also, side note, I need to know what songs you sang more than I need an iced coffee.

STELLA

Please for the love of God tell us everything.
Right now.

"Well, according to my siblings, you're my boyfriend," I say, pushing the phone aside. I know I need to straighten things out with them, but I can't right now. I don't have the energy for their antics. Not before this hangover has subsided.

"Okay then," he says. "Maybe we do need to come up with a plan."

We fall silent again, I assume both thinking of our next steps, but that doesn't last long. Linc's apartment door slams open, then shut, the sound echoing off the walls.

"Lincoln Kincaid! Where the hell are you, and what the fuck did you get into last night? And when did you get a girlfriend!"

"Fuck," he groans, letting his head fall back as he pinches between his eyes.

My eyes are wide as I look back toward the sound of stomping heels clicking furiously down his hallway. I can't see who it is yet, but it's clearly a woman. And she's clearly mad.

"Linc! Is that...do you have...Oh mylanta! Am I a fake mistress?"

He shakes his head. "No. Worse. She's my publicist."

10

line

"WHAT THE HELL?" KATIE YELLS AS SHE MARCHES INTO THE kitchen. It takes her a second before she sees Ainsley, which earns us another scream. "What the *hell*? Why is she here?"

Dang. Three-ish swear words in less than thirty seconds. I really am in trouble. Which now has my mind wondering what kinds of pictures got posted from last night.

"Katie, there is actually a very easy explanation," I say, trying to calm my publicist down while also doing my best to ease away the panicked look on Ainsley's face. That also explains why her mouth is hanging open. Panic and shock means she's not going to speak.

Dang, I might be a better boyfriend than I thought if I'm remembering that detail from last night.

"Oh, you better," Katie says as she slides her iPad down to me. "Because *this* is what I woke up to this morning."

Ainsley's sitting to my left, half covering her eyes like she's about to watch a murder scene in a scary movie. I inch closer to her, bringing the iPad between us.

"We'll look at it together," I whisper. "Last night was a tag-team effort. And so is today."

She slowly moves her hands away from her eyes and gives me the most timid nod I've ever seen. "Together."

I bring the iPad fully between us when the headline on some sports gossip blog is big, and bold, and honestly…only half wrong.

MORE TROUBLE, AND A NEW LOVE FOR NASHVILLE FURY'S LINC KINCAID

Linc Kincaid and mystery woman seen together at downtown bar. See pictures, and video, of the Fury tight end fighting over his newest lady.

Early verdict: Not as bad as the time with my first team when I was photographed leaving a mobster's poker game in Vegas—I swear I didn't know he was in the mob—but I'm guessing for someone like Ainsley, who apparently doesn't drink but was taking shots like a champ last night, this is really, really, bad.

I feel like I'm scrolling forever through pictures and screenshots that Katie has put together. And it's almost a chronological timeline of our night.

The photos start with when I first came over to her, when Dr. Dipshit was manhandling her. Someone even has the video of me jumping off the stage and stalking toward her table. Damn, I didn't realize I was that intense in the moment.

The rest of the pictures look like we are a happy couple enjoying a night out. Cuddled up in the VIP section. A few of us kissing. I can't help but smile when I see those, even though I know that's not the response that Ainsley or Katie want to see from me. There are even videos of both of us singing.

But the video that has likely set Katie ablaze is from toward the end of the night, when Ainsley had to literally jump into my arms to stop me from laying Dipshit on his ass. I didn't see the whole interaction between them—as I was walking back to the VIP section I saw her fall and then I saw him put his hands on her. I saw the panic in her eyes when she realized it was him.

And then all I saw was red.

I was going to hit him. I wasn't even trying to talk myself out of it. I was going to lose my career over a woman I barely knew. And I still don't know if I would've been sorry. The fucking asshole deserved it.

Then Ainsley saved me. Literally. When she jumped in my arms and distracted me just enough to bring me back to the present, I felt calmer. More collected. It was like I could feel my blood cooling with every second our lips touched.

I know she said that I saved her last night, but I don't know how much she realizes that she saved me too.

"Well? Do you and apparently *her* have anything to say?"

"I think the pictures tell the story pretty well," I say. "Oh, Ainsley, this is my publicist Katie. Katie, this is Ainsley."

"Nice to meet—"

Ainsley stands up to shake her hand, but Katie's crossed arms and quick glare make Ainsley sit right back down.

"What the hell, Katie?" I ask, wondering why she's so bent out of shape about this—*and* treating Ainsley like some gold-digging homewrecker. Granted, she doesn't know her. But Katie's usually pretty level headed. Nice to literally everyone. She wasn't even this mad after the first fake fight picture, which in my opinion was much worse if you put them side by side. "Listen, it's a few pictures and a few headlines."

"Headlines that talk about you fighting in bars over random women."

"Hey! She's not random," I say, suddenly feeling protective of the closest thing I've had to a girlfriend since, well, ever. "And I didn't fight. No punches were thrown. Just a lot of looks and some threatening words. And for that, I don't think you're giving me enough credit."

"Quit trying to be cute, Linc," Katie said flatly, finally uncrossing her arms but only so they can hold her up as she stands at the island. "I'm sorry I came in hot. I just wasn't ready for this. I thought after our incident a few weeks ago, we had an understanding that you were going to stay out of trouble."

She turns her gaze to Ainsley, who sinks back into the couch like she's praying it swallows her.

"Hey, this isn't her fault," I say, because I refuse to have Ainsley catching strays for a situation I escalated. "I recognized her from the hospital visit earlier in the week. Her ex, who I didn't know was her ex at the time, was bothering her. I stepped in. And I'd do it again, so fucking drop it."

I glance over to Ainsley, who's looking up at me with wide eyes. Like she's somehow shocked that I'm defending last night.

But I mean it. Every word. And I'd do it all again without question.

"So she's not your girlfriend?"

"No," I respond. Also, why is that the question she asked and not asking me why I almost got in fight? "I just made it up to try to get her ex away from her. But he wasn't leaving, so we kept up the act."

"And I need to apologize," Ainsley jumps in. "I got carried away at some parts."

Katie shakes her head, looking more resolved now. "So all of this was just a bar stunt?"

"Yes," Ainsley and I say together. We lock eyes after we do so, both of us looking a little sad. But why? We both knew last night was an act. Albeit, a fun one. But that's all it was. So why do I feel like I'm getting punched in the gut right now?

Plus, it's not like I could actually date her. Sure, when I first met her at the hospital, I had an idea of getting her number. Maybe seeing what she was about. But now that I know her better, I know that in no way, shape, or form can I date this woman. For one, I'm about to start the football season, which is the absolute worst time to get into a relationship. And second, I've known this girl for a total of maybe fifteen hours and I already know that she's too damn good, and too fucking pure, for me to taint.

And I would. That's who I am. No sense in denying that fact.

"Yes. Just a stunt," I say. "We don't know what to do next, so we're hoping you can use your PR magic?"

Katie doesn't answer for a second, instead grabbing her phone when an obnoxious nuclear fallout siren sound starts blaring from it. I glare at her, realizing she has likely tied my name in the media to that notification sound on her phone.

"Katie? What's—?"

"Shh!" She scolds, not looking up at us but instead very invested on whatever is on her phone. When she looks back up at us, gone is the angry look from a few minutes ago. Instead it's replaced by a smile that's a little…unsettling.

"Katie? Why are you smiling like you're a villain that just came into her origin story?"

She laughs off my comment. "Because, Linc. Apparently you never needed to hire me to repair your image. Apparently, all you needed was a girlfriend."

I reach out and grab Katie's phone, holding it so Ainsley and I can both see whatever is on her screen. I didn't know what I was going to see, but what I wasn't expecting was to be trending on social media.

For being a *boyfriend*.

"Social media is a crazy place," Katie says. "Because apparently, somehow, you two, overnight, have become the Fury's favorite couple."

"Holy moly…" Ainsley whispers as I scroll through post after post with words that have never been associated with me.

Posts with words like, "find someone who looks at you like Linc Kincaid looks at her." Which, that's a good one, because I *am* looking at Ainsley like she's everything. I believe this was during her final performance, when she was trying to be seductive. She was, but in a weirdly adorable way.

But as I keep scrolling, I'm seeing pictures and edits that have painted me in a good light for the first time since I started playing professional football. Then again, that's probably more to do with Ainsley than me. I have a feeling she can shine a bright light on the darkest of situations.

"What does all of this mean?" Ainsley asks.

Katie takes back her phone, and for the first time today, looks at Ainsley like she's not a parasite. "It means that as of right now, you and Linc are officially dating."

"Excuse me?" Ainsley asks. Which, I'm glad she asked, because her asking for clarification was a lot nicer than how I was going to put it.

"You're dating. You're a couple. As the kids say, you're *shipped.*'"

"No, we're not," I say. "You're crazy."

"Not crazy. Strategic. For the first time since you brought me on, I see the long game," she says, but pauses for a second before she continues. "We've been searching for something, anything, to make headlines to repair your reputation. Anything to show that you've moved on from your troubled past. And that thing is going to be the love of a good woman."

What are the words coming out of her mouth right now? "Katie, you can't be serious. You're saying you want me and Ainsley to keep dating *for my reputation?*"

"That's exactly what I'm saying," she says, point blank. "I'm not saying you have to sleep together. And it's probably better if you don't. Makes things confusing. But according to the public and the media? Linc Kincaid is officially off the market."

I don't even have to look over to Ainsley to know that her eyes are probably bugging out of her head.

"Fake date?" I ask again for clarity. "Who the hell does that?"

"More than you know," Katie says. "Before we get too far, who knows that last night was a sham?"

"Wyatt," I say. "Maybe Maddox."

"My best friend Mia," Ainsley says quietly.

Katie nods. "Good. Containable. It needs to stay that way."

"Can we slow the fuck down?" I ask. "I didn't agree to this. Neither did Ainsley. Plus, who the hell is going to believe this?"

"My siblings do," Ainsley says, her voice a little louder. "They know me better than anyone, and they were already asking me all kinds of questions today. And I'm the least likely of my family to start randomly dating a celebrity. So if I can make them believe it, anyone can."

Katie dramatically points to Ainsley. "See! That's what I'm talking about! This is going to be great!"

I stand and shake my head, because the more she talks, the more this doesn't feel right. "Ainsley, I'm going to go talk to Katie for a second. Wait here, please?"

Ainsley just nods and quickly looks down at her hands, as I summon Katie toward my door. Because I'm about five seconds away from kicking her out and telling her to come back when she has a better idea.

"You're nuts," I say. "No way this will work."

"It already is," she says, holding up her phone to show me a new video. This one is of us kissing, edited to some pop song I've never heard of. They've mixed in photos taken of us last night, but keep cutting back to the kiss. Which, I'll admit, was a damn good kiss.

"Linc, all I'm saying is that in a matter of hours, the headlines went from 'near fight' and 'back to his old ways' to no one giving a shit about any of that. All anyone is talking about is the woman who tamed the Fury's bad boy."

I pinch the bridge of my nose. Sure, it would work. I know it would. But I feel guilty using Ainsley to help fix my career.

"I can't do this," I say. "There has to be another way."

"I'm not taking that as a no," she says, as she rubs her hand up and down my arm. "Just think about it. Because if you really want to become a new Linc Kincaid, having a pretty girlfriend, who just happens to work at a children's hospital, isn't the worst way to do it. In fact, it might be the only way."

I don't get to say anything else as Katie brings her phone to her ear and promptly exits my apartment.

I keep thinking about it as I head back down the hall to Ainsley, who is probably having a small stroke over all this drama. A public relations relationship? That sounds like shit out of the movies, not something in my real life. Fake dating was one thing when we were making Dr. Dipshit jealous. But to do this on a long-term basis? Asking her to give up part of her life to help me? That's something I can't ask her to do.

"Hey, I'm sorry," I say as I take my seat back next to her. "What Katie suggested, it was un—"

"I'll do it."

I don't know if I'm more surprised that Ainsley cut me off or what she said. "Ainsley, I'm going to tell her no."

"Or you can tell her yes."

Where's the shy woman I met last night? Or the one I bumped into at the hospital who said three words? "It's not that simple."

"It actually is," she says. "See, there's this thing called a cell phone. And when you call her, you say 'yes, we're in.'"

Now I'm laughing. "Sarcasm? Not what I expected from you."

She shrugs. "It's the caffeine. Makes me sassy."

God, she needs to quit being adorable or I'm going to say yes to this crazy idea.

"I appreciate you wanting to do this. But really, you don't have to."

"I know. I want to. For both of us."

Damn, I didn't expect this kind of stubborn from her. "Ainsley, I say this with all of the love a fake boyfriend can, but are you still drunk?"

She laughs and stands up from the island, making her way to my living room like she already lives here. I follow as if I'm under a spell. And you know what? Maybe I am. That has to be it. She's drunk, and I'm hexed.

"Katie's right, this will help you," she says as she sits on my couch. "I was scrolling some social media while you two were talking. I can't believe just from a few photos how…every-where….we are."

"It's nuts. And it won't get better if we do this. But are you ready to have cameras following you around?"

"My building has great security. And as long as they stay off of hospital property, I think I can survive."

I appreciate her courage, but I can tell in her voice that she's trying to talk herself up to this more than anything.

"And then there's the whole Jonathan situation."

Oh. Yeah. Dipshit. "He's the reason we're here in the first place. I guess it would help you to have a reason at work to tell him to go fuck himself."

She laughs. "The day I tell someone to go eff themselves is… well…who knows, now? I got drunk last night and sang karaoke. And I thought those things would never happen."

Her lightness relaxes me a bit, letting me truly look at this woman. She's willing to give up so much for me. I'm a virtual stranger. Sure, having a fake boyfriend to fend off an ex is conve-nient, but the long and short of it is that she's giving up a lot more for me than I am for her.

"Ainsley, are you sure about this? You'd be giving up your life, for however long this would go on. I'm sure you have dates to go on. Actual ones with guys who can give you futures. I'm not that guy, and I don't want to be the one to hold you back. Especially when I know that I can never be anything more than fake to you."

There. I said it. Cards on the table.

Part of me expected her to nod her head, agree with me, and gather her things and go. A shake of the hand maybe for an interesting night.

Then I remembered I've learned this woman is stubborn. So not only does she not waiver, she moves in closer and takes my hand.

Seriously, who is this enigma of a woman?

"First of all, there are no dates. Which should probably be more embarrassing to admit, but it's the truth."

She has to be just saying that. Men should be pounding down doors and starting wars for a chance with her. Hell, I almost did.

"And then there's this." She holds up her phone and shows me text messages from Dr. Dipshit. Just the sight of him in her phone sends my blood simmering. "When you were talking to Katie, Jonathan texted me, demanding I talk to him before work on Monday. He still doesn't believe we're together. That he'd like to go into work with us patched up and already a couple again. And I don't want that, so believe me, Linc, this helps me just as much as it'll help you."

"Okay, but—"

She sticks a finger to my mouth, giving me a playful wink to go along with it. "Aren't you the one last night telling me to get out of my head and do something scary?"

I give a small laugh as I feel a smile creeping in. "Using my own words against me?"

"I use whatever weapons I have," she says. "So what do you say, Kincaid? Let's do something scary and fake date."

guide to love rule #37

Fake it till you make it. Just don't fall in love.

11
ainsley

Did I just say that? Did those words really come out of my mouth?

I think they did. I heard them.

Linc was right, I must still be drunk.

I've never asked a guy out—fake or real. Well, I did once in third grade when I asked Tommy Hatcher to be my boyfriend. He told me he'd let me know after recess.

I'm still waiting.

But even though he never gave me my answer, that one time was enough for me to realize that putting yourself out there is scary and that I never wanted to do it again. And I haven't. Until now.

"You sure about this?" Linc asks, his green eyes giving away how conflicted he feels right now.

"I am," I say, trying to be as confident as I can be. "I mean, we probably need to come up with some logistics. A backstory. And maybe I should know your middle name. Things like that. But yeah. I'm sure about this."

He laughs. "My middle name?"

"I don't know? It feels like something people in a relationship would know about each other. Mine is Mae."

"Ainsley Mae? How Southern are you?"

"Very," I say, leaning into my faint drawl a little harder. "We moved to Rolling Hills when I was at toddler. But before that my family lived in Georgia. Every member of my family for generations has gone to the University of Tennessee. I only went to Vanderbilt because of the nursing program. But just wait until you meet my mother. The only thing stronger than her drawl is her sweet tea."

Linc lets out a huff of a laugh as he shakes his head. "At this time yesterday I was planning for a day of never leaving my house. Twenty-four hours later I'm in a conversation about meeting the mother of my fake girlfriend."

I can't keep the smile off my face. "So we're doing this?"

Again, who am I? Why am I the one insisting on this? Am I that starved for a relationship that I'll take even a fake one? Do I need a buffer that much from Jonathan that I'm willing to become a part-time actress to make it happen? I must be. That's the only explanation I can think of.

Or at least, the only one I'm willing to admit to myself.

Linc looks at me, his eyes softer than they've been since Katie barged in here. "I'm not going to lie; this would help me. A lot. This is a really big season for me, and anything I can get to help me both on and off the field, I'd be a fool to send away."

"I'm happy to help."

He shakes his head, taking his hands in mine and pinning me with his stare. I barely known this man, but I've already learned so much about him through his eyes. They're so expressive, and I don't even know if he realizes they possess that power.

"I know you are, because you're a good person. I barely know you, and I know that much," he says. "But this is going to be a lot for you, Ainsley. I'm not the biggest star on the team, but I've starred in a lot of negative headlines over the years, so the gossip rags know I'm an easy target. And all of them were my fault. I'm not known for the best choices, and trouble seems to find me, even if I try and distance myself from it. But I'm trying to become a better person. A better man. And if you did this…I don't know how I could ever repay you."

The sincerity in his tone right now is hitting me straight in my heart. How can I not help him? "Linc, I don't know if this is too much, too soon, but I'm going to be honest with you. I was in a weird place mentally before last night. I was lonely. Depressed. So much so that I actually considered calling Jonathan."

Well, *that* gets his attention. "Is that why he showed up?"

I quickly shake my head. "No. I didn't call. But when he appeared, it threw me. At first, I thought that it might be a sign. That if I thought about him, and then all of a sudden he's back, maybe it was a signal we should work it out."

"Ainsley, I don't care if you're struck by lightning, *never* get back with that idiot."

That makes me laugh. "I know that. Well, now. It was just…I know my mental state going into last night. If he would've showed up, and you weren't there… I don't know what I would've done."

I watch as Linc's jaw ticks, which…why is that so attractive? I know last night that he was playing up the protective role when Jonathan was around. But seeing it today? When it's just us? Oh, sweet baby Jesus…

"Well, then, that settles it," Linc says, popping up from the couch and holding out his hand. "Yes, Ainsley Mae. I'll be your fake boyfriend."

I can't keep the smile off my face as I stand up quickly— maybe a little too quickly as I wobble, suddenly lightheaded because that breakfast sandwich Linc ordered for me went untouched.

"Whoa," he says, grabbing my arms just hard enough to steady me. "You okay?"

"Yeah. Just need some food."

"I know the perfect spot," he says. "Come on, girlfriend. Let's get a real hangover breakfast."

———

"Here we go, Linc. One garbage omelet. And one avocado toast and fruit cup for the lovely lady."

"Thanks, Mel," Linc says, grabbing a bottle of hot sauce as I stare at the omelet.

"Have you never seen a garbage omelet?"

I shake my head at Mel's question, which makes the seventy-plus-year-old Greek man chuckle. "I didn't think any portion of food could be so big."

"That's why it's a garbage omelet. Just a bunch of things thrown together. Cleans out the fridge. Garbage."

"That makes sense," I say as I twist my head to get another angle. "But did you clean out an industrial one?"

"Oh, I like her," Mel says. "Even if she only ordered toast."

I immediately open my mouth to apologize—because I really did want to try an omelet but my stomach rebelled at the thought—before Linc put his hand on my forearm to stop me. "Quit giving my girlfriend shit, Mel. She'll eat what she wants."

"Girlfriend?" he says. "You've been coming into this place every Saturday for six months and not once did you tell me you had a lady! Why've you been hiding her? Is it because she only eats toast?"

Now it's my turn to laugh. "Toast is just a today thing. I promise when he brings me back next week I'll try an omelet."

Mel nods and gives me a wink. "I'll hold you to it. You two enjoy."

I laugh as Mel winds through the small dining area of his hole-in-the-wall restaurant back to the kitchen. "He's a delight."

"He's something," Linc says. "I hope you don't mind that I told him that you're my girlfriend. He's one that I felt safe to try it out on who wouldn't think I was full of shit, but also at the same time, if he didn't believe me, he'd call me out."

I shake my head as I pick up the slice of sourdough piled with bright green mashed avocado. "Not at all."

"Good. But is it scary how easily it rolled off my tongue?"

"You had practice last night," I say. "Now it's just a continuation."

"True. That, and the looks we got this morning probably helped."

I've never done a walk of shame in my life. I've heard about them from Quinn and Stella. Maeve likely did them in her time, but she's never shared the stories. But since I never slept with any guys in college, there was no shame to be had.

But this morning, as I walked out of Linc's apartment building wearing the same rolled-up pair of gym shorts and oversized T-shirt he gave me earlier, I had a taste of what my sisters were talking about. Though they were just regretting decisions they made the night before, I was getting stared at by the people in his building and even received a few side-eye glances and whispers as we walked the few blocks to Painter's Alley and then around the block to this hidden gem of a diner.

Linc was right. He's a celebrity in the sense that people know who he is, but not enough that paparazzi were waiting outside of his building. But still, it was unsettling knowing that people now know who I am, just by association.

"So—"

"Do—"

Our words come out at the same time, and our moment of awkwardness is followed by laughter.

"Why is this so weird?" I ask.

"Probably because 'how do we fake date' isn't a conversation you have every day?"

He has a point there. I'm also very glad we're the only ones here. I already don't know how to act around Linc, so having to have this talk, while not having to deal with people staring, is a blessing.

"I mean, I've never had it," I say as I take a sip of my orange juice.

"I'll take you one further," he says. "I've never had any kind of relationship talk. Ever."

Now that does surprise me. "You've never been in a relationship?"

He shakes his head. "I wasn't kidding when I told you that I'm not the forever guy, Ainsley. I have baggage. Scars. A past full of bad decisions that I'm paying for every day. I never wanted a relationship then—I was too selfish and busy burning my life down."

"And now?"

His eyes turn sad. "And now I don't want to burden anyone while I work through my demons. Playing for the Fury, this is my last chance at a career. I'm twenty-eight, which is middle-aged in football years. If I can put together a season to remember, then maybe I bought myself a few more. But if I can't get out of my own way—which is the story of my life, mind you—I'm done. And there's no backup plan. So I told myself no distractions this year."

Well, now I feel bad. Did I really force this on him? I'm not forceful. Am I?

"And then I came along…"

He smiles through the pain and reaches over the table, grabbing my hand like it's the most natural thing in the world. "That's not what I meant. I'm glad we're doing this. The more I think about it, the more it makes sense. All I'm saying is that there's never been a time in my life when I've thought about being a boyfriend, fake or otherwise, so to say I'm out of my depth is an understatement."

That makes sense, even though it hurts my heart to know that he went through a past that he still feels like he's atoning for. I want to ask him about it, but I know this isn't the time or the place.

"Well, then, we're really up a creek," I say. "Because if you think I know what to do, you're sadly mistaken. My only adult relationship experience is with Jonathan, and you see what a gem he is. And I'm not the best at making decisions."

"Really? You seemed just fine today deciding that we were going to do this."

"I think you were right. I was still drunk. Because that's not me." My joke coaxes a smile out of him. "But what about you? Weren't you the one last night who swooped in and played the hero? Declaring yourself as my boyfriend? That seemed pretty decision-y."

He gives me an almost shy shrug. Which is adorable, because I didn't think there was anything shy about Linc. Though I'm seeing a different side of him this morning than I did last night. "That was a split-second decision, and believe me, those usually don't pan out for me. Actually, that might be the first time in my life an impulsive decision didn't end up with me in a fight or in jail."

I can't hide my surprise. "Jail? You've been to jail?"

"A few times," he says. "Minor arrests. Nothing with extended sentences."

"Still," I say. "I've never even gotten a speeding ticket."

"That doesn't surprise me," he says. "Okay, so this is the blind leading the blind?"

"Pretty much."

Linc puts down his fork—after taking the biggest bite I've ever seen—before resting his elbows on the table. "Okay, let's start easy. How is this going to work?"

"That's the easy question?"

"Maybe easy wasn't the best word. More like necessary."

"True," I say. "How about we lay out what we absolutely need to get out of this. And then we can figure out what we need to do to make those things happen?"

"Look at you, taking charge," Linc says with a wink. "I like it."

I feel a blush creeping in, which I do my best to push down.

If that's all it takes for my cheeks to turn red around this man, then I need to figure out a way to build a better defense system.

"For me, I need for Jonathan to get the picture and leave me the heck alone. So I'm going to need to be able to talk freely about you being my boyfriend."

Linc raises an eyebrow. "That's it?"

I shrug. "I think?"

He shakes his head. "Oh, no. I told you last night we're going to make that man jealous as fuck. And I don't know if we really did a good enough job last night, since he's still texting you."

He moves a chair over, sliding into me and grabs my cell phone.

"What are you doing?" I stare at him, jaw hanging, as he flips my phone toward me to open it with the Face ID.

I watch for another second as he navigates to my camera. I'm still in shock as he holds the cell phone in front of us, snapping a selfie as he kisses me on the cheek.

"Linc!" I say with a giggle. "What was that?"

He holds it in front of me. "Our first photo."

I take a look at it, and if you ignore the mess of hair that's thrown on the top of my head with a hair tie I found in my purse, the fact that I have no makeup, and not a lick of my normal morning skincare routine, we do look cute.

"I'm sending this to myself, which then also means you now have my number."

"Oh yeah. Probably need that."

"You should make that your wallpaper, just in case Dr. Dipshit sees your screen." Linc navigates around my phone for a few more seconds before handing it back to me.

"You done?"

I watch as this man takes two more random selfies, and then a few of me, likely looking exasperated with my new boyfriend. "Now I am."

"You're a lot, aren't you?" I ask.

He winks at me as he moves back to his side of the table. "Oh, you have no idea."

I'm going to blame the sudden knot in my stomach from the lack of food I've had today and the abundance of alcohol last night.

"Okay, so you need me to go into overdrive and make Dr. Dipshit get the picture that he's not a part of your life. Easy enough. Call me boyfriend whenever you want. Hell, come up with a pet name for me. I'll also make sure to send plenty of flowers to the hospital. Lunch deliveries. Coffee drop-off. Impromptu patient visits. He'll see me so much he'll think I work there."

"That seems like a lot," I say. "Plus, isn't football season starting? Would you even have time for all of that?"

"Ah, see, the thing about football schedules is that we're very regimented. Every week, unless we have a Thursday or Monday game, is very structured."

"So the opposite of mine," I say. "I work mostly days, but the shifts are long and can fluctuate."

"That's why this will work," he says. "So when I randomly pop in with your favorite coffee order, it won't be random at all."

"Well, I don't drink coffee, so you'll have to think of something else."

Now it's Linc's turn to be shocked. "You don't drink coffee?"

"Nope. And that Coke I had today was a hangover exception. I do drink sweet tea though"

He shakes his head. "With every word you say, I'm more intrigued by you, Ainsley Mae."

I have to look away, because there's no fighting this blush. Linc calling me that is making my body react in a way that is definitely not appropriate for a Saturday afternoon in a dive diner. Only after I take a few breaths can I look back to my boyfriend, who's just looking at me with…gosh I can't describe it, but his eyes are soft and warm, and I have a feeling I'm going to need to remind myself on a daily basis that this is not real.

"Thanks," I say. "So with your season starting, what will you need from me?"

He sits up a little straighter as I turn back the conversation. "I'm guessing Katie is going to make sure we're seen out. So dinners, when we can squeeze them in. I have some charity things and team functions that people would assume you would attend with me. And of course, if you can make it to games—that's the easiest."

"That should be no problem," I say. "Oh, just wait until I tell my brother I'm going to be going to Fury games. He's..."

The words die on my lips as I look out of the window of the diner. I watch four very familiar people looking around outside on the street, acting as if they're lost, until they spot me staring at them through the window.

"What?" Linc says, looking out the window in a panic. "Is someone watching us?"

I nod, but I don't blink. "Yes. My siblings."

12
linc

I LOOK OUT THE WINDOW OF THE DINER, NOT REALLY SURE WHAT I'M about to see.

And somehow, without knowing who Ainsley's siblings, are, I know when I see them immediately.

"I'm going to kill them."

I choke on a laugh, because what I'm looking at right now is downright comical. Three of them are wearing all black. The fourth has long, dark hair and is wearing normal casual clothes for a Sunday. She also looks annoyed as hell at the other three. There's one guy among them, and he's pushing a stroller. The two black-clad women are looking around like they're auditioning for the next spy movie. Honestly, I'm ready for the blonde to start jumping on cars.

"What are they doing?" I ask as I watch the guy quickly look away from the window, clearly trying to do his best to look casual but massively failing.

Ainsley shakes her head and throws in an eye roll. "Not having boundaries."

She throws down her napkin and pushes away from the table, marching to the front door.

"What are you idiots doing?"

I look back through the window to see all of them freeze at Ainsley's yell.

"I told you she'd see us," the non-black-wearing woman says.

"She wouldn't have if you would've worn black, Maeve!"

"It wasn't the black, dumbass," she replies to the man. "It's that she was sitting in front of a window, and you're not stealthy. You're on the downhill slope to forty and pushing a baby stroller."

"How dare you!" he yells.

"Will you four just get in here? You're causing a scene, and I've had enough over the past twenty-four hours."

I stand up from my chair realizing that I need to think quickly right now.

This is Ainsley's family. I know they were already worried about her today, based on her reaction to the group texting. But for them to track her down and come here, and clearly with some level of planning, feels like a lot. Is this a normal family thing? Or just a her-family thing?

I've never met a family in the capacity of a boyfriend. Actually, I've rarely met families. In high school and college, I didn't have serious girlfriends, so I never had to deal with a dad greeting me at the front door with a baseball bat. Even my friend group wasn't the kind who had moms who were inviting us over for Sunday dinners. The only one who would've done that was my Gram, but she hated my friends and told me they were bad influences.

She wasn't wrong.

The only time I've ever met anyone's family was at Mississippi State. Wyatt would always make sure to invite me to dinner when his parents were in town. I knew why he did it—Gram was too old to travel at that point, which meant I never had anyone coming to see me play on Saturdays or take me out for a decent meal—but they never made me feel bad about it. I always appreciated that.

But this is not that. The Atkinses were trying to make me feel included.

Ainsley's family is ready to put me under the interrogation lamp.

"Well, well, this must be my sister's new boyfriend."

I swallow the sudden lump in my throat, and wipe my hand on my shorts just to make sure I'm not sweating. "I am. Linc Kincaid."

"Oh, I know who you are." The male looks me up and down, trying to seem intimidating. Also, the stroller he was pushing doesn't have a baby in it. Which is weird.

"Oh, save it," Ainsley says. "Can we just all sit down and cool off? Also, why do you have an empty stroller? Where is my niece?"

"It's part of my cover," he says as we all take a seat. I pull out Ainsley's chair for her, making sure she sits before I get into mine. I might not know how to be a boyfriend, but that just feels like bare minimum.

Once I focus back on the siblings I'm glad I did. Four pairs of eyes are staring at me, and they're all giving me different looks.

The blonde, who looks about the same age as Ainsley, is just smiling.

The one not wearing black is shooting eye daggers at me.

The other sister wearing all black is sitting back in her chair, looking very casual. And I'm pretty sure she's wagging her eyebrows.

And the guy? He's still trying to look scary. I hate to tell him that he's not.

"Quickly, let's get this out of the way," Ainsley says, "Linc, these are my siblings. That's Stella; I don't know why she's smiling like that. Maeve is trying to decide which question she wants to ask first. Quinn is being inappropriate, and I apologize for her. And Simon? He's not that tough."

"Yes, I am!" he protests, leaning in closer to me. "Now, we have some questions for you, Mr. Kincaid."

"Hold up," Ainsley says. "Before we get into the interrogation, what are you idiots doing here? Also, do you know the definition of boundaries?"

"You didn't answer us today," Stella says. "We were worried."

"So you decided to dress up as amateur ninjas and, what, use my location tracker to find out where I was?"

All four of them sit back with guilty looks on their faces.

"We just wanted to make sure you were all right," Maeve says. "It's not like you to go radio silent."

"And we saw the pictures and videos," Quinn says. "You were drinking and singing karaoke. And then there's this guy, who, the last we heard you just met last week at the hospital and now is your boyfriend. You should have known we were going to come looking for you."

Ainsley's shoulders slump a little. "I'm sorry I didn't respond. It's just been….well, let's just say today's been a little crazy."

I don't know if this is the right thing to do, but I don't think about it as I reach under the table for her hand. From the little bit I know of Ainsley, this girl does not like to be the center of attention. And yet here she is, with four interrogation lamps set on her. When she feels my hand connect with hers, she slowly turns to look at me. I watch as a little stress leaves her shoulders. She squeezes my hand back, but doesn't let go.

"Guys! Look at them!" Stella croons. "They're freaking adorable!"

Ainsley blushes and turns back to her siblings, but doesn't let go of my hand. "I'm guessing you guys have questions."

"Only a thousand," Stella says.

"Can we just get rid of the elephant in the room and ask when the fuck did you two start dating and why did the internet find out before us?"

Oh shit…what's our story?

I assume that if her siblings wouldn't have shown up, we

would've gotten around to figuring out our story that we're telling everyone. But we didn't yet, and judging by the ghostly white color painting Ainsley's face, she's not sure what to say.

"That's my fault, so I'm sorry about that," I say, giving our joined hands a squeeze, silently hoping to convey that I got this for her. "I don't like to go public that I'm dating someone until it's secure, you know? But, unfortunately, snooping cameras and Ainsley's ex, had other plans."

"Wait!" Maeve yells. "Why is Jonathan a part of this story?"

"I thought he lived in Texas!" Stella blurts out, looking alarmed.

Ainsley just nods. "He's back. I didn't know it until he showed up last night. He obviously didn't know I was seeing someone, so he got a little close. That's when Linc stepped in."

"No wonder you drank," Quinn says. "I'd be drunk too if my douchebag of an ex showed up out of nowhere." The look Ainsley shoots her direction suggests Quinn might get drunk for a lot less. Got it—she's the fun one.

"I prefer to call him Dipshit," I add, which earns me a smile from Quinn.

"Oh, I like this one, Ainsley."

God, does this woman go five seconds without blushing? It's adorable. And it also makes me wonder: if she blushes that easy in her cheeks, does the rest of her body?

No, Linc. Stop. Stop that right the fuck now. She's your fake girlfriend, emphasis on fake, and you're meeting her fucking family. Mind out of the goddamn gutter.

"Can we back up a second?" Maeve asks. "Didn't you two just meet last week? How the heck did you go from strangers to a couple in a week?"

"You want to take this or me?" I ask. To them, I hope it sounds like a simple question. In reality, I need to know if I'm making this shit up or she is.

I see her square her shoulders, and I suddenly feel a wave of pride that she's going to go out on this limb. Though it's probably for the best, since I have no idea what she's told her family.

So I sit back and listen, interested to hear our origin story.

"You're right, we did just meet at the hospital visit," she says. "I didn't think much of it, but then the next day, this guy shows back up again."

I pick up my cue with a smile. "I did. I didn't have a chance to get her name or number after she mowed me down and ran away."

She gasps. "Excuse me? *You* ran into *me*."

"If I remember correctly, you were looking everywhere but ahead. I had the right of way."

"Awwwwww." I look up to see Stella and Quinn with hearts in their eyes, clear approval of our not-so-fake meet cute. I think we're halfway to convincing them. Maeve is still keeping an even face. And I wonder if at any point her brother is going to stop scowling at me.

I turn my attention back to Ainsley, who's now going on about how I asked her for coffee that day.

"Which is when I learned she doesn't drink coffee."

My interruption earns me a smile from Ainsley. "Which is also when we pivoted and went to get smoothies."

When I was young, I'd make up elaborate stories. More for entertainment than anything. As I got older, those stories became me trying to create alibis for myself, or reasons why it really wasn't my fault for what I clearly did. When you're that kind of liar, it rolls off the tongue, sometimes too easily.

But with Ainsley? I would bet my contract that this woman has never told a lie in her life. Yet, right now, she's making up our first date, and the days after, like it's nothing.

I don't know whether to be proud or frightened.

"So we ended up texting and talking all week. Then last night, he asked if I wanted to meet up with him and some of his team-mates. I was a little nervous, obviously, especially when he said they were going to a karaoke bar. But then he said I could bring Mia, so I agreed. Things were fine until Jonathan showed up, and then…yeah. The rest, I'm pretty sure the whole world saw."

"Wow," Stella says with a shake of her head. "I feel like that was quite a whirlwind."

"The best things are," I say, putting my arm around Ainsley for a little emphasis. It clearly works with Stella and Quinn. But I still can't crack Maeve or Simon.

"That's all well and good, but this makes zero sense." Maeve focuses on Ainsley, who I don't think is breathing. She must be the family lie detector. "I mean, I know it's not like you were in some sort of recovery program, but in all the years I've known you, there's not been one time where you've even *wanted* a drink. And suddenly last night you're drinking, singing—which might've been more shocking than the drinking—and have a pro football player boyfriend. I'm sorry, it just all feels like a lot. And it doesn't feel like you."

I start to reply, suddenly getting the feeling like I did last night when Dr. Dipshit was berating her. I don't know why I have this overwhelming urge to protect Ainsley, but I do.

"Maeve's right, Ainsley," Simon says. "You could've put yourself in a dangerous situation. You aren't used to—"

"She's a grown woman," I interrupt, because they need a reality check. All of the siblings eyes turn to me, which is good. "She wanted to blow off some steam. She was in a safe place with me, Mia, and ten other professional football players, who weren't going to let a thing happen to her. Despite the night of debauchery you think you saw, we had fun. *She* had fun. So maybe back off a little, considering you guys just blew in here and bombarded her after a very stressful morning of processing the consequences of dating someone like me."

It's silence for a few seconds, including Ainsley, who out of the corner of my eye I can tell is slack-jawed. This is also how I know that I have no clue how to be a boyfriend, because I'm pretty sure you don't tell your girlfriend's siblings basically to fuck off after knowing them for twenty minutes.

"Well, damn," Quinn says, breaking the silence. "Ainsley's got a live one."

"She does," I say. "This wasn't the way we wanted to tell people. Things got out of control last night, and for that, I do apologize. But your sister is a grown woman and one of the most responsible people I've ever met. She can make her own decisions. And we're in this now. Together."

I look over to Ainsley, who's smile about knocks me out of the chair. It's the same smile she gave me when I saved her from Dipshit. It's the same smile she gave me so many times last night, thanking me but without saying the words.

And it's a smile that I need to make sure I don't let break through to my heart. Because if I did, I'm pretty sure it would ruin me.

Or worse, ruin her.

"Okay then," Simon says, pinning his eyes to me. "But I do need to ask you one question."

I've been waiting for this. If this guy went to Tennessee, then he follows SEC football. Which means he likely knows about my history: What I did in college. Why I didn't get drafted. Why it took me years to land with a team. And frankly, if he didn't ask, I'd be questioning his big brother status.

"Understandable." I say, taking a deep breath. "Fire away."

"I have two," he says, clasping his hands in front of him. "You can clearly see that we love our sister, and we're very protective of her. So I need to know, what are your intentions with our Ainsley?"

"Oh mylanta," Ainsley says with a groan. But I just smile. Somehow, this answer is the easiest one I'll have to answer all day.

"I want to take it slow, see where this goes," I say before looking over to her. "This week has been fast and crazy. I want to slow down a bit and continue getting to know her. And hopefully, she keeps me around for a while."

There. A committed answer that a boyfriend would give while also giving us an out for when the time comes that we call this quits.

"I can accept that," Simon says. "Now, most importantly, I know your history, which is why I need to know…"

I suck in a breath as I brace myself for the uncomfortable questions.

"Are you guys going back to the big game this year?" he asks, shocking me, and I think the rest of the table. "I just need to know if I should put money down on the early odds. Also, are you starting? Or is that insider trading? Because if I can put down an early line for you to lead in receiving yards this year for a tight end…well, that could be a pretty payday here in a few months."

"Simon!" Ainsley yells. "Are you seriously asking my boyfriend for gambling advice?"

He shakes his head. "No, because that's against the rules that Linc here has to abide by. But, this guy won me a shit-ton of money last year." He turns his eyes to me, the scowl that he wore before now gone and is replaced with more of a fan-boy look. "That catch? Gave me the over for the game and hit on a parlay that won me five grand. Clearly I need to know what the team is looking like, and since my inside man retired a few years ago, I now need to use the resources I have in front of me."

"Um, we're looking good?" I say, still confused. "Also, inside man?"

"Did my sister not tell you? Wes Taylor, former tight end? He's one of my best friends."

Now it's my turn to fan boy. "Are you serious? The guy who's position I now play? He's one of my fucking idols!"

"Do you want to meet him?" Simon pulls out his phone. "I can call him right now."

We start talking as Simon dials a number before I hear a squawk of irritation from next to me.

"Can you two stop?" Ainsley snaps, taking everyone by surprise. "Actually, can this be done? I'm very hungover, and since I've only been hungover one other time in my life, this is really the worst. I'd like to go home and sleep and not wake up until tomorrow. So can we adjourn whatever this has turned into?"

I'm guessing that no one is used to Ainsley yelling like that, so the siblings quickly gather their things and I hustle up front to pay for our meals. We all say our goodbyes—Simon hugs me and promises to arrange a lunch with Wes—and even Maeve doesn't scowl at me before getting in her car.

All and all, not the worst it could've gone.

"Step one, done," Ainsley says. "Do you think they believed us?"

I bring her in for a side hug as we start walking back toward my apartment. "One hundred percent."

13
the banks family group chat - minus ainsley

So we don't believe her, right?

Absolutely not. It once took her a week to decide what earrings to wear with a dress she had bought two months prior. No way she's all of a sudden dating Linc after a week of knowing him and two-ish dates.

I know this isn't the topic of conversation, but I found a video of her singing. The girl sang a sex song!

Send it immediately.

Can you two focus? What are we going to do?

I say we let her roll with it. If she wants to think that we're buying it, we let her.

QUINN

So you want us to lie to her and let her pretend?

MAEVE

Really, Quinn? You, of all people, are going to get offended by someone lying about relationships?

QUINN

I didn't lie. I just didn't admit. There's a difference.

SIMON

Listen, I say we let them do what they need to do.

STELLA

Since when did you become the sensible one?

SIMON

I've always been sensible.

MAEVE

Absolutely not.

SIMON

As long as he treats her right, and gets me some tickets, I'll believe whatever they want me to.

MAEVE

Why are you acting like a broke-ass who can't buy his own football tickets? Last I checked, your six-figure income is plenty to afford some nice seats.

SIMON

I mean sure, I can. But why should I when my future brother-in-law is the starting tight end?

STELLA

Easy, brother. This is fake, I'm 99% sure of that. I highly doubt Linc Kincaid is going to become the next Banks-in-law.

SIMON

A guy can hope. I mean, my brothers-in-law are my business partner, a man who invents video games, my favorite bar owner, and now a football player? I'm in man heaven!

STELLA

You're ridiculous.

SIMON

So I've been told.

MAEVE

Okay, to round this up: We all think this is fake. But we're all in agreement that we're going to go along with this until further notice? Agree.

QUINN

Yes, Mama Maeve.

STELLA

Noted.

SIMON

I can't wait to go to games this year!

MAEVE

Why do we even try with you...

guide to love rule #28

When entering a fake relationship, have safeguards in place to make sure you don't fall for your faux boyfriend.

14

ainsley

For the most part, I love who I am as a person. I love my empathy and the way I can find good in most situations. I love my job and helping people. I have good friends, am a good sister, and being an aunt is the best title in the world.

But I hate—no, loathe—that I'm an overthinker.

It's the actual worst.

Because tell me why, I, a fully capable and grown woman, is sitting her in apartment, alone, staring at her phone, wondering if she should text the man she's apparently dating.

I mean, I can, can't I? He made sure to give me his number earlier today when we were at breakfast. When we said our goodbyes, he told me that we'd talk soon to figure out our next steps. But did that mean he would reach out to me? Me reach out to him? I'm not exactly sure what I would say, but I have questions that we didn't get to today due to my siblings interrupting us in the worst game of ninja spies ever.

First: How long am I going to be the girlfriend of Linc Kincaid? Are we talking weeks? Months? Years? What have I signed up for?

Oh, and the question of sleepovers. Does he expect things to happen? I don't feel like he does. I stayed at his house last night, and he put me in his bed and slept on an uncomfortable recliner when I was there for the vulnerable taking. But I'm not, as my sisters say, experienced. I've slept with two guys in my life, and both of those were very forgettable. Or really, unforgettable, because of how bad they were.

At least, I don't think they were good? I don't have anything to compare it to. I just know if *that* was good, then I have no idea what my sisters talk about or what I read about in romance novels.

I want to talk to him about these things, but if I text him, am I weird? Clingy? I don't want to be a stage-five clinger, but I'm starting to feel like a stage five crazy person.

Just as I'm about to toss my phone down on the couch to get it out of sight, I feel the vibration in my hand of a text coming through.

BOYFRIEND

Hey, I need your help with something.

I read it a few times. And yup…he did that.

AINSLEY

Did you put your name in my phone as boyfriend?

Of course. That's what I am, aren't I?

I feel my smile coming on, and there's nothing I can do to stop it. Especially because it's accompanied by little butterflies in my stomach.

This isn't real, Ainsley. He's not really your boyfriend. He's just playing into the part. Don't get giddy.

Okay, *boyfriend*. What can I help with?

I need a new show to watch, and I can't decide.

I can't help but laugh as I snuggle into my couch.

And you're asking me? I wasn't lying today when I said that I'm the queen of decision paralysis. I've been wanting to text you for an hour but talked myself out of it because I couldn't decide to do it.

An hour?

Yes, but let's not focus on that. Back to your problem.

You can text me whenever you'd like. Please don't overthink that.

But I really need help. I have nothing to watch, and Wyatt is no help. Maddox will suggest a freaking British baking show or some shit like that.

Oh, I love those! They're so competitive but so nice at the same time.

Come on, Ainsley Mae...not you too...

I'm just saying, they're delightful. Especially at Christmas.

You're not helping.

Okay, let's find you something. What do you like to watch? Is there something you're in the mood for?

Comedy? No...thriller. Maybe a cop drama? I don't know. All I know is that it's football season and I want something to occupy my mind when I'm not at practice or studying plays, because I don't want to get the itch to go make stupid decisions. And there are going to be times when you're working, so I need something to fill my time. So if I have something addicting, I'm more likely to stay home. Does that make sense?

> Totally. But, I hate to tell you this, I'm no help in those genres. The shows that I tend to watch are more on the romantic side. I'm actually doing a rewatch now of my favorite hospital drama of all time. Totally addicting. There's drama and blood, but also love and scandal. Really, something for everyone. And it's been going on for like twenty years, so there's plenty to binge. Would totally get you through a football season.

> You lost me at love.

My heart sinks a little at that. Though it shouldn't. Linc has been up front that he's not a love, or forever, or a commitment guy. In fact, I should save a screenshot of this text to remind me of that when I start feeling those stupid butterflies.

> Suit yourself. But I think if you want an addicting show, that's your bet.

> I'll keep scrolling.

> Fair. Do you want to know the name of it, just in case?

> I'm good, thanks. Maybe I'll try a baking show...

I smile and almost put my phone down, but I don't. I need to ask him at least one of the questions. He said I could, plus he opened the texting door. No need to overthink this.

I audibly laugh at that thought. Because yeah, right. That'll be the day...

> While you're deciding, can I ask you a question?

> Of course.

I know we talked about some logistics today, but…I feel like we need to cover a few more things.

Such as?

I know we laid out what we could both use from this, but how long is this going to go?

Trying to get rid of me already?

No. Not at all. I'm just wondering, because this can't go on forever. And I need to prepare for things. I know this might come as a shock to you, but I'm not good with spontaneity.

No…really?

I know. Shocker. But if I know what our timeline is, I'll feel much more comfortable.

I mean, I guess I didn't think about it. You know, because I don't think. I save that for you.

Happy to help.

Linc doesn't respond back immediately, which doesn't freak me out. Actually, I like that he's taking his time.

But, what does freak me out is ten seconds later when I see "Boyfriend" pop up on my phone, accompanied by one of the selfies he took of himself as a FaceTime call appears.

"How much did you do to my phone? You had it for less than a minute."

He laughs, and I can't help but stare as I watch him lay back on his couch. He has his free hand behind his head, unintentionally showing off his tattooed bicep that is straining against his gray Fury T-shirt. His brown hair is messy, and he has a little scruff on his normally clean-shaven face. I've always been a fan of clean-cut men and smooth faces, but suddenly I'm having an appreciation for a little scruff.

"I move quick, Ainsley. Gotta be on your toes."

I smile as I pull my blanket up to my chin as I lay on my couch. "I didn't take you as a phone talker."

"Usually I'm not," he says. "But there are just some conversations that shouldn't be done over text. This is one of them."

I smile again, appreciating this gesture. "Thank you."

"No, I should be thanking you, every day," he says. "I know I said it earlier, but I feel like I'm getting so much more out of this. You're saving me."

"We're not going to keep score. But I do feel like you have more of a timeline need than I do. My hope is that Jonathan will get the hint. Or even better, find another job, so I never have to see him again."

"And the city of Nashville would be better for it."

I laugh. "Exactly."

We pause for a second as I watch Linc gather his thoughts. I know this is hard for him, based on what he told me, so I have no problem waiting. I just appreciate the effort.

"I told you a little about this today, but this football season is the most important few months of my life," he begins. "I'm only signed with the Fury for one year. If I can have the season of my life, I'll either re-sign with the Fury, or another team will want to pick me up. But if it goes south? If I'm in trouble, or don't play well, or the black cloud that's followed me around my entire life decides to pour on me, I'm done. There'll be no more football."

I know that I'm still getting to know Linc, but if I've learned anything, it's that this man shows his feelings in high definition. I can see the look of determination, mixed with some sadness, in those green eyes. Where some guys play things close to the vest, I don't think that's the case with Linc. He acts first and thinks later, and I believe that's how he shows himself as well. He puts it all out there, no questions asked.

"Well, then that settles it," I say. "This is going through football season."

His smile is slow, and it comes with a little shake of the head. "I thought you said you weren't good at making decisions?"

I blush at his teasing comment. "Maybe I just needed someone to boss around."

Linc's smile turns a little mischievous. "That can be arranged."

My face is now a tomato. Which isn't exaggeration, because I can see myself on the FaceTime.

Oh Ainsley…what are you getting yourself into?

———

BOYFRIEND

HE'S MARRIED? WTF!

I don't know what surprised me more—the robot voice coming through my earbuds announcing that I had a text from "Boyfriend" or the cryptic message that came with it.

AINSLEY

What are you talking about?

The doctor! McDreamy! He's married!?

I bust out into laughter, nearly falling onto the fruit that I'm cutting up for my week's meal prep. Oh my gosh, he's actually watching…

I thought you said you weren't going to watch it? Something about no love for you?

I wasn't.

But…

But then I got curious. Like what kind of show could be on television that long? So a few Google searches and I figured out the one you were talking about. I turned on the first episode just to see what it was about.

And…

I just finished the first season. I haven't slept much. Which sucks, because I have practice today, and this isn't the way to start my first week of the season.

Welcome to the fandom.

I'm about to become addicted, aren't I?

I'll get you a box of tissues. You're going to need them.

———

There is so much sex in this hospital. Is there that much sex that happens at hospitals? I know we haven't talked about sex, but I need to make sure you're not having sex in hospitals.

No. But there is some. Ask Mia the next time you see her. And trust me, there's no sex for me in hospitals.

Hard pass. And thank God.

That was my window. That was the window that I could easily say "Hey, Linc. So…you know…sex…do you plan on us having it?"

I told myself I wasn't going to overthink things with Linc, but this one I am. And not only that, I'm going to chicken out on this conversation entirely.

How far in are you?

A few episodes into season two. Because we open on Thursday night, our practice schedule is a bit out of the norm. I had to go in for some walkthroughs today, and we have a long day tomorrow.

Then I suggest you stop for now. It's getting late.

It's 7 p.m.

I know, but you're getting into the good stuff, and I don't want you up all night. You've probably already gone too far.

It's just a television show, Ainsley. I can turn it off whenever I want.

Famous last words…

———

What the actual fuck just happened!

Code Black?

How'd you know?

Just a feeling. Also, have you slept? It's six in the morning.

Not important. Does this show have some sort of drug in it? You know, I get drug tested. And for the woman I'm asking to help keep me out of trouble, this feels very much like you trying to get me *into* trouble.

LOL. Yes. Consider me your dealer.

Also, I'm going to have to go to practice today, exhausted as hell, and when the guys ask me why I look like shit, I'm going to have to blame you. Because I can't tell them the real reason and since this is mostly your fault, you're getting the blame.

Me?! I did nothing wrong here!

Do you think I'd be watching this show if you hadn't come into my life?

Oh…sorry?

Now I need to get you back. Maybe our first real date will be to a karaoke bar. Repeat performance?

You wouldn't.

I have the song list already in my head…

———

I'm mad at you.

I try not to laugh, but it's useless. Oh, the poor man. He wasn't ready. And frankly, none of us were the first time we watched it.

I'm sorry. I didn't want to spoil anything.

It just…This fucking show!

I know. Though I must say, I kind of wish I was watching with you. I've never seen anyone else watch it for the first time. I'm sure the reactions are priceless. Especially for things that are going to come up.

You know you can, right?

I stare at my phone for a minimum of thirty-six seconds, give or take three, not sure how to respond.

Is he asking me to come over? Does he want me to? Or is he being nice? That's probably what it is. Maybe.

Oh God I'm so bad at this...

> Oh. No. I didn't. But yeah... well...if you'd ever like company...and if you wanted me to come, I could probably do that. But only if you want me to.

> Overthinking over text is a different kind of skill, Ainsley Mae.

> It's my superpower.

> Well, I want you to know that you have an open invitation.

> Oh, that won't do. I'll never use it because I'll assume you're just being nice to me, and I don't want to inconvenience you. I'm already thinking that anyway.

> You really do overthink everything, don't you?

> It's a gift and a curse.

> Speaking of invitations, what are you doing Thursday night?

> Working. Last day of the week for me. Why?

> Katie was seeing if you were planning on coming to the game. But no worries.

My heart sinks at the mention of his publicist wanting to know, and not him. Which is silly. This isn't real. Him putting boyfriend as his name in my phone is part of the bit. And frankly, him mentioning that she wanted me there and not him is another reminder that this is all for show. Because frankly, all this texting this week has me forgetting sometimes that this isn't real.

It's been nonstop. The only time we're not texting is when he's at practice. I rarely check my phone during work hours, but I've found myself doing it more and more this week to see if he's messaged. I also apparently have a "Linc smile," according to my coworkers. Which is good for this charade, but bad for my heart.

Because I can already tell what's going to happen. I'm going to fall for this man and forget that it was never real to begin with.

I can't forget. I won't let myself. Linc is a great guy, but he's been nothing but honest that he's not a forever guy. And I'm a forever girl.

I need to do something to remind me that this is fake when it's feeling too real. Or when he invites me to his apartment. Or when he FaceTimes me shirtless. Oh! Maybe I need to do that rubber band trick and snap myself every time I start getting a little too smiley. Yes, that's what I need to do.

Yeah, I get off work right when the game starts. And Lord knows because I'd have to leave on time, or maybe early, that a baby will start to be born right then and there. I'm sorry. Sunday games will be easier for me.

No worries. How about Friday? I have the night off since we played the night before. Can I take you to dinner? Our first official date?

I reach across the desk at the nurses' station and grab a rubber band and slip it on my wrist before answering. At least it's pink and matches my scrubs.

Sounds good. Where are you thinking?

Are you asking because you need to look at the menu before we go?

You already know me so well.

I've got a few places in mind. I'll send them
after my position meetings.

Sounds good. Do good at practice today.
Catch all the balls!

Did you just make football sound dirty?

Not on purpose.

You really are something, aren't you, Ainsley
Mae?

"Drat," I whisper to myself before snapping the rubber band
on my wrist. "I'm doomed."

15
linc

"ALL RIGHT BOYS! BRING IT IN!"

There are some hoots and hollers, and a round of in-unison claps, as we run back to the center of the field where our coach, Hunter McAvoy, has just called us in. Like clockwork, because we've all done this thousands of times in our football lives, we remove our helmets and take a knee, ready to listen to whatever our coach says.

And we all listen—intently—because it doesn't get better than the man in front of us. And he has the championship rings to prove it.

"Good practice today, and frankly, all week," he begins. "It's never easy starting the season with a mid-week game—personally it throws my timing all off—but y'all are handling this like the pros you are. I have no doubt that Charlotte isn't going to know what hit them on Thursday night!"

That gets a little bit of a reaction from the guys, but I don't say anything. The season opens in two days. In forty-eight hours, I'm going to be running on the field as the starter in a season opener. It's something I've never done before. And something I'm not taking for granted.

"Make sure everyone gets the treatment they need before

they take off," Coach McAvoy says. "Tomorrow is just going to be meetings and a quick walkthrough before we report to the hotel tomorrow night. All right, let's bring it in!"

We all rise from our knees and lift our helmets in the air for the final huddle of the day. Our captain, quarterback Bryce Donald, waits for us to quiet down before he parts us with his words of wisdom.

"I'm proud as hell to be out here with you guys, and more so, that we've all had our eyes on the prize since the end of last season. Let's start this week with a fucking bang and show the league we aren't fucking around this year. Bring it in, three in four, on three! One…two…three…"

"Three in four!"

We all start making our way back to the locker room at our practice facility, cheerfully jostling each other and joking. "Three in four" is the motto we adopted on the first day of training camp. It's a reminder that we have the chance to do what few professional teams ever have a chance to do—win three championships in four years. It also serves as a daily reminder that we lost last year, or we'd be going for an unheard of four-peat. It's perfect to remind us that we need to work hard, and if we do, we'll cement our dynasty.

Dynasty. How in the hell am I a part of a team that is one of the greatest of all time? I figured if I were ever in this position, it would be on the practice squad, or second-string special teams. I want to pinch myself that I'm here, but the sweat dripping down my face and burning my eyes is enough of a reminder.

For the first time in my life, things are looking good. I have a starting spot. A guaranteed contract. Hell, I even have a girl-friend. Sure, she's of the fake variety, but I can't deny that it's been nice having someone to talk to besides Wyatt and Maddox.

It feels weird to be on the upside of anything. And while part of me is waiting for the inevitable bad thing to happen, the other part of me is breathing easy for the first time in a long time.

"Why's Kincaid spacing out?"

I look up to see Maddox pointing at me, while Wyatt just shakes his head as we enter the locker room.

"Probably thinking about his *girlfriend*." Wyatt says, teasing me like we're seven years old. "I mean, he's texting her all the time. He took her to his breakfast spot on Saturday. We're going to lose him, Maddox. Pretty soon, it's just going to be us in the bachelor section."

"Damn, really?" Maddox says as he starts taking off his pads. "Wait! That girl from karaoke the other night? You two are dating now?"

"Yeah, we are," I say, trying to seem as natural as possible. And praying that he doesn't start questioning timelines. "She's a great girl. Name's Ainsley."

"Yeah, she seemed nice," he says. "I mean, I hate to tell you this, but I wasn't paying a lot of attention to you guys. Not when I had a bachelorette party that was keeping me quite entertained."

I roll my eyes at my manwhore of a teammate and friend. If it was anyone else but Maddox who just said that, we'd be slapping him upside the head. But it's him, and the asshole is charming enough to get away with it.

How do I describe Maddox Gallagher? There's no one word to totally explain him. Because he's a weird, manwhore enigma with a heart of gold.

Men want to be him. Women want to fuck him—and frankly, he usually doesn't turn them down. I've heard from fans that he's both the husbands' and the wives' hall passes. Sometimes together. He's second on the team in jersey sales, and that's only because the league's best quarterback is our captain. But Maddox is a fourth-year safety from Iowa. That's not supposed to be how that works.

Now, one would think if a guy is that popular he'd have the ego to boot. Wrong. Somehow he's the nicest and most genuine player in the locker room. He does more for the team's charities than anyone, along with the one he started himself that promotes STEM activities in afterschool programs.

If he wasn't my friend, I'd hate him.

"Well I'm happy for you," Maddox says. "And if she brings you luck and makes it so you're catching a hundred yards and a touchdown a game, I'll like her even more."

I laugh. "You know I'm not superstitious like you are."

In my defense, no one is. This is a twenty-six-year-old man who has to drink milk before every game because he did it once when he was six, apparently had the best game of his life, and has done so every game since.

Maddox shakes his head as he grabs his shower caddie. "I'm just saying, if you start earning out those brand-new contract bonuses, and it has anything to do with her, you will be. And quick."

Maddox heads off, leaving Wyatt and I alone in front of our lockers.

"Well, safe to say he's on board, and didn't question the odd timing," I say quietly, not wanting anyone passing by to overhear this conversation.

"Nah, you should be good," Wyatt says as he starts undressing. "The guys who were there that night aren't going to ask you specifics. And the rest? The rest you can tell them as much or as little as you want."

I look around the locker room, taking in my team. It's a good balance of young guys and veterans. And not just any veterans —ones who know how to win. Since the team brought Coach McAvoy on seven years ago, they've improved every year to become one of, if not the best, team in the league.

And now I'm here. I'm a part of this. Sometimes it doesn't seem real. I mean, being in locker rooms is one thing. But knowing I'm contributing? Starting? Sometimes I feel like I'm going to wake up and this was all a dream.

"What are you doing Friday night?" Wyatt asks. "Rare free night. I think I'm going to head to the cabin for the weekend.

Don't tell anyone I invited you, but you're more than welcome to come."

"While I'm flattered for my first-ever invitation, I can't," I say as I pull off my sweaty practice jersey. "Taking Ainsley to dinner."

He wags his eyebrows. "Look at our boy, going on dates and shit."

A few of the teammates laugh at Wyatt's comment, which earns him a towel thrown to the head. I lean down, like I'm picking it up, but it's just so I can talk lower.

"Katie told us we need to be seen out. So we're going to dinner. Some fancy restaurant where I won't know what fork to use. Don't be thinking this is real."

Wyatt knows more than anyone that I don't date. At least, not romantically. Yes, I've been out with women. Scratched the itch when I needed to. But every one of them knew it was only going to be one night. I certainly didn't plan romantic dates at five-star restaurants.

When I told Ainsley earlier that I had a few ideas in mind, that was my stall tactic to Google nice date night restaurants that I think she'd like, while also putting us in public to make Katie happy that we're being seen out.

"Where you taking her?" "Wyatt asks.

"Not sure," I admit. "Any suggestions?"

"Oh no," he says as he pats me on the shoulder as he stands up. "You went and got a girlfriend. You're on your own, brother."

"Fuck you." We both laugh and just as I'm about to grab my shower caddie, I hear my name being called across the locker room.

"Kincaid! Coach McAvoy wants you in his office."

Because this is a professional football locker room, and we're all a group of grown men who mostly act like we're eight, a chorus of "ooohs" and "you're in trouble" come echoing as I tug on a clean T-shirt and shorts before making my way to the coach's office.

"What'd you do this time, Kincaid?" I look over, eyes narrowed as Brad taunts me from in front of his locker. "Or should I ask, who'd you punch?"

I don't mean to slow down my stride, but I can't help it. I need to calm down, breathe in and out, but every word this guy says gets under my skin. He's been goading me since the minute I walked into this locker room, and it only got worse when he realized that I wasn't some random injury fill-in. He thought I was going to be some lowly, former-practice-squad player who couldn't hack it. And frankly, he was right about most of that.

What he didn't know was that I was a man determined not to blow my last shot.

After that catch last year, his glares went from dismissive to angry. I know he fucks with me because he's scared. And he should be. I'm the guy taking his job. So he wants me to fuck up. He knows that I'm living on my last life here, and if he can push me over the edge, his spot is back open.

If it were anyone else here, I'd feel bad that their season ended on an injury like his. ACL rehabilitations are a bitch, and there's never a clear timeline on when you can come back. But when you're a dick like Brad, you don't get sympathy. And if I wasn't one fight away from the team kicking me off, his face would've met my fist a long time ago.

"What are you doing here, Rockwell?"

He stands up, a little wobbly since he's off crutches. "Being a good teammate. I'm going to be back any day now; I don't want the rapport to have gone away. Or for anyone to forget who their real tight end is."

Fucking liar. I know he's at least six-weeks away, and even that's being generous.

"Glad to have you here," I say, a touch of sarcasm in my voice. "That way you'll have a front-row seat when I break the league's tight end receiving yards record this year. Wouldn't want you to miss that."

My words hit the mark as Brad puffs out his chest, bumping it to mine as I hold my ground. I'm not going to hit him—that's what he wants. No, my fists are going to stay firmly in place at my sides.

Clenched. But in place.

"You were a flash in the pan last year," he says. "Just wait until I'm back and you have some real competition."

I laugh, stepping up a little closer. "Funny how you think that when you come back there'll be a spot for you. Face it, Rockwell, you were then. I'm now. And you can't fucking stand it."

My words hit the mark, and Brad gives me a shove. All I do is send him a cocky smile as I feel a host of hands pull me back. Which I get. I wasn't about to throw, but with me, it's better to be safe than sorry.

"You just have to instigate, don't you?" Wyatt says as he pushes me aside. I take another step back, but Brad can't get anywhere near me. Not with one of our captains, Cole Campbell, blocking him.

"Don't be starting shit, Rockwell. Get your stuff, go do your rehab, and get the fuck out of here."

I can't see Brad—only because Cole is the biggest motherfucker I've ever met in real life—before I hear my name called again.

"Kincaid! My office! Now!"

Wyatt pats me on the shoulder and I take a second to cool down before heading into Coach McAvoy's office.

"Take a seat," he says as I close the door behind me. I know he didn't ask me to, but I've been part of these meeting enough times to know that closed doors are protocol.

"Coach, about that," I say, wanting to get ahead of the talk I know I'm about to get. "I apologize for snapping at Brad. I—."

Coach McAvoy shakes his head before I can finish speaking.

"All I saw was the end, but enough to know that Rockwell likely started it."

Wow. I wasn't expecting that.

"He's not handling his injury well," Coach continues. "He was always a cocky guy. But it never crossed the line that became toxic for the team. But the guy who's rehabbing now? He's a different player than the one we signed two years ago. And I'm telling you this because, if you haven't figured it out yet, he's not fond of you."

I laugh. "Yeah, he's not exactly playing that close to his chest."

"Just keep your head down," he says. "I'm going to be having a talk with him, believe me on that. He might not be active right now, but that doesn't mean he's still not under contract. If he continues to cause disruptions like this, there will be consequences."

And this is just one of the reasons I love Coach McAvoy. It doesn't matter if you're a seasoned veteran, or a new guy he recruited off the streets, everyone is treated the same.

"Thanks, Coach."

He holds up a finger, signaling that he's not quite done. "And while I'm glad you didn't hit back today, I think we need to talk about your actions this past weekend."

He tosses a few pieces of paper on his desk, and I don't need to lean in too far to see that it's the first headlines that came out —the ones that leaned into how I almost clocked Dr. Dipshit.

"Do we need to talk about this?"

I shake my head, lowering my eyes for a second before I realize that I need to face this head-on with the man who's giving me my life right now. "No sir. Temper slipped for a moment."

He sits back in his desk, clasping his fingers together. "Over a girl?"

"Yes, sir. She's...my girlfriend."

The slight stutter was more because I don't think I've actually said that word out loud since that night. It was one thing that night, when it was a game. But it's not a game anymore. Well, not the same one. The stakes feel bigger.

"Wow," Coach says. "No offense, but I didn't see you as a commitment kind of guy."

"None taken," I say. "I guess you could say that when the right woman comes along, everything changes."

"Don't I know it." I watch as my coach goes from this stern authority figure to his eyes softening as he looks over to a picture of his wife and their two sons. "I'm not going to tell you how to live your life, Kincaid, but you know you have a lot riding on this year."

I nod, not needing to say anything else. He and I have gone over the terms of my contract, and behavior clauses, extensively.

One-year contract. If things go well, they plan to re-sign me. And when it comes to fighting? There are no three strikes. No second chances. The first time I throw a punch, I'm out of here.

Which I know means that my football career would be over. Completely.

"I understand, sir," I say as I stand up. "I apologize for it almost happening this weekend. But in my defense, it was my girl's ex, and he's a dipshit who doesn't listen to a woman saying no."

This earns me a smile from my normally serious coach. "That helps. Slightly."

He stands as well, reaching out for my hand. "I'm happy for you, but make sure this isn't a distraction. This is a big season for us. For you. Just be smart."

I nod in understanding. He's right. It's not just big, it's huge. It's everything.

And I can't—no, I won't—fuck it up.

guide to love rule #63

There's a lot to learn about football when fake dating a player. You have to learn terms, signals, and to not stare at him in his pants.

16
ainsley

AINSLEY
Good luck tonight! Catch all the balls!

BOYFRIEND
You really like that phrase, don't you?

I do. I mean, that's what you do, right? Catch the balls? I'm still not sure what a tight end does.

It's mostly what I do. And hopefully score touchdowns. But you realize you're the girl who doesn't swear and you're making my sport, and my job, sound dirty?

The beauty in my humor is the subtlety.

That it is, Ainsley Mae...that it is.

But seriously. Good luck tonight. I'll be watching. Mia's taking me to a sports bar. She says it'll make it feel more authentic. But I know she just wants an excuse for beer and wings.

If you can't be at a game, a sports bar is the way to go. Just make sure to wear a Nashville Fury shirt. Then you'll fit right in.

I don't think I have one.

Well, I'll have to change that.

You don't have to do that. I already feel bad enough that I can't be there.

It's fine. Probably better.

What do you mean?

Can I tell you something?

Of course.

I'm nervous for tonight.

Why?

I've never started in a season opener. Hell, I've barely been on active rosters at the beginning of a year. And there's so much riding on this season. On tonight. What if I forget plays? Or have more drops than catches? What if I get hurt and I have to do fucking rehab with fucking Rockwell?

Hey. What's this overthinking? Quit trying to copy me 😄

Oh God, I am…Is this how your brain works every day?

Yup. And double time on Sundays.

Damn…I'm sorry. This sucks.

It does, but I'm a pro. So this is what we're going to do. You're going to go play football. Be the best tight end (whatever that means). Catch all the balls and score touchdowns. Clear your mind of the rest, and let me overthink it for you.

I'm not sure that's how it works.

Let's try. Just take a deep breath. Do what you do best, and I'll do the same. And just know, I'll be watching and cheering for you, and doing all the overthinking for both of us.

Promise?

Cross my heart.

———

"Can I get you another round?"

Mia grabs her tall beer glass and tips it back, finishing the contents of whatever beer she's drinking. "Yes. One more. Because if this game is about to go into overtime, I'm going to need this and a round of shots."

My stomach recoils at the word.

"You got it. Anything for you?"

I shake my head. "Just another water would be great."

The waitress gives us a nod, while also clearing away the smattering of appetizer baskets that we've gone through during this game. Wings. Mozzarella sticks. Jalapeño poppers. Cheese fries. More sides of ranch than any one table should have. If I knew that watching football also came with endless apps, I'd have start coming with Mia to watch years ago.

"Still not drinking?" Mia asks, and I shake my head before the question is out of her mouth.

"If you do order shots, can you make sure it isn't Fireball? That might send me over the edge."

This makes her laugh as the game comes back from commercial. The score is tied, and it's been back and forth since the first quarter. There's five minutes left of the game and the Fury have the ball, but if there's one thing I know about football, it's that five minutes takes a very long time. At least, that's how I remember it when I went to my yearly UT football game with the family.

I don't think I've ever watched a football game as intently as I have tonight. And I've been holding up my end of the bargain in the overthinking department. How does he not get hurt? What if he does get hurt? Is the yellow line on the television real or just for us at home? Are they allowed to go to the bathroom during the game? Why does the quarterback just shout random words? Thankfully, Mia is an amazing teacher and hasn't rolled her eyes at me once.

I also finally know what the yellow flag means.

As for Linc, he's been catching most of the balls. Mia reassured me that rarely, if ever, does anyone catch every single pass thrown to them, which made me feel better. According to the stats that I've been keeping up with on my phone, he has caught for ninety-eight yards tonight. He was close to a touchdown in the second quarter, but there was a penalty on the play that negated it.

I knew that because of the yellow flag. I think it was holding. Which I still can't tell what that is, but I know it's against the rules.

"Let's go!" Mia yells, clapping her hands for emphasis as the Fury offense runs onto the field. "One more, boys!"

I never understood when people would yell at the television when watching a game. It's not like they can hear you. But I must say, more than once tonight I've found myself doing the same thing. It's oddly therapeutic.

"Okay, what needs to happen now?" I ask as the players line up and Bryce starts calling a play.

"So when it's tied like this toward the end of the game, it's all about strategy," Mia explains as he hands the ball off to the running back, both positions I learned the names of tonight. "The goal is to score, obviously, but you want to do it while also wasting as much time as possible. The quicker you score, the more time the other team has to come back, and you don't want that."

"Makes sense," I say. "How do they take their time?"

Mia laughs as another play is about to begin. "That's a lesson for game like three or four. Just know, for tonight, the longer the Fury has the ball, the better their chances are."

Fair enough. My brain is already flooded with football knowledge I never thought I'd have. I think I'm tapped out for the night.

I don't think I blink as the Fury slowly makes their way up the field. At some point, I've stood from the high-top chair I'd been sitting on, my arms crossed in nervousness as each play unfolds.

"Is every game this intense?"

Mia shakes her head as the Fury converts another first down. "God, no. This one is on another level."

That makes me feel slightly better. Because if this is what I signed up for this season, I don't know how I'm going to have any nails left.

The Fury leaves the huddle and lines up. Linc is on the field and like many plays tonight, all I do is watch him. It guarantees I don't miss anything, even if the play doesn't go to him. But it's been fascinating to watch. I didn't realize how much football was like dance choreography. Everyone has a place to go and timing in which they have to get there. If one person does their job wrong, it sends the whole group off. I might not know what they're doing, or how they know what to do just by Bryce bellowing out words, but they do, and it's a beautiful thing to watch.

Now the tackling? I could do without that.

Bryce gets the ball snapped to him and he runs back, looking for a player to throw it to. My nails are to my lips again as I see Linc running to the center of the field, and like so many times tonight, he leaps above the defender, catching the ball out of the air before falling to the ground. And because it went past the yellow line that's only on television, I now know they got a first down.

"Yes!" I scream and jump up and down, hugging Mia. "That's over a hundred yards!"

"Fuck yeah, it is!" Mia says. "And now they're in the red zone. That means they're within twenty yards of the end zone."

"Good to know," I say, quickly taking a drink of water as the team comes back together. My eyes roam around the bar, taking in all the Fury fans who came out tonight. It's a home game, and I knew that downtown would be crazy, which is why Mia and I found a place a little outside of town, hoping it wouldn't be as crazy.

I was wrong about that. The bar is packed. I still don't know how we found a table. Hordes of men are gathered around, yelling at the television for every play, good or bad. There are a few women here, but none of them are watching as intently as Mia and I. And if I'm not mistaken, a few of them have sent glances my way. My brain automatically assumes that I have something in my teeth or toilet paper stuck to my shoe, but I also saw them looking at their phones before looking at me, and I remember that I'm not unknown Ainsley Banks anymore.

I'm Linc Kincaid's girlfriend.

"Okay, we're back," Mia says as she rubs her hands together. "A few more run plays then let's put this baby in the end zone."

As if she had a copy of the Fury playbook, the team does exactly that. Two running plays, which puts them around the ten-yard-line with a minute twenty left.

"Is it time to score now?" I ask. And gosh, I hope so. I need them to just win so my stomach can quit doing flips.

"Soon," Mia says. "Depends what McAvoy has up his sleeve."

Now that name I know. Hunter McAvoy is a legend in this state. It also helps that his sister lives in Rolling Hills, and *my* sister is his and his wife's interior decorator.

"Come on," I mumble, my feet rocking back and forth before I suck in a breath as I realize that Linc is running toward the end zone.

I don't blink. I can't. Not when the ball is launched at him as he comes across the center of the end zone. He has to jump a little to get to it, and just as he's about to, and in mid-air, a defender jumps into him, sending him to the ground and batting the ball along with it.

"Hey! I don't think you can do that! That's mean!" I yell, and apparently I'm right. Because every single person in the bar is yelling at the television as I see the yellow flag being thrown. "What just happened?"

"They just fucked up," Mia says before the ref comes on television and announces that Charlotte committed pass interference, and that it's now penalty and a first down.

"Oh, we're so close!" I say as I see the big number ten behind where the Fury is lining up and the end zone just a few yards away. "Mia, why am I so nervous?"

"Because you're a football fan now," she says, and luckily for me and my breathing, Charlotte takes a time out, and I get a chance to sip—no, gulp—my water before the final plays.

"Are you having fun?" Mia asks.

"I am!" I say genuinely. "It's a whole different experience when you have someone to watch and vested interest."

"I bet."

I raise a questioning eyebrow. "I mean, so do you."

"What's that mean?"

"Are you saying you aren't watching differently now that you and Wyatt…"

I trail off because I assume that they hooked up that fateful night, but she never came out and said so, and I don't want to assume. But Mia waves me off.

"It was one night of fun," she says dismissively. "Not like he's my boyfriend."

"But he could be."

She shakes her head. "You know I don't date football players."

"If I can, you can."

"But are you?" she asks. "I thought you two were just pretending."

Thankfully the bar is loud enough that I doubt anyone heard her say that. "Well, yeah. But we're friends. And tomorrow we're going on a date. So it's kind of real? But it's not."

Out of habit, I reach over to my wrist and give the rubber band that I've rarely taken off a snap. Though if I keep this up, I'm going to have to get a new one, as I've almost worn out the elastic.

"Just be careful," she says as the game comes back from the commercial. "I know you can catch feelings easily. And I don't want to see you get hurt."

"I won't. I promise." Well, other than my wrist hurting, but she doesn't need to know that.

The cheers of the bar pull us away from the conversation, and I resume my position, standing with one arm wrapped around my stomach as I bite the nails on my free hand. There's less than a minute on the clock, and according to Mia, this is probably the time they need to score.

I'd like it to happen now, please and thank you.

"Come on…" I whisper as Bryce gets the ball. The players start running to their spots, and my eyes are trained on Linc as I see him come across the center like I've watched so many times tonight. I suck in a breath when Bryce guns the ball his way, and then I stop breathing all together.

Linc leaps.

The ball is in his hands.

He brings it into his chest.

And then he falls to the ground.

But he never loses hold of it.

Touchdown Fury.

Touchdown, Linc.

"Oh my gosh!" I yell, cheering and jumping up and down in the middle of the bar. But I'm not the only one. Mia is randomly high-fiving the table next to us before running over to me and picking me up, spinning me in a circle.

"You're boyfriend is a fucking beast!" she yells. "That's right! My girl is dating Linc Kincaid, and the Fury are going back to the championship!"

That earns a few hoot and hollers from the crowd as I focus back on the television, where the camera on the field is now zoomed in on Linc.

"What's he doing?"

I don't answer Mia as I watch the camera zoom in on Linc, ball still in his hand. I feel the goofy grin on my face as I see how happy he is, while also knowing how much relief he has to feel after having a game like he just did.

When the camera is just inches from him, I watch as he points to it...all before he makes an "x" across his heart.

"Why'd he do that?" Mia asks. "I've never seen him do that after a touchdown."

I bite my lip and fumble to find the rubber band on my wrist and snap it. Because I think know.

Cross my heart...

He...that was for me. Don't ask me how I know, but I do. And not in an overthinking kind of way. No, Linc looked right in the camera and made the motion. It felt intentional. And even though he's across town, playing in a stadium with sixty-nine thousand fans surrounding him, and thousands more watching this game around Nashville, at this moment, I know that this is a moment for us.

Gosh darn it...I'm really going to need another rubber band.

guide to love #102

First dates are nerve-racking even when they're with your fake boyfriend.

17
ainsley

"Nope. Next option."

I turn to Stella, who's sitting on my bed, looking me up and down in a way that I'm not too sure I like. "What? Why?"

She shrugs. "I don't know…it just needs something."

I look back at the mirror and check myself out in the white, floral tea-length sundress that I picked for the night. I mean, sure, maybe a necklace or bracelet, but other than that, I don't know what "something" could mean.

"I think I have some jewelry I can wear," I say, walking to my vanity. But Stella doesn't answer me. Instead she jumps up from the bed and marches into my closet. "What are you doing?"

"Finding you something else to wear."

I look to the mirror, trying to see what she doesn't like. "I like this dress. I feel pretty in it."

"You are. You're gorgeous, and that's not what I'm saying." She trails off, and as I look over, I see articles of clothing actually flying out of my closet. "But it's a white floral dress for a date night. At a dark-lit, fancy restaurant. That's not a sundress occasion. You need something…more."

"Well, I don't know what 'more' is, but I don't think you're going to find it in my closet. Not since you moved out."

If there's a fashionista of the family, Stella is the clear winner. Funny enough, Simon comes in second. She's always wanted me to dress a little edgier on certain occasions, or wear something a little more revealing, but I've always politely declined. Thankfully, we're not the same size so she can't force me to wear a crop top or a form-fitting dress. I'll stick to my sundresses and rompers, thank you very much.

"Do you still not own anything fitted?"

I laugh and sit down at my vanity, figuring I'll finish my makeup while Stella digs for things that don't exist. "I think you know that answer."

"I don't know why you're against the notion of a bodysuit," she says. "You can pull it off. Your curves would look fucking amazing in one."

"It's not a body image reason, I just don't feel comfortable," I defend. "And shouldn't you feel comfortable in the clothes you wear?"

Stella lets out a bark of a laugh. "No. Comfort has no place in clothing. Or in shoe selection."

I love my sister, impractical shoe collection and all. When I told her I had a date tonight, she didn't hesitate to tell me in no uncertain terms that she'd be coming over and helping me get ready. Because that's what she's always done when I've had a date in the past. No mind that I'm twenty-nine years old and am plenty capable of getting ready on my own. But this is what we do. I have a date. She comes over to talk me down from my nervousness. She tries to get me to wear something out of my comfort zone. I tell her no with a smile.

I needed this tonight. Stella being here is the one thing giving me normalcy for a date that's in no way normal. She's my best friend in the world. She's the sibling closest to my age. We grew up sharing a bedroom and then lived together after college. She knows me better than anyone on this planet.

Which is why it's killing me that I can't tell her that the date she's getting me ready for is nothing but a publicity stunt.

When Linc messaged me the name of the restaurant the other day, he confirmed to me that there would be "random" cameras that we might see when we enter or exit the restaurant. Then, I received a text from Katie, who apparently now has a group text going for the three of us, confirming the cameras and how we're supposed to act.

We always need to be holding hands or some sort of touch. We need to look happy. But also we need to make sure we're never looking directly at the cameras.

So now, not only am I nervous because the restaurant Linc picked is super fancy and I have no clue what I'm going to order, despite studying the menu nonstop for two days, but now I have to not think about people taking our pictures from bushes.

My brain hurts, and for the first time in my life, I think I actually need a drink.

"What's your schedule like the rest of the week?" Stella calls from the closet.

"I work Sunday, Tuesday, and Wednesday. I might pick up another shift, but then Friday before being off for the weekend."

"Just wanted to know what days you're free for me to take you shopping," she says. "If you're dating a Fury player, we need to do something about your wardrobe."

"My wardrobe is fine," I say. "But I do need some new shoes if you want to go still."

The word "shoes" is always a solid way to get my sister's attention. "Shoes, you say? What do you need? Heels? Wedges? Boots?"

I shake my head. "No. It's that time for some new work tennis shoes. Mine have worn out."

Stella's shoulders slump. "Get me all excited just to tell me we're going for some white sneakers with three-inch cushions."

"Exactly," I say as my phone vibrates with an alert. "Oh. Linc's here."

Now, normally for a first date I'd meet the guy at the restaurant. Dating 101 dictates that it's better to have an out and not be committed to using him for transportation in fear that it goes bad. But Katie was adamant that Linc pick me up, just in case someone realized that we arrived separate, and I'm now being greeted at my door by my fake boyfriend.

"Okay, let me look at you," she says as I stand up, grabbing the white designer purse Maeve got me for my birthday last year. "Are you sure you don't have anything form fitting? Maybe in the little black dress variety?"

"I think you would've found it by now."

I give my sister a quick kiss on the cheek and tell her thanks when I hear a knock on the door. I know I shouldn't feel nervous, but I am. Though, that can probably be chalked up to never going on a fake date before, and the fact that I'm *just* now starting to overthink all of this as I open my door should indicate how nervous I am.

"Hey…" I meant to say more, but that one word died on my lips when I see Linc standing in my doorway.

The crisp white shirt he's wearing pops against his tanned skin. He's paired it with a pressed pair of khaki pants and brown dress shoes. Which, when I look down is when I realize that his cuffs are rolled to his forearm, showing his sleeve of tattoos.

Also, when did forearms become sexy?

I quickly look back up, realizing that I'm staring, which is when I see that he's staring too. At least I think he is. Maybe. I don't want to assume and be conceited. But he hasn't blinked, and I'm now wondering if I left on my eye masks.

"Hey to you, too," he says just before running his hand over his mouth.

Neither of us say anything more for another moment, and it's just about to become awkward when my sister comes in to save the day.

"Well, then," Stella says, sliding up next to me. "Maybe the sundress was the right call. You two kids have fun tonight. Don't do anything Quinn wouldn't do."

———

"Right this way, Mr. Kincaid."

Linc places his hand on the small of my back as we follow the hostess to the booth in a low-lit, five-star restaurant just off of Broadway. We're seated against a window—which I'm guessing is on purpose—but I can't complain. Not with the view of the Cumberland River at dusk.

"Welcome," our server says. "Can I start you both off with a cocktail? Martini? A craft beer? Bourbon?"

I shake my head. "Can I get a club soda with a splash of cranberry and a lime? And a water with lemon, please?"

Our waitress just smiles and nods. "Absolutely. And for you sir?"

"Just water," Linc says.

"No problem. Please let me know if you have any questions on the menu. And our appetizer special tonight is Oysters Rockefeller. We also have a dry-aged prime ribeye with a roasted bone marrow butter and charred cipollini onions."

Our waitress is a few steps away before I watch Linc open his menu. I do the same, wondering what the heck I'm going to eat, because it's not whatever she talked about. I'm not exactly a fancy eater, but normally I can find something that I know what it is and might even enjoy it.

But as I read through the menu today, and yesterday, and the night before, and now, I'm not quite sure what I'm looking at. And I'm clearly not going to ask the server a question about anything, because I'd rather suffer than ask for help that I'm sure she'd be glad to give me.

I look over to Linc, who's reading the menu as intently as I was earlier. He hasn't said much to me since we left my apartment. Actually, now that I think about it, he hasn't said anything.

Oh no…what did I do?

I retrace our steps since leaving my apartment. He offered to get us a ride share so I didn't have to walk in my wedge sandals, which I thought was very gentlemanly.

Except he didn't say anything in the ten-minute ride to the restaurant.

When we arrived, Linc was polite, getting out of the car first to make sure he came around to my side, giving me his hand to help me out of the car. His hand was on the small of my back as we took the few short steps from the car to the doors of the restaurant, and even inside, he always had some sort of contact to me.

Which was exactly what Katie told him to do.

Okay, so maybe it isn't me. Because I don't know what I could've done. I look at him across the table as he intently studies the menu, trying to figure out what he's thinking. I feel like I'm getting to know him a little more every day, but I don't know him well enough yet to know all his looks and tells. He looks stressed. Uncomfortable. Like this is the last place he wants to be.

Oh gosh…is he rethinking this? I mean, he has every right to. He said he's not a relationship guy, and maybe even this is too much for him? We agreed the second that this wasn't working for us anymore, that we'd cut ties. No questions asked. But I didn't think it would end before it really even began.

Or maybe I should've bought a little black dress…

"Hey," he says, almost startling me. "You okay?"

I nod, setting down the menu that I've barely looked at, yet also memorized. "I'm fine. I was actually wondering the same about you?"

He smiles and sits back against his chair, seeming relaxed for the first time tonight. "You know you don't have to overthink for me when it's not a game?"

My smile, and the blush on my cheeks is instant. "It never turns off. But that doesn't change my question. You haven't said much, and I just want to make sure that I…"

I trail off, not wanting to sound like some sad-sack

complainer. I try to find words to finish that thought when I feel Linc's hands taking mine.

"Hey, this has nothing, and I mean nothing, to do with you," he says, training his eyes to mine. "And, I need to apologize."

"For what?" I ask, ignoring the sudden sweat my hands are feeling.

"Not telling you before right now how absolutely beautiful you look tonight."

"Oh." It's the only sound I can muster out. "Um, thank you. You look handsome as well."

"Thanks," he says with a grin. "Wyatt wouldn't let me leave until I had his seal of approval. He was convinced because I don't date that I don't know how to dress myself."

I laugh, wondering if Wyatt was also terrorizing his closet. "Stella tried to get me to wear something else. She said this wasn't fancy dinner appropriate."

He shakes his head. "I don't care if it is or isn't, that dress is perfect on you. And for future reference, if there's an option to wear or not wear the sundress, wear the sundress, Ainsley Mae. Always wear the sundress."

Thank goodness the restaurant is dark, because I'm pretty sure my face is completely flushed right now from Linc's words.

And why is there a tingle...down there. That was...well, unexpected.

Gosh darn it...why did I think I could go tonight without wearing the rubber band. It looked odd, so I took it off.

Bad move, Ainsley...bad move.

Linc looks around before leaning into me. "Does this feel ridiculous? And before you overthink, not meaning a date with you. But this whole night?"

"Oh my gosh, yes," I say in relief. "This is a lovely restaurant, but between Katie telling us the cameras were lurking—and I'm pretty sure we're supposed to be holding hands right now—I feel like I just have a giant camera on me at all times. Also, I don't know what to order, because I don't know these foods."

"Thank God it's not just me," he says. "I know I'm not a dater, but even I know that this isn't how it's supposed to go."

"You're not wrong," I say. "I mean, I'm not some pro at it. But I'm pretty sure we're not supposed to spend our date looking over our shoulders, all while trying to figure out something to order at a place that clearly neither of us want to eat at."

That makes him laugh. "What gave me away?"

I shrug. "You crinkled your nose more than a few times. And I'm pretty sure you don't even read your playbooks that hard."

"Guilty," he says. "Whoa! Wait! Why didn't you say anything, if you didn't want to eat here either?"

I shrug. "Because even more than being a Grade-A worrier, I'm a people pleaser. So if this is the restaurant you chose, I was *not* going to be the one to object."

"Oh, Ainsley Mae..." The smile he gives as he laughs under his breath hits me straight in the heart. This. This is the man I've come to know over the past week. Light. Easy. Not having to put on a show for anyone. "Can I possibly tempt you with a suggestion for the rest of our night?"

This sends my eyebrows up. "Linc, if you put one drop of alcohol in front of me..."

He laughs again, tossing his napkin on the table before standing up. He holds out his hand for me, and now I'm even more confused. "Nothing like that. But how about we defy orders and get the hell out of here?"

I look out of the window, where I happen to see someone with a camera walking by. "But aren't we supposed to stay here? For pictures that aren't happening or something? Katie will flip if we leave. I already think she doesn't like me very much, and if I go along with this, she'll dislike me even more. And, I think you realize this by now, but I'm not the kind of girl who gets in trouble, and I really don't want to get in trouble on our first date."

Linc gives me a wave of a hand. "I'll deal with Katie. Plus, if these photo people are real journalists, they'll figure out that we bounced and they'll chase us down. What'd ya say, Ainsley Mae? Want to do another scary thing?"

My stomach flips, but in a good way, at the thought. I really don't want to eat here—I can't pronounce most of the sauces, and if I can't pronounce it, I don't eat it. Clearly, Linc would feel more comfortable somewhere else. Maybe he's right, if the cameras really wanted pictures, we should make them work for them.

And if that wasn't enough, the glint in Linc's eyes is enough to push me over the edge.

As well as send a tingle up my spine.

"Okay, boyfriend. Where do you suggest?"

18
line

"I DON'T CARE IF THIS IS REAL OR FAKE, LINCOLN KINCAID, THIS IS the best first date ever."

I laugh and sit back as Ainsley organizes the trays of food that were just delivered. "And here I thought a good first date would require me getting dressed up, picking a fancy restaurant, and eating a seventy-dollar steak prepared in sauces I've never heard of."

"Nope," she says. "Chicken tenders and sweet tea. This is the key to a girl's heart."

If this is what it's like to date Ainsley, then this year is going to fly by.

I laugh as I watch in a little shock, and a whole lot of awe, as my prim and proper "girlfriend" brings a ranch-soaked chicken tender to her mouth. Her head is tilted, as if she's going to try and catch any dripping dressing with her tongue. I'm also ignoring the fact that I'm slightly turned on by this. "Do you want a tender with that sauce?"

She shakes her head. "When it comes to chicken tenders and ranch dressing, the limit doesn't exist for too much."

"Agree to disagree," I say as I take a tender of my own, but dip it in the correct tender condiment—barbecue sauce. "Barbecue is clearly superior."

Ainsley feigns shock, and even adds her hand over her heart for added effect. "I don't know if this relationship can continue if we have that kind of divide. I mean, Linc, how would we raise the children!"

The more time I spend with Ainsley, the more I realize just how funny she is. She had me laughing that first night, but I figured that was the alcohol and the ridiculousness of the entire situation. But every time I talk to her, I find myself laughing. I didn't expect her to have a subtle sarcasm. Or the perfect one-liner. And to do it all looking hot as fuck in that sundress.

"Well, that's easy," I say. "We don't have any."

I don't miss the way Ainsley's face falls a bit before she quickly regroups. "Shit. I'm sorry. I didn't mean for it to come out as a dick thing to say."

She shakes her head and takes a drink of her tea. "No, it's fine. It's not like this is..." She trails off to look around. But luckily, since we're in a hole-in-the-wall restaurant on the outskirts of metro Nashville, it's so packed no one can hear us. "I just want a family, and usually I don't date someone that doesn't have that goal. Doesn't make sense to waste someone's time, right? But sometimes it's easy to forget that we're not...I'm sorry. I shouldn't have reacted like that."

"No apologies necessary," I say. "But if it helps, and if anyone asks, I'll tell them we want a litter. *All* the babies."

She laughs. "You can stop at three. That's my max."

"Good to know," I say before studying a french fry a little too intently. I normally do a pretty good job of keeping my sad childhood pushed aside, and I don't know if it's the actual talk of family, but suddenly those feelings are starting to uncomfortably bubble to the surface.

"Hey." I feel Ainsley's hand on top of mine, and when I look up, those blue eyes are pleading with me. "I'm sorry if I made things weird."

I shake my head, pushing aside the thoughts of dead parents, passed-on grandmothers, and all the reasons I've come up with not to get close to anyone. "You didn't. That was all me."

I can tell Ainsley's trying to give me an out. Because that's the kind of person she is. And while I'm not ready to tell her all about my fucked-up past, I need to give her something.

I want to give her something.

"My grandma raised me," I begin, not wanting to get into the dead parents quite yet. "It was just her and me for a lot of years. And then she passed when I was graduating college."

The words trail off and I feel Ainsley's hand holding mine tighter. "I'm so sorry, Linc. That had to hurt so much. You've been on your own for a long time."

I've been on the receiving end of sympathy many times in my life. Most of it felt disingenuous. But this? Those few words from Ainsley? Somehow I can feel her sorrow for me through those few little words and her kind eyes.

"It did. Then it was just me. No other family. So I think I just don't know any different."

She nods in understanding. "I get that. Then there's my family, that has zero boundaries."

I chuckle thinking back to that. How was that only a week ago? "Yeah, it was a lot."

She shakes her head and I feel like we're getting back on the right track. "They mean well. We all do, when it comes to our siblings. But with me I feel like they're too much."

"How so?"

"I'm not the baby of the family, but I've always been the most delicate," she says, absently grabbing a french fry, but not eating it. "I was the good one. The one who didn't care about tattling, because rules were in place for a reason. And I followed them, every single one. I was also a bit of a crier. And when I say was, I mean am. You put on the sad puppy adoption commercial and I'm a puddle."

"I mean who isn't? Those eyes? That song? Take my money and then also give me that dog."

"Exactly," she says. "But yes, combine all of that together, and I was definitely the most sensitive of the five of us. As we got older, and it was clear that I was the one who wasn't going to take the risks or push the boundaries, I became the most breakable. So when they saw the news about us, and the pictures, I get why they did what they did."

"The black was a nice touch," I joke as I grab another tender. "Can I ask, though, how does a girl who doesn't swear, only drinks when pushed to her limit, and gets nervous when breaking the smallest rule, is related to four siblings who launched a ninja expedition to try to spy on their sister in broad daylight?"

"Oh, if we were trying to spy on another sibling, I would've been right there with them," she says. "The day I first met you—"

"Do you mean the day you ran into me or the day I became your boyfriend?"

It's not hard to make Ainsley blush. And I don't know if I'm ever going to get tired of it.

"Ran into you," she says, her shy smile gracing her beautiful face before continuing. "That night, we all ganged up on Quinn's boyfriend's mom, and fooled her into thinking she was getting a lot of money in order for her to not try to get custody of a baby."

I blink rapidly, trying to follow that line. "Excuse me, what?"

She laughs. "It's a long story for another day. But that was my way of saying that if shenanigans are happening, I'm all about them. I just need them to stay on the right side of the law."

"Wait, does your family break the law?"

She shakes her head as she takes another bite of a ranch-dipped tender. "A few arrests, but no convictions. My sister Stella, though, was once picked up by the FBI for questioning."

I drop the tender I was about to put in my mouth. "The FBI? As in the Feds?"

"Yup," Ainsley says, like that isn't a bombshell. "But it all went away after we got her ex to admit to a dominatrix that he set her up."

I stare at her, jaw dropped, because no way those words just left her mouth. "You're lying."

"Cross my heart."

We both pause for a second after she says it. I don't think she meant to, but the second it came out of her lips, she realizes what she said.

Kind of like me last night when I scored that touchdown. I didn't even realize what I was doing until I did it. But in that moment, the first person I thought of was Ainsley.

Because my mind was clear. During that entire play, it was like every other worry or possibility left my head. All I saw was an open field and six points.

I know rationally that Ainsley didn't magically fly into the stadium and wave a magic wand to clear my mind from the noise. But she also did. Which is why when I found the end zone and my teammates started flooding me in celebration, it was just her blonde hair and blue eyes I could think of.

I'd wondered if she saw it. Knowing Ainsley the little I do, I doubted she was going to bring it up. But between how her breath stopped just now, and the flush in her cheeks, she did. And that's good enough for me.

"So you're saying that I, the man who has also never been convicted, but was damn close a few times, picked the right sister to date?"

Ainsley gives me a genuine smile with a coy shoulder shrug. "Stick with me, Kincaid. I'll have you volunteering and not swearing in no time."

I don't know what draws my attention from Ainsley to out the window, but I do. Which is when I see a not-so-sly passerby not passing by. And aiming a camera right through the window.

"I think we've been found," I say. "Want to keep them on the move?"

Ainsley looks out the window, then back to me. "Can ice cream be involved?"

"Can it be involved?" I stand from my seat, holding my hand out for her to help her up. "Not only can it be involved, I think it's required."

———

"So if you weren't playing football, what would you be doing?"

"Oh yes! The twenty-questions part of the first date!" My sarcastic comment earns me a side-eye as we walk with our ice cream cones along the Cumberland River. "I'm kidding. But yes. It was football player or bust."

"But you went to college? What did you major in?"

"Communications, which in athlete terms, meant I was majoring in football," I say. "And if your next question is 'Linc, what would you do with that if football didn't work?' The answer is play football. I needed a major, and it required the least amount of science and math classes."

"Unlike my major, which was all math and science," she says before taking a lick of her sugar cone filled with strawberry ice cream. I opted to go with a waffle cone of cookies and cream. "That was the only thing that almost stopped me from becoming a nurse."

"And let me guess, you were a straight-A student, even while taking stupid hard math and science classes?"

She bashfully shrugs. "Yes. But I had to work for them. I think organic chemistry almost killed me."

"We had a very different college experience," I say. "The only thing that tried to kill me were summer workouts."

"But you didn't start at Mississippi State, right? You transferred?"

"Did someone do their homework on me?"

Again with that shy shrug. It's fucking adorable. "Yes. But in my defense, Mia also told me your entire bio, and my sister Stella is an unofficial FBI member. So I had help."

I take the final bite of my ice cream cone and thank the heavens Ainsley remembered to grab napkins, as we find an empty bench looking at the river. In the skyline is the Fury stadium, and right now, at night, with the reflection of the water in front of it, I don't know if there's a more beautiful sight.

Well, there is, and it's the woman next to me. But I need to do a better job of keeping those thoughts at bay.

"I wasn't the best student in high school," I say, still not wanting to put a damper on the night with my sad sob story. "Gram did the best she could, but even back then, I had a reputation of using my fists to talk, so I was in detention more than I was in class. When I discovered football, that helped me a little, but even then, I was doing just enough to stay eligible."

Ainsley doesn't push or ask more. Most people would if I left things open like that. But not this woman. No, she just turns to me, her toned legs bent slightly as she listens intently to every word I'm saying.

"Because my grades were barely Cs, I wasn't getting college offers. But there was nothing else I wanted to do. Trades didn't appeal to me, and I knew I didn't have the grades, or the focus, to do well in college, so my coach suggested junior college. He hoped that in a smaller setting I could figure out what was next, and also use the time to get grades up where I could maybe head to college and play big-time football. God love that man for seeing a future in me that I never dreamed possible."

"The good teachers and coaches have that way about them," she says. "They see things in us that we never could."

"He did. I went to a JUCO, got decent enough grades—and more importantly, stayed out of trouble—and after two years I made it to Mississippi State. And the grades might've been better, and I technically have a degree, but even with all that, it was still pro football or bust."

My throat starts to tighten just thinking about the next part of the story. If I'm not ready to talk about my parents, I'm definitely not ready to talk about the incident that nearly ruined my entire life.

I don't know if Ainsley can tell, which I don't know how she could, but thank goodness she takes the reins of the conversation.

"I get that feeling, it was nurse or bust for me," she says. "I never went through a phase as a child when some days I wanted to be a teacher and the next day I wanted to be a space cowgirl."

"Space cowgirl?" I tease. "I feel like that's the most un-Ainsley thing to do. Zero gravity and horses?"

She laughs as my arm goes across the back of the park bench, like it's the most natural thing to do. I try to tell myself it's for the photographers that could be following us that Katie set up, but I know it's a lie.

"Exactly. I could never. But luckily I didn't have to think about it because the first time I put on my toy stethoscope, I wanted to be a nurse."

I remember that feeling, only it was the first time I put a football in my hand. "What made you want to be a children's nurse?"

"That I'm not sure," she says. "I just remember being fascinated by it. I used to beg my mom to take me to the doctor, just so I could see my nurses. I'd try and tag along with my siblings when they had appointments. I was a volunteer at the local hospital the minute I was old enough. Being a pediatric nurse was all I ever dreamed of."

"And look at you now. Living the dream."

"Kind of," she says. "It's veered and now I'm in labor and delivery."

"I still can't believe you literally bring human life into the world," I say. "I can't be trusted to keep a plant alive. I've never even had a pet."

"It's amazing," she says. "Though sometimes I do miss being in the units like the one I met you in."

"You mean the one where you ran into me?"

She gives me another side eye, which I can't deny is becoming one of my favorite looks on her. "Are you ever going to let me forget that?"

"Maybe, but not anytime soon."

She playfully bumps her shoulder into me, and it takes all the willpower in the world in my body to not bring her into my side.

What is it about this woman? I know this is fake. My brain is saying it. No, *screaming* it. Yet, with every minute I spend with her, I can't help but want to touch her. To get to know her.

Which is bad. So very, very bad.

"That day you came in, it actually reminded me of the reason I wanted to be a peds nurse. To give those kids hope and light when there are days that all they know is darkness."

"I had to keep reminding myself of that," I say. "I went through some shit as a kid, but them? Going through cancer or other sicknesses that run their lives? I can't imagine dealing with that at such a young age."

Ainsley's eyes roam to look out over the river, which gives me a chance to sit here and take in just how fucking gorgeous she is. There's a slight breeze, pushing her hair back off her shoulders. I don't mean to, but my fingers can't help it as they start slightly tracing lines along her back. She has to feel them, but she doesn't say anything, instead just keeping her focus ahead.

"Teachers and veteran nurses told us in school that there would be hard days," she continues. "I knew some patients were going to come in and weren't going to leave. But nothing can prepare you for the first time you lose a child."

"I can't fucking imagine."

"I couldn't do it," she says. "I wanted to, but it hurt too much. So that, combined with a horrible ex-boyfriend doctor who worked on my floor, it was an easy enough to decision to ask for a floor transfer."

"I didn't realize he worked on your floor."

"Used to. Though, he has made it a point to stop by labor and delivery every day this week."

My blood pressure immediately spikes. "He has? Why didn't you tell me?"

"It's fine," she says, though I don't think it's fine at all. "He hasn't bothered me. Really."

"Really?" I say, my jaw ticking back and forth. "Ainsley. That's why we're doing this. For him to stay away from you."

Her hand goes to my heart, and I don't know what kind of voodoo this woman possesses, but her touch immediately begins to calm me. "You have. It's convenient that every time he comes up to the floor, I happen to get a phone call from you that one of my fellow nurses announces with absolute glee. You have impeccable timing."

That makes me feel slightly better, but I think it's about time that I reintroduce myself to Dr. Dipshit. "If he bothers you, I don't care if I'm at practice, or even at a game, you call me. Deal?"

She nods and pats my heart before removing her hand. "Cross my heart."

There it is again. A phrase so common, yet it's somehow become ours.

Ours.

No. This isn't an "ours." This isn't an "us." We're just two people helping each other out. A transaction. Nothing more, nothing less.

Even though it feels like more.

A lot more.

Every cell in my body is screaming to kiss her. She's so close. Her perfect pink lips are just inches from me. It would be so easy just to lean in and take them into mine. If cameras are around, they'd probably love getting that picture. But I don't want them to see that. No, if I did kiss her, I wouldn't want the world to see. That would just be for us.

But that can't happen. There can't be an us. If I've learned anything tonight, it's that this woman is way too good for me. She delivers babies. Her smile literally lights up a room. In no way should she be with a former juvenile delinquent from Detroit turned last-chance football player who still has a reputation for fighting.

So I can't kiss her. I can't ruin her.

But God, I want to.

guide to love rule #132

There is never a good way to ask your sisters how to give a
blow job.

19
ainsley

"There she is, the most popular woman in Nashville."

I roll my eyes as Quinn walks into Maeve's house, Grace in her arms. "I'm not the most popular woman in Nashville."

"Maybe not the most popular, but one of the most envied." Stella offers her two cents as she walks into the expansive living room of Maeve and Logan's mansion. I don't even know if mansion is a big enough word. This house could have its own zip code.

"You guys are exaggerating." I do my best to play off their words as I set down the two large pizzas and breadsticks we ordered for our girls' night. "This town is filled with country legends and actresses and beautiful people everywhere you look."

"That may be true," Stella says as she brings up something on her phone. "But not every one of those people has the Fury's hottest player looking at them like this."

When Stella shows me her phone, I actually lose my breath for a second. I knew there were pictures of Linc and I from our date two nights ago. I thought I'd seen all the pictures that magically showed up on social media the next day.

But I didn't see this one.

We're sitting at the bench at the river. Our ice cream is long gone, and Linc's arm is draped on the back of the bench. I'm transported back to that moment, his fingers lazily tracing random patterns across my skin. I had goosebumps all night, and it wasn't from any chill in the air. I don't know what he said in this moment, but I can tell I'm laughing. Relaxed. Not worried if we were being photographed or overthinking a single thing.

Then there's Linc. While my eyes are looking down at the moment, his aren't. They're looking right at me, the dimple in his cheek enhanced by his small smile.

And I think he wanted to kiss me.

I had this thought that night as well, but I chalked it up to the romantic setting of the moonlight hitting the river and the show we'd been putting on for whoever Katie sent to follow us. But seeing this? Now I'm not so sure.

Could he? No. He's been adamant about this not being real. But would he have done it for the plot? Maybe. But would he have looked at me like this? If so, maybe his job after football should be acting, because just looking at this picture, my body is tingling and the butterflies are butterflying.

Snap.

"Why'd you do that?"

Biscuits! I didn't think anyone was paying attention to me when I pulled on my handy dandy rubber band. "Nervous habit I've developed. Anyway, how is everyone?"

Maeve's eyebrow raise tells me she doesn't buy it, but luckily my oldest sister doesn't press on. "I'm fine. But don't think you're off the hook just yet."

"Yes. Because I need to know if this look led to a kiss, because holy shit that look almost got me pregnant."

"You have a man, Quinn," Stella says. "I'm sure Porter will get you good and pregnant whenever you're ready."

"Oh no," she says, setting Grace up on the floor in front of us with a host of toys. "Was just a figure of speech, baby sister. Miss Ma'am here is all we can handle for a little while."

As if on cue, Grace lets out an excited shriek, clapping her hands for extra effect. Because we're dutiful aunts, we return the applause, and for just a minute, I think that the spotlight is off of me and onto the cute toddler.

I could only be so lucky.

"Okay, so was there like, a lot of tongue? He's one of those guys that takes your face in his hands and puts you where he wants you, isn't he?"

"For fuck's sake, Quinn…"

"What!" she exclaims to Maeve. "I've been waiting years, emphasis on the plural form of year, to have this kind of talk with Ainsley. Years!"

"We were out in public," I say, which isn't a lie. I know where Quinn wants to take this conversation, and I hate to tell my sister she's about to be vastly disappointed.

"That didn't stop you at the karaoke bar."

I level a look to Stella, who's giving me a fake-innocent smile. "That was extenuating circumstances."

"So what you're saying is that if you're drunk, you'll kiss in public?"

"Really, Maeve? You too?"

She just shrugs and sits back with her wine glass in hand. "Just calling it like I see it."

"Fine," I concede. "Yes, the kissing in public was a product of what was a crazy night and random circumstances that I guarantee will never happen again. From here on out, all kissing that I choose to do will be in private."

"I don't know," Stella says. "If Emmett looked at me like that? I don't know if I could've waited for privacy."

I might say I wanted privacy, but Stella's not wrong. I wouldn't have cared if cameras were right next to me. A full country concert could've been playing behind us, and I probably wouldn't have known. If Linc would've kissed me in that moment, I'd have been done for. And no rubber band could've snapped me out of it.

"Well, we did," I fib, because I can't tell them that he didn't. That would make them ask more questions. "And it was a very nice kiss."

"Nice?" Quinn asks as she reaches over to grab a slice of pepperoni. "You say nice about flowers. Actually no, nice is reserved for a bouquet of carnations or an ugly sweater that Great Aunt Doris knitted for you that you have to pretend to like."

"We have a Great Aunt Doris?" I ask.

"Is she the one on mom's side who makes the pies but the crust is always burnt?"

Maeve shakes her head to Stella. "No, that's Dad's cousin, Leslie."

"We don't have a Great Aunt Doris! It was hypothetical and not the point!" Quinn takes a few calming breaths and assures Grace that everything is okay. "All I'm saying is that if a kiss with Linc is only nice, then one of you is doing something wrong."

"Don't say that," Maeve says, slapping her arm. "Let this girl have her moment. And her own adjectives. If it's nice, then let her have nice."

Nice is a safe word to use to describe my foggy memory of kissing Linc. Because what I actually remember is fire and heat and never wanting to stop. But I'm sure that was a product of the crazy night and the liquor. So for now, we'll go with nice.

"Thank you, Maeve," I say. "Now, can we talk about something else?"

I take a breadstick out of the box, and one of the many cups of ranch that came with it. I knew the conversation would be like this when Maeve suggested that we come over for pizza and wine—and my water. It's been a while since the four of us have hung out, and Logan was taking her son to the arcade for some bonus dad-son time, so we have the house to ourselves. Which means no prying ears of my eight-year-old nephew, giving my sisters cart blanche to ask me whatever they want about Linc.

Sure, there's Grace, but she's one. She can't understand us. Hopefully. She does live with Quinn, though.

"Sorry, can't do," Stella says. "Because Quinn's right, we've been waiting years for this conversation. And we have to know…"

"Know what?"

The three of them look to each other then back to me. I don't know the rest of Stella's question, but judging by their looks, heightened eyebrows, tilted heads, I think they think I should know.

I don't.

"Damn, she's so innocent," Quinn says. "How's the sex? And if you say nice, I swear to fucking God I'm going to riot."

"Quinn! Language!" I say, reaching down and picking Grace off the floor. I cover her ears for dramatic effect, but really, I'm trying to stall while I figure out how to answer this.

"It's fine. If she learns it now, I won't need to have the sex talk with her when she's older."

"Lucky her," Maeve says sarcastically.

The two of them start bickering in only the way sisters can, which is great for me. And Grace even helps me out by reaching for my cell phone. She knows Aunt Ainsley has the good games for her to play.

What do I say? I have to speak the truth. I'm already telling them a gigantic lie that's killing me inside. My conscience can't add another. Plus, these are my sisters. The women who know me better than anyone in the world. Sure, they might be hoping that Linc and I are having sex, but when I tell them we're not, they're going to think something is up. Or worse—they're going to judge me in that sisterly way.

Unfortunately, I feel like that's my best option.

"I'm sorry to disappoint you, but Linc and I haven't slept together yet."

"Ah, man," Quinn groans. "I really wanted to know if he could actually pick you up and hold you against a wall."

My eyes double in size. "What are you talking about? Why would he do that?"

Quinn winks at me. "Well, he could go down on his knees so he has a better angle to—"

"Stop!" I yell, not wanting to put images into my head that I won't be able to get out. For better or worse. "What is it with you and Mia and men holding you against walls?"

"Just you wait and see, sister. Just you wait and see…"

I don't let my mind go down that rabbit hole. "Well, that hasn't happened. Nor has much else. We've only been dating a few weeks, and our schedules are crazy. Plus, we kind of started this in a whirlwind. We're good with taking the other things slow."

There. Was it a fib? Yes. But at least I'm now not having to make up the sex things we've done that I'm sure would either be wrong or so boring that Quinn would demand to take me to a Kama sutra class.

"That's understandable," Maeve says. "We know you like to take your time with things, so I, for one, am glad that you two are waiting."

"Thank you," I say.

"Yes, sorry if we bombarded you," Stella adds. "It was just fun to think about, considering our sister is now in a hot relationship and not with…"

Stella trails off, but Quinn finishes the thought for her. "Doctor Dweeb."

Normally I'd defend Jonathan, and say he wasn't that bad, but after how he's been acting since he arrived back in town, dweeb isn't a strong enough word. And what I really want to call him I won't, because it's words I've never said out loud before.

"In all seriousness, I need to ask," Maeve pauses before finishing. "You and Jonathan had sex, right?"

Okay, truth time. This I can handle. "Yes, we did. It was… fine."

"Oh shit! Fine is worse than nice!"

I nod to Quinn. "And it really wasn't that fine."

Quinn laughs and tips her wine glass to me. Stella and Maeve join in the laughter as Grace slides off my lap, taking my phone with her.

"I'm not saying you can judge a man's bedroom performance by the cover, but if you told me that man was making you come, and there was no faking involved, I would've been floored."

I shake my head to Quinn's statement. "Cover was judged appropriately. It was okay. No fireworks or screams. Honestly, sometimes I didn't know if it happened."

"He didn't make you suddenly start swearing?"

I laugh at Stella's joke. "Not even a little bit. Well, maybe in frustration, because how can a medical doctor not know where certain parts are? He knows they aren't made up."

All three sisters either spit out, or choke, on their wine. "Holy shit, Ainsley. You've got to prepare us next time you're going to say something like that."

I level a look to Quinn. "Why? Because you give me so much notice when you crack a joke?"

"Look at our sister," Stella says. "Linc's making her sassy."

"I wouldn't go that far."

"I don't know," Maeve says. "Clapping back? Getting drunk? Being okay with random people taking your picture in public? This isn't the Ainsley Banks we know."

Now that's true. Each morning when I wake up to my text from Linc, I have to pinch myself that I'm doing this. This is the most unlike-me thing I've ever done. Yet, at the same time, it's the most fun I've had in a long time. And it all started one night when I was convinced to go to a karaoke bar.

"Okay, the question has to be asked." I turn to Maeve, wondering what question is going to be asked, and whether or not I'm telling the truth. "When you were with Jonathan, did you ever have an orgasm?"

Phew. Truth. "No. I don't think I've ever had one. Ever."

You can hear a pin drop in the expansive room. I'm pretty sure even Grace put her game on pause to look up at me in wonderment.

"Never?" Stella asks. "Like never ever?"

I shake my head. "I've only been with two people. The first was a college boyfriend, and it didn't last long. After that, I wanted to make sure to wait for someone who I thought I was going to spend my life with. And with Jonathan, I did. He was someone I saw a future with at the beginning. Even if the sex was…how do I say this nicely…"

"You don't," Stella interrupts. "The pencil dick never made you come, and if I remember correctly, didn't he cry after you had sex the first time?"

"What!" Maeve and Quinn yell in unison.

I rapidly blink because I never told anyone that. "Wait! How did you know?"

I've never shared a lot of my sex life—tonight is a first, even with my sisters. I never even told them small details of the semi-good things, so I know for a fact I never would've told them about that.

"Oh, my dear sweet Ainsley, must you forget that we once shared an apartment."

I feel the color draining from my face. "You heard his crying?"

She nods. "Honestly, at first I thought it was you. And I was about ready to bust down your door and kick the shit out of him. And then I heard you comforting him, telling him it was okay. How you didn't hear me laugh, I have no idea."

"I'm so pissed you didn't tell me about this," Quinn says. "Dr. Crier has such a good ring to it."

I know it says more about him than me, but still, the story doesn't bring me joy to think about. "I hate that I'm twenty-nine and I've never…" I can't bring myself to finish that sentence, and it's not because I don't want to say the words. It's because I'm embarrassed. "I've never even given a…"

Quinn's eyes pop out of her head. "Are you about to say you've never given a blow job?"

"She's Ainsley," Maeve defends. "Do you think she was a secret freak on the weekends, giving head to any guy who walked by?"

"I don't even know what that means," I admit. "But it's true. Jonathan never wanted one. Said they hurt. And since I really didn't know how to give one, and I would've died of embarrassment to ask y'all, I just never did."

"Wow," Stella whispers.

"Yup. I'm twenty-nine, I've never had an orgasm, and I don't know how to give a BJ."

I just admitted that out loud. And now I want to go find the nearest hole to crawl into.

"Hey, nothing to be ashamed about," Quinn says. "If it makes you feel better, you just made my whole day by saying 'BJ.'"

I give her a side eye. "You're welcome."

"Also, it's easy," she continues. "You suck on it like a lollipop, and most importantly, don't bite it."

"I know that," I say. "Well, the biting part."

"Then you're golden."

"Now that our sister has given you such eloquent advice, I'll wrap this up," Stella says, scooching Quinn out of the way so she can put her arm around me. "I remember what it was to be like with a man who left things…lacking. You feel like you wasted so much time and wondered what could've been."

"You're right," I admit. "I stayed with Jonathan because I thought I loved him. And maybe I did at the beginning. But I wasted years on a man who wasn't a fit, is now borderline stalking me, and I don't even have an orgasm to show for it."

"Just remember," Maeve says, coming to sit on the other side of me. "You're the romantic of the group. The one who has said for years that one move, one insignificant moment, can change the outcome of everything. You're on the path you're supposed to be on. And whether Linc is it for you, or just a stop along the way, don't take it for granted. Have fun. Live your life. And if it happens to come with orgasms? Then so be it."

I smile as I lean my head on her shoulder. "What would I do without you three?"

"Not know how to give a blow job, apparently."

We all start laughing at Quinn's joke as arms wrap around me in a group hug.

I love these women more than anything. And even though most of this conversation revolved around the lie of my life, I'm so glad that I finally opened up to them about everything.

It was a little scary, but I did it.

I feel lighter. Freer.

That's until we break from the hug and I happen to look down.

Where Grace is with my phone.

Only it's not the game she's playing.

It's a phone call.

An active one.

To Boyfriend.

20
linc

I DON'T KNOW WHICH FOOTBALL SCHEDULING GOD TO THANK, BUT I'm praying to them today, because due to our game schedule to start the season, we have a light day today. Just walkthroughs and film sessions. Which is good, considering I barely slept last night.

I mean, how was I supposed to when all I could see every time I closed my eyes was Ainsley licking my dick like a lollipop?

The answer is I didn't. I stared at my ceiling all night, thoughts of Ainsley with my cock in her perfect mouth. The mouth I wanted to kiss the other night more than I wanted my next breath.

"I don't think I've ever..."

I should've hung up then. Actually, I should've hung up when I realized that I was baby-dialed and was listening to a conversation that was not intended for my ears. But apparently I'm a glutton for punishment. Because while I now know entertaining facts, like that Dr. Dipshit is a crier and can't handle a blow job, I also know that Ainsley has been severely, and I mean severely, underappreciated in her relationships.

When I heard the sadness in her voice as she was admitting

to her sisters the disappointment she had sexually in her past relationships, it broke my heart for her. How could a woman that good, that beautiful, not know what it was like to see fireworks? Have excitement? It kept me up all night. All I could see every time I closed my eyes was Ainsley coming apart by my fingers. My lips. My cock.

Me.

I couldn't get the images out of my head. I took a cold shower. Well, I did after I jacked off in said shower. I tried to watch that damn show she has me hooked on. Hell, I even tried to read football plays. Nothing worked.

I've never been baffled by something like this. I don't know how anyone who calls himself a man could be with a woman like Ainsley and not want to make sure she sees stars. If she were really mine, she wouldn't know a day without them. She wouldn't be able to leave my orbit without knowing how beautiful she is, inside and out. Because she is. She deserves the world.

A world I can't give to her. I know that. But I can give her something else.

I can give her the stars.

I came up with that idea around five in the morning. I'd always felt like I was getting more out of this arrangement than she was. Maybe this is how I even the playing field?

That is, if she wants it. It's her decision. But I did promise that I'd be the best fake boyfriend I could be. I feel like offering orgasms should be part of my duties.

Which is why I'm here at her work, dinner and a sweet tea in hand.

I aimlessly wander the halls of labor and delivery for a second—the floor layout is much different than the others that I've visited here—but when I finally find my way to the nurses' station, it's not Ainsley's blonde hair I see. Instead, it's a bad hair piece.

Oh! A bonus treat...

"Dr. Dipshit! Fancy seeing you here."

He turns around, his face morphing into disgust at the sight of me.

"Kincaid."

"Aw, you remember my name." I croon as I lean against the desk, putting my delivery on the counter for him to see. "I'm honored."

I watch as his face turns red. Man, it doesn't take him much to make him mad. Oh! I wonder if I can make him cry? It can be like a couples activity that Ainsley and I share.

"What are you grinning about?" he spits out.

"Don't you worry about it, buddy," I say condescendingly, giving him a slap on the back. "Have you seen my girl? I haven't talked to her all day. So I brought her dinner for us to share."

If his face was red a few seconds ago, it's about ready to explode now. "She's not your girl."

"Huh, that's funny," I say as I pull out my phone. "Then what's this?"

I've never been so thankful for Katie sending me an article as I was driving over here. It's of pictures from our date this past weekend, but the headline is new:

How Linc Kincaid and his new woman spent their weekend off.

"If she's not my girl, then why is *US Daily* writing articles that she is? You know, my coach's wife is an editor there. They wouldn't print lies, especially about Fury players."

Except they are, because we're so damn good no one knows it.

Dipshit does his best to puff out his chest and step up to me. I might not be originally from the south, but I've been here long enough to know when a "bless your heart" is best used.

Bless his heart…

"I don't know what you have on her, or why she's doing this," Dipshit spits out. "But this can't go on forever."

"Oh, but it can," I say. Sometimes I scare myself with how good of a liar I am. Or how easily I'm able to pretend that what Ainsley and I have is real. "Do I deserve a woman like Ainsley? Hell no. She's too good for me, so that I agree with you on. But I know when I have a good thing in front of me. And unlike some people, I know that I'd be a fucking fool to throw it away."

Dipshit's jaw ticks before a nurse steps up to us. "Dr. Ainsworth? You're needed back on your floor."

He nods his head at her before she takes a step back, but not before sending me a knowing wink. I don't know who this nurse is, but she's about to get added to the drink and food delivery list.

"Ainsworth? You mean her name would've been Ainsley Ainsworth? Oh, absolutely the fuck not."

He was just about to walk away before he turns back. "Not would. Will. She'll come back to me. Just you wait. You're going to fuck this up, Kincaid, just like you've fucked up everything else in your life. And when you do, I'm going to be waiting. Just you see."

"I beg to differ, my man." I step up close to him, my height towering over him even more. "Get it through your head. She doesn't want you. And she'll never have your name. But Ainsley Kincaid? Now that has a ring to it."

We stare at each other for another second before I feel a familiar, and calming, hand on my arm. "Is everything okay here?"

Ainsley's sweet voice cuts through the testosterone that was just flowing between me and Ainsfuck.

I really should learn his name…

"Everything's fine," I say, throwing my arm around her shoulder and bringing her in so I can kiss her temple. "Isn't it, Doc? Nothing to *cry* about, is there?"

He stares at me for another beat before looking to Ainsley. He doesn't get the joke, but the way she stiffens in my hold, she knows exactly what I'm talking about.

"Everything's fine. I have to get back to my floor."

He storms away, and just as he turns the corner, I step in front of Ainsley. "Surprise!"

The color is draining from her face, and I'd bet all the money in my wallet that her brain is spinning out of control trying to figure out how she's going to explain the phone call last night.

"Yeah, surprise," she says quickly, speedwalking around the nurse's station to grab one of her three water bottles. "You didn't tell me you were coming."

"What kind of surprise would it have been?" I turn to her coworker, who I'm now more certain than ever made up that important need back on Dr. Dipshit's floor. "I'm Linc Kincaid. Ainsley's boyfriend."

"Oh, I know who you are. We all do." She says with a knowing smile. "I'm Liza."

"Nice to meet you, Liza. I'm sorry I didn't bring you anything, I didn't know your order. Next time."

She waves me off. "No need for that. As long as you keep making this girl smile like you have been, that's all I need."

"I do what I can," I say as I look at Ainsley, who is doing her damnedest to not make eye contact with me. "Hey, Liza, I know my girl here is busy, but I brought her some dinner and wondered if I could sneak her away for a break? I know she's working late tonight, and I haven't gotten to see her in a few days."

"I can't, Linc," Ainsley quickly says. "You know, there are… babies. And mothers. And babies. Just so many babies."

"No, there aren't," Liza says with a shake of her head. "No mamas are about to go into labor. You go eat dinner. I'll call you if something happens."

Ainsley narrows her eyes at my new best friend. "Liza, I really shouldn't leave you—"

"Girl, it's fine. You're already working extra hours to cover today. You can take some time. I've got you covered."

"You're the best, Liza," I say, leaning my elbows on the top of the counter of their expansive desk. "Are you sure I can't bring you back something?"

"Maybe a Cherry Coke?"

I pat the top of the desk. "You got it. And thanks with the Doc back there."

"I didn't even have to meet you to know I liked you better," she says. "Now you two kids go have fun."

"Thanks, Liza!" I grab our dinner and drinks and when I turn around, I see Ainsley all but sprinting down the hallway. Damn, she can move.

"Get in here," she says as she opens a door to what seems to be a staff break room.

"Wait! Is this the sex break room?"

She rolls her eyes as she stands in front of me, hands on her hips. "This is labor and delivery. There is no sex break room."

"I'm actually kind of glad about that," I admit as I put down our takeout containers and drinks. "But enough about that. I hope you're hungry. I have chicken tenders, coleslaw, Texas Toast, and they threw in some banana pudding because they're big Fury fans. I told them—"

"Why are you here, Linc?"

Apparently Ainsley has bypassed the speechless, surprised stage to a panic stage of some sorts.

"Can't a boyfriend bring his girlfriend dinner?"

She gives me a raised eyebrow as she sits across from me. "He can. But your timing seems suspicious."

"Nope, nothing suspicious," I say, a little tease in my tone. "Since you told me Dipshit was bothering you at work, I wanted to come up here. I also needed to eat. Since you were working late, and I have light days on Mondays, I thought this would be the perfect way to kill a few birds with one stone."

She tilts her head to study me as I hand her one of the carryout containers. "That's it? No other reason?"

I should be the nice guy and let her off the hook. Tell her

what I heard. But what's the fun in that? "I don't know, Ainsley. What would another reason be?"

Our stare down is intense. She knows I know. I know she knows I know. But there's one thing about me, and it's that I hate to lose. Especially this fun little game of cat and mouse.

"Is it because…" Ainsley's words trail off.

"Because what?"

She bites her lip so hard it might start bleeding. She wants to ask. I can see it in her eyes. Sure, she might still be the shy girl I first met, but every time we're together, I see her breaking out of that shell a little more.

"Last night…my sisters…oh, you know what. Never mind."

"I don't think so." Ainsley tries to turn away from me and start digging through our now-lukewarm chicken tenders, but I don't let her. I pull my chair closer to hers, turning her so she's now facing me. I make sure to pull her in so close my legs have to spread to put her into my orbit. I nearly get lost in her sweet, floral, scent, but I push it aside, because I need this more. "Use your words, Ainsley Mae. You can do it. Do something scary and ask me what you want."

The blush on her cheeks is instant. God I hope she agrees to what I'm proposing just so I can see what else I can do to make those cheeks pink.

"Did you hear the conversation with my sisters?"

I take her hands in mine. "I did."

"How much?"

Once I figured out what was going on, I knew I was entering midway through the conversation. But I know what I heard. And that was enough for me.

"I heard that Dr. Dipshit didn't deserve a woman like you. That you have been massively neglected for a very long time. And that, if you want, I can be the man to change that."

I feel her hands go limp in mine. She hasn't blinked. Was that the best way to approach this? Probably not. But Ainsley needs decisiveness, so why not rip off the sexual Band-Aid?

"What do you mean?"

I take a breath, because I might've just dropped that bomb, but I want to make sure I get this right. "I know I probably shouldn't have listened last night, so I do need to apologize for that."

Ainsley shakes her head. "I mean, my niece called you without me knowing, so there's honestly nothing to apologize for."

Oh, now that makes more sense. "Remind me to buy her a really good Christmas present this year. Because I'm glad she did."

"Really? You wanted to hear my horrible, and minimal, sexual history?"

"Not for the reasons you're probably thinking. Ainsley, you are too beautiful of a woman—too good of a woman—to doubt yourself like the way I heard you talking last night. I hate that these schmucks who call themselves men have made you feel anything less than the incredible woman you are."

"Linc, I—"

I put my finger in front of her mouth. "No, let me finish. Because I have a feeling you're going to try and dismiss the words I just said. But please don't. I know you're not the kind of girl to sleep around. You're a commitment girl, and that's admirable. So I know this probably isn't something you've ever considered doing. And you're probably going to tell me to go to hell for suggesting it."

"That would require me saying that word."

I can't contain my laughter. God, this woman...she really is something else.

"All I'm saying is that if you want to feel those fireworks—if you want to know what it can be like—then let me help you."

She doesn't say anything. Which is what I expected. She's surprised, so she's quiet. That's how Ainsley operates. And a proposal like this might put her into a coma.

"Just think about it." I bring her hand to my mouth and give the top of her hand a gentle kiss. "Whatever you'd want to do, whatever you'd want to explore, let me be the one to show you what it can be like."

I stand up, ready to leave, so that way she doesn't have to sit in shock in front of me, but I'm barely up before I feel her pull on my hand.

"Why?"

She's now standing, her blue eyes big and questioning.

"Because I can't give you forever. But I can give you this."

guide to love rule #58

Lists are necessary for order in life. They're also overrated when you're being kissed like you've never been kissed before.

21
ainsley

I DIDN'T MEAN TO TAKE AN EVERYTHING SHOWER FOR SEX PURPOSES. I really didn't.

It's just because of a series of really odd events that I'm now standing at my fake boyfriend's apartment building, asking to be let in, because I think I want to accept his offer to become my sex teacher.

Maybe. I'm still not sure. Probably. I think.

It started with a normal length shower. I always take one when I come home from work. But then I started—okay, continued—thinking about Linc's proposal, and things got out of hand.

So I washed. And conditioned. And exfoliated. And shaved. And shaved some more. Before I knew it, I'd taken an everything shower on steroids that ended with freezing cold water and being even more confused than ever.

I can't give you forever. But I can give you this…

Who says lines like that? Fictional men, that's who. And more important, how am I, the hopeless romantic who is already having a hard enough time remembering what Linc and I are doing is fake, not supposed to fall in love with this guy? And oh yeah, he's offering me orgasms.

The second I got out of the shower—and moisturized, because I'm not about to let this go to waste—I grabbed a notebook and a pen. There, sitting on my bed criss-cross-applesauce, head and body still wrapped in towels, I made a list of pros and cons of his offer.

Pros:
*** Finally have an orgasm. Hopefully. Probably.**
*** Get to actually contribute to my sisters' sex conversations.**
*** Not have my last sexual partner be Jonathan.**
*** Be with a man who doesn't cry during sex.**
Learn to give a proper blow job.
Cons:
*** Will probably fall in love with my fake boyfriend.**

It's only one con, but it scares me the most. Because I will. I know me. I've already gone through four rubber bands since we started this.

But the pros are pro-ing…

No. I need to tell him no. That I appreciate the offer.

Even though I want to.

No. I don't.

But I do.

I really, *really* do.

And that might scare me more than anything.

I take a deep breath as I prepare to call Linc to let me in, but before I can, my phone vibrates in my hand.

BOYFRIEND

You look really beautiful when you overthink.

I look around, because is there a secret camera? Is he tracking me? I keep looking, only to hear a telltale laugh not far from where I'm standing.

When I turn around, Linc's standing against an SUV, his arms crossed, and the smirk on his face is making me forget the one and only con.

"How long have you been there?"

He pushes off the vehicle, and holy smokes…why does he look so hot right now? He's wearing what he had on earlier—perfectly fitted jeans and a black T-shirt—but somehow it looks sexier now. And believe me, he looked good earlier—though there was the added effect of him going toe-to-toe with Jonathan. But now? Now I might become a puddle on the sidewalk. Because the way he's looking at me with such intent…with a mischievous sparkle in his eye…it's enough to make me say yes right now with no objections whatsoever.

Or I'm just horny.

Oh my goodness…am I horny? I've never been before…

"Long enough to know you've changed your mind probably six times."

Add another con to the list: He already knows me too well, and that's before seeing me naked.

Oh my gosh, Linc would see me naked. I'd see *him* naked.

I'd see his tattoos. All of them. Including the thigh tattoo that's haunted my dreams.

"How about we go upstairs," he says, putting his hand on the small of my back. "Because I don't know what just hit your brain, but your eyes are bouncing around like you don't know which way is up."

"Good idea," I say as I let him guide me inside his building. I haven't been back here since the fateful morning. Gosh, was that only a few weeks ago? It feels like forever. But I remember it like it was yesterday. Sitting at his counter, recounting our crazy night. Katie suggesting we keep the lie going. Me insisting that we do it.

What had gotten into me that morning? Was it part of my hangover and confidence from the night before? It had to be. Is that girl still here? Does her spirit live at Linc's apartment? Because I could use some of that girl's confidence tonight as I sit on his couch, wondering if I can say yes to something that is so far out of my comfort zone it has a different country code.

"I didn't know when I'd hear from you."

"If you think I've gone a second without thinking about this, then you don't know me as well as you think you do."

He laughs and hands me a bottle of water as he sits next to me on his sectional. "I figured you were. But how long that took before you came to a decision was up in the air."

That's true. I could have overthought this one until the season was up and then I wouldn't have had to make a decision at all.

Oh…now there's an option…

No. I need to nip this in the bud. Or I'm not going to sleep tonight. Or ever again.

"I've thought about it."

"You don't say…"

He gives me a playful wink, and he's really lucky right now that he's hot and I'm going insane. "Do you want me to say yes to this or not?"

That straightens him up real quick.

"That's what I thought." I take my oversized tote off my shoulder and pull out the notebook.

"Did you really make a list?"

"Of course," I say as I flip the page to the rules that I wrote down for this to happen. He doesn't need to see the pro-con list on the first page. "Did you expect anything less?"

"Actually, I didn't," he says as he inches closer to me, his hand going across the back of the couch. "All right, Ainsley Mae, lay it on me."

I turn toward him and do my best to resist the sexy smirk he's giving me. "Okay, if we're going to do this, and I'm going to say *if* because I don't want you thinking this is a done deal—"

"I never would."

"Good. Then, in the hypothetical if we were to do this, we need rules."

That takes him back a little. "Rules?"

"Yes, rules," I say. "Because this is already very out of my comfort zone, and if I have rules, it will help me not feel like I've been body snatched."

He can't hide his grin.

"This is serious, Linc! Are you going to be my sex teacher or not?"

He coughs and sits up straight. "Yes, ma'am. Please, tell me the rules."

Part of me—the one who's chicken about actually going through with this—hoped that my threat of rules would make him take his offer back. I mean, he has a bad-boy reputation. He has to hate rules, right?

Apparently not.

"Well, okay," I stumble a bit because I truly didn't expect him to go along with this so fast. "First, I guess, isn't a rule, but more of a general understanding of how this would work. Do I ask for things? Do you come up with a lesson plan? And if there is a lesson plan, are there tests? Do we have certain areas that we concentrate on per night? Is it go with the flow? Do I come over here, or you come to my house, with the intention of—"

I don't get a chance to finish my sentence because as I'm reading from my scribbled notes, the notebook is ripped from my hand.

"Linc! What are you doing?"

He doesn't even look at my notebook before throwing it to the side. "Fuck your list."

My mouth drops open, and I don't have time to be stunned because before I know it, Linc's hand is behind my neck, pulling me in for a kiss that's so sudden, and so hot, I've lost all brain capacity.

Holy frick…

All thoughts of lists and rules and guidelines are gone from my brain as I sink into Linc's touch. Yes, we've kissed before. But this is different. Intentional. Every swipe of his tongue, every nip of my lips, is Linc showing me that he knows exactly what I need.

And I know he does. With every fiber of my being.

He pulls me up to his lap, his hand still on my neck and the other now holding my back as he deepens our kiss. My arms wrap around his shoulders, wanting to feel him closer as our tongues explore wherever they want.

Goodness gracious, this is a good kiss. No, a great one. Epic. I haven't kissed many men—shocking, I know—but with each one of them it took time to get the rhythm right. Which way were our heads turning? Were we using tongue? Me wondering why they were biting my lip, because from what my sisters told me, there wasn't supposed to be biting.

But this kiss? I don't know how Linc's doing it, but there isn't a thought in my head. All I'm thinking about is how his lips taste —like mint and trouble and pleasure—how his hands feel as they pull me closer to him. How my body is heating more and more with every swipe of his tongue.

"Linc..." I hear the moan come out of my mouth before I can stop it. I've always been too shy to vocalize any feelings or sensations during sex—and I've never really had any that made me want to—but I can't keep his name inside as he starts kissing across my cheek and down my neck. My head falls to the side, wanting to give him all the access he wants as he starts gently fluttering his lips at my pulse. He has to feel it quickening. My heart is pounding, my body throbbing.

Everywhere.

And I mean *everywhere*.

Linc slowly starts laying me down on his couch, and I feel his body weight on me as he pulls back his kiss.

"Well, that's one way to get me to stop thinking."

He laughs and kisses the tip of my nose. "I'll have to remember that the next time I see those wheels turning."

The next time...there's going to be a next time.

I'm doing this. We're doing this. Holy frick, I'm doing this...

"Hey." As promised, he leans down for another kiss. "Stop that."

I wrap my hands around his neck, gently playing with the hair at the nape of his neck. "Easier said than done."

"I get that. And I'm not saying I don't want you to think at all. I quite like it when your brain starts spinning." He pauses to kiss me again. It's like he can't stop. "I don't need a list to know what you need, Ainsley. I just need you to want this. And to trust me. Can you do that?"

Since the moment I met Linc, I knew I could trust him. That first night, I trusted him with my safety. After that I felt confident enough to be willing to live a lie. And now I'm trusting him with my body.

Now my heart? That's another story.

But I'll worry about that later.

And that right there may be the scariest thing I've ever done.

"I can."

He smiles back as he looks down on me, his fingers gently pushing aside a lock of hair behind my ear. "Good. Then let me take care of you. That sound good?"

I nod as I tug him closer. "If I want something, am I allowed to ask for it?"

His grin is downright sinful. "Of course. What do you want, Ainsley Mae?"

"I want you to kiss me again."

22

linc

How can I say no to that?

I can't. And I don't.

My mouth is back on hers in an instant. It's only been a minute, but I already miss her sweet taste. How her body was starting to come alive just from my lips.

She's so fucking soft and so fucking flawless. Her curves have made my mouth water since the second I felt her against me in that hospital before she ended up on the floor. But now that I have her here? Getting to feel her body under me? My hands just starting to explore the flare of her hips? She's even more perfect than I realized.

My hands have a mind of their own as they start wandering her body. They're about to go under her shirt, wanting to feel her skin more than I want anything in this moment, but I need to make sure she knows one thing.

Because I might know what she needs—and I do—but this is her show. And she needs to know that.

"If there is anything I do that you're not ready for, you stop me. Immediately. Do you understand?"

Her eyes look drunk as she nods. Only this time she's not

drunk off cinnamon whiskey. It's me. And she's just getting her first taste.

"No, Ainsley. I need you to say it."

She cups my face into her hands. "I will. I promise."

"Good girl," I say, feeling a weight off my shoulders. "Now I promised you fireworks. I think it's time for the first show."

I watch as her crystal blue eyes darken as I tug her up, pulling her to my lap, taking my time as I pull up her fitted T-shirt and toss it to the floor. I suck in a breath as I stare at the vision in front of me. Tits that I can't wait to have in my hands—and more so in my mouth—stare at me as they are held in by a white lace bra that is so Ainsley, yet so fucking sexy, I might come right now.

"Fuck," I groan, my mouth on her chest like a magnet is pulling me toward it.

I place slow, lingering kisses across the top of her chest, her back starting to arch as I take my time. My hands slowly start pulling down her straps before I reach around with one to take off her bra. The fabric falls away from her, and I guide it down her arms before completely removing it.

"Even more perfect then I imagined." I cup each in my hands, loving the weight as I bring one to my mouth.

I feel her body tense and then start to writhe against me as I start sucking on her peaked nipple. Her hands are now in my hair, pulling ever so gently as I move my mouth to the other, wanting to make sure it has just as much attention.

"Linc..." My name dies on her lips as I start flicking her nipple, her back arching so much I need to move my hands just to make sure she doesn't fall. Shit, she's so responsive. So expressive. How the fuck did Dr. Dipshit, or any other tool she'd been with, not realize that Ainsley wasn't enjoying herself? This girl hates lying; I doubt she was faking orgasms.

"You like that, don't you?" I ask, taking my mouth away for just a second so I can watch her face as I tease each of her nipples.

"Yes," she breathes. "But I want more."

My cock twitches at her words. "More, huh?"

Her head bobs up and down, her eyes half open as I start to grind my dick into her. "Yes."

"Always so polite," I say as I lay her down on my couch, sucking on a nipple one more time before I position myself next to her. "Now what do nice girls say when they want something?"

Her eyes open for me, already dazed, and I haven't even made her come yet.

Yet being the operative word.

"Please."

It's barely a whisper, but I heard it. And I want more.

"What was that?" I ask as I slide down her leggings. "What is it you want?"

"More…please."

"That's my girl." I lean up, planting my lips on her again as my hand travels down to the spot that I've been dying to touch.

Fuck, she's soaked. I can feel it through her white lace panties. Ainsley is drenched from that little bit of foreplay. I don't plan on having sex with her tonight—baby steps is the name of this game—but I can't imagine what she's going to feel like when I finally have that wetness around my cock.

Our kiss deepens as I slide my fingers around the damp fabric, slowly teasing her entrance. Her hips are already begging for more, and so is every other movement she's making. She's pulling at my hair. Her chest is pressing up into me. The little moans leaving her mouth are quite possibly the sexiest sounds I've ever heard in my life.

So I do as she asks, and I slide one finger in. Her gasp is loud, and I almost lose myself right there, feeling how goddamn tight she is around me. If she's like this for my finger, her pussy is going to squeeze my dick like a vise grip.

"That's it," I whisper, slowly working my digit around to warm her up. "I've got you."

There's so much I want to do right now. I want to kiss her again, because I'm pretty sure I'm already addicted. I want to suck on her perfect tits, but I have a feeling that's going to be a daily occurrence now that the flood gate has been lifted for that. But no, above everything else right now, I just want to watch her.

I want to watch her face as she feels my finger—now fingers —inside of her. I want to watch her find the pleasure in something that I'm going to guess by her reaction she's never felt before.

I just want to watch.

"Feels...so..."

"I know," I say, enjoying every moment, maybe more than she is. I know I said this night is about her—and it is. And I knew that I'd enjoy myself. But even I didn't realize how much I'd get lost in her body. In her touch. In how with every movement she makes in response to me, I want to give her that much more.

I start speeding up my movements, sensing she needs more. And I'm right. My fingers are working in and out of her, and for every push I make, her hips rise more and more in the air. Like they're begging me to finish her off. Fuck, she's so hot right now. My cock is begging for comfort, release, anything, as I watch this gorgeous woman chase a high only I can give her.

"You've got this," I say, rubbing her sensitive nub a little faster. "Let go, Ainsley. Just let go."

And she does. I feel the second her orgasm hits her. Her body shakes. Her hands grip onto my arms like she needs it to hold herself to this Earth.

"Linc! Oh my God! Yes!"

That's it. Hearing my name being screamed by her as she holds me hostage is the death of me. Literally, as I feel myself come in my pants like a fucking sixteen-year-old.

Worth it.

"Fuck, Ainsley," I groan, my body convulsing along with her, but mine more of a surprise than hers probably was.

Holy fuck...that's never happened to me. I've always been able to control myself. Then again, I've never been around a woman like Ainsley Banks before.

"Holy Moses," she says, her voice shaky as her breathing starts to come down. "That was..."

"Yes, it was," I say, kissing her lips to help bring me down as well. "You're beautiful, you know that right?"

There's the blush. I just fucking came in my pants but I swear just with that little bit of color in her cheeks, I'm hard all over again.

What is this woman doing to me...

"Thank you," she whispers, her yawn coming almost immediately.

"You don't need to thank me. Ever," I say. "I'll be right back."

I kiss her one more time before maneuvering off the couch to head to my bedroom. I quickly strip from my jeans and boxers, throw a new pair on with some Fury joggers, and grab a washcloth for her. When I make it back to the living room, I smile as I see that it didn't take long for her to fall asleep.

"Sweet dreams, Ainsley Mae," I say, bringing a blanket to drape over us after I clean her up. "I know I will."

———

"What has our boy smiling like that?"

"Smiling like what?" I try to play Maddox's comment off, but I know the cheesy smile on my face is giving me away. "Can't a guy be happy?"

"He can. But he usually isn't when it's our long day of practice and Coach is in a particular mood."

I wave Maddox off. "I don't know what you mean. The sun is shining. It's not scorching hot outside. We got a win last week, and we're going to win again this week. All reasons to have a smile on my face."

Maddox looks at me with a raised brow, and I think he's

going to drop it before Wyatt comes sliding into the conversation.

"Or, does it have something to do with the fact that Ainsley spent the night last night?"

Again, because a grown-ass football team is comprised of ten-year-old boys, teammates not even involved in this conversation give me an "ooooohhhh."

Though I can't blame them. If this was Wyatt or Maddox, or really anyone, I'd be doing the same damn thing.

"How the fuck did you know she stayed?" I ask as I finish putting on my gear for today's practice.

"Saw you walk her to her car," he says. "Ten out of ten on the kiss goodbye."

I roll my eyes. Though he's right. It was a damn good kiss. "You're an idiot."

He gives me a slap on the back. "I'm proud of you. You've got yourself a good one."

"We ever going to see her again?" Maddox asks. "I feel bad that I didn't properly get to know her the night of karaoke. Maybe she has a friend you could introduce me to?"

"She doesn't," Wyatt snaps.

"Damn," Maddox says, holding his hands up in surrender. "Okay then. Maybe a sister?"

I shake my head as I sit down to tie my cleats. "Three, but they're all in relationships or married. Sorry, buddy. You'll have to continue your manwhore ways somewhere else."

"I'm not a manwhore. I'm an equal opportunity lover."

That he is. I swear, one week I saw him go home with a girl who was barely out of college and the next someone who was old enough to be his mother.

"Kincaid, did I hear that right? You've got yourself a girl?"

I stand up as Bryce approaches me. We're tight in the locker room. He's my quarterback, after all, and we have to have some sort of relationship. But since he's married and has a kid, he doesn't come out a lot with the single guys on the team.

Though I guess I'm not one of the single ones anymore. Or am I?

"Yeah, I do."

"That's awesome," he says. "She coming to the game this Sunday?"

"I'm not sure," I say. "She's a nurse at Nashville Children's. I'll need to see what her work schedule is."

"Let me know," he says as I grab my helmet and we start walking to the practice field. "My wife Lucy and my sister Brenna have a suite. It's easier when they bring the kids with them. They love meeting new partners of players. And that way she has friendly faces surrounding her during the game. You never know what kind of crazies will be in the stands."

"Thanks, man," I say. "I'll talk to her tonight and let you know."

Bryce jogs off as I trail behind. Fuck, I'm glad he said something, because I've never requested tickets for anyone. Ever. Gram was unfortunately too old, and at the end, too sick, to come see me play in college. No way she could've made the trip from the suburbs of Detroit to Starkville. And by the time I got to the pros, for the few pro games I did dress for, she was already gone.

What will it be like knowing Ainsley's in the stands? Knowing she's there to watch me, hopefully with my number on her back? I knew she was watching during the opener, but her watching on television versus her being there in person is a whole other thing. I suddenly have a whole new motivation for this Sunday's game. Because it's not going to be enough just to beat the Philadelphia Kings on our field. No, I want to make a mark.

And I want Ainsley to see it.

"I'm headed to the doc today. Rumor has it he's going to clear me."

I swallow a groan and do my best not to ball my fists as I

hear Brad's snide words somewhere behind me as I'm about to leave the tunnel.

"Good for you."

I try to keep running, wanting to ignore him so my good mood doesn't turn sour, but I can't as he steps in front of me. "When I'm back, this honeymoon you're on is over, Kincaid. I'm taking my job back. And did I hear that you have a girlfriend now? She'll probably dump you when your ass is back on the bench."

I purposefully don't react to his Ainsley comment. If he knows that triggers me, it's only going to add to his arsenal. "You can try. But while you're still getting your knee wrapped and figuring out which size brace you'll need to wear, I'll be catching another touchdown. Maybe two this week. I'm feeling good about the matchup."

Brad's face reddens as my cockiness is clearly getting to him.

"I'm taking you down, Kincaid. And when I'm back, you're going to be yesterday's news."

"You can try," I say, taking another step to him. "But you won't. Have fun at PT. I'm going to go turn some heads."

I jog off, doing my best to push the impending return of Rockwell to the side of my mind.

If he is cleared, I don't have room for error. I already didn't. He might be a Grade-A prick, but the guy can play ball. He was in the top five in receiving yards for tight ends last year before he got hurt. You never know how someone is going to come back from injury, but I have to go under the assumption that he's back and better than ever.

Which just means I have to up my game even more.

Now I have another goal for this Sunday: Make Ainsley proud. And keep my fucking job.

guide to love rule #21

Don't overlook the good girls. They have a mean streak you won't see coming.

23
ainsley

"Oh my gosh! You're Ainsley! Linc's Ainsley!"

I don't know how I hear my name over the noise filling the air as Quinn and I walk toward the Fury stadium, but I do. And I'm glad I did. Because as soon as I turn around, two women around my age are sprinting toward me.

"Um...hi?"

"I can't believe we're seeing you!" one says as she digs her phone out of her clear bag. "Can we take a selfie?"

I hear Quinn snickering behind me as I try to wrap my brain around what's going on. "Um...sure?"

Each of them stand on either side of me as I smile toward the phone. I do my best to have a genuine smile, but it's hard because I don't know how this is real life.

"I can't believe we saw you!" the one who took the selfie says. "We met *the* Ainsley."

"I'm just Ainsley," I say, trying to temper down this fangirling. For one, it's a little embarrassing. Two, my sister is never going to let me live this down. "But it's really nice to meet you two. Big Fury fans?"

"Of course," they say in unison before the selfie taker continues. "And we used to have the biggest crushes on Linc. But not anymore, because he's with you, and you two are basically perfect together."

"For real you two are couple goals," the other says. "I swear to God, I died dead when I saw the photos of him walking you to your car this week."

Not going to lie, I melted a little too when I saw those. Neither of us had any idea that anyone was around. I mean, it was eight in the morning on a Wednesday. Must've been a slow news day. And I wish I could thank whoever took them, because the moment he kissed me goodbye before I drove off… Yeah, I'm glad I get to relive that moment forever.

"Thanks. I'm a pretty lucky girl."

We chit-chat for a few more minutes, and then they ask for another picture before they head off with the rest of the crowd to head inside the stadium.

But me? I stand outside the suite entrances a bit stunned, because how is this my life?

"Oh, just wait until the group chat hears about this."

I groan as we walk toward the entrance. "Please don't."

"Oh, dear sister, if you don't think I'm going to report on every minute of this, you don't know me at all."

"You know, I didn't have to bring you here today," I say, really hating that Mia had to work. "I could've asked Simon. Or I'm sure Stella would've loved to come."

"But you asked me, so now you must suffer the consequences." We each show the security guard our suite badges before we go through a metal detector and head to the elevator. "Now come on. You need to become a WAG, and I've got nachos to eat."

When Linc asked me if I wanted to come today, I obviously wanted to support him. It was even better when he said I could bring a friend. I assumed we'd be sitting in regular seats in the stadium, which is when I asked Quinn to come along. Then I found out that we'd be in a suite with other wives and girlfriends.

I really should've brought Maeve.

I love my sister, but she's the most unhinged person in my life that I'd want with me at a football game. Especially a game where I'm trying to make a good impression on the other wives and girlfriends. I know Linc and I aren't really for real, but I still want them to like me. Especially if I'm going to be here for multiple games this season. So maybe it wasn't my best idea to bring Quinn, who would have no qualms about starting fights with referees, or other fans, if something happened she didn't agree with.

Just the headline Linc and I need:

Linc Kincaid's girlfriend banned from games after sister fights with fan

"I need you to promise me you'll be on your best behavior."

She puts her hand over her heart as the elevator takes us to the suite floor. "I solemnly swear. Though I'm a little insulted that you felt the need to say that."

"Really? Are you not the person who organized egging a referee's house back in high school because he made a bad call?"

"It was a clear fumble and it cost us the game," she defends. "And it wasn't eggs. It was toilet paper."

"Apologies," I say, shaking my head at my sister. I love her, but sometimes I wonder how we share DNA.

When the elevator stops at our floor and we step out, we're quickly guided down a long hallway. Fans are gathered in and out of the suites, all wearing some sort of Fury merchandise. I feel a few eyes on me, but not like earlier. Though I'm guessing that's because I just passed country star Dustin Wild. Compared to him, I'm small potatoes.

"Right in here," the attendant tells us. "Enjoy the game. Oh, and nice jersey."

The older woman gives me a wink as I walk into the suite. I didn't know if I should wear this today—it felt a little cliché to wear your fake boyfriend's jersey to your first game. But after the note he left with it when he had it delivered to my apartment yesterday, how could I not?

I THOUGHT YOU COULD USE SOMETHING TO WEAR TO THE GAME TODAY. I'D BE HONORED IF YOU WORE IT.
   <3 LINC

That man. He might say over and over that he's not the kind of guy who can give you forever, but every day he does some-thing to contradict that statement.

And I'm now on to my fifth rubber band in three weeks.

"Oh! Hi! You must be Ainsley!"

I smile as two women come toward me, one holding a toddler and the other with a very tiny baby strapped to her chest.

"Hi! Yes, I'm Ainsley. And this is my sister, Quinn."

"So nice to meet you," the brunette holding the toddler says. "I'm Lucy Donald, Bryce's wife. This here is my best friend and sister-in-law, Brenna Campbell."

"Nice to meet you," Brenna says. "And welcome to the WAG Hut."

I look around, and I don't know what I was expecting, but it's not this. For some reason, when I thought of suites, I thought of booze all around and platters of food that couldn't possibly be all eaten by the time the game ends. And yes, there is food. I do see a small refrigerator with an assortment of beers and small bottles of wine. But what sticks out more are the piles of chil-dren's toys scattered about. A play mat and a pack-and-play. And instead of the game being on the television, it's a children's show with the blue dog that I've seen more than a few times playing in the hospital.

"I hope you don't mind, but this is the boring suite," Brenna says. "Once upon a time we were the young, hot WAGs. Drinking vodka sodas, wearing cute clothes to games."

"And then we had kids," Lucy says as her son runs off to something that caught his eye. "I hope you don't mind."

"Oh not at all," I say as her son comes back over, handing me a toy car. "I might not be a mom, but this is definitely more my speed. I'm not much of a drinker. And thank you for the car, buddy. I love it."

He gives me a big, toothy grin as he runs back to his pile, bringing me another.

"I'm sorry, but you're his new best friend now," Lucy jokes. "Come on, let's get you settled."

Lucy shows us the food and beverages, as well as that there are a few rows of seats outside the glass windows that give you a perfect view of the field.

"Help yourself to any of the food," Lucy says.

"Thank you kindly," Quinn says, circling back to the buffet like she's never eaten before.

"Pardon my sister," I say. "I broke her out of the institution this morning. She's forgotten what real food is like."

She throws me a middle finger as Lucy and Brenna laugh at our antics. "Oh, I like you two. Just what we needed in the Hut."

"And we're not the only ones who sit in here. I don't want you to think that we're the outcasts," Lucy says. "Other partners come in and out. It's open to anyone that's dating or married to one of the players. It's fun to sit in the stadium. But sometimes you just need to get out of the crowds, especially if there are kids involved."

"Totally understand," I say. "I work at Nashville Children's, so I understand wanting to have a separate place for you and the kids. Especially for newborns."

"Yes! That's where I know you!" Brenna yells. "You weren't my nurse, but I saw you on the floor."

I think back, and yes, I do remember a Campbell baby a few

months ago. "Oh my gosh. Yes. How are you? How are you feeling?"

Brenna and I start a conversation about her birth, and how her daughter, Everly, is doing. Before I know it, a few more of the WAGs have come in, each introducing themselves to me, and I fall into a natural conversation with them all.

I was nervous coming here today. On my scale of "doing scary things" initiative that I've been on, this isn't at the top, but it definitely cracks the top ten. It normally takes time for me to open up and meet new people. But as I'm talking to these women, I feel at home. Like I'm strangely supposed to be here.

"Ainsley! There you are!"

Any thoughts I had about this starting to feel a little too real are quickly brought back down to Earth as Katie walks into the suite. "I hope you don't mind me coming in, but I heard you were here today and I wanted to stop in and say hi."

"Oh, yeah, hi," I say. I haven't seen her at all since this whole thing started, but I know Linc talks to her most days and meets with her a few times a week. "How'd you know I was here?"

"Linc silly," she says, the fake smile she gave me the first day we met in full form right now. "How nice of the veteran WAGs to let you watch the game with them."

"Hey! That makes us sound old," Brenna complains. "We're not vets. We're *seasoned*. Also, who the hell are you?"

I swear I see Quinn's face light up with Brenna's words. My sister might've just found her new best friend.

"She's Linc's publicist," I say. "How about we go to the outside seats and watch the start of game?"

"Sure," Katie says, giving a look to Brenna before we make our way out. "These seats are nice. I rarely watch a game from the stands. I'm more of an on-the-field girl."

Did she need to say that? That felt a bit forced. Also, I'm pretty sure publicists don't watch games from the field, but I have bigger questions to ask her about. "Is there anything I can help you with, Katie?"

I take in her dress for the day, which also doesn't seem very publicist like. Not that I expect people to dress in business casual every day, but she's chosen to come to today's game in a cropped Fury shirt, cowboy boots, and denim shorts. It has a number on it, but I don't know whose, and I can't see the back to check the name. The attire matches the two girls I met out front. For them, it makes sense. For Linc's publicist, I'd think she'd want to dress a little more professional.

"I just wanted to check in on you. See how everything is going?"

The question seems simple, but this woman is one of three people who knows what's going on with me and Linc. Does she really want to talk about our secret where others could hear? Sure, this is a loud stadium, but it's certainly not private, so I'm not about to spill secrets where anyone could hear them.

"I'm doing great," I say. "Work is going well. Linc's great. We've been finding some times between our schedules to see each other. Couldn't be happier."

"That's ah-mazing," Katie says. I got the fake vibe from her the first day we met, but now it's a little more over the top. "I saw you spent the night the other night. *Love* that for you two."

She gives me a shoulder bump as I notice that the Fury offense is taking the field. I quickly scan the players, and there he is, number twenty-four.

"Yeah, I did," I say. "I'm guessing you saw the photos?"

I can't ask her outright if she sent anyone to take them, at least not here. But I have wondered if they were random or if those had Katie's fingerprints on them.

"I did. Was a little shocked, to be honest. I didn't know you two had graduated to sleepovers?"

I take my eye off the game for just a second, wanting to assess her. Because I know I overthink a lot, and make up things in my head because I'm paranoid, but I'm ninety-five percent sure this woman is digging for information.

"We did," I say, glad right now that I have to stay in girlfriend character. "It was a lovely night. One to remember. I'm so glad that the cameras were there that morning. It was a night, and a morning, I want to remember forever."

My words hit the mark as I watch her neck start to turn red. Is she jealous? Surely not. She suggested we do this. If she had a thing for Linc, making us date would be the stupidest idea in the world. But before she can formulate a response, I hear Quinn running through the suite to the outside seats.

"They're in the red zone. Let's fucking go!"

I stand up and start clapping my hands with the fans as Linc and the rest of the offense line up out of the huddle. I was nervous last week when I watched him on television, but this is even more intense in person.

I start to bite my nails as Bryce calls for the ball. My eyes never leave Linc as I watch him race a few yards ahead before running toward the middle of the end zone. My heart drops into my stomach as Bryce fires the ball to him, who has to jump a little to catch it. I suck in a breath as I watch him fall to the ground, but the ball never leaves his hand.

"Touchdown! Fury!"

I scream and start jumping around, hugging Quinn as she cheers along with me. A few of the other WAGs came outside to watch the drive, including Lucy, who gives me a high-five. I glance at the Jumbotron, who has the camera on Linc, who crosses his heart with his finger before pointing the ball to the camera.

Cross my heart...

Everyone around me is still cheering, music now pumping through the stadium, when I turn to Katie. She's not cheering or dancing like the rest of us. Actually, if I had to put a word to it, she looks miffed.

"Everything okay? Your client just caught a touchdown. Shouldn't you be excited?"

"Oh yeah," she says. "I think I'm going to get going. We can talk later."

Katie starts walking back through the suite, and normally I'd let her go and just enjoy the game with my sister and the women who have welcomed me into their group. But today I'm feeling some kind of way. It might be because I had caffeine this morning. It might be because I've now had an orgasm. But she's not leaving quite yet.

"Katie!" I call out, quickly looking around to make sure we're alone in the hallway. "I'm onto you."

She scoffs. "Onto me? What are you onto?"

I don't want to outright accuse of her anything, because I don't know what her end game is. But I'm not getting a good feeling, and I refuse to ignore my intuition.

"If you don't like what's happening between Linc and I, I'd remind you this was your idea," I say, low enough that we don't draw attention. "I don't know what you're trying to pull, or what your motives are, but I'm going to be watching you. Because I care about Linc. And hear me when I say this, if I see you do one thing that's going to hurt him in any way, you're going to hate the day that you decided to put this plan in motion."

She narrows her eyes at me, but Quinn interrupts before she can say anything.

"Everything okay out here?"

"Just fine, sis," I say. "I'll talk to you soon, Katie. Enjoy the rest of the game."

We wait a second to make sure Katie exits before we turn back to the suite.

"Who was that snarky Ainsley? I didn't know snarky Ainsley existed!"

I laugh as we turn back to the suite. "I didn't either. But I'm learning a lot about myself these days."

"Remind me to thank Linc. Whatever he's doing, I'm a big fan."

So am I, Quinn…so am I.

24
linc

"THAT'S HOW WE FUCKING DO IT, BOYS!"

Our sideline is fucking pumped up about that last touchdown. As we should be, it was a beautiful interception by Maddox, who ran it back sixty yards to seal the win for us.

There's two minutes left in the game, and unless something crazy happens, me and the rest of the offense can take the rest of the game off and walk away as winners. Two-and-oh to start the season…not bad. Not bad at all.

"Fuck, yeah," Wyatt says, slapping my back as I watch Philadelphia's offense try to make a comeback. "Good fucking game, Linc."

"You too. The line played out of their minds today."

And I'm not saying that because my best friend anchors the right side. They were blocking everything, giving Bryce all the time in the world to make his passes. Which is why I had a hundred and twenty yards receiving and two touchdowns. Our running backs rushed for another hundred-and-fifty yards.

It was a great all-around game, and I hate to jinx things, but if this is how we're going to play this season, it's going to be hard to stop us.

Three in four, baby…three in four.

"A bunch of us are going to go out tonight. Dinner and a few drinks. Nothing crazy. Want to come?"

I start to answer him, but as I do, the Jumbotron plays one of our favorite victory songs—and it's one that our fans have embraced. I don't usually watch the board, but since this game is wrapped up, I let my eyes wander.

And then they pan to Ainsley. She and Quinn are dancing in the front of the suite, Brenna Campbell and Lucy Donald next to them. The crowd roars when they see the four of them, and that only doubles down their dancing and excitement. I step back and drop my helmet so I can watch for as long as the camera will let me. I know I'm smiling like a fucking fool, but I can't help it. She's fucking gorgeous and smiling ear to ear, having the time of her life.

And she's doing it in my jersey.

"I'm going to assume you have other plans tonight," Wyatt says as he steps next to me.

"Yeah...I think I'm busy."

I don't know who said what, but all four of them start hysterically laughing before it zooms in on Ainsley. She happens to look over to the camera and gives it a wave with the biggest smile I think I've ever seen on her before it pans away.

"This is still what it started as, right?" Wyatt asks. "It hasn't become...more?"

I get what he's saying, and I appreciate his choice of words. "Still the same. A few other perks, but that's it."

Sure...keep telling yourself that.

Wyatt shakes his head. "Just be careful, man."

"About what?"

He looks at me, then to the box where the girls are sitting, then back to me. "Your smile."

Okay, what the fuck is he talking about? "My smile?"

He nods and puts his hand on my shoulder as the game clock expires and the crowd roars to life once more. "That smile doesn't happen for a guy who's faking it. That's not even the one you'd have if you knew cameras are around. No, that's the smile of a guy who's in love. And I know how you feel about that subject."

I scoff at him. "I'm not in love. Believe me, nothing has changed. We're just having fun."

He just laughs as we jog onto the field to shake hands. "You keep telling yourself that."

———

I've never showered so fast in my entire life.

Sure, it helped that I had to do a formal post-game press conference, and our media team likes us put together and not still in uniform. But even if I didn't, I would've still broken the team record for fastest to leave the locker room.

Because I have plans. And they involve Ainsley. In my jersey. And that's it.

"See you tomorrow," I say to Wyatt as I grab my duffel bag. "Have fun tonight."

"I'd say you, too, but I already have a feeling you're going to."

I couldn't keep the smile off my face if I tried. "Oh, I will."

I wave goodbye to a few guys as I walk out of the locker room. I'm just about out when I hear my name.

"Good game, Kincaid. Too bad—"

"Nope! Not fucking today Rockwell," I say without even giving him a second glance. "Not fucking today."

I push through the doors, leaving a likely pissed Rockwell behind me. I don't give a shit. I don't care about him or his empty words and taunts. That's all they are—him trying to get in my head because he's scared shitless that he's about to become second string. Or worse, traded. The rumors are starting to circulate, but that's all they are. Rumors. I'm not going to let myself buy too much into them until I see it for myself.

But no matter what, at some point he's going to be cleared,

and I have to go under the assumption he's still a member of the Fury. And if he is, I just have to keep showing the coaches what I've been doing since last season. I'm making plays. Being a good teammate. Arriving early and staying late. My production is top of the team through the first two games.

I know me contributing at all to a team is still something new, but I can safely say I've never felt like this before. And I have a feeling the woman I'm walking to, the one wearing my jersey with a smile on her face that could light up this whole stadium, is a big reason why.

"Hey you," I say, dropping my duffel bag to properly hug her. "Come here."

She takes a step toward me, letting me easily lift her off the ground as I hug her close. I want to kiss her—you know, for the bit and no other reason—but I'm not sure how sober Ainsley feels about PDA. Especially in front of fans, my teammates, and her sister.

"Oh, you two are just the best," Quinn says as I put her down. "You're my favorite of Ainsley's boyfriends."

"You're just saying that because you sat in a suite today," Ainsley teases.

"Possibly. I also really hated Dr. Dweeb."

"Oh, I like that one. I usually call him Dipshit," I say as I give Quinn a quick hug. "Rolls off the tongue."

"Oh, I like that too," Quinn says. "Also, I need to thank you. Two touchdowns? My fantasy team, My TDs are Real, appreciates it."

I choke on my own spit. "That's your fantasy name?"

"Of course it is. And of course they are. I love a good double entendre."

"Quinn..." Ainsley groans, but I just laugh and kiss her temple. "Please, Quinn...I beg of you..."

I don't know what Ainsley was going to say, or what Quinn's likely hilarious comeback would've been, because we can't help but hear someone coughing. Loudly. Like they just swallowed twenty bugs in a dramatic fashion.

"Katie?"

Why is my publicist here when I'm not in trouble? And why is she dressed like that?

"Hey, Linc! Great game today!"

"Thanks?" And yes, it came out like a question, because I'm honestly not sure why she's here. Katie's role is to help me off the field and to make sure I stay out of trouble. When I'm here, the Fury's media team handles interviews and anything game day related. Technically, this is a day off for her. "Did you come to the game?"

"Of course I did," she says, her cough magically gone. "Just wanted to come down and see you. Make sure everything was okay."

I shake my head. "I'm good. Everything is going great. We're just going to have an early night in, so nothing to worry about on your end."

"Oh, great," she says with a bit of fake enthusiasm to her voice. "Ainsley, it was fun hanging out with you today!"

What? She saw Ainsley? I'll have to ask her about that later.

"I'm sorry, we haven't been introduced," Quinn says, stepping up in front of Ainsley. "I'm Quinn. Ainsley's sister. I saw you earlier, and I didn't get to say hello. I didn't want to interrupt your and Ainsley's conversation. You're Linc's publicist? Did I get that right?"

Katie's eyes narrow a bit at Quinn. "That's me. His publicist. Or assistant? Maybe manager. I just do so many things for him in his life."

While that was true in the off season, since we've started back up, and since Ainsley and I concocted our grand plan, I really haven't needed Katie or the dreaded iPad anymore. Which is strange considering I saw her daily in the offseason.

"Interesting," Quinn says. "Also, why are you wearing a

jersey like a desperate fan girl? And whose is it? Got a favorite player that isn't Linc?"

Katie huffs at her insinuation. I notice then that she's wearing number 88. Which is Rockwell's number. "I can be a fan of my client's team. And I just had this shirt laying around."

She could, but that seems awfully suspicious.

"Anyway, Linc. I talked to Ainsley today. She said things were okay. Just making sure she isn't leaving anything out that I need to be aware of?"

I'm a little confused, but that's when Ainsley steps slightly in front of me. "Yes. We did have a chat today. And Katie knows where everything stands. Don't you?"

Ainsley and Quinn are staring Katie down. She's trying to give it back to them, but I see a "dare me" look in Quinn's eyes. And Ainsley? If I wouldn't know better, that's a little bit of possessiveness in her gaze.

And it's fucking hot as hell.

"All right ladies, we're going to get going." I take Ainsley's hand back in mine, because if we stand here any longer, she might scratch Katie's eyes out. "Katie, we'll catch up this week before we hit the road."

If she says anything, I don't hear it as I lead Ainsley, Quinn following, to the parking lot where players and family can park.

"What was that?" I ask as we're out of earshot.

"Nothing you need to be concerned about," Quinn says.

I look over to Ainsley, and clearly it *is* something I need to concern myself with, and I make a mental note to talk about it later.

"Quinn, thanks for coming," I say, trying to change the subject. "But if it's okay, I think I'm going to steal this one for the rest of the night."

"Okay? I fucking love it!" she says as she walks over and gives me a hug. "Have a good night. And don't do anything I wouldn't do. Note, I do a lot."

I laugh as she pulls back to give Ainsley a hug.

"You're a pain, you know that right?" she says.

"But you love me," Quinn sings. "Have a good night you two. Oh! Ainsley! Remember, just don't bite it!"

I spit out a laugh as Ainsley's entire body goes red in embarrassment. "Your sister is a fucking hoot."

"She's something," she says as she we approach my SUV. I click the fob to unlock it, and I feel her starting to pull away.

"Where are you going?"

She looks back to me as I hold her hand tighter. "To my side?

"Oh no, you don't." I drop my bag and step into her, pinning her against the car. "You don't open doors. I might not be a forever guy, but I know that when you're about to drive away with a beautiful woman next to you, she doesn't open a door. Ever."

"Oh...I—"

I cut off whatever she was about to say with a kiss so hard I feel it in every single cell. I wanted to kiss her the second I saw her after the game. Hell, I wanted to leave the sideline, climb up to the suites, and kiss her when I saw her on the big screen. It's been two days since I've kissed her, and frankly, that's just far too long.

I pull away, more because if I don't then indecent things are going to happen here, and I know for a fact Ainsley isn't ready for that.

"Linc?"

"Yeah?"

Her hand travels down the outside of my pants, lightly touching my already aching cock. "I'm ready for more fireworks."

guide to love rule #7

Swear words are appropriate sometimes. Orgasms are one of those times.

25
ainsley

"Ainsley Mae…what are you doing?"

I lean over the center console, letting my hand graze where it just was a few minutes ago. "I don't know what you mean?"

He gives me a side eye before turning his focus back to the short drive we have to his apartment. "You're trying to kill me. That's what I mean."

Who am I, and when did I get so bold?

If I really sat back and thought about it, every single bold, scary, and frankly, out of character thing I've done can all be tracked back to the night I met Linc Kincaid.

But today? Today is even surprising me.

First, I threaten—well, the Ainsley version of threaten—another woman on the suspicion of nefarious intentions. Do I have proof? Nope. Just going off a vibe. I also danced with a camera on me that was displayed on the Jumbotron, took selfies with strangers, and now I'm rubbing my boyfriend's penis in a moving vehicle.

Oh, and I realized I'm probably in love with Linc.

It's been quite a day.

"I don't know what you mean," I say as I lean a little closer.

The low tone of how he mutters the f-word as I continue lightly stroking him might be the hottest thing I've ever heard.

"Ainsley, we have two minutes until we pull into the parking garage."

"Oh, so are you saying you want me to stop?"

I start to take my hand off of the top of his pants, but I'm barely an inch away before Linc grabs my wrist, putting it back where I just was.

"No, don't stop," he says, hissing in a breath. "Don't you ever fucking stop."

I do what I was doing before, gently gliding my hand back and forth across his length. I don't know if I'm doing this right. Jonathan wasn't a fan of foreplay. I believe his words were, "Why mess around with this stuff when we could just have sex?"

So right now I'm going on intuition and watching every little reaction on Linc's face. His sharp jaw is ticking back and forth. A few times he's let his head hit the back of the seat. And the noises he's making? I never knew noises could turn me on.

But they can. Oh mylanta they can…

Linc speeds into the parking garage under his building, slamming on the brakes as he whips into his parking spot.

"Don't move." Linc shuts off the car and all but jumps out of the driver's seat. I do take off my seat belt—I might have been giving a mini hand job, but I was still going to be safe—just as Linc opens my door.

"There's my little tease," he says leaning in and kissing me just as hard as he did before we got in the car. Only this time, it's with his hand cupping my center. "Are you wet for me Ainsley Mae?"

"Yes," I moan as he continues rubbing me over the denim fabric of my jean shorts.

"Do you know how long I've been wanting to touch you? Taste you?"

I let my hand travel back down to the spot it became quite

familiar with on the short drive here. "Then what are you waiting for?"

The challenge I send sparks something in Linc, and before I know it, he's pulling me out of the car, only to hoist me over his shoulder.

"Linc!" I scream out, laughter laced through. "You're going to drop me!"

"Never, Ainsley Mae. Never."

Thankfully, Linc's car is parked only a few feet from the elevator. He puts me down when we're in, but only for him to pin me against the wall, his mouth crashing back onto mine.

How is it that just from a kiss I can feel so much? I've kissed guys before. I might not have slept with many, but I kissed my fair share over the years. But never in all that time did I feel a kiss all the way to my toes. Is it because he's holding my face like he never wants to let go? That he's pressing into me, showing me how much he wants me?

Or is it because it's Linc—the last man on Earth I thought I'd fall for, who's now the only man I want.

Gosh, I'm really up a creek with this…

I feel the elevator stop underneath me, slowly opening its doors just as Linc pulls back from me. Luckily, no one is in the hallway to see him hoist me back up, carrying me fireman-style.

"You know I can walk, right?"

"Quicker this way," he says, and though I'm protesting, I'm not really. I've never been actually carried by a man before. Then again, I never dated six-foot-five muscled beasts who don't break a sweat when carrying their girlfriend fifty feet down a hallway.

No. Fake girlfriend. Not real. Remember that, Ainsley.

In my defense, my brain isn't thinking much now, not when I can only think about the possibilities of what's going to happen next.

Oh! Is he going to hold me against the wall? Can I ask him to hold me against the wall? I bet if I did, he'd do it. Mia and Quinn would be so proud of me.

Just as I'm about to ask, the man reads my mind. The second we step into his apartment, he brings me off his shoulder, but my feet never touch the ground before I feel the hard wall against my back. My legs instinctively wrap around him as our mouths come back together.

Oh, they're right, this is hot. Knowing that he's holding me, pressing into me while our mouths move in a hungry harmony? My hands combing through his brown hair as his fingers grip into my thighs? I now see the hype.

I'm a fan. A big, *big* fan.

"Linc…" His name spills out of my mouth as he starts kissing across my cheek and down to my neck. My head falls back against the wall, and I don't even know if it hurt. All I can feel is his tongue lapping over my pulse, which is apparently connected to my center as I start grinding into him.

"I need to taste you, Ainsley." He slowly brings me down, my legs a little wobbly as I watch him go to his knees. "Are you ready for that?"

"Yes." I don't think about it, but I don't need to. There's not one iota of overthinking that needs to be done in this moment. Because what I want more than anything right now is to feel Linc's mouth on me.

My breathing picks up as I watch him slowly lift up the jersey, delicately unfastening the buttons on my shorts. To help speed up the process—I'm efficient if nothing else—I start to lift up the jersey. But it's barely off my skin when I feel him grab onto my hands.

"No," he says. "Jersey stays on. But everything else goes."

His green eyes are burning, so I do as he says and put it back down. His smile is now wicked as he goes back to my shorts, slowly pulling them down my thighs, taking the hipster lace panties down with them.

"Ainsley Mae and lace," he says on a sigh as I step out of them. "The perfect combination."

I've never had my pussy actually throb before.

And yes, I just thought the word pussy.

I might not say it, but holy molasses, I can think it.

Because it is. It's like every second he teases and makes me wait, the more it aches for him.

The hurt suddenly goes away, and somehow gets ten times worse, when I feel his tongue on my bare skin for the first time. I scream out an unintelligible noise when I feel his mouth latch onto my center.

Goodness gracious, I think this man is going to make me swear…

He lifts my leg up, draping it over his shoulder as his mouth continues to work me. My hands are in his hair, pulling at it for some sort of relief, but also making sure he doesn't stop.

I don't want him to *ever* stop.

His tongue starts picking up the pace, rapidly flicking over my clit at a speed I didn't know tongues could reach. It's too much. It's not enough. It's everything I've ever wanted, and everything I didn't know I was missing.

Then again, I'm pretty sure no other man can do this. This is a skill and a feeling solely reserved for Linc Kincaid.

"Linc…" His name comes out in a beg. "I feel…"

The orgasm I had the other night was sudden. I didn't know it was happening until it did. And then holy geez, did I know it.

But right now? I feel it starting in my stomach. The sparks and sensations are coming together in a ball of fire, and if something doesn't happen in the next three seconds, I think I might actually explode.

"That's it, Ainsley Mae. Come. Come on my face and let me lick you clean."

Linc's dirty words, and his mouth back on me in an instant, does me in. It's like he flicked a switch.

"Holy Moses!" What is happening to me right now? My body is physically shaking. The one leg I'm standing on nearly gives out. The only reason it doesn't is because Linc is there, holding onto me as he brings me down from the high.

"That was fucking beautiful," he says, kissing my thighs as he stands back up. "My beautiful girl."

I grab his face, pulling him in because I don't have words right now to tell him how I feel. I don't even know how I feel. It's…so much.

But what I didn't think about, because I've lost that ability, is that I can taste myself on his lips. If you would've asked me a month ago if I'd ever kiss a man after oral, I'd laugh at you, get very embarrassed, and probably say something about it not being sanitary. But now? Linc's lips are like a drug. Knowing that he did that to me? Knowing that he wanted me so bad that he ate and licked me like I was his last meal? It has me feeling some sort of way.

And it has me wanting to give him a blow job.

He ends the kiss, breaking away with a wicked grin, but before he can say anything else, I take a page out of his book and go to my knees.

"Ainsley?"

"It's your turn."

I'm a little shocked, and a little hurt, that his first motion is to pick me up under my arms and stand me back up. "Ainsley, you don't have to."

"What if I want to?"

I take his hand in mine, walking him into his living room. He sits down, but I don't go next to him. No, I go to my knees, because today I'm a new person, a bold person, and I don't want to let this feeling go to waste.

"You probably heard, but I've never done this before," I say as I start to unbutton his blue jeans.

"I did." His voice is low and vibrating. And sexy as heck.

"But I want to. I feel bad that I'm the only one having fun."

"Oh, Ainsley Mae…" He pauses, only to groan as I pull down his jeans. "If you think I'm not having fun then you haven't been paying attention."

I smile, still a bit nervous as I reach for the waistband of his boxer briefs. His eyes don't leave mine as he takes off his T-shirt. "Well, I'm glad. But I still want to do this."

He nods slowly. "I want it, too."

To anyone else, those words wouldn't mean much. But to me? Hearing Linc saying that he wants this? If I had any doubts about wanting to do it before, they're all erased.

"Good," I say. "Now…will you teach me?"

I don't think I've ever seen a person's eyes dilate before in real time. It might be the most intoxicating look I've ever seen.

"I start here, right?"

Linc nods but doesn't say a word as I bring down his boxer briefs. And…

Holy. Forking. Shirtballs.

Linc is huge. Like, I should be scared of it huge. It's somehow long and wide, and I was never good at physics but this doesn't seem possible.

"Ainsley, you don't—"

I stand up just enough to find his lips. It's my turn to kiss him quiet. I'll figure out the logistics later. "I want to do this for you. For me. Now, are you going to tell me what you like, Linc Kincaid, or do I have to figure it out for myself?"

He smiles at my challenge, giving me one more kiss before I go back to my knees.

"Take me in your hand. Don't be afraid. As much as you can grip."

I do as he says, and I'm glad he's starting here. This I can handle. Well, kind of. My fingers barely fit around his girth.

"Now what?" I ask as I start moving my hand up and down.

"Just like that. Start slow." He closes his eyes and lets his head fall back. His smile is faint, but I can tell that he's enjoying what I'm doing. "All the way down, and all the way up, Ainsley. Feel every inch of me."

I follow directions—which is right up my alley—and do what he says. I try to keep my stroke even, going all the way to the tip before all the way back down to his base.

"Good girl," he says. "Now a little tighter. That's...that's it. Keep going just like that."

Linc has praised me before. His little words of affirmation have hit me in different ways. But this? Oh, this is hitting different.

"Is this all you want?" I ask. "Or do you want my mouth on you?"

He nods rapidly, slowly opening his eyes. "Yes, Ainsley. Let me watch as you put those pretty lips around my cock."

A surge of confidence, and maybe a bit of delusion pours through me. I lick my lips, hoping the little bit of moisture helps as I do the thing I've always been scared to do.

Just don't bite it.

"That's it. Take your time," he says, slowly gathering my hair in his hand. "Just the tip first. Nice and slow."

I take a breath for confidence as I open my mouth, doing as he says as I put my lips around him.

"Now go up and down, just a little, work me up and down just like your hand did."

I follow the directions, letting my mouth travel a little down, then back up. I don't know what I thought it would taste like, but it wasn't this. His skin is velvety and smooth inside my mouth. There's a faint taste of salt, and I wasn't prepared for how that would make me want more.

"Can you go a little more, Ainsley? Can you take me deeper?"

I don't know if I can, but I want to try. I let go for a second, needing a breath, before taking him back in my mouth. The rumble from Linc is all the encouragement I need to do a little more.

"That a girl," he says as I feel him wrap my hair tighter in his hand. "You're taking me so good."

He didn't tell me to, but I start going faster, his words spurring me on. I feel my saliva starting to coat him, each pass of my mouth making his dick more and more wet.

First pussy and now dick. My brain is thinking all kinds of naughty thoughts tonight.

"Now use your hand, too," he says. "Stroke me while you suck me."

My brain tries to quickly think about the order of operations for that—do I go in the same direction or is it opposite?—but as if he can read my mind, Linc puts his hand over mine, guiding it as he wants it as my mouth continues to do the work.

"You're doing so good, baby," he says. "Hold me tighter. Just like you did earlier. Hold me tight as you suck my cock."

I don't know if you can have an orgasm from praise, but the way my pussy just clenched, I think it's possible.

Knowing this is now what he likes, and feeling more and more confident as I go, I take my other hand and wrap it around him also, using both to stroke him in tandem. I open my eyes just enough to watch his head fall back, a look of pure ecstasy on his face.

I'm doing this. Me. My hands. My mouth. I'm making this big, tough, strong man fall apart.

I never thought I'd enjoy this. I heard my sisters talking for years about them, but it sounded like nothing I'd want to take part in. Part of me didn't mind when Jonathan said he wasn't a fan.

But I was wrong. So freaking wrong.

Seeing this? Seeing his reaction to me as my mouth gets a little more confident with every pass? Taking him just a little deeper each time? I don't know if I've ever felt more powerful in my sexuality in all my twenty-nine years.

"Ainsley, I'm close baby," he says, his hands gripping the couch like he needs it to keep grounded. "I'm—fuck!"

He quickly pulls my mouth up, his breathing heavy as he pumps himself twice before letting his release pour out onto his stomach.

"Oh my gosh. I'm sorry! Was I supposed to…did I do it wrong?"

He grabs his shirt, quickly wiping himself off before tossing it to the side and bringing me to his lap.

"Don't you dare fucking apologize," he says, his mouth on mine in an instant. His kiss is hard, and his tongue is claiming. It makes me want to do this all over again. "You did nothing, and I mean, absolutely nothing wrong. You were absolutely perfect."

"I don't know," I say, feeling emboldened. "I think I can do better. Maybe I should practice more?"

"I mean, practice does make perfect," he says as he lays me down on the couch, finally peeling the jersey off. "In fact, I should probably practice some more too."

26
the banks family group chat - minus ainsley

You can't keep me waiting anymore. What's your assessment?

Honestly? I don't fucking know.

How do you not know? You spent an entire football game with her. Did you stick with her after to see them together?

I did. And they were a normal couple. He hugged her and gave her a polite kiss on the cheek when they were in the meeting place with people around. He kissed her a few times, but nothing scandalous. She made pleasant conversation with the wives and girlfriends we were sitting with. Danced and got put on the Jumbotron. It was a really fun time.

Well, that doesn't seem super romantic. If anything, that gives "doing it for the cameras" energy.

SIMON

Still pissed that she asked you to go and not me.

QUINN

Suck it up, brother. But once I tell y'all what else happened, it's going to be good that I went and not you. Because Stella, there is some tea.

STELLA

Oh! Details. Now.

MAEVE

I swear to God our lives are a fucking telenovela.

QUINN

You're not far off, Maeve. So Katie is Linc's publicist. And she came to the suite—that's just supposed to be WAGs, their kids and special guests like me—but she tried to make this whole fake-ass show about wanting to come check on Ainsley. But she was dressed like a fan girl and in another player's jersey.

STELLA

His publicist was? What the fuck?

QUINN

Exactly. Now, she and Ainsley went outside the suite to talk, and I let her have the space, but y'all, I've never seen this look on Ainsley's face before. It was…dare I say…mean.

SIMON

No!

MAEVE

Really?

STELLA

That a fucking girl.

QUINN

Right? That's what I said. I tried to make sure everything was okay, and y'all…the only way to accurately describe the look Ainsley was giving her before she sent her away was "don't fucking try me, bitch."

MAEVE

Ainsley!? Our sister?

QUINN

Yup. And it was the same when we left, because the bitch showed up *again*. I've never been so proud of Ainsley in my entire life.

SIMON

What did Linc do?

QUINN

Looked confused at first. I think this Katie person has some wool pulled over his eyes, but he clearly saw that Ainsley didn't want to be around her and got her out of there.

SIMON

That's good. If he took Katie's side I'd kill him. Even if he did get me twenty-one points today in fantasy.

QUINN

But this is where things are confusing—the way he looked at her when she stood up for herself? How he looked at her when she hugged him after the game? Y'all, this man is not faking it. And I don't think our sister is either.

STELLA

So it's real?

MAEVE

From the details you gave, my guess is that they're together, but bless their hearts, neither of them realize it yet.

QUINN

Honestly, that's where my money is too.
Because if they're still faking it, they're the best
actors in the world.

STELLA

And we know that's not our sister.

SIMON

Are we placing bets for when they realize this?

MAEVE

Of course, who do you think we are?

27

linc

PEOPLE ALWAYS THINK THAT THE FOOTBALL SEASON IS A GRIND, AND it is, don't get me wrong. We're only in Week 5 and my body is already starting to feel some mid-season soreness. However, the good part of the season is the regimen. Every day I know what I'm supposed to be doing.

And every Monday is the same.

Treatments, lifting, meetings, film review. An early day wrapped up around three o'clock.

Then it's off to my favorite part of every Monday—taking Ainsley food at work and sharing her break with her. Yes, it might have started to remind Dipshit that I'm here and he needs to back the fuck away from her, but it's now become part of our weekly routine. And since we had an away game yesterday, and I didn't get back until after midnight last night, I haven't seen her since Friday.

And that's just way too long.

> Hmm…okay…can we do Mexican? If that's okay with you.

> Look at that! I'm so proud of you. And you never have to ask me if Mexican is okay. The answer is always yes. I could eat a burrito every day and never get tired of it.

> Good to know. I really just want chips and queso. But I feel like just ordering chips and queso is wrong, like I'm cheating the system, so I'll get a burrito too.

> Ainsley, what do you really want?

> The largest chips and queso on the menu. And like one taco.

> Then that's what you'll get. See you in a few hours.

> Can't wait. I meant to text earlier, but a baby decided that it wanted to be delivered immediately. But are you okay?

I let out a deep sigh, running a hand through my hair in frustration as I sit in front of my locker. Headlines on a Monday morning should be all good, especially when you have another game with a touchdown. But somehow, and completely out of left field, a headline sprang up today in a national publication that I didn't see coming.

Linc Kincaid's season might be off to hot start. But let's not forget the man he is.

The column was a hit piece. Painted me in the worst light possible. Brought up shit that I hadn't thought about in years.

The problem is nothing in it was wrong. Every one of the things that the clickbait columnist wrote happened in my life. I just thought it was all finally in the past.

He pointed out my past history of fighting. Somehow got confirmation of the fights that I used to get into back in high school, which I have no idea who he talked to that knew about those. And of course, he brought up the infamous fight that ended my draft prospects and kept me a bouncing around as a practice squad player for most of my career. He even went into detail about how I started boxing in the off season to make some money, which hardly anyone knows about. As he put it, "once a fighter, always a fighter. So when will we see this side of Linc Kincaid again?"

The man knew everything. And I don't know how. He didn't interview me. He didn't reach out to the media relations team here or any of the coaches. Everything was attributed to a "source who knows Kincaid well," but for the life of me, I don't know who could go by that title and want to see me painted in that light.

Needless to say, it motivated me for a hell of a workout today. But now I just want to put it behind me, go have dinner with Ainsley, and then maybe, if I'm lucky, have her for dessert later.

Yeah. I'm fine. Katie says she's taking care of it. And the team's communications team is doing some digging for me. It's just...I didn't do anything, and shit like this is still popping up.

I'm so sorry. What can I do?

Nothing. Just be you, and when I bring you food tonight, pretend it's a normal Monday. Tell me all about whatever craziness your siblings are up to, and I'll tell you the shenanigans from the road trip.

That I can do.

And…I meant to tell you about all of this. I want to. My past. More than the column went into. It's just…I hate talking about it.

Whenever you're ready, I'm here. Always. But also know, whoever you were then is not the man I know today. I know that. Your teammates know that. So everything else? It's just a bunch of crap.

Only Ainsley can say the word "crap" and make me smile enough to almost snap me out of my funk.

Crap? That's a borderline bad word, Ainsley Mae.

If you think that's bad, you should've heard what was going through my mind many times last week.

Woman…are you trying to kill me?

Me? That doesn't sound like something I would do. But I have to go. See you soon.

I'll get extra queso.

Best "boyfriend" ever!

I stare at the last message she sent, the quotation marks around boyfriend sticking out like a sore thumb.

Obviously she put them there on purpose. The purpose is

me. I've been the one saying all along that I couldn't give her more than this. But every day I spend with her—every time I kiss her, every time I taste her, every time she's in my orbit—I refuse to think about what's going to happen at the end of this season when she's not part of my life anymore.

And I hate it. I hate it so fucking much.

"It's one headline man, don't let it get to you."

I snap out of it when I hear Maddox and feel him slap me on the shoulder. "Oh. Yeah. It's bullshit. I talked to Coach. He knows it's bullshit too."

Maddox takes a seat in front of his locker, which is just a little down from mine, but we're the only two still here besides the coaches and a few players working out with the physical therapists.

"Do you know why he wrote it?"

"No fucking clue," I say. "It's not so much that. The thing that's bugging me is that the writer kept saying that everything was coming from a someone close to me. But I have no idea who the hell that is, and if they are, why they're trying to do me like this?"

"Damn, really?" Maddox shakes his head a little. "Is it anyone from the team?"

"Not that I can think of," I say. "Wyatt is the only one who really knows everything about my past. You know the next amount, but I don't think it was everything that was written. And the only one who has it out bad enough for me to plant that shit is Rockwell, but again, he'd have to be working with someone to find out about some of those things that happened almost fifteen years ago."

The reporter did his homework. He described a fight I got in at school where I bashed a kid's head into the pavement. I was thirteen. What he left out was that it was the first day of school after my parents died, and the kid called me an orphan. I snapped. But again, no one knows that part. Hell, only a few knew about that fight. Whoever his source was, they know every one of my skeletons. Even ones I thought were buried.

Shit, are there more that I've forgotten about? I'm not a paranoid guy, but I can't help but feel it right now.

"Well, we all have your back," Maddox says. "I know if any one of the guys here are asked about you, they're going to tell the truth—that you're a hell of a teammate and the past is the past."

"Thanks. I appreciate it. I just hope they don't ask Rockwell."

Maddox waves my comment off. "Fuck that guy. I hope the rumors are true, and he gets traded. He's a cancer in the locker room. Plus, he doesn't have the karaoke voice you have."

I laugh at Maddox's successful attempt to turn my mood around. "That was a crazy night."

"It was," he says. "Speaking of, how is Miss Ainsley?"

"Good. Really good," I say as I start gathering my things into my duffel bag. "Actually heading to the hospital now to see her."

"Really? Mind if I tag along?" Maddox asks as he grabs his bag from his locker. "And I'm not trying to kill your vibe; I just like to go do some impromptu visits every now and then."

"For real?"

He shrugs it off like it's not a big deal as we make our way out of the locker room. "I hate seeing those kids like that. Most days, what they have to look forward to is hopefully not getting worse. If I can swing in and brighten some spirits? It's the least I can do."

This man is a fucking enigma. One minute he's bedding half of Nashville and the next he's making secret visits to a children's hospital. He's the one columnists should be writing about, but instead of his football prowess, they should be talking about what the hell goes on in his head.

"That's fucking awesome," I say patting him on the back. "I usually take dinner to her and we eat on her break. If you don't mind making a stop for food, you're more than welcome. And maybe I can do some visits after?"

"Hell, yeah," he says. "And did I hear dinner? What are we getting?"

I laugh as we get our bags and make our way out of the locker room. "She wants Mexican. Specifically queso."

"Fuck, yeah, I want Mexican," he says. "Grab me a steak quesadilla. But I'll eat it later. I'd hate to interrupt date night."

"It's not date night," I say as I pull my phone out of my pocket and find the closest Mexican restaurant to the hospital so I can put in our order and pick it up on the way. "It's just what we do on Mondays."

"Yes. Exactly. Monday night date night. It's quite adorable."

"You're an ass," I say, taking a second to make sure I order my entree, the largest order of queso possible, salsa in case she wants it but forgot to tell me, extra chips because that feels like the safe move, and a taco. Except she didn't tell me what kind. Better get a chicken and a beef, just to be safe.

"So how are things going with you two?" Maddox asks as we get into my car.

"All good. We're getting into a groove. You know, with football season and all."

"And is this still a fake relationship, or are you two actually dating?"

I shoot him a look, and I can't hide the shock on my face. "You know?"

"Of course I know," he says. "Don't worry, your secret is safe with me."

I let out a breath. "I assumed you didn't. You never said anything."

"I know when to keep my mouth shut," he says. "I realized pretty quickly at karaoke that it was a swing in and save the girl moment. Which, maybe I should've done it. Maybe Ainsley could be my girl right now."

I grip the steering wheel tighter and don't care about keeping my eyes on the road so I can shoot daggers his way. "Back the fuck off, Gallagher."

He laughs, shaking his head. "I'd never now, man. That's your girl. I saw the way you were looking at her after the last home game. How you made sure to FaceTime her before we got on the plane to come home yesterday. You might still think this is just for show, but newsflash, my tall, pass-catching friend, you're done for. It's time to accept your fate."

"I'm not done for," I argue as I make the easy drive from our facility to the Mexican restaurant. "Ainsley and I know where each other stands. Everything you're seeing is part of the act."

"You keep telling yourself that," Maddox says as I pull into the restaurant. "I'll go get the food. You think about it. And when I come back out, maybe you'll realize you're in deeper than you realize."

Maddox jumps out of my car, but what he doesn't know is that I don't need a moment. I know exactly what I am.

Fucked. That's what I am.

Ainsley is perfect in every way.

Hell, I think I started falling for her the second she ran into me.

But that doesn't change who I am. And maybe, if things were going good, I'd be able to think that I'm not who I was. But then there are articles like today that remind me that the guy I was is never far away.

That's who I am. Who I'll always be.

And that man isn't good enough for Ainsley.

So I'm going to take what I can get. Keep being the "boyfriend" and the selfish bastard who holds her as she comes apart in my arms. All while knowing that the only woman I'd ever let in is the one woman I have to keep out.

"Oh shit," Maddox says as he climbs back in. "You really are done for, aren't you?"

I nod, because there's no use denying it. "So fucking screwed my man. So fucking screwed."

guide to love rule #76

Sometimes you need to put your foot down to make your point heard. And sometimes you have to cuss a little.

28
ainsley

LINC WARNED ME THIS COULD HAPPEN. HECK, IT DID HAPPEN AT THE beginning of all of this, when I was the new shiny toy of Nashville and sports gossip blogs. But then it was just a few pictures, mostly of Linc and I, and a few headlines about "Linc Kincaid's new woman." Yes, my name was dropped. Apparently that wasn't hard to find. Neither were my age or occupation. And that didn't bother me.

But today's blog offering hit a different nerve.

Who is Ainsley Banks and why she's the perfect fake girlfriend for Fury star Linc Kincaid

I read it for the twenty-eighth time, though with every pass it doesn't get better.

When it comes to me, there were the normal things that have been written before. But whatever "source" this gossip blog found really wanted to make sure that they painted me in the worst light possible.

Or if anything, the most embarrassing.

The article called me a stick in the mud. Someone who wasn't fun, and how could I date a professional football player when I'd never ridden a roller coaster before?

One, I don't know how they knew that and two, those things are terrifying. The conspiracy theory I'll die on is that big amusement parks pay off OSHA to say that those speed traps of death are safe.

The article painted me out to be the scaredy-cat, meek girlfriend that I probably am. Oh, and they of course went after my appearance. That I'm average looking. Hips a little too big. Why would Linc be dating a "basic woman" when he's in a city flooded with country stars and influencers are far as the eye can see?

That's the one that hurt the worst.

Then, of course, the real point of the article was questioning the validity of our relationship. How we were nothing and then everywhere. And, what guts me the most, how because of Linc's "dark past" that he's using a "do-gooder nurse" to fix his image.

They make it sound like he's the devil. He's not. He still hasn't told me everything that's happened to him. But I know in my bones it's more than people write about.

The problem is that everything is true. And you can't sue for libel when it's true.

My phone buzzes to notify me that Linc's here, and while part of me is relieved to see him, I'm also not ready to. Anything could happen when he walks in here. He could say that we need to ignore it and keep going about our business. He could also say that if one article saying this has come out, more are likely to come. And with that, our time is over.

And I'm not ready for that. Not in the least.

I take a few deep breaths as I walk to my door. I try to calm my brain that's already in overdrive thinking of every possibility that could come the second Linc walks in. But as I turn the handle and open the door, my brain is immediately quieted when Linc pulls me in, his hands cupping my face as he kisses me like he hasn't seen me in days. Like he needed to feel me to make sure I'm still here.

I'm here, Linc…as long as you want me to be.

He pulls away, a little too quick for my liking, but his hands don't leave my face.

"Are you okay?"

I nod. "I should be asking you that."

He doesn't say anything as he steps inside my apartment, kicking the door closed behind him. "Oh, no. This one isn't about me today. I'm used to this shit. Today went after you, and that's not fucking okay."

I hold his hand as I walk him into my living room. I let go so I can sit on one side, giving him room to sit as well. Except that apparently today we're not going to be sitting apart, as Linc grabs my hand and pulls me to his lap.

"You know this couch is big enough for both of us," I tease, trying to break the tension.

He shakes his head. "Not today, Ainsley Mae. Not today."

We don't say anything for a minute as Linc holds me. My head is resting on his shoulder as my hand lightly rubs small circles over his chest. I've now seen the tattoos across his chest. Each time I do, I want to trace them, try to memorize them for when this moment is gone. I try to remember each one, but I can't. I'm too focused on the speed of his beating heart. Though, the longer we sit like this, I feel it start to slow.

It's then I realize that sure, he wants to comfort me. He wants to make sure I'm okay, because today is the first day that headlines were aimed directly at me in a negative way. But maybe he needs this too.

No. Don't think like that, Ainsley. Nothing has changed.

I take in a few deep breaths, because now I need to recalibrate my heart. Because I swear to heaven and Dolly Parton, this man makes it harder and harder every day to not fall in love with him.

"I'm okay," I say. "It wasn't that bad. Embarrassing? Yes. Made me feel exposed? Also yes. But it's not like it said I killed puppies. If that happened, I'd be calling my brother to get me a lawyer. Because I'd never kill puppies."

It wasn't a real joke, but I don't even get a hint of laughter from Linc.

"Talk to me," I say, adjusting myself so that I'm now straddling him, because I want to look him in the eye for this conversation. I usually don't push him. I know he's pretty closed off, and I want to respect those boundaries. But if he's here to really check on me, then I need to know what's going through his mind. Because I won't be okay either until I know he is.

"I just want to know who the hell is doing this," he says. "While I have ninety-nine percent confidence that whoever is leaking these stories is out to get me, I have to ask: Is there anyone who would want to hurt you? Another ex I don't know about that is worse than Dipshit?"

"None that I can think of," I say. "There was only one other person I seriously dated, and that was back in college. We haven't spoken in years. Last I heard he lives in Cleveland with his husband and their two kids."

It takes Linc a second to process what I just said. But what he says after shocks me a little more. "You're meaning to tell me, that you've only had two serious relationships in your life? How?"

My eyes leave his, but he quickly brings them back up with a lift of my chin. "I didn't mean that against you. In no way is that a fault of yours. I just want to know how many men over the years saw you, could be with you, and chose not to? That's fucking insanity to me."

"Not as many as you think," I say. "I was focused on my studies. And I've always wanted forever. I never saw the appeal of dating just to date. If I was going to be with someone, I had to know it was for the long haul. For both, at the time, they were forever. Just so happens one was gay and the other was a putz."

My choice of words makes Linc laugh. "In my opinion, they're all putzes."

We take in the moment of levity, before it's my turn to ask him the hard question.

"Do you think someone is leaking these stories? That someone is out to get you?"

Katie's the first name that comes to my mind, but I also know that sounds ridiculous, so I don't offer it as a suggestion. I'm still convinced something isn't right about her, but it's also her job to keep his name out of the press. No way would she sabotage her career to ruin him.

"Believe me, I've been trying to figure out all of this. Who, why. The timing. Everything," he says. "For weeks, there's nothing. Hell, months, aside from a few random articles because of a few random pictures. That column at the beginning of the week, why was it written now? Most of that shit was written last year when I started making my name known. So why bring it back up? Why feel the need to drag you, and therefore, try to drag me too? Nothing about this makes sense."

"I wish I knew," I say, even though I know he was talking in rhetoricals.

"I mean, Brad Rockwell fucking hates me," Linc continues. "He's getting cleared after the bye week, and I know he's going to make my life a living hell. That's if he doesn't get traded. But assuming he doesn't, I wouldn't put it past him to try to fuck my world up. Try to distract me so I'm off my game and coach gives him his starting spot back."

"Have you talked to Coach McAvoy about this?"

He shakes his head. "I might hate Rockwell, but until I have proof, I can't go around throwing out an accusation like that. Once something like that hits the locker room, it would be chaos."

"Well, maybe I can?"

Linc leans me back, a very confused look on his face. "Not that I want you to, because I'm going to say this now, I don't, but how do you think you're going to get a hold of my coach and tell him that the other tight end is being mean to me?"

I giggle, because when he puts it like that…

"Well, I have a few ways," I begin. "His sister, Whitley, lives in my hometown. I go there once a week to see my family, so I could conveniently run into her and maybe drop it in her ear to maybe drop it in her brother's?"

"You know Coach McAvoy's sister?"

"I do. Such a sweet girl," I say. "Or, I can have my sister Maeve call him. Or maybe his wife? Which one do you think would work best?"

I've never dropped a man's jaw before. But right now Linc's is on the ground.

"And before you ask, my sister worked with Hunter to design and decorate his wife's new office. She's the reporter, right? Could we call her? Maybe she can investigate around?"

Linc shakes his head as he snaps out of his daze. "She is. But you won't. Is there any other line of communication you have with my coach that I don't know about?"

I think about it for a second. "Besides Wes? I don't think so. But I could use him. He was always my favorite of Simon's friends. Or! My family has a way of making things happen. I can call my sister Stella, and she could do two Google searches and figure out who's behind this. Then Quinn would key their cars. Simon would actually sue them. And Maeve? Well, she'd coordinate the chaos. We're pretty versatile in vigilante justice."

For the first time since he's walked into my apartment, Linc gives me a genuine smile. "While I appreciate it, your family doesn't have to come to my defense."

"They don't have to. They'll want to."

My directness seems to take him by surprise. "But they don't know me, Ainsley. Why would they want to come to my defense?"

"Because I care about you, Linc. And if I say that it's time to rally the troops, the troops get rallied. That's how our family works. No question about it."

Not that I've ever had to say those words before. Until I met Linc Kincaid, the worst thing that I'd need my family for is to help get my car out of a ditch because driving and I have never really gotten along. But I know in my heart of hearts that if I said that one last Banks family shenanigan had to happen, and in the name of Linc, they wouldn't bat an eyelash.

"I don't want to do that to you," Linc says, though I can feel my stomach dropping as he looks at me, sadness running through his beautiful green eyes. "I never thought that any headlines would go after you the way they did today. They shouldn't be prying into your personal life like that."

"I knew it could happen," I say, trying to put on a brave face.

"We both knew, but it doesn't make it right. I'm guessing this is going to get worse before it gets better. So yes, if you need to take legal means to clear your name, I wouldn't blame you. Hell, I wouldn't blame you if you wanted this to end tonight."

My stomach drops at his words. Fake or not, I'm not ready for this to be over. "What are you saying, Linc?"

First it was sadness. Now it's just pain in his emerald gaze. My heart hurts for him right now. Hurts for me. For us. This can't be how it ends. I won't let it.

"This isn't what you signed up for," he continues. "This was supposed to help clear my name and give me a good story. But instead, someone is now using us to take me down. Using you. I won't put you through that. If I'm going down, I'm not taking you with me."

There. He said it. This is over.

Except no. It's not over. Because I'm not that easily scared. At least, not anymore.

"The hell you're not."

I cover my mouth.

I just swore out loud.

Judging by Linc's wide eyes, he's just as surprised as I am.

I haven't sworn out loud since I was seven. It was the f-word. I heard Simon say it, so I thought it was okay. It wasn't. I was grounded for three days, and that was the last swear word I ever said.

But this warrants it.

And it's about to warrant it again. Because that one word just opened the Ainsley Banks flood gates.

"Did you just cuss at me?"

I nod, suddenly feeling much bolder than I did a minute ago. "I did. And I'll do it again if your stubborn ass thinks you're getting rid of me that easily."

29

linc

This is it.

I'm either in or out.

I told Ainsley up front that I'm not the forever guy. And I meant it.

Then.

And why would I have been? Everyone in my life has left me. I know it wasn't by their choosing, but for an angry kid who didn't understand the world, it made sense to me.

For my entire life I've thought that. Sure, I have Wyatt. Maddox. I had coaches in the past who were in my corner. But no one has wanted, or was able, to go directly into the fire with me.

But here's Ainsley. Not only willing to, but volunteering to get burned right by my side.

Oh, shit. And apparently she's still talking and I wasn't listening. I need to work on that if I'm going to do the scariest thing I've ever done.

No, not if. *Am.*

"…the scary thing I did today was I'm choosing to fight this with you. Whoever's out to take you down—take us down—they're going to have to go through me first. I told you I was going to help you, and I don't back down on my promises. I'm in. All in. However much you'll let me be. Whether it's continuing to be your friend, your fake girlfriend for the press, I'm in. Or..."

I don't let her finish. If she would've been reading from her notebook, I'd have tossed it to the side like I did before. I just kiss her. I kiss her with everything I have in me. I kiss her with the promise that I'm going to do my damn best to give her what she deserves.

Love. Happiness.

Forever.

My entire life I've been the man who's made the wrong decisions. I think it's about time I made the right one.

She pulls away, a little confused about what just happened. "I hate to assume what that meant, Linc, so I'm going to need you to explain what that kiss was for."

I lean in to give her one more small one before I adjust her in my arms.

"That means there's no more fake." I stand up, bringing her in my hold as I start walking toward her bedroom. She's silent as I take the short walk down the hallway, kicking open her bedroom door before laying her on her bed. "From this point on, you're mine. But more than that, I'm yours, Ainsley Mae."

I watch as her eyes and smile catch up to the words I just said. But I'm not done.

"Let them write what they want. If they want to call us fake, let them. Only we know what we are. What we have."

"We have each other," she says. "Together."

"You and me."

Our words are whispers as I lean down, kissing her deeply. This is how I should've known she was special. From the first time we kissed—drunk and a little crazy on the high of the night and the act we were putting on—our kiss was seamless. Our tongues knew where they wanted to go, and how they wanted to connect. Our mouths never stumbled, always knowing how to take and give in the perfect balance.

"So fucking beautiful," I grit out as my mouth starts kissing down her neck and chest. "So fucking mine."

My cock hardens as the words leave my mouth. Never did I think I'd ever call anyone "mine." And maybe before, that was true. But I didn't know Ainsley then. I didn't know that everything could change when you found the person who made you whole. Who made you smile. Laugh.

Love.

"You feel so good," Ainsley breaths out as I quickly take off her shirt and bra. "How do you make me feel so good?"

"I could ask you the same question," I mumble as my tongue circles over her nipple before I latch onto it, squeezing the other as her hips start bucking underneath me. "Do you see how hard I am for you? You do this to me, Ainsley. Only you. Only ever you."

She nods as I stand up, pushing down the joggers and boxer briefs I have on before using one hand to pull off the Fury T-shirt I'm wearing. When my cock springs free, I see the heat flick on in Ainsley's eyes. I start stroking myself, and if I had any questions on whether we're on the same page for what's about to happen, my girl gets on her hands and knees and starts crawling across the bed to me.

Holy fuck…my good girl isn't so good anymore…

"So if I'm yours, and you're mine, does that include this?"

Her hand travels to my cock, stroking it just like I taught her to. "Yes."

When did my Ainsley Mae get a dirty side to her? It's like with two minimal swear words, the flood gates opened.

But I'm not mad about it. Not at all. Especially if she continues to touch me like she's doing.

"I want you, Linc. I want you to have me. All of me. Nothing between us."

I forget to breathe for a second. "Ainsley? Are you sure? Don't think you have to—"

She cuts me off with a kiss. "Yes. I've been on the pill for years. I'm clean."

"I am too," I say. "We're tested regularly. And I've never gone without."

Ainsley traces a finger gently up and down my sternum, my breath hitching along the way. "Then take me, Linc. Make me yours."

Ainsley will never have to ask me twice for anything in this life. And surely not this.

Our kiss this time is full of fire and passion, my hands on her waist as I lay her back down on the bed. My hands travel down from her back to her hips, down to her thighs where I part her legs.

"You're so wet for me already," I say, licking my lips as one finger enters her. "Do you want my cock, Ainsley Mae?"

"Yes," she breathes heavily as I slowly insert a second into her. She's so tight already, I have to try to even my breathing just thinking about how she feels when my cock enters that sweet pussy.

"You know, one day I'm going to get you to say that word," I tease as I continue working her. "And it's going to sound so good coming out of those pretty little lips."

"Linc!" I don't think she's hearing anything I'm saying. Her eyes are closed, and her body is begging me for more. I have her so close to the edge she's about to explode.

"Shhh," I say, slowly taking my fingers out of her. Her eyes flash open, just in time for her to see me lick one off.

"Open your mouth, baby," I say, taking a risk that she might not be able to say the true dirty words yet, but that my good girl is a little dirty.

She does as I say, her eyes heating as I place my one finger on her tongue.

"Now close. Taste yourself. Taste how wet you are for me."

Ainsley doesn't say a word as she does what I ask. Her swollen lips close around my finger before I feel her tongue circling me. Just like it did on my cock.

"Such a good girl," I say, her legs spreading wider on instinct. "Are you ready?"

She nods her head, still silent in the anticipation.

"I'm going to go slow," I say as I lean down, pressing kisses along her jaw line. "If it's too much, if there's anything you want me to do, good or bad, you tell me. Do you understand?"

"Yes." Her breathing is starting to pick up with every word I say. "I'm ready, Linc."

With one more kiss I fall back to my knees, taking a deep breath as I line myself up at her center. I push in just the tip, and the gasp that comes from her lips is enough to make me come right there.

But I don't. I won't. Not until I give her—us—the night we're both craving.

"I got you, baby," I say, slowly pushing in. "I've always got you."

Ainsley's breathing is heavy as I do my best to enter her slowly, allowing her to adjust for my size. "Just breathe. Relax. I promise I'll take care of you."

Have I ever said those words before? I don't think I have. Certainly not to sexual partners who were either one-night company or drunken mistakes. I haven't had family in years, and when I did, I certainly wasn't taking care of anyone. Yet right now, that's all I want to do. I want to take care of her in the bedroom, making sure that she knows not only how beautiful she is, but how she makes me feel. I want to take care of her out in the world. To know that she doesn't have to do the scary things by herself.

Neither of us do. Not anymore.

"There you go," I say, her body starting to relax as I press in more.

My strokes are slow and steady, needing to move or I'm

going to finish before we begin, but also knowing I need to warm her up.

"You feel…so…I feel…so…full," she finally mumbles out, her head turning back and forth as I keep pumping into her.

I keep my eyes on her as my thumb goes to her clit, rubbing it in circles as I'm finally able to fully press into her. I find the spot just in time, a yelp leaving her mouth as her back arches, her tits in the air and looking like every fantasy come to life.

"That's it," I say, my speed starting to increase. "You're taking my cock so good."

Her eyes flutter open, straight fire blazing out of her normally crystal blues.

"Say it again," she says, her words as breathy as I've ever heard them.

Wait…does my sweet Ainsley have a praise kink?

Because if she does, I'm going to go buy a ring tomorrow. And there will be nothing fake about that diamond.

"What? That you're taking my cock like a good girl?" I wrap my hand around her back to bring her into me, my dick never leaving her sweet heat.

"Yes."

Her hands are around me, her nails digging into my back. "Did you like when I said that?"

"I did."

"Well, you are," I say. "Do you want more?"

She nods as she starts to become more comfortable, moving up and down on my cock. Fuck…I might lose it the first time she rides me if she feels this good. "I do. I want more, Linc."

"Say less, Ainsley Mae. Say less."

I kiss her as I bring her back down to the bed. I want to do so much more—give her so much more—and I will. Eventually. But right now, between her tightness, her newly unlocked praise kink, and the fact that I'm figuring out in real time that I'm with the woman of my dreams, I don't think I'm about to last much longer.

"Give me that leg, baby," I say as I put it on my shoulder, allowing me to press into her farther than before. "That's it."

I lose my words as her fingers find my chest, scratching me, begging to hold onto something as I drive into her. She was already tight around my cock, but the second her orgasms hits, I'm finished. I can't hold back anymore, and neither can she, as we come together in a way that almost has me blacking out.

Holy shit. I've never done that before. My body is shaking as I spill into her, and so is hers. Our holds on each other are the only thing keeping us grounded as the highs slowly start to wear off.

"Holy Moses," Ainsley says as I bring her into my arms.

Holy Moses is right. And if I could speak, I'd say that. But I can't. I think I'm done for.

In more ways than one.

30
linc

I DON'T KNOW WHAT TIME AINSLEY AND I FELL ASLEEP LAST NIGHT.

I know I lost myself in her twice, and I could've a third time if I didn't see the blissful exhaustion in her eyes.

I'm exhausted too, in the best way. Yet, I can't seem to stay asleep.

It's like my brain won't shut off, and only one question is rolling through it: How did I get here?

This, being in a true relationship with someone, is never something I wanted. Never thought I could handle. Or maybe, deep down, deserved. Not after the life I chose to live. Or the one that was handed to me.

Yet, here I am. The most amazing, beautiful, kind, smart, too-good-for-me woman, is laying on my chest. Her naked body is pressed against me, wrapping me in her arms like she needs to hold onto me to sleep.

Then there's my career. Without a doubt, this is the best year of my life. I'm on pace to break records. I'm the top tight end in the league statistically. I'm in the top five of all receivers in the league, which is almost unheard of. At this point, even when Rockwell does come back, Coach McAvoy would have a hard time benching me, considering what our offense has been doing from week to week.

I'm the happiest I've ever been. If I could get the fucking gossip blogs and clickbait columns to stop writing shit about me, my life would be pretty close to perfect.

Which is why I'm staring at Ainsley's ceiling, watching the fan go round and round. Because I can't help wondering when the other shoe is going to drop.

"If this is what my overthinking feels like to you, I apologize," Ainsley says, her voice gravelly. "Brains are really loud."

I softly laugh as I kiss the top of her head. "I'm sorry. I didn't mean to wake you."

"Do you need anything? Are you not comfortable? I know my bed is probably too small—"

I roll over, pinning her under me. Out of a habit that I didn't know I formed, I lean down to kiss her. It's like I can't help myself. When I see those perfect rose-colored lips and those blue eyes staring up at me, I'm a goner.

"Everything is perfect," I say, peppering a few more kisses on her neck, and then one on her tits just because I can before I roll back over, bringing her with me, my chest to her back.

"Then why haven't you slept more than a few minutes?"

I relax into her touch as she starts aimlessly tracing the ink on my arms. I feel her fingers over the letters—LK and MK. Their initials.

"My parents were Laura and Michael," I begin, closing my eyes as I transport myself back to that night. "My parents had tickets for a show in Detroit for their anniversary. We lived about thirty minutes outside the city, and my mom loved live music. Would always dance around the kitchen to whatever was on."

"Sounds like my kind of lady," Ainsley adds as I pause for a breath. "If there's music on, why wouldn't you dance?"

I smile at that thought. Sometimes I don't feel like I remember my mom at all. But then little moments like this I do. And she would've loved Ainsley.

"They were excited. And I was too. A friend of mine was having a party. Girls were invited over, but the guys were staying the night. You know, one of those parties in eighth grade when you thought you were so cool to be invited and the pretty girl was going to be there?"

"I do. Only mine was seventh grade, and his name was Ben. But I left once spin the bottle started. I was not comfortable in that situation. Seven minutes in heaven? I think not."

I laugh, because only her. "Are you going to hold it against me if I started the game at mine?"

She chuckles in my hold. "I kind of expected it."

"Well, if I would've just stayed making out with Caitlyn Morrow, maybe things would've been different." Not the best segway in the world, but I don't know how else to really tell this story. "Things were going fine. Your normal thirteen-year-old party, until a few guys I knew signaled for me to follow them outside. I knew of them. Not my crew, and to this day, I don't know why they were there. But me and a few of my friends followed them like the teenaged idiots we were."

I can still feel the cold in the air as we walked outside into that frigid February night. But of course, I didn't put on a jacket because I was a middle school boy. Jackets were for losers.

"They had a joint," I continue. "I don't know where they got it, or why they asked me and my buddies to come out and smoke it. Before I know it, I was a walking stereotype of the story teachers give you about when you're first asked to do drugs. And, like the idiot I was, I fell for the peer pressure and took a few hits."

Ainsley rolls into me, but making sure to lace her fingers with mine before I go on. It's like she knew this is where the story is about to take a turn.

"Of course, we got busted, because we're dumbasses. The party ended, but all of our parents were called to personally pick us up."

I feel my throat starting to tighten up, but I breathe through it and lean into Ainsley's touch, to keep going.

"My parents had to leave their concert early. I heard my mom screaming on the other side of the phone when she was told what happened. And remember, they weren't supposed to pick me up. I was supposed to stay the night."

Tears start welling in my eyes—just like they do every time I think about what happened next.

"It was February in Detroit. The roads were shit. And a car in front of them hit a patch of ice on the highway. Eight cars were in the accident total. My parents were the third car in the pileup and…"

I trail off as I can't keep the tears at bay. Ainsley wraps her arms around me, holding me as I cry into her shoulder. I'm squeezing her so tight, having not thought about, let alone talked about, that night in God knows how many years.

"If I would've said no, not been a stupid fucking kid, they'd have stayed at the show. They wouldn't have been driving then. They…they'd still be here."

"Oh, Linc," she says as she sits up against my headboard, moving me to lay across her lap. I feel her gentle fingers combing through my hair, the other rubbing my back. "I'm so sorry you had to go through that. Have had to live with that. I can't imagine."

"I was already a rebellious kid. Pushed the limits of what I could get away with," I say through the tears. "But after that, the rebellion turned into anger. I had no limits."

"Where did you go? After they passed."

"My grandmother," I say. "I was an only child. So were my parents. Grandma was the only one I had left."

I'd spent plenty of nights at her house growing up. Grandma was never not in my life. But I remember the first time walking into her house, knowing that it wasn't just for a visit. I cried that entire night. I believe it was around three in the morning when she came into my room and just sat with me. We cried together for what we both lost. She told me that parents weren't supposed to bury their children; that she was supposed to go first. That teenagers shouldn't be staring over graves of their parents. That sometimes the world wasn't fair.

Those words have stuck with me for a very long time.

"She did her best," I continue. "But I was so mad at the world. Getting in fights almost daily. Went to juvie for a few days to try and scare me straight. Nothing seemed to work. That is, until I discovered football."

I go on to tell Ainsley about the high school coach who got me mostly under control. The fights never fully stopped, but while I was playing, or training, it seemed to keep my temper, and my fists, at bay. I tell her about my journey from high school, to junior college, all the way until Mississippi State.

"I'm glad you found an outlet," she says. "And someone who believed in you."

"It helped. But the problem with me is that I've never been one to make the best decisions. And while football might've kept me out of trouble, the temper and the anger were never too far away."

"Is this the fight before the draft?"

I nod in her lap, figuring at this point she probably read about it. But no one has ever learned about the whole story. "We were at the combine. I still couldn't believe I got an invitation. Only the best of the best get the invite, but that means you work out in front of scouts from the entire league. And I didn't have a fallback plan. It was pro football or bust."

On the field, I killed it that week. Ran the best forty time I'd ever run. Was catching everything. I was unstoppable. As for the interviews you do with teams? Those could've gone better. They all asked me about a few fights I was in during college. About how every coach they talked to made some sort of mention about my temper. I thought I'd talked enough to convince them I was worth taking a chance on.

But then, my world crashed down.

"It was my last night there, and I got a phone number from a Detroit area code. It was the hospital. My grandma…she'd been sick. I knew she was. I was planning to go visit her after I left the combine, but…it was too late."

Ainsley moves my head from her lap, but only so she can hold me in her arms. She doesn't say anything. She doesn't need to. I feel every ounce of support and comfort just from her touch alone.

"I went into the hallway and lost it. I hadn't even told my agent yet that she'd died. I just went and hid. I was a mess. I was twenty-two years old at the time, but I suddenly felt like an orphan, even more than I did when my parents died. And suddenly, the anger came back. I was angry at God for taking away the only one I had left before I could say goodbye. I was still angry for my parents' deaths. I was just so–fucking–angry."

I close my eyes and back away from Ainsley's hold, needing to get the rest off my chest. "I thought no one could see me. I was in a random hallway that I'd found, but two guys came walking through. And apparently they were still twelve-year-old shit heads, because instead of asking me if I was okay when they saw me crying against a wall, they started digging at me. Calling me a pussy. A crybaby. That to man up and not cry or I wasn't going to get drafted. They all assumed that's why I was crying. And…I snapped."

I just saw rage in that moment. They had no idea what was going on in my life, and instead of telling them just to leave me the fuck alone, or walking away, I made the worst decision of my life.

"I beat the hell out of them, Ainsley. It was two-on-one but you'd never know it, the way I left them. For a second I thought I killed one. I threw him against the wall, and his head bounced. All I was seeing was red. No one ever asked me what happened. I was just sent home and I fell off of every single person's draft board. I squandered my entire career in that one moment."

I wouldn't blame Ainsley in the slightest if she backed away from me now. Held me at an arm's distance after I admitted I gave a man a concussion and that I was lucky it wasn't much worse. But she doesn't. Instead she comes in closer, wrapping me back up in her arms.

"When I got home, the anger didn't stop, only I was mad at myself. Mad that I lost it. That I let down Grandma. My parents. Everyone. That was my rock bottom. And I've been clawing like hell to come up from it every day since."

"That's all you can do," Ainsley says, her legs now wrapping around me as well. "And the man I know? The man who saved me? My boyfriend? He's not that guy anymore. I hope you don't think that."

I shake my head before it falls into her shoulder. "Sometimes I do. Many times I did when I was sitting watching a football game on TV, knowing I could've been out there, but instead I was boxing for cash and hoping a team had a practice squad opening. Living in a delusion that one day a team would pick me up."

"Intrusive thoughts are the worst, but that's all they are," she says. "You've made a change. You're a good man, Lincoln Kincaid. You visit kids in the hospital, even when there aren't cameras around. You stay after games and sign autographs. And I also know that you arranged for Caden, the patient you met on your official Fury visit, to go to a game this season. Bad guys don't do things like that."

I shrug off her praise. "But even with all of that, I feel like it doesn't matter."

"Maybe not to some, but to me? To your teammates? Your fans? It means the world to them. And those should be the only ones you care about."

"Thank you," I say. "But this is now the problem, and frankly, why I couldn't sleep. Things are good. Too good. I don't want to get comfortable. What if the other shoe drops? What if these articles get worse and people believe that I'm back to the angry guy who hit first and didn't care about the consequences? Or worse—what if something happens to you? I swear to everything, Ainsley, if someone hurt you, I wouldn't just hit someone, I'd kill them. And I wouldn't feel bad about it."

She shakes her head as she gives me a reassuring kiss. "I'm not going anywhere. And don't worry about having to kill someone for me. If something like that were to happen, my brother will hire someone to do it. He knows all kinds of guys. I'm sure he has someone for that."

I appreciate her joke, but that doesn't change anything. "This is the scariest thing I've ever done, Ainsley. I don't want to mess it up."

"You won't," she says. "And I was told once by someone that it was good to do scary things every once in a while."

I can't fight my smile. I never have with this woman. From the first time she ran into me, to the time she tried to seductively sing karaoke to me, to right now when she's trying to break down my last wall, she's always had a way to make everything seem easy. Happy.

Less scary.

"I don't know how to do this," I admit, linking my hands behind her back. "But I want to. I want to be the man you deserve."

"You are," she says as we fall back down to the bed. "And the same for you. I want to be the best person I can be for you. This is a partnership, Linc. We're in this together. All of it. You and me."

I kiss her forehead, feeling more relaxed now than I have in who knows how long. "We're really doing this, aren't we?"

"We are," she says. "Should it feel different?"

I shake my head. "No. Let's be real. We were the worst fake daters in the history of PR relationships."

Her laughter fills the room. "We were pretty bad. But now there's no more pretending."

"No more watching what we say."

"No more snapping rubber bands on my wrist when you did something sweet."

Wait...what did she say? "You did what?"

"Oh, yeah," she says as the blush takes over her face. "I realized pretty quickly that I was going to fall for you. So every time I had a thought that was wanting to make this real, I snapped my wrist to remind me it was fake."

Shit. I had no idea. "Is that why your wrist was always red?" I ask.

She shrugs. "Yes, and can we never bring that up again? In return, you can talk about how I ran into you until the end of time."

I pretend to think about it for a second. "Fine. Deal. Just promise you'll stop doing that?"

She moves her hand between us, her finger gently on my chest. "Cross my heart."

Our lips find each other again, a soft kiss, but one that means so much.

No more fake. No more PR. Just us.

"You swore at me," I joke as our lips come apart.

I swear she has the sweetest laugh I've ever heard. And right now, on this date, I vow to myself that I want to make her laugh at least once a day. I think if that happened, we'd live a pretty good life together.

"I did. But it worked, right?"

I spit out a laugh. "Yup. That was it. Hearing you call me a stubborn ass sealed the deal."

"Well dang, if I would've known *that* I would've swore at you weeks ago."

I roll her on top of me, about ready for round three. "Yes, the swearing snapped me into reality. But falling for you? It was so much more than that."

She tilts her head with a soft smile, her naked body lying on top of me. She feels perfect there. Like she was meant to be.

And maybe she was. I was just too stubborn to admit it.

"It was you, Ainsley. You're like no one I've ever met. From the moment you walked into me, I think I knew you were different."

She blushes. "You did?"

Now it's my turn to take my fingertip and gently make an X over her heart. "Cross my heart, Ainsley Mae."

guide to love rule #9

Good girls can still say dirty words.

31
ainsley

I've never been so glad to get cut in all of my years as a nurse.

We had a really hard birth this morning. Luckily, baby and mama are going to be fine, but it was scary for a while.

Then I thought my day was getting better when I had a delivery at lunch. I'd told Linc last night that I was weirdly craving tomato soup and grilled cheese. So when the reception desk called to tell me I had a delivery, I was excited for what I thought was Linc being Linc. Especially since he's on the road for an away game.

It wasn't him. It was flowers from Jonathan, with a note asking if he could take me to dinner tonight to "see where I was at."

I took the flowers to a patient's room. They were nice flowers and shouldn't go to waste, but I didn't want to have to look at them any longer than I had to.

So when we were slow on the floor—babies come when babies want to come—my charge nurse asked for volunteers to leave early. I couldn't have raised my hand fast enough. Which is why I'm now speedwalking to the elevators, one Stanley in hand, my cell phone in the other, as I'm ready to get home and shower off the day. All I want is to talk to Linc before he has to report for curfew and enjoy my day off tomorrow away from the hospital and watching my man play against the New York Vipers.

AINSLEY

Leaving work early. I had a day. Hope to talk to you tonight

Linc doesn't respond, which I figured he wouldn't. I know he has team meetings before they're dismissed for dinner. But he did tell me to text him when I left work, and I'm proud of myself for not overthinking whether or not to text him earlier than he expected.

Look at me go.

The elevator comes and I hit the button to take me to the employee parking garage, but unfortunately, it stops two floors away.

"Ainsley! What a surprise."

The groan I let out echoes through the elevator. "Jonathan."

He steps into the elevator, but strangely doesn't press a button. I don't think this is a surprise. I don't know how he knew I was leaving—no one on my floor would tell him anything, let alone my comings and goings—but this can't be a coincidence. Especially not after the flowers today.

"Did you get my present?"

"I did."

I stare at the lights as they move from floor to floor. Normally these elevators are pretty fast. Today they're moving at a snail's pace.

"So since you're getting off early, and my on-call shift is over, do you want to take me up on that dinner date?"

"No, Jonathan, I don't."

I don't look at him as I respond, instead thanking the heavens above as the doors open to lead me into the parking garage, where I'm only a few cars away.

"Ainsley! Can we talk?"

Why is he following me? Also, why can't this man take a hint? It's not even a hint at this point. It's a loud, flashing sign accompanied by the crazy inflatable waving-arm tube man outside the car dealership.

I turn on a dime, though I didn't realize how close he was to me. I'm a few steps from my car, and Jonathan is so close I can feel his breath.

"Jonathan! Get the hell away from me."

The strength in my voice—and my use of hell—takes him back slightly, but he's still too close to me for my liking.

"Why are you acting like this?" he asks.

Me? He's asking me that? "I could ask you the same question. And frankly, I'd rather dig into that. Because why won't you leave me alone? I've moved on. And you should too."

He rolls his eyes. "Really, Ainsley? You're still pretending with that guy?"

"It's real!" I yell, my voice echoing off of the cement walls of the garage. "You're the one choosing not to believe that, and I don't know what else I can do to make you understand that I want nothing to do with you!"

He shakes his head, taking a step toward me. I was already close to my car, and his movements make me reverse until I feel my back hit the metal. Both of his hands reach out, essentially pinning me against my practical Honda Civic.

"What's he done to you?" His voice is low, and it sends a chill down my spine.

"Jonathan. Back up. Now. Or I swear I'll scream."

He rolls his eyes again, but slowly does what I ask.

"I don't know who you are anymore," he says, shaking his head in disappointment at me. "You don't raise your voice. Or swear. You don't go out drinking. Or partying. And PDA? What was that about? Where did my Ainsley go?"

He could be talking about the karaoke bar, but I have a feeling if he knows when I'm leaving the hospital, then he saw photos on social media this week of Linc and I kissing in public. He has two away games in a row, so we took Tuesday to have a little date night.

God forbid a girl kiss her boyfriend after he takes her for ice cream.

And gave her an orgasm in the car. But nobody else needs to know that.

"Your Ainsley? I was never *your* Ainsley." Sure, I might've thought that when we were together. But now that I'm with Linc? Now that I truly know what it's like to be wanted and desired by someone—and vice versa—it's laughable that I thought I ever had that with Jonathan. "I might not be the Ainsley from the past, but every day I'm learning who I truly am. I'm happy. I've moved on. You need to as well. For good."

Just as I finish my monologue, my phone starts ringing, and I let out a sigh of relief when I hear the song that Linc made his personal ring tone. And yes, it's the song I sang to him badly at karaoke. And judging by Jonathan's face, he clearly remembers.

"This is Linc. Would you like to tell him why you sent his girlfriend flowers today and stalked her into a parking garage? Or should I?"

Jonathan's eyes narrow as he contemplates his answer. "I'm not giving up, Ainsley."

"You should," I say as I hit the accept button for the FaceTime call. "Hey, babe. How are you?"

I hold the phone up, but I'm not looking directly at him. But I can tell he's a little confused, because in the nearly two months we've been together—real and fake—I don't think I've ever called him "babe."

"Still at work? I figured I'd catch you on the drive."

I don't reply yet, making sure I keep an eye on Jonathan as he slowly retreats to the elevator. Once he's in and I see the lights start moving, I finally let out a breath.

"Baby? You okay? What's going on?"

"Jonathan," I say as I hurry and throw my things in my backseat before I tear out of the parking garage. And by tear I mean going five more miles over the speed limit with my seatbelt securely fastened.

"What the fuck do you mean, *Jonathan*?"

I try to slow my heart rate down, because the more I'm worked up, the more I'm going to work up Linc. And considering he's in Chicago right now, worrying about me the night before a game is the last thing he needs to do.

I shake my head as I pull to a stop light. "I'm fine. Just a little shook up."

"You're more than shook up, but I don't want you telling me all of this while you're driving."

"Okay. I'll call you back when I get to my apartment?"

I see him shaking his head. "Absolutely not. I'm staying right here. And I'm just going to sit with you so I know you get home safe."

I nod and feel tears starting to form in my eyes, the adrenaline wearing off as I make the fifteen-minute drive from the hospital to my apartment. I have my phone on a dock, so I give a few glances to Linc, who's lying on a bed in his hotel room. What I wouldn't give to be driving to him tonight, knowing that his touch would be the exact cure to wipe away thoughts of this insane day.

What is Jonathan's deal? Yes, he's never been one to get the hint. The relief I felt when he moved to San Antonio was immense. But this seems extreme, even for him. Mia wanted me to file for a restraining order before he moved. Maybe it's time I consider it.

Luckily, the drive home is quick tonight, and I'm walking to my apartment before I know it. Linc hasn't said anything, and even if it's just through the phone, I do feel more relaxed knowing he's with me.

"Okay, I'm here," I say, literally dropping all of my water bottles and my bag onto the floor as soon as I walk in. My tennis shoes are off just as quickly as I physically fall into my couch.

"Are you okay?"

He already asked me that, but I can tell by the worried look in his eyes he needs confirmation. "I'm fine. Just…I don't know. Something is up."

I go on to recount the day—well, the parts involving Jonathan. With each detail, his face gets redder. A vein in his neck starts to pulse, and while it's slightly sexy, I'm more worried that I'm about to give this poor man a stroke.

"I'm going to kill him, Ainsley," he says. "Contract or not, I'm going to fucking kill him."

"While I appreciate your willingness to give up your career in my honor, let's try and make it not come to that," I say. "But I do think I need to go to human resources about this on Monday."

"You absolutely are," he says. "And I'm going with you."

"Linc, you don't have to do that."

"I know. I want to."

The seriousness and worried look in his eyes hits me in the heart. "Okay. Thank you. And thank you for staying on the phone with me."

"You don't have to thank me. I'm glad I called when I did. I'm also proud of you. Standing up to him like that? That took balls, Ainsley Mae."

"Thanks," I say with a shrug, like it's not a big deal. Even though now that I think about it, it was a big deal. "It was a scary situation, and I was more confused than anything. But telling him off? That felt pretty freaking good."

"Damn right it did."

We share a smile as I make my way into my bedroom and sit on the side of my bed. My heartbeat is finally back to normal, thank goodness, and frankly, all I want now is to talk about anything other than Jonathan. "Are you by yourself? Where's Wyatt?"

I see Linc relax a little more as well. "He and a few of the guys went to dinner."

"Why didn't you go?"

He shrugs as he puts his arm up, propping his head against his hand, which perfectly shows off his sleeve of tattoos. The sleeve I've become quite familiar with. I was pleasantly surprised to learn that Linc's sleeve goes through to his chest, and that there are other ones scattered on his body. Two on his calves and one on his thigh.

That one's my favorite.

"My options were going to a fancy steakhouse where I'd have to pretend to know half the things on the menu, or I could order delivery, eat in peace, and get to talk to my girl. It was an easy decision."

"Well, I'm glad you did," I say, falling to my bed. Normally I'd take my scrubs off before doing this, but the weight of the day has finally taken its toll on me. "If you can't be here, then this is the next best thing."

"I never minded away games, but now I have a beef with them," he jokes. "Who am I supposed to cuddle with tonight? Wyatt?"

The thought makes me laugh. "I bet he'd let you be little spoon."

"Nah. The fucker is selfish." I giggle as I watch Linc's expression soften. "And the only little spoon I want is you, Ainsley Mae. That ass rubbing against me? Feeling your body in my arms? There's not much better than that."

Linc's words begin to heat through me. "I like it too."

I don't know what in those four words flip a switch in Linc, but I can tell the second they do.

"What do you like? Tell me, Ainsley."

His words are direct, almost an order. Part of me wants to tell him—I bet he'll give me some sort of reward if I do. But the shy girl that still lives in me doesn't know if I can say the words he wants without him here next to me.

"You want to know what I like?" he begins, clearly knowing me well enough to realize I need a minute to gather the courage.

"I love holding you. I love feeling those tits in my hands as your ass rubs against me. The little moans you make when I kiss that spot on your neck that you love so much."

I sit up against my headboard, because lying down is not going to help me right now when I want to teleport to Chicago and dive into Linc's bed.

Who knew sex was addicting? I sure as heck didn't.

"I love it too."

Linc's smile is wicked as he positions himself against his headboard. "Can you show them to me?"

My eyes go wide at his request. "You want me to…strip?"

He nods as he reaches behind his back and pulls his T-shirt off with one move. "Take off your shirt, Ainsley Mae. Show me what I want to touch."

I know we're both alone. But there's something so *naughty* about this. "I've never…on FaceTime. Or real life, for that matter."

"Good," he says possessively. "Do you know how much it turns me on to know I get some of your firsts? That I want to invent new ones to have just so they'll be mine?"

His low voice, and the excitement of the request, has me clenching in all the right places. Oh my gosh, maybe tonight I'll finally use the toy Quinn got me for my birthday last year that I've never had the courage to use.

Oh! Could I use it with Linc sometime? I think that could be fun. Not now. But in the future. I should put it on the list.

"Okay," I say, having more confidence to take this leap with him. I go to put my phone down, but just as I do, I hear his objection.

"No, Ainsley. Pick it up. Find something to prop it on. I want to watch."

The idea of Linc watching me strip is…exciting. I didn't expect to have that reaction, but as I put my phone against my bedside lamp and lift my shirt over my head, I can honestly say I'm turned on by doing this. Especially when I reconnect with his gaze. I don't see his other hand, but I can see movement in his arm.

And…oh my…is he…to himself? That's freaking hot.

"That's it, Ains—" he stops mid word as he realizes that I'm not done, deciding myself that if he wants to see me, then I'm going to show him. He's speechless as I reach around and unclasp my bra, letting it fall down my arms.

"Fucking gorgeous," he says. And if he wasn't stroking himself before, he surely is now. "You know what I'd love more than anything? What first I want more than my next breath?"

A million possibilities run through my head. "What's that?"

"To hear you say every dirty word that goes through that head of yours."

I reposition myself on the bed. "Are you saying you want to teach me how to talk dirty, Lincoln Kincaid?"

He gives me his signature smirk. "Just because you're mine now, doesn't mean the lessons are over."

I feel my nipples peak at the request. A small part of me doesn't think I can do it, then I remember I'm the woman who cussed at her boyfriend for being stubborn, screamed at her ex today for being crazy, and is topless on FaceTime.

If I can do that…I can say the words. I know them. I'm thinking them. I just won't think about them beforehand. This feels like a do-it-in-the-moment situation.

"You want to, don't you?" Linc asks.

"I do."

"I know you do. I see it in your eyes, Ainsley. You're a good girl, but I know there's some bad in you. And I want to hear you say every last filthy thing."

"Okay," I say with a breath, wishing now I also took off my pants, because they're feeling very restrictive.

"We'll start easy," he says. "What is one thing I just said that I loved?"

I take a deep breath, thinking that I need to gather the

courage. But I don't. Not with the way Linc is looking at me, heat and want in his eyes. "That you love my ass against you."

"That's right, baby," he says. "What else?"

I look down for a second, then back to him. "That you love my tits in your hands."

"Damn right I do," he says. "Will you touch them for me? Pretend it's me. Do what makes you feel good."

A month ago even considering something like this would've been laughable. Heck, a day ago I'd have said that I could never do something like this. But there's something about Linc that makes me want to try. That makes me want to explore. That makes me want to do something scary.

Because apparently scary things can also make you feel good.

"Like this?" I ask, taking my right breast into my hand, massaging it just like he likes to do. Well, not exactly like him. His hands are so big they cover almost all of me, and I do well for myself in the chest department.

"Just like that."

"Linc," I moan, closing my eyes as my hands explore. I gently twist one of my nipples, loving the little pain that gives me a lot of pressure.

"That's it, Ainsley. Do you like it when I do that to you?"

"Yes. And I love when you suck on them."

I open my eyes to see Linc lick his lips. "Yeah? Do you like that more than when I eat that pretty pussy?"

And I'm wet.

Yup. Panties about to be ruined because of my boyfriend's filthy mouth.

"It's pretty close," I admit as I try to nonchalantly move my hand down to give myself some relief. "But I think the second thing is my favorite."

"Come on, Ainsley Mae. You know you want to say it. Be my good girl and tell me."

It's like he knows when I hear that the flip switches in me. I never knew that was going to be my kryptonite. Or maybe Linc is, and the two combined are enough to end me here.

But what a way to go.

"I love it when you…when you lick me. Taste me. I love when you eat my pussy."

I've seen Linc turned on before. Many times. But I don't think anything will rival the look he's giving me right now. His eyes are dilated. His face is flushed. The little vein that pops out in his neck when he orgasms is starting to pulse.

Me. I did that. My words. My body. The thought of me is making this man come undone. He's not telling me that I sucked his dick too hard. Or that I couldn't be on top because I might crush him. Or that my C-cup boobs were just average. No. This man is looking at me like I'm his greatest fantasy come to life.

So if dirty talk is what Linc wants, that's what my man is going to get.

"Can I tell you the things I still want to try?"

He nods and grunts out an agreement.

"I want to sit on your face."

Linc's eyes go wide, clearly not ready for that.

"Is that okay?" I ask.

He furiously nods. "Suffocate me, for all I care. I'd die a happy man."

"Also, can you…when you come over tomorrow, can you…"

Why is this one so hard?

"What, Ainsley? Tell me. Tell me what you want. Rub that clit like I know you're doing and tell me what you want."

"Can I be on top? I want to ride your cock, Linc."

I see him physically react, his body nearly jerking with my words. "Are you telling me?"

My hand speeds up, because the thought of this is too much to handle. I start coming undone with every word that spills from my mouth. "I've never been on top. I want that first. I want to ride you. Can I do that? Check another first off my list?"

"Fuck….yes…you…can…"

I feel my orgasm hit me as I watch Linc's eyes close and his face tighten. The groan of relief he lets out is amazing to watch.

"Holy shit, Ainsley Mae."

I giggle as I grab a tissue from my bedside table. "Holy smokes is right."

He laughs. "All of that and you can't say holy shit?"

"Baby steps, Linc. Baby steps."

32

linc

"KINCAID! WE'RE GOING OUT TONIGHT WHEN WE GET BACK. You in?"

My immediate thought to Maddox's suggestion is "fuck no I don't want to go out. My girlfriend told me last night that she wants to ride my dick because she's never been on top, and I haven't been able to get that out of my head all day."

But today was a really good win. Chicago's one of the best teams in the league, and this was a potential championship game matchup. I had a touchdown and eighty yards receiving. Plus, we're about to be on our bye week break. So yeah, I want to go celebrate. And I want my girl with me.

"Do you mind if Ainsley comes?" I ask. "We had plans, so I don't want to cancel."

Plans. Ha. Sex plans, more like it.

"Hell, yeah, bring her," Wyatt says. "And you know, see if she wants to bring Mia too. You know, for moral support."

I lift an eyebrow. "Really? My girlfriend needs moral support?"

"We wouldn't want her to be the only woman," Wyatt says. "I'm just looking out for her."

"Sure you are," I say as I grab my phone.

LINC

Would you by any chance want to come out with me and the guys when we get back?

AINSLEY MAE

As long as I don't have to sing karaoke, I'm in.

Cross my heart. 😊 Oh, and Wyatt wants you to call Mia. For your moral support. Nothing about him wanting to see her. 😏

Ha! I knew those two had something going on. Unfortunately, though, she's working. I'll text her to see if she can meet us when she gets off.

Sounds good. Meet me at the facility in about forty-five minutes? I'll send a ride share for you so you don't have to deal with your car all night.

You're the best.

Nah. Just one less thing for us to worry about when I'm going to want to Irish goodbye from the bar because I have had certain thoughts on my mind since last night.

Same. Oh. And I have a few more ideas. I made a list.

You're killing me, woman.

See you soon 😊

"Damn, dude, you're blinding me with that smile," Maddox says from across the aisle of the team plane.

"Our boy is in love," Wyatt says. "But it looks good on you."

"Thanks," I say. "I know she's too good for me. And I probably don't deserve her, but I'm not going to look a gift horse in the mouth."

"As you shouldn't," Maddox says. "Come to think about it,

between the game today, Ainsley, and the news of the week, all things are looking up, Kincaid, if I do say so myself."

He's not wrong. It has been an overall good week. Highlighted by the news that the Fury traded Brad Rockwell.

Like we all knew was coming, he was finally cleared from injury. I knew it was coming, but it still gave me anxiety knowing that Coach McAvoy would have to make a decision of who was starting and how reps were going to be divided. I swear it was minutes after we got the news that he was cleared that he was also packing his bags and heading to Milwaukee.

A team that happens to be our next opponent after the bye week.

Kincaid versus Rockwell. Just like it was back in college. A battle of two standout tight ends.

One I'm not about to lose.

"Okay, between you and me," Maddox says as he leans in from across the aisle. "How much did you celebrate when you got home that night? You threw a party, didn't you? You and Ainsley popping bottles and shit?"

"I wouldn't say a party," I say with a smile. "Okay, fine. There was a party and Ainsley got us a cake because, according to her, when there's an excuse to eat cake, you eat the cake."

"I like her," Maddox says. "Did she bake it? Scratch or box? What kind of frosting did she use?"

Wyatt and I look over to our friend with very, and I mean very, confused looks. "Why are you asking me baking details? For one, she bought it. Some bakery we found on the West End. And two, even if she would've, how the fuck would I know?"

"There's a new bakery?"

This man is the best cornerback in the league, with the attention span of a gnat. "Do you want me to get the address from Ainsley? Also, do you have a secret baking hobby that we don't know about?"

"No," Maddox says, though the way he waves his hand at

the statement has me thinking that the answer is actually yes. "I just enjoy a sweet treat."

"Who the fuck says sweet treat?" Wyatt asks.

"Me. I do. Got a problem with it?"

"Not at all," Wyatt says as it's announced that we're making our descent into Nashville. "You keep playing the way you are, and I'll buy you sweet treats for life."

We all laugh and sit back for the final minutes of our flight. I grab my phone, order Ainsley a ride, then begin to aimlessly scroll. I'm not big into social media, but I'm not offline either. Usually just something to kill the time.

I scroll and see some headlines from games around the league today. Apparently Brad caught his first touchdown of the season, though the headline does say it looks like he lost a step.

Not going to lie, that made me smile.

The Philadelphia Kings picked up a win. A talking head made an ass of himself, predicting a team to win by a huge margin, only for them to lose on a field goal at the end of the game. I check out a few more headlines before stopping when I see my name flash in front of me. And it's not in a football-related headline.

Honeymoon over? Linc Kincaid's woman spotted with another man

My blood spikes in temperature as I frantically click on the link. In my heart of hearts I know that Ainsley would never cheat. The woman once ate two grapes at the grocery store and then told the cashier about it to adjust the weight. But that little devil on my shoulder that's convinced myself for years that I can't have good things happen to me needs to know what the fuck this is about.

"Hey, you okay?" Wyatt asks.

I don't answer as I frantically bypass whatever bullshit words are on the article, scrolling until I see a picture. If the headline is going to say spotted, I'm assuming that there's "proof."

It only takes a few more scrolls to see it. There's Ainsley, who's leaned back against her car. A man is standing in front her, hands on both sides of her, caging her in. He's leaning in like he wants to kiss her.

"Holy shit," I hear Wyatt say. "What the fuck is that?"

"I don't know," I say as I enlarge the picture. I can tell that's Ainsley's car. The photo is a little grainy, clearly taken from far away and zoomed in, but I can tell that it's her silver Civic. It looks like they're in a garage of some sort, and I'm going to guess the hospital, because she's in her scrubs and carrying one of her three emotional support water bottles.

But it's not her car I'm focusing on. Or even her. I need to know who the fuck is around Ainsley, which will then tell me who I need to kill.

I move the picture to get a better view when I see it. Him.

Fucking Dipshit.

"Who's he?" Wyatt asks. "Wait! Is that the guy from the bar? Her ex?"

"It fucking is," I grit out. "This was taken last night."

"How do you know?"

"Because he fucking cornered her when she was leaving work. I FaceTimed her as it was happening."

"Are you kidding me?"

"No. She was shaken up for a second, but more because she told him to take a fucking hike."

I scroll back up to see what this "writer" is spewing. According to the article—AKA the lies—Banks, Linc Kincaid's normally shy and reserved girlfriend, is using Kincaid's time away from Nashville to canoodle with a mystery man.

Who the fuck says canoodle?

I speed-read the rest, because it's a lot just about us and our timeline of dating. Or at least, the one we've let the public know about.

"This makes no fucking sense," I say as I turn my phone off. "Who is doing this? Why is someone in her hospital's parking garage waiting to take a photo? This isn't random. This feels fucking staged."

"It does," Wyatt agrees. "But who? Do you think her ex set it up?"

"The thought crossed my mind," I admit. "It's all too much of a coincidence."

"Has Katie messaged you yet about it?"

"No, she hasn't," I say, double-checking my messages to make sure I didn't miss anything. "Hopefully that means that she's taking care of it."

I send her a message, demanding to talk to her when I'm off the plane. Thank God we're about to land. I'm going fucking crazy in this seat. I need to check on Ainsley. I'm not sure if she's seen it yet. If she hasn't, I don't want to send it via text when I'm on a plane. She'll panic, think she did something wrong, then worry herself to death.

She did nothing wrong. But I'm now sure more than anything someone is doing this to us.

At first I thought the photos were random. The ones back from camp, when it looked like I was throwing a punch at the arcade. The karaoke night. The random other headlines. They all were far enough apart for me to just think people were bored and needed clicks.

But this? This feels calculated. Now I'm wondering if nothing was accidental.

The plane comes to a stop and I'm off in a matter of minutes, though it feels like hours. I bypass any need to go inside the facility and head straight to my car. According to the ride share app, Ainsley's a few minutes away. But when I make it to the parking lot, I realize I have a visitor waiting for me.

"Katie. Thank God. Thanks for coming," I say. "Are you taking care of it?"

She looks up at me, and that's when I see the bags under her eyes. It looks like she's been crying for a week. Also, why is she dressed in all black like she's ready to go to a funeral? "Taking care of what?"

Of what? The woman is chronically online and has alerts set up on her phone for when my name is mentioned on any form of social media. There's no way she doesn't know about this. Also, why is she here, if not to talk about this?

"I'm not in the mood for jokes, Katie. Please tell me you're doing something about this."

I hold out my phone, praying that this really isn't the first time she's seeing it. "Oh that. That's nothing."

"What do you mean it's nothing? This blog is now just outright making up lies about Ainsley. And I'm pretty sure her ex is in on this."

"Those are about Ainsley, not you," she says. "My job is to keep your name out of the tabloids. Actually, if anything, I think this helps you."

I think I'm in some sort of bananas world right now, because what?

"Please, tell me in what world that lies about *my* girlfriend are being spread and you think that *helps* me?"

Katie rolls her eyes. Rolls them. And at this point, I'm now madder at her than I am at the gossip blog. "She's your fake girlfriend. I don't know why you're getting so bent out of shape over this."

"Actually, I'm his *real* girlfriend, so if you're going to talk about me behind my back, at least use my correct title."

I don't know when Ainsley got here, but as always, her timing is impeccable. And she looks *pissed*.

Oh shit. I have a feeling I'm about to see a side of Ainsley I've never seen before.

"Real?" Katie says, clearly not believing Ainsley, even with my arm now around her. "Remember, Ainsley. I know. This? You and him? My idea."

"Sure, that's how it started."

I thought she was going to keep talking, until she steps in front of me. I'm still slightly confused even when she pulls me by my shirt for a kiss that's so hard our lips might bruise.

Ainsley breaks away and turns back to a stunned Katie. I'm left stunned. "This is how it's going. Now you're caught up."

Jealousy.

Holy shit, that's what I'm seeing in her right now.

She just claimed me. She came here, and not only stood her ground next to me, but with me. All while telling Katie, and whoever else is pretending to hide behind their cars to watch this drama, that I'm hers.

Not going to lie, this is pretty fucking hot.

Katie's eyes are narrowed at Ainsley before she sets them on me. "Is this true, Linc? You're actually *with* her?"

"I am. Is that a problem?"

"Yes it's a problem!" she cries, though it comes out more like an upset toddler. "You saw the photos. She's cheating on you! You should be breaking up with her!"

"Funny how you think pictures of me looking terrified constitutes as cheating. Which I'm not, by the way," Ainsley says. "Also, how did those pictures come about Katie? Anything you want to share?"

Katie ignores Ainsley's claim before turning her sad eyes back to me. "Linc. You don't need her. I know this was my idea, but she's only dragged you down. It's time to end this."

Who is this woman? It's like I don't even recognize her. Gone is the Type-A publicist who ran my media life over the summer. Gone is the kind girl who always tried to break news to me gently. The woman in front of me is someone I don't recognize.

And it's time for her to go.

"Actually, Katie, what I don't need right now is you."

It's like for a second she doesn't hear me. Then I watch on a delayed timer as my words finally register.

"What did you say?"

"I said that we're done. Thank you for the work you've done for me, but I think it's best if we part ways."

"But—" she shrieks, and I don't look, but I'm pretty sure Ainsley has a smug smile on her lips. "You need me, Linc. Remember?"

"I don't think I do," I say as everything comes into place. "Since the season started, what have you done to help my image? To make sure that if misleading or horrible headlines have happened, to squash them? Because they seem to be coming up more and more, and you seem to be doing less and less. Today was the final straw."

"I was trying!"

"Clearly not hard enough," I say as I step a little closer to her. "We're done, Katie. I'll call my agent and let him know that we're parting ways. He'll be taking care of the rest."

She steps back, a hurt look on her face, but that's quickly wiped away in favor of a scowl.

"This is your fault," she hisses as she points at Ainsley.

"You keep telling yourself that," Ainsley says as she steps closer. "I told you that I had my eye on you. To watch your back. You did this to yourself. So now it's time for you to take your iPad and leave us alone. Understand?"

I've fought many of my battles before, often leaving me and someone else bloody. But watching Ainsley fight for me? And with nothing more than words and glares? I've never been defended like that before.

Katie doesn't say anything else, instead just lets out a huff as she turns on a heel and stomps away. Ainsley and I both watch as she gets into her car before speeding out of the parking lot.

"Holy shit," I say, bringing her into my arms. "Where did that come from?"

She coyly shrugs. "No one messes with my man."

"Your man, huh?"

"Damn straight."

She adds a wink, and I can't resist anymore. I don't care what kind of commotion we've caused; I need to kiss her. For real. Not the one she did to show off in front of Katie. Not one we'd do to be polite. Or to give cameras their shot. No, I need to feel this woman's mouth on me.

Because yeah…she's mine. In every sense of the word.

But I'm hers. Maybe even more so.

"I've got an idea," I say as I open my car door for her.

"If the idea is scrapping plans with the guys and going to your apartment because it's technically closer and not having on clothes for the rest of the night, then I'm in."

I pull her in, hearing "oohs" and kissing sounds from my teammates as I give her a kiss that promises what's to come.

She defended me. She defended us. She fought a battle with me. Next to me. For me.

Because this woman loves me.

And I love her. So fucking much.

guide to love #70

When you find your person, you realize how different things were before them. And what true love really is.

33
ainsley

WE WEREN'T EVEN TWO STEPS INSIDE LINC'S APARTMENT BEFORE WE were stripping each other. It was a matter of seconds until he was kissing every inch of my body, his hands touching every part of me his mouth wasn't. Within minutes he was inside of me, thrusting into me like a man possessed.

And I loved every second of it. It mirrored what I felt in the moment as I was telling that horrible woman how it was.

Linc's body was saying, "She's mine."

And when I was facing her, that's the only thing that was going through my head. *He's mine.*

This shouldn't surprise me. Linc has always known what I've needed. Even before we began the physical part of our relationship, the man somehow has always had a sense about me.

He knew when I needed help that night at the bar.

He knew how to navigate the first meeting with my siblings.

He knew how I needed to be touched when I didn't have a clue.

And now, as we lay in his bed—his fingers gently stroking my back as I aimlessly trace the ink on his chest—we both know that we needed this. The silence after the passion. To process everything that's happened in a matter of hours.

"Am I stupid?"

His question surprises me, and I turn to look at him, needing to know where that came from. "The initial answer is no. But now I need to know why you asked that?"

I roll off his chest, propping my head up with my hand, but Linc makes sure I'm not far away, pulling my body into him. "Katie. I trusted her. But the way she started acting recently? I don't know…something was off, and I ignored it. I feel like I've been played."

I bring his hand up to my lips, gently kissing his palm in hopes of some comfort. "My answer stands that you're not stupid. We put our trust into people, and she was no different. She probably did have your best interests at heart at some point, but something happened along the way. We just don't know what."

"You happened," he says. "The second you came into my life, things shifted."

I had that thought, but didn't want to say anything and sound conceited. "I knew she never liked me. That was evident from the first day we met. But, being me, I assumed I was reading into things that weren't there. That changed when she showed up in the suite that first game I went to."

"What did happen that day? You never filled me in."

Oh, shoot. Now I feel guilty. "I meant to, I promise, Linc. But after we had that little exchange in the tunnel, we got in the car and then we came here and…"

"Then you sucked my dick wearing my jersey," he says with a wink. "I guess I can forgive you for that. In my defense, I forgot everything that happened before that as well."

I relax, and of course, blush a little, because that day was pretty hot. "I really didn't mean to hold out on you. But then after that, I didn't really see her again. I'm assuming she saw you, but she avoided me. I honestly didn't think about it until today."

"It's okay," he says, kissing my forehead for good measure. "It's just…something's not adding up."

"I have theories, but they don't make sense."

"What are they?" he asks. "Because I'm clueless."

"My first one is that she has feelings for you."

"Really?" he asks, clearly not thinking on the same path as me. "Besides being a little touchy-feely, she's never come across that way."

"I know," I say. "It was my first thought. But then, why would she set us up? If she truly had feelings for you, getting you a fake girlfriend is the worst idea in the world."

Linc lets out a breath. "What's always bothered me was the game she showed up to wearing a Rockwell T-shirt. She knows he hates me, and my feelings are mutual. I'm not saying she has to ride at dawn with me, but that always rubbed me the wrong way."

"And was she dismissive? That's what it always felt like to me when I overheard your conversations, and even today from what little I heard as I was walking up. It's like she didn't care."

"She didn't. But do you think…did she have something to do with all the negative stuff?"

I shrug because I honestly don't know. "I hope not. The glass-half-full Ainsley wants to say that those are separate and she's just really bad at her job. But now? Now I don't know what to believe."

Linc pulls me back into his embrace, rolling me over with ease as he balances his weight on top of me. "No matter her intentions, I do feel like I need to thank her. Because her suggestion of you and me dating? Best thing to ever happen to me."

His lips descend on mine, and while I have a gut feeling that this Katie thing isn't over, I'm done thinking about her tonight.

"Do you think we really would've never seen each other again?" I don't want to give Katie any more brain space, but now that he's put that out there, the overthinker in me is taking over.

Linc's smile says it all. "Like I could've stayed away."

He sits up, bringing me with him. My hands immediately circle his neck as he looks at me like I've never been looked at before, making my heart swell so much it might burst.

"I love you, Ainsley."

Holy crap. Did he just say…

"Oh, the shocked face. I missed that look," he says as he comes in for a quick kiss. "That's the look you first gave me from the floor of the hospital, and I remember thinking that you were the most beautiful woman I've ever seen."

"You did not." The man is going to make me blush as I fight back happy tears.

"Oh, but I did," he says as he pulls me in tighter. "I looked for you after you left. I knew you were…what did you say?— 'Leave, car, go'…but I looked. I needed to see you again."

Yup. Crying. Tears. Happy tears. And I'm not even ashamed.

"When I saw you that night at karaoke, I couldn't believe my luck. I didn't even know your name, but there you were."

"And then you were my boyfriend."

"Damn right I was," he says with a quick kiss. "All that is to say I don't think I could've stayed away from you if I tried. I looked for you that first day, and I know I would've looked for you again. You were in my bones from the second I met you, Ainsley Banks. Even if we had said our goodbyes that day at my kitchen island, I know that I'd have made as many hospitals visits as I needed to see you again."

He pauses to gather his words. Which is good. I need a second to gather myself.

My entire life, I've dreamed of the moment. The moment when you realize that you're in love and you're loved back just as much. I prayed for this. Wondered when it was going to be my turn.

But now it's here. This man who I literally didn't see coming, yet changed my entire world.

And it's all because I did the scary thing.

"I love you, Ainsley Mae," he continues. "I don't know much, but I know our story wasn't supposed to end that day. And if I have my way, it's not going to end for a very long time."

"I love you, Linc," I say before kissing the heck out of this man. I have so much more to say. But more than that, I want to show him how much I love him too. How much he saved me that night. How he showed me a side of myself that I didn't know existed.

No more hiding. No more being scared.

Just being happy.

Being me.

Being loved.

Reading me like he always can, Linc gently lowers us back to the bed, our lips never leaving each other as I feel him growing hard on top of me. I open my legs, knowing that he doesn't need to get me ready to take him. My body is always ready.

Plus, all that talk about love? That's foreplay enough.

Linc lines himself up, slowly entering me, my back arching as I feel him filling me. I still don't understand the logistics of all of this— but what I do know is that when he's inside me, slowly pumping in and out of me, I've never felt more complete in my life. And so for that, I'm going to choose to not overthink it.

Instead I'm going to focus on Linc. On how he looks down at me like I'm his whole world. How his lips always need to be on my body in some way. How he moves in and out of me, his pace always in tune with what the night calls for.

Earlier was about heat. Raw emotion. We both felt it after our run-in with Katie, and we both needed the release.

Right now is just about us. About love. About each other.

Holy Moses…this isn't sex. This is making love. What I've dreamed of, wanted, for years. This is what my sisters always talked about. Sure, they discussed some adventurous things, but underlying in all of it was how their partners made them feel whole. Beautiful. Wanted. Cherished. Loved.

And that's what's happening right now as Linc brings his

hands under my back, holding me against him as he makes sure that I feel every inch of him inside me.

My arms and legs are wrapped around him, needing to feel him as close as possible. He buries his lips into my neck, kissing and sucking as our movements start speeding up. My nails dig into his back as I feel my orgasm start to build, and as much as I want the release, I want to feel more of him just like this. I want this moment to last longer.

I want it to last forever.

My body moves, signaling to him that I want on top. I know we talked about this the night before, and I figured at some point it would happen tonight, but I never knew it would be like this. The smile on Linc's face is one I wish I could take a picture of. It's a little devilish. A little love drunk. And a whole lot satisfied.

I put my hands on his chest, bracing myself as he lines me up and helps me ease down onto him.

"Oh God," I say in a moan. "This feels so good."

"Take what you want, baby. I'm yours."

And I do. I grip onto his chest as I move up and down on his length, loving how it feels the same, yet so much different. His hands reach up for me, playing with each of my breasts as I start riding him a little faster, wanting to feel more and more of him with every movement.

"I love you, Lincoln Kincaid," I say as I change my pace, slowing it down to more methodical movements. "I love how you make me feel. I love how I can be every part of myself around you. I love that you help me do the scary things, and if I fail at them, I know that you'll be there to catch me. I love that you know to get me eight sides of ranch with everything. And I love how you love me. I…I just love you."

His hand is behind my neck in seconds as he pulls me down for a kiss that I actually feel in every cell of my body. He has me rolled over in seconds, our pace now furious as our mouths are taking everything we want.

Not that I'm complaining.

"Linc!" I scream as I hold onto him for dear life. I detonate the second his finger connects with my clit, flipping the switch that just sent me into a new orbit. He follows right behind me, letting out a grunt so loud that it's possible Wyatt could hear him three floors away.

We both come down from our highs, but our embrace never breaks. His arms are around me, holding me close as I do the same. Neither of us say a word. We don't need to.

We love each other. And that's all we need for whatever is thrown at us.

guide to love rule #111

A true test to see if your partner is the one is to have him hang out with your family. If he survives that, he can survive anything.

34
ainsley

Along my journey to learn football, I asked Linc how the league determined the bye weeks. To my Type-A leaning brain, they felt very random and chaotic. He admitted he didn't know how or why, but that he always believed they had a way of coming at the right time for every team.

I now believe that statement. Because I don't know if the rest of the Fury needed the off week, but Linc surely did.

Linc had to go talk to his agent about the proper steps to fire Katie so she had no legal recourse. And while that went well, and his agent apologized profusely for being the one to suggest they work together, the Katie drama wasn't quite over. Yet another blatant lie of an article came out last night—which we both believe, but can't prove, was Katie's last eff-you to us. This one said that not only were we fake, but insinuated that I was actually being held captive. We actually laughed when we read it, as his head was on my lap, while wearing my eye masks because he wanted to see what they felt like, and I was playing with his hair in a face mask of my own. Yeah. I'm totally being held against my will.

Needless to say, mentally, the bye week came at a good time. But we were both feeling a little cooped-up in Nashville. So, I suggested what I know to be the best medicine one could ask for —a night out in Rolling Hills.

"Let's raise our glasses, especially Ainsley, who for the first time around us is having an actual cocktail," Simon says as the large table in the middle of the bar is filled with each of my siblings and their significant others. "I'd like to propose a toast to each of my sisters, who, I must say, has impeccable taste in men."

Even though the compliment is to us, Linc, Emmett, Logan, and Porter, all share fist bumps and high-fives in congratulations to themselves.

"But, I want to say thank you specifically to Linc." As Simon pauses, Linc puts his arm around me and pulls me close. "Thank you for protecting our sister. Thank you for being there for her. Thank you for bringing out a side of her that we always hoped was there. And thank you for making her smile. Welcome to the family. We're chaos, but we're a damn good time."

Simon and Linc share a head nod as we all clink our glasses together. I use the time to wipe away the runaway tear that trickled out. If Simon's going to be like this tonight, what's he going to be like when we get engaged?

Oh my gosh, are we going to get engaged? Is this it? I mean, I want to. Someday. Not tonight. But yeah, I want to marry Linc Kincaid.

And for the first time in my adult life, I'm truly believe I'm with a man who wants to marry me too.

"This is so exciting!" Stella claps. "Ainsley's having a drink. She and Linc are for real. We're all in love. I love this so much!"

I almost spit out the vodka and cranberry I agreed to have while Linc chokes on his beer. "What did you say?"

Stella's eyes go wide as she realizes what slipped out of her mouth. "Oh. Yeah. Um…"

She looks to Quinn for help, who I'm guessing has been waiting for this moment for weeks. "Settle the bet. How long have you two been fake before you became real? There may or may not be a hundred-and-sixty bucks riding on this."

I look around to the table of my siblings and all of their partners. "Y'all bet on this?"

"Hell, yeah," Porter says. "This was the first Banks family bet I could be a part of. I wasn't turning down that action. It'll even be better if you tell me that the winning date was three days ago."

Linc starts laughing, and all I can do is shake my head. "Did any of you believe this for any amount of time?"

"We knew from the second we crashed your breakfast date," Maeve says. "But, it seemed like it was really important to you both to go with this, so we let it go. We knew you'd tell us when you were ready. Or someone wouldn't be able to keep their mouth shut. And here we are."

Everyone shoots a look to Stella, who holds her hands up in innocence. "It slipped! I swear. But you two just looked so happy, and I'm tired of texting behind your back."

"What!" I gasp. "There's a side text? That I'm not a part of? I'm always included!"

"Now you know what it feels like," Quinn says. "But none of that matters now. You're here together. And for real, because you two can't keep your hands off each other. The Fury is undefeated so far this season. And you're about to tell me that you dropped the fake act a week after we saw y'all at breakfast so I can win. All is right in the world!"

I feel Linc laugh next to me as I just shake my head. "Sorry, sister. Linc? Would you like to tell them who the big winner is?"

"I'd be honored," he says as he sits up a little straighter. "A drumroll please, Ainsley Mae?"

He gives me a wink as I pat my hands on the table. "Whoever had the Thursday before the Vegas Aces game, you're the winner."

My sisters all open their phones, doing mental math of the schedule in comparison to the date Linc just told them. But as I watch them scramble, and Simon silently throw a tantrum because he knows he lost, I watch as my brother-in-law Logan smiles from ear-to-ear, putting his hands behind his head as he leans back in his chair.

"Really?" Porter yells, getting everyone's attention. "The billionaire won?"

"What can I say, I looked at the data. Figured out the odds. Ran a few tests."

Maeve clearly doesn't buy that. "Just say you guessed. No one likes a know-it-all."

"Maybe I did, maybe I didn't," he says as he kisses her cheek. "But what I will say is, 'pay up, wife.'"

Everyone except Logan, Linc, and I groan as they fish twenty-dollar bills from their pockets or purses. Simon and Charlie say their goodbyes since my niece is sick tonight, but they didn't want to miss out. But during that, I notice Logan leans over to Porter and passes him the pile of cash.

Apparently, Linc notices too.

"Do I need to pick up the family tab at some point? Is this a thing the men do? I mean, I can. I will. But I don't want your family to think I'm a scrub."

I shake my head. "No. Logan's a billionaire video game developer. Created SpaceCraft. He doesn't always pay, but does this a lot. You're safe."

Linc's eyebrows shoot up. "You're...he's—" Before I know it, I realize I've lost my boyfriend to the lore of my brother-in-law. "I fucking love the new game you just came out with! The guys and I play all the time!"

Logan laughs and stands up from the table. "Thanks, mate. How about we talk about it over a game of pool? Guys? Doubles?"

"Ah man!" Simon pouts as his wife starts dragging him out of the bar.

We all laugh as each of the guys start standing up.

"You good if I go play?" Linc asks.

"Of course," I say, kissing his cheek. "Go have fun."

A genuine smile crosses his lips before he kisses me goodbye. He's not even two steps away before Emmett comes over, slapping him on the back, which I have a feeling means he's going to be talking all things football, Fury, and video games for the foreseeable future.

"You're happy."

It takes me a second to realize that Maeve's talking to me. "I am."

"That's what happens when you're getting good dick."

Stella smacks Quinn since she's the closest to her. "Jesus Christ, Quinn."

"Ouch," she rubs her shoulder, but then sets her eyes on me. "And speaking of JC, blink twice if you've seen him or cried out his name."

I smile, blink twice, and add in a wink for good measure.

"Fuck yeah!" Quinn yells. "Honestly, that makes me happier than anything."

"Can I admit something?"

"Absolutely," Maeve says. "And don't think because Quinn is staring at you that you have to tell more than you want."

I glance over to Quinn, who's giving me some wagging eyebrows. I love her, but she's ridiculous.

"For years, I've always wanted to talk sex with all of you. I was always so jealous you had these times to reminisce about. And I had nothing I'd experienced that even came close to what you guys were describing, and I always felt so left out."

"We're sorry, Ainsley," Stella says, wrapping me in a hug. "We just figured that you had them, but didn't want to share."

"Or that you were a virgin. We never figured out how to actually ask that one."

"That's fair," I say to Quinn. "But for all those years, I thought y'all had to be exaggerating. That sex really wasn't like that."

"But now?"

You'd think that question would come from Quinn. But no. It's Maeve, giving me a look like only a knowing older sister can give.

"It's so much more," I gush. "It's…I see…he did…"

"She's speechless, ladies," Stella said. "That's the first sign of good sex."

"Second," Quinn chimes in. "Sore legs are first."

"You're right!" I say and clap my hands. "And I know that now!"

We all start laughing, tipping our glasses to each other. As Stella and Maeve take a sip of their drinks, I take the opportunity to lean into Quinn.

"Also, I thought you'd like to know, I didn't bite it."

Quinn laughs and hugs me tight. "I'm so fucking proud of you."

I'm proud of me too. Not for not biting Linc's penis. That is a low bar. But what I am proud of myself for is that I'm not ashamed or scared for sharing myself with my sisters. Not self-conscious in what I'm going to say or share. And that I did the scary thing and allowed myself to have the experience that led me here—to being with a man who loves me, who I love right back.

"While we're very glad for you," Maeve interrupts. "We do need to know that you're okay. The latest headline was a doozy."

I turn to my oldest sister, who's giving me the most comforting "Mama Maeve" look she can. Every time a headline pops up about us, they all make sure to check on me. I always say I'm fine. But I know this has to be worrying them.

"I'm not lying when I say I'm fine," I say. "Some get to me a little more than others."

"Who's doing this?" Stella asks. "Because at this point, someone is clearly after Linc, and by proxy, you."

"I have a feeling I know who, and hopefully now she won't be a problem anymore."

Quinn's ears perk up. "Please tell me you're talking about that bitch from the game. What was her name? Cunty?"

I laugh, because it should be her name. "Katie. His publicist. Or I should say, *former* publicist."

"Oh, thank God," Quinn says. "She was something. And when I say something, I mean a cunt."

I start filling my sisters in on details I hadn't bothered them with, but to my surprise, they know a lot of it.

Thanks, Quinn.

What they don't know is what happened two days ago. The blow-up. The scene we caused in the Fury facility parking lot. The way she just went ballistic seemingly out of nowhere.

"Oh shit," Quinn says. "She's full-on boiled bunny."

"Exactly," I say. "She had the crazy eyes."

"Thank God she's gone," Maeve adds.

"I'm not sure," I add. "Linc fired her, and his agent terminated all of their contracts. But something still feels off. It's like… I don't know…I'm waiting for the other shoe to drop or something."

"Do you want me to do some digging?" Stella asks. "I rhinestoned an FBI hat, and I only got to wear it once."

"Can you?" I ask. Who needs private investigators when you have Stella Banks at the ready? "I hope I'm just being paranoid and overthinking this. But the look she gave me when she walked away? She's not going away quietly."

"You aren't," Maeve says, bringing me in for a side hug. "Trust your gut, Ainsley. If something feels wrong, don't ignore it. And, lean on us when you need to."

I nod in thanks. "I'm sorry I didn't tell you guys about the arrangement. We thought it would be better if no one knew the truth."

"We understand," Quinn says. "It was funny, though, thinking you pulled one over on us."

"I thought we did so good," I say. "Linc was especially proud of himself."

"Oh, that man was worse than you were," Stella says. "That whole breakfast…the way he looked at you? Let you lead the conversation? Didn't flinch at Maeve's intimidation, or Simon's attempt at it? That man was a smitten kitten from the jump."

I look over to Linc, who I happen to catch looking back at me. I'm greeted with a wink before Porter has to slap him on the back to signal that it's his turn.

"I really love him," I say. "I know I've been acting a little strange since we met, but I promise you, I've never felt more me in my life."

"We can tell," Stella says as she holds my hand. "Through all of this, the one thing you always looked was happy. And I think everyone will agree with me that's all we want for each other, is to find love that makes us happy."

I look back at Linc, who's now laughing with my sisters' partners.

This is what I wanted. This is what was missing from my life. A man who loves me, whom I love in return. Who gets along with my family. Who wants to be part of this with me.

I finally found it. And like hell I'm going to let Katie, or anyone else, tear this away from me.

35

line

We knew today was going to be the hardest game of our season. Not because Milwaukee is that good; I mean, they're decent, but we were favored in every aspect.

The only thing that we needed to be aware of was that we knew Brad was going to give to his new team the full scouting report on how to stop our offense.

AKA: Me.

The man might as well have given his new team a photocopy of our playbook, that's how ready they were for us today.

Anytime they could put double coverage on me, they did. I don't have a touchdown today and barely have fifty yards receiving. It's by far my worst statistical game of the season. Thank God our coaches are the best in the fucking league, because even though they've essentially stopped our offense, our defense has been playing out of their minds. Rockwell doesn't have a catch. They've limited their offense to only field goals. Unfortunately, that's all we've been able to do as well, which is why the game is tied with a minute left.

"All right boys, I think I can speak for everyone when I say that I want nothing to do with overtime," Bryce says in the huddle. "Two plays, one touchdown, and let's get the fuck out of here."

Everyone nods in agreement as we lean in to hear the play call. "Five wide. Play action left. Tight end leak. On two."

The play call shocks me. "Are you sure? They've been on my ass all game."

Bryce shakes his head. "You do what you do. Get open. I'll do the rest."

The man is a league and championship game MVP. Like I'd doubt him. "You got it, Cap."

He repeats the play call again as we break from the huddle, and I line up in my stance. I do my best to read the defense, hoping they're going to play me soft so I can find my seam. They haven't all game, but teams in this situation usually play to prevent the big play, opting to give up the shorter ones.

All I know is that if they give me an inch, and I can find the route, I'm going to go a fucking mile.

I hold my hand out, signaling to the referee that I'm an eligible receiver and to make sure I'm lined up correctly. My gaze happens to fall on Rockwell, who I'm sure by no coincidence at all is standing in my line of sight.

Prick. I don't know why the man still thinks he needs to make my life miserable, but he is. Joke's on him. He got traded to a mediocre team and will probably have to take less money next year when his contract expires. I'm leading the league in receptions for tight ends, have a beautiful woman watching me somewhere in this stadium, and am living a life I never dreamed of. So he might think he's getting in my head, but I couldn't give two shits.

I hear Bryce start his cadence, and I take one more glance at the defense before I take off on the count. I fake the block that the play calls for before sneaking out to the right. Like I thought, the defenders are playing to stop the big play, or covering the receivers we had lined up on the opposite side of the field, which leaves me wide open in the flat. Bryce and I lock eyes, and before I know it, he's gunning the ball to me.

Catch. Turn. Go.

I knew I could make it a few yards, and just out of the corner of my eye, I see one of the safeties heading toward me. I stop on a dime, juking him out as he whiffs on the tackle. Which is when I realize that I have twenty yards to victory.

And I take off. Twenty yards never seems far in practice. Or doing a warmup. And in reality, it's not. But when all you can see is the end zone, a victory, but also knowing you have defenders on your ass doing their best to chase you down, it can seem like a mile.

I see out of the corner of my eye teammates flanking behind me, having my back to try to stop any potential defenders from tackling me. I glance out of the corner of my eye, which is when I see Maddox losing his shit on the sideline, and another teammate just pointing to the end zone.

And the second I cross it, not a soul tackling me, I hold up the ball like it's a fucking trophy.

Because Brad Rockwell be damned, I fucking won.

"Holy shit!" someone yells as Wyatt runs to me and hoists me in the air. I slap his pads a few times before he puts me down. There's still thirty seconds left on the clock, so we have to get off the field before we get a penalty. But that doesn't stop me from doing what I've done after every touchdown this season, crossing my heart for Ainsley.

"What the hell was that?" Bryce asks as we make our way to the sideline.

"You said two plays. Figured if I could do it in one, why not?"

He laughs and slaps me on the back. "Good game, Kincaid. I know they were on your ass. You overcame. Kept your head down and grinded. That's how you do it."

"Thanks, man," I say as we exchange a handshake. A few more teammates come over and congratulate me, and just as I'm catching my breath, the game clock expires, and the Fury have another win on the season.

8-0.

Fuck yeah.

I run out onto the field with my teammates for the post-game handshakes. Luckily this isn't college where we all have to line up and tell everyone good game, meaning I don't need to face Rockwell. However, he apparently missed me because he's in my face just as I get to midfield.

"You held on that last play," he digs, which all I can do is laugh.

"You know I fucking didn't. Then again, you didn't get flagged for shoving Maddox in the second quarter, so who knows what you think should be called on the field."

Sometimes I wish I could still hit people, because I want to punch the smarmy smile off of his smug face. "Oh, I missed you Kincaid. Though, I do get to keep up with your antics in the news. How's Ainsley, by the way? She realize she can do better than you yet?"

I clench my fist at my side do my best to calm my breathing. "Talk about me all you want Rockwell. I don't care. But you keep my girl's name out of your fucking mouth."

"Or what?" he says with a laugh. "You going to punch me? Going to fuck up your contract for some woman?"

"For her? I would. In a fucking heartbeat."

I feel hands pulling me away, and fuck, I gave Rockwell too much. The smile on his face now looks like a damn comic strip villain.

"Come on," Wyatt's words bring me back from wondering what actually constitutes as a punch. "He's not worth it."

I know he isn't. But the look he's giving me now is more sinister than ever. Sure, his favorite pastime was to mess with my head. Try and get me to throw a punch. But now? Now I feel like I inadvertently upped the stakes.

And he's going to take full advantage.

———

"Back to where it all started!"

I laugh, and roll my eyes a little, as Maddox brings over a bucket of beers, as well as a club soda and cranberry for Ainsley. "All right, what are we going to sing?"

"I'm not singing a damn thing," I say as I put my arm around Ainsley as we sit on one of the couches in the VIP area the karaoke bar has made permanent for us. Apparently Maddox is a regular here. "I'm here to observe and to hang out, so none of y'all give me shit."

It's not a normal thing for us to go out and celebrate after a win. Usually we're tired, sore, and just want to collapse into bed. But today was a big win. A hard-fought one. And frankly, after a run-in with Rockwell, I could use a beer. So Wyatt, Maddox, myself, and a few other guys decided to go out and celebrate. But of course, I was only coming if Ainsley could come.

Because yes. I'm a fucking simp for my girl, and I don't give a shit who knows it. It doesn't hurt that she's wearing a dress that has patches of my jersey sewn into it. And she's paired it with cowboy boots and a bow in her hair that makes her look like the innocent girl everyone thinks she is.

Except I know she isn't.

"Ainsley?" Maddox says, tilting his head to the stage. "Do we get a repeat performance?"

"Absolutely not," she says. "That was a one-night-only thing."

"Oh come on, you were great," Maddox says. "What would it take for you to sing again?"

She thinks about it for a second. "Win it all. Then I'll sing whatever you pick."

"Fuck yeah!" Maddox yells as they shake on it. "You got yourself a keeper there, Kincaid."

"Don't I know it." I kiss her temple as we sit back and listen to three members of our defensive line sing an iconic boy band song. They're terrible, but the song is too good to not sing when at karaoke.

We're listening to the performance when my eyes start gazing around the bar. People watching is always phenomenal in Nashville. Being a Sunday, there are a ton of people wearing Fury gear. A fair amount of Milwaukee fans, too, because we always get a host of out-of-town fans who want to visit Nashville and also see their favorite team in one trip. And…what the fuck…

"Am I going crazy, or is that Katie and Dipshit? Together?"

Ainsley sits straight up and looks to wear I'm pointing. And yup, there they are, sitting close together at a high-top table near the bar. She seems to be looking very interested in whatever he's talking about while he's trying his best to pretend to be interesting. At least, that's what I'm going to assume, having known both of them.

"Okay, that's freaking weird," Ainsley says. "Can it be a coincidence that they met on a dating app and they picked this bar out of all the bars in Nashville to go for their date?"

"I believe in coincidences, but not one like that," I say. My spidey-senses are tingling. I don't know what's going on there, but it's nothing good.

"Hey," she says, holding my chin in her fingers. "Ignore them. I'm going to try to. I've missed going out like this. Which I never thought I'd say. So let's try and not have them ruin our night."

"I have too," I admit. I felt like it was the safest thing to do when the headlines and photos started becoming more attacking. Though that didn't seem to help. "I'm sorry I've kept us caged up."

"No apologies. Let's just hope that's all behind us and we can hang out with friends like a normal couple."

"Agree," I say before I lean in. "But if you want to leave, just say the word. We'll get out of here so fucking fast."

"And why is that?"

Little minx knows exactly why, but if she wants to hear the words, why would I hold back?

"Because, I love it when my good girl wears dresses like this. When I can keep it on her as I bury my cock into her pussy. To see my cum drip down her leg. And from the moment I saw you tonight, that's all I could think about. Because when we get home, I'm going to press you against the door, lift up your skirt, and fuck you from behind until you scream."

I pull away just enough to see her eyes heat and her body squirm at my words. "Does that sound good, Ainsley Mae? Or do you want to stay here?"

She nods. "Take me home, Linc."

That's my girl.

In true Irish goodbye fashion, I take Ainsley's hand and pull her up, giving Wyatt a quick nod so he knows we're out, but I'm not spending the next twenty minutes shaking hands with my teammates, who I'll see tomorrow. It's also why I don't bother looking for Maddox, though we do pass him as we head to the elevator to take us to the first floor. He has his eyes on his conquest of the night. I can tell she's older than him, probably in her mid-thirties, but my man doesn't seem deterred. If anything, he's all in.

Good for him.

We duck and weave our way through the crowd and make it to the elevator, making sure we avoid Katie and Dipshit. When we step off, I wasn't prepared for the crowd we'd be walking into on the first floor. I hold on to Ainsley's hand as I snake our way through the crowd. We're almost to the door when I get bumped by someone. Next thing I know I lose hold of Ainsley, but when I turn around to try to look for her, I'm pushed from behind. I assume it's just because the bar is packed; that is, until I turn around and see the man I never want to see again.

"What the fuck are you doing here, Rockwell?"

The bastard has a smug smile on his face that gives me an unsettling feeling. "We're on a bye this week. Told the team I needed to pack up some things at my old place. Figured I'd come out for a drink. Place isn't my style, a little too juvenile. But it'll do for the night."

I don't know why this man is walking around town like he has the biggest bank account out of all of us. He wasn't even the highest paid Fury player, and his contract went with him to Wisconsin. And, the locker room gossip is that if the Fury couldn't find a trade, then they were going to release him mid-contract for behavioral issues inside the clubhouse.

"Well you have fun." I turn back to look for Ainsley, hoping that she's not too far. I can see over most of the people, and I try to look for her hair and the bow she's wearing, and just as I get an eye on her, I feel Rockwell pull me back again.

"You have a lot of nerve, you know that, right?" he says.

"What the fuck are you talking about?"

"I'm in fucking Milwaukee because of you."

"Or maybe you're there because the Fury saw a toxic player and didn't want to infect their locker room. And when they have a better player who doesn't like to start shit with teammates, they choose that option. As far as I'm concerned, this is your find-out stage, Rockwell."

He narrows his eyes. "You've been a pain in my ass since college. Why won't you just go away?"

I step up closer to him, getting right in his face. "You did this to yourself. Now, I need to find my girl and you need to fuck off."

He gives me a shove, and I think about pushing back. For just a second. But I can tell in his eyes he wants this. But I do the thing that I know pisses him off even more. I just turn and walk away.

I keep looking for Ainsley, and I finally spot her toward a side exit that the guys use from time to time to avoid the crowds. I start making my way toward her, when I notice she's literally being pulled out by someone.

Fucking Dipshit.

"Ainsley!" I yell, all but throwing people out of my way to get to her. Which is how I don't notice that I nearly walk over Katie.

"Oh, Linc! Funny seeing you here!"

"It's really not," I say, not having time for her bullshit.

"Where you going?"

"Leaving. Which doesn't concern you."

She's on my heels, following me as I finally get to the exit.

"Let me guess, need to find your girlfriend?"

I don't answer her—again, I feel like silence here is the best way to go—and I'm glad I don't. It's why the second we step out of the bar, I hear every word out of Ainsley's mouth.

"You crazy fucking bitch!"

Stunned doesn't even remotely come close to what I'm feeling as I watch my normally reserved, sometimes shy, never cursing, girlfriend, shriek words I never thought I'd hear coming from her mouth as she all but tackles Katie the second we exit the bar.

"Holy shit! Ainsley!" I go to grab her, pulling her off Katie as she starts pulling her hair. "Not saying that she probably doesn't deserve this, but want to fill me in?"

"Her!" Ainsley points to Katie, who's trying to play the sweet and innocent card. "She did this. She did *all* this. We were right. She set us up."

I have no idea what Ainsley's talking about specifically, but judging by Katie's smug look, she does.

"I don't know what you mean, Ainsley?" Katie pretends to be sincere. "If anything you should be thanking me. I'm the reason you two lovebirds are together."

"So you're going to deny that the reason my ex here decided to follow and stalk me to my car was because you encouraged him to? And that you weren't parked behind a car somewhere, getting every horrible picture you could?"

Katie just shrugs. "I don't know what he told you, but that can't be true. That doesn't sound like something I'd do."

She might've said those words, but the scathing look she sends to Dipshit, who's now cowering away in his guiltiness, says more than her lie just did.

"You're a fucking horrible person," Ainsley says. And out of everything that's happened in the past twenty minutes, Ainsley dropping f-bombs is still the most shocking. "I don't know what your motivation was. Why you wanted to tear Linc down. But we're not going to let you."

"How you going to do that, Ainsley? Fight me? I thought that was Linc's job in this relationship."

I start to open my mouth, but Ainsley beats me to it. And not only that, but she pulls away from me and actually shoves her. "I fight for what's mine. And that includes slapping bitches who fuck with those I love."

Holy shit…my sweet Ainsley Mae might fight a bitch.

"You…you! You ruined everything!" Katie yells, lunging at Ainsley. I hurry and react, picking up Ainsley to get her out of the way, which only sends Katie flying and nearly running into the brick of the building.

"We need to get out of here," I say to Ainsley as I set her back down. When I do, I notice a familiar look in her eye. I've seen it on myself before.

She's ready to fuck someone up.

I try to pull her away, despite the "come at me" stare she's giving Katie, which is why I don't see Dipshit running toward me. That, and he's short.

"Get your hands off of her!" he yells as he tries to tackle me. "She's mine! She's always been mine!"

I turn just in time to see him, and I swing my arm, trying to stop him. The only problem with that is because I don't know what's happening with anything right now, and he's short, Dipshit runs into my outstretched and accidental fist.

"What the fuck?" I mutter as I watch him fall to the ground.

"You hit me!" Dipshit cries out, holding his nose. And yes, I technically did, but no way could I have hit him that hard.

Oh shit…I hit him…

"Oh no, what happened?" Katie says with a vengefulness in her voice I've never heard before. "Looks like someone got in a fight."

"It's…" I don't have the words because I have no idea what's happening right now. I look around, stunned, as Ainsley comes back to my side.

Which is when I see it. Him.

My downfall.

Brad Rockwell. Standing against the building. Phone pointed right at me.

guide to love rule #121

Family will always be there for you. Especially when shenanigans are involved.

36
ainsley

AINSLEY

I just need you all to know that something is going to come out today. There was…a bit of a fight last night after the game. Both Linc and I were involved. It's too convoluted to explain over text, and we still don't know when the pictures or videos are going to come out, but I just wanted to give y'all a heads up.

QUINN

You? Fought? People?

AINSLEY

I did. Wasn't my proudest moment.

QUINN

Was it the bitch?

AINSLEY

Yes.

QUINN

Then worth it.

MAEVE

Let's back up here. What happened?

AINSLEY

It's really too long to text. I'm fine physically, and so is Linc. We're just in a holding period, but I'll message when we know exactly what we're dealing with.

SIMON

I'll sue them. Whoever it is, I don't give a fuck. I've got a guy who could ruin their lives in a week.

STELLA

If you figure out who did this, I'll stalk them until they don't know peace. And then I'll sic Quinn on them. They'll regret the day that they fucked with a Banks.

QUINN

I'm locked and loaded.

MAEVE

We're here if you need us. If you can't tell, the troops are ready to be activated.

LINC HASN'T SAID A LOT TODAY. NEITHER HAVE I. I KNOW HE DIDN'T sleep, and that's because every time I woke up from the hour I dozed off, he was squeezing me tighter than he ever has before.

When we knew we were being photographed and followed, it was one thing. We didn't know what the pictures were going to look like, but we had an idea. We could be prepared.

But for this, we have no idea what's coming. Or when. We know it's going to be nothing good. Not when the three people who hate us most are involved.

As soon as we got home, Linc called his coach and the communications team, letting them know what happened. That there was a dust up, he was trying to break it up, but that he accidentally hit someone. He thought it was best that he owned up to it immediately, given the state of his contract. While Coach McAvoy was glad he did, they were still going to have to investigate. He said he'd talk to the front office and the communications team and be back in touch with us today.

So now we just wait. Wait for whatever photos or video they took to hit the internet. Wait for the Fury to decide Linc's future. I'm convinced that the police are going to show up at my front door any minute and arrest me for assault.

Waiting is the worst.

"How the fuck did all of that happen last night?" he mutters as we sit together on the couch. It's as far as we've been able to get this morning. "One minute everything was fine. Then the next it was just chaos."

"I don't know, but it doesn't feel like an accident."

Once we saw Brad videoing the entire fight, Linc grabbed my hand and we all but ran to his car two blocks away. We half-expected the photos and/or video to come out last night. The fact that nothing has come out yet is more shocking than anything.

It's also making it worse. The longer this drags on, the more anxious we both are.

We're back to silence when a banging on my apartment door makes both of us jump in our seats.

"Stay here," he says as gets up. I don't know who could've gotten through the security in my building. It's not like we have a door man or anything, but there are three security measures to get in.

I turn from my couch to look back, nervous when the knocking keeps coming.

"Who is it?" Linc yells.

"The cavalry!" Simon says. "Now let us in!"

I stand up from the couch, simultaneously laughing and tearing up as Linc opens the door for each of my siblings, as well as their significant others, to come piling through.

"What are y'all doing here?

Maeve raises her eyebrow like my question is dumb. "You

can't send texts like the ones you did this morning and not expect us to react in this exact fashion."

"How did you get in?"

Stella holds up a keycard. "Tracked your location. Still had my key card from when I lived here. Also conveniently ran into someone from the second floor who remembered me. Now tell us what's going on before Simon blows a gasket."

"I'm fine," he says. "I just have three lawyers and a guy who I'm not sure what he actually does for a living on ready in my phone."

Normally that joke would make me laugh, but as we all find seats in my living room, there's nothing to laugh about. Especially when we fill them in on everything that happened.

Of course, the story takes longer to tell, because there are interjections throughout. Those included, but were not limited to:

"You've got to be shitting me!"

"You swore! And slapped her! I'm weirdly proud."

"That whore!"

"Can I rip out his other ACL?"

And, my favorite, of course, from Quinn: "I hope they are together. He doesn't like his dick sucked, and she looks like she gives terrible head. All teeth, I bet."

That helped break up the heaviness in the room.

But it didn't last long.

"So what are you two thinking?" Maeve asks. "Because the more you talk about this, the more I feel like this wasn't accidental."

"We've both been thinking the same thing," Linc says. "If it was just Rockwell? Sure. He's a dick and likes to antagonize. Katie's fucking crazy. And Dipshit isn't far behind. If this was individual, we could chalk it up to just the coincidence of being at the same place and tempers getting heated."

"Side note: I love you call him Dipshit," Stella interrupts. "Sorry. Continue."

"Because he is," Linc says as he and Stella exchange a head nod. "Except last night he was more calculated. He and Katie were definitely working together. I don't know how they joined forces, but that's a thing. The part about Rockwell, though—did he just see a chance and took it? Got lucky that he was at the right place at the right time?"

A light bulb flicks on over me. "You said that he normally never went to that bar with y'all, right?"

Linc nods. "He was never part of our crew. It's not a secret that we go there a lot, especially since Maddox has dubbed it our place, but I don't buy that he's in town for a night and just got an inkling to go and check out a karaoke bar."

"Is it normal for players to stay behind after away games?" Maeve asks.

"It's not typical, but exceptions have been made," Linc says. "If he told them he didn't have time to move all of his things, and they had a bye anyway, I can see them giving him the green light."

"It's just all too coincidental," Stella says as she digs her phone out of her purse. "Did Katie and Brad know each other?"

All eyes are on Linc as he thinks about it for a second. Except Stella, who's been activated into private investigator mode. "Not that I know of. I was introduced to Katie through my agent, but Brad isn't represented by him. Then again, Katie's an independent publicist, so she might work with a lot of sports agencies, for all I know? And she was randomly wearing a T-shirt with his name on the back once. I don't fucking know anymore."

"And where does Dipshit fit in?" Quinn asks. "God, that name just feels right."

"If Katie is as crazy as we think, she could've found him easily," I say. "I still have old pictures of him on social media. I'm sure that line isn't hard to draw. And now that I think about it, I bet that first blog that came out about me? That had to all come from him. He would've been the only one to know those kinds of details who would've talked to her."

"And I'm convinced now that Katie is the one who was the source for all the hit pieces against me," Linc says. "I had to tell her everything when I hired her. She used it all against me."

We all fall silent, letting all the possibilities run through our minds, when an alert goes off on Linc's phone.

"It's the Fury," he says as he answers. "Hello?"

The room is silent as we watch every reaction he has. Because if the photos and videos are as bad as we think—and if the Fury doesn't believe him—that's it. Season over.

And that can't happen. I won't let it.

"Okay, thanks. I'll see you guys in an hour." Linc says as he puts the phone down, the color draining from his face.

"Are they out?"

He nods and navigates to something on his phone. "It's not good."

I suck in a breath as I look over his shoulder. I'm guessing everyone else is reading along with us on their phones, judging by the gasps and cuss words floating in the room.

The Brawl on Broadway: Nashville Fury's Linc Kincaid and girlfriend get into heated fight for all to see

The headline takes some liberties. Sure, the bar was on Broadway, but we were in an alley. And for "all to see" is also a stretch.

But that doesn't matter when there are photos and videos of everything.

Me running toward Katie. Me slapping Katie. In my defense, Jonathan had just slipped up and told me that Katie reached out to him and said she had a way to get me back, but he needed to help her.

But the worst part of the whole video is the clip of Jonathan running into Linc, which is cropped and framed in just a way that absolutely makes it look like Linc punched him.

My heart sinks when I see it. This could be it for Linc. And all because of me.

"I'm so sorry," I say, wrapping my arms around him. "This is all my fault."

"Don't you fucking dare," he says as he pulls me onto his lap. "A smart woman told me once that we were a team. And that's what we are now."

We sit in silence for a second, forgetting that my siblings are all around us, as we try our best to comfort each other. The problem is, there's nothing we can do when we don't know what the future holds.

"He clearly ran into you," Maeve says. "Is he really trying to say he was punched?"

"Apparently," Linc says. "That phone call was also to let me know that Dipshit plans on suing me for injuries and emotional damage. So I guess I need a lawyer."

"Don't you worry, it'll be taken care of," Logan says. "I have plenty at my disposal. Simon does as well. You just tell us what you need and it's done."

"Thanks but—"

He shakes his head. "No buts. It's done."

Linc nods and tears come to my eyes, everything starting to hit me.

"What else can we do?" Quinn asks. "What else did the Fury just say?"

Linc's face is covered in defeat. "They want to talk to me in an hour. Our head of communications. Coach McAvoy. My agent. It doesn't look good. And if everyone is in that talk, and I'm really being sued, I have a feeling I'm about to get suspended. And that's if I'm lucky."

"He could lose his contract," I quickly explain. "He could get cut."

"Absolutely the fuck not!" Simon yells. "And I'm not just saying that because I'm winning two fantasy leagues with you."

Linc just shakes his head. "There's nothing we can do.

Pictures and videos are out. Even if the Fury believes me, it's all the media is going to be talking about. They'll cut me because I'm a distraction. No team will want the drama. I'll be back to where I started, unemployed, with no hopes of ever playing again."

"Like hell we're going to let that happen," Quinn exclaims, rubbing her hands together like she's about to stir some shit up. Which she probably is.

Linc shakes his head. "I appreciate whatever you're thinking of doing, but I don't know what you can do. Plus, this isn't your fight."

"Oh, but it is," Maeve says. "You're family now."

The tears are flowing as I watch each of my family members, and in-laws, looking at us like they're ready to go to battle. I grab hold of Linc's hand, because I can only imagine how overwhelming this is for him.

"This is kind of what we do," I explain. "Let them help us."

He nods. "Thank you. All of you."

Quinn lets out a hoot. "I knew we had one more shenanigan left in us!"

"You shouldn't be this excited about it," Porter says.

"Like hell I shouldn't be," she says. "Plus, Ainsley swore. *Swore*, Porter! And she hit a bitch! This is about to be the most epic takedown the Banks family has ever done!"

"Can I ask a dumb question?" Linc says. "Exactly what is going to happen?"

Stella laughs as she holds up her phone. "I've already been doing some digging, and I'm pretty sure I've just found the gold mine. So what we're going to do is clear your name and take down those three in the process."

Everyone's eyes go wide, and I pray to God I'm not getting my hopes up for nothing. "Really? You found something?"

"Oh yes," Stella says. "And if this works, Linc's name will be cleared, we'll prove that last night was, in fact, a setup, and the trio of trouble will never show their faces in Nashville again."

37
linc

Suspended pending investigation.

It's the best outcome I could've hoped for. Because my contract clearly states that if I'm involved in an altercation where fists are thrown, that I'm going to be removed from the team and my contract is null and void.

I never thought I'd be thankful for video being released, but because it was, Coach, my agent, the general manager, the communications team, and everyone who has a VP in their title, could see what happened. That I did not attack Dipshit. That he ran into me. However, because the video is out there, the team felt it would be best to suspend me until further notice as they investigate the situation.

When I told Ainsley and her siblings the news, they were happy for me, but apparently they don't trust other people's timelines. When this family gets an idea in their heads, they move quickly. Which is why we're here, two days later, in a hotel in Nashville, ready to serve what I've been told is Banks Family Justice.

Whatever that means.

"This seems like a lot," I say as I watch Logan fire up a massive computer system.

"You'll say that frequently about our family," Maeve says. "But you get used to it."

As an only child, I don't know if that will ever happen. Because there's being a part of a big family, then there's being welcomed into a family who's currently setting up a high-tech surveillance system in a hotel room to help you clear your name.

"I'm having deja vu," Simon says.

"Have you guys done this before?" I ask softly as Logan turns on the screens to show a crystal-clear picture of the adjoining room. One that's registered to Brad Rockwell.

"Once," Ainsley whispers. "Only that time Logan wasn't running the cameras, and we had a dominatrix involved."

I have to blink a few times because why was a dominatrix involved, and why is Ainsley saying it so casually? "Excuse me?"

"How is Natasha doing?" Quinn asks as she overhears our conversation.

"Really good," Stella adds. "We got coffee last week."

I feel like I'm going to be saying this a lot, but what kind of family am I getting myself into?

"I'll fill you in later," Ainsley promises as she wraps her hands around my forearm. "Let's just concentrate on today."

I wish I could, but the pessimist in me doesn't see how this is going to work. "Not that I don't trust you guys, because clearly this isn't your first rodeo, but this seems a little far-fetched. Are we sure this is going to work?"

"Oh it'll work," Quinn says. "We're putting a psycho, a narcissist, and a douchebag in a room together. What could go wrong?"

A million things sprint through my brain, but I can't think about them when I hear a voice come through on a speaker Logan has set up. It's Porter, who is down in the lobby with Emmett as our lookouts, with some sort of high-tech ear pieces and microphones.

"Boiled Bunny entering the building," Porter says. "And from what I can tell, she's taking the bait."

Here we fucking go…

When Stella started uncovering the tangled web that Katie, Brad, and Jonathan weaved, the plan we came up with felt a little too crazy. A little ridiculous. But the Banks siblings told me it would work. The partners all gave me affirming head nods.

And so far, much to my surprise, it is. It began with Simon and Logan getting into Brad's hotel room earlier today when he was at the gym to plant the surveillance equipment. I had my doubts they could pull it off, but apparently a well-placed bribe and Simon "knowing a guy" did the trick. And now, step two is complete, as Katie has taken the bait. That one I had more faith in. All that took was Logan sending Katie an email from "Brad" —well, the mirrored email he created to send it to her—asking her to come see him before he left for Milwaukee.

And being that she's his former mistress, she couldn't come fast enough.

That's right. Stella dug. And that's the goldmine.

"She's pulling the trench coat in the hotel move," Porter says. "This is going to be epic."

"Aw, I remember when I did that," Quinn says.

"We don't need to hear story time right now," Maeve whisper-yells. "Plus, we need to keep our voices down. Be safe about this."

That's not a problem for Ainsley and me. We've been holding our breaths since we got here. Not that I don't have faith in the Fury for doing a solid investigation, but if we can get proof that we were set up, and it just so happens to land on their desk, then this saga is going to finally be over with.

Logan adjusts the cameras, one facing the hotel door, another facing the room hooked onto a lamp, and the other expertly hidden in the headboard. It lets us watch every angle on each monitor.

"Showtime," Logan says as we watch Brad's expression of surprise when he hears a knock on the door.

When Brad opens it, he steps back a little, clearly not ready to see Katie standing in the hallway, jacket wide open, and not much underneath.

"Hey, Pookie. Did you miss me?"

She pushes him into the hotel room, Brad stutter stepping back, as she tackles him onto the bed.

"Katie, what are you doing?" Brad asks in a muffled voice as Katie attacks his lips, straddling him, jacket still on.

"What do you think I'm doing, silly? Everything worked. We can be together now. Eeek!"

Katie dives into Brad's mouth, and I watch in horror, but Ainsley turns away.

"I don't think we should be watching this," Ainsley says. "Just tell me when this is over."

"Oh, sweet Ainsley," Quinn says. "Even when she's having sex, she's still our innocent girl."

"It's not that. No one should be watching this."

She's not wrong. I never saw Katie kiss before, but it's like she's trying to swallow Brad's face like she's in some sort of alien movie.

"Ew," we all say in accidental unison. I have to shake out the chills because…no. Just no.

"Katie, Katie, baby," Brad says, doing his best to lift her off of him. "As happy as I am to see you, you've got to catch me up. How did you know where I was staying?"

Katie laughs and playfully smacks his chest. Only by Brad's reaction, I don't think it was very playful. "You told me in your email, Pookie."

"I have no clue what the fuck you're talking about," he says, standing from the bed, I'm guessing to be saved from another attack.

Katie drops her trench coat to the ground, fully revealing a barely-there lace number.

"I love when you play hard to get," Katie says, sitting on the bed, legs crossed. "You wrote me and said that everything worked. That we ruined his life. You got what you wanted. And now because of that, we can be together again!"

Another in-unison chorus comes from our room, only this time it's "oh shit."

Because holy shit…

This is what we needed. Confirmation of the affair. Because if our theories are right, this is what started it all.

Stella did some digging—the woman astounds me with what she can scrape from just from a few social media and Google searches—and found some old photos of the two of them together. Enter Logan—who apparently, along with developing video games, has a hacking hobby—was able to find old texts and messages sent last season between Katie and Brad. Most of them required all of us to wash out our eyes after what we read, but in between the horrible sexts and nudes I'll never be able to unsee, this is what we put together: They were fucking. Brad was married. Brad's wife found out. Brad called off the affair, and his wife still left him. And all of that happened the week before he tore his ACL.

His life literally blew up in front of his eyes. Then I came along and poured salt in every wound.

And if they just keep talking, we could figure out their entire plan.

"Katie, I never sent you that email," Brad says, as he tries to hand her back her coat. "I told you that we were done. The other night was the last time."

"Of course he'd get his dick wet one more time," Quinn says. "Asshole."

"No, you didn't!" Katie screeches. "You told me to ruin his life. Get him cut from the team. By any means possible. And if I did that, you'd take me back. And I did it! It worked. He's suspended but I bet he's getting kicked off soon. I fed every columnist I knew all his dirty laundry. Let every one of them quote me as a source. I ruined my career for you! So why are you breaking your promise, Bradley?"

"Don't call me that. You know I hate being called that."

"Well, I hate being lied to, *Bradley*, so tell me why you don't love me!"

"She's cuckoo for Cocoa Puffs," Ainsley says as I let out a whistle.

"That's an insult to Cocoa Puffs."

The two continue going back and forth when we hear a signal from Emmett.

"Dipshit entering. I repeat, Dipshit on his way up."

"He better have loose lips again," Ainsley says. "I still can't believe he admitted all of that to me."

"What did he actually say?" Stella asks. "I think, in the chaos, we never got back to that part of the story."

"He pulled me away from Linc, conveniently when Brad stepped in front of him," Ainsley begins. "It was all the distraction needed to separate us. Kept going on and on about how he knew that we were fake. That we weren't real. That I could drop the act. And when I told him it wasn't an act, that we were dating, he dragged me outside, but that was so he could yell at me. Which, okay, throw a tantrum. But in that tantrum, he slipped and said that Katie told him we were fake and that if he helped her, that she could guarantee we would break up. Whatever he said after that I'm not sure, because that's when I lost it."

"And that's when you called her a 'crazy fucking bitch!'" Quinn exclaims. "Not going to lie, I've watched that part of the video multiple times."

"She is. And that's why I'm hoping she'll slip today. I have to know her motives," Ainsley says. "She ruined Linc. She tried to ruin me. Was it all just to get Brad back? Was everything just for that?"

"We'll see," Logan says. "Because Dipshit has entered the chat."

"How did you get him here?" Ainsley asks. "You never told me."

Maeve, Stella, and Quinn all give each other guilty looks.

"What did you three do?"

"It wasn't bad," Stella begins before Quinn finishes her thought.

"We just…may have texted him, pretending to be you, and that you broke up with Linc and wanted to see him."

Ainsley gasps. "What? Why would you do that?"

"Because we didn't know what would get him here," Maeve defends. "We know he and Katie weren't actually together. This was the only surefire thing."

"But don't worry," Stella says. "You're not going anywhere near them."

"Damn right she's not," I say as I pull her in front of me.

"Absolutely not," Quinn says. "Because I have a feeling these idiots are about to show their asses in three…two…"

Quinn's countdown is stopped by Dipshit's knock on the door.

"Who the fuck else is coming?" Brad walks over and opens it without looking into the peephole. "What the fuck are you doing here?"

"You aren't Ainsley," Dipshit says as he walks in, carrying a bouquet of flowers. "Katie? Why are you here? And half naked?"

She rolls her eyes. "Ugh. I really need you to stop talking about Ainsley. I thought she was going to be my ticket. Turned out she fucking ruined everything."

Keep talking, Katie. Bury yourself…

"I thought she was perfect! The perfect plan to do what you asked me to do." She turns to Brad, and while I can't exactly see her face from this angle, it's almost like she's reaching for him. "You wanted him gone. You told me though I had to play the long game. That we couldn't do it too quick. We had to let him bury himself. And what better way to bury yourself then by being a shitty boyfriend?"

Gasps echo in our room.

"That's why she pushed for us," Ainsley says quietly. "She thought we'd fail."

"Showed her," I say, kissing her temple. Though, her idea wasn't a bad one. When I first brought Katie on, and she asked me about my dating history, I simply told her there wasn't one. That I wasn't a relationship kind of guy. When she saw the opportunity in front of us, she had to think I'd fuck it up, and she'd be right there to exploit it in the name of Brad Rockwell.

"But no…" Katie continues. "Linc has to go and fall in love with her. But I ramped it up for you, Brad. I planted those articles. Painted him bad. I even fucked this guy for dirt on Ainsley. Lot of good that got me, since all he could tell me is that she's the most boring woman on the planet!"

"Hey!" Dipshit speaks up. "That's the love of my life."

"I think I'm going to puke," Ainsley says. "Also, am I that boring?"

"You're not boring, baby," I say. "You just save up the excitement for special occasions."

All of her siblings laugh at that one. But not too long, because Katie's talking again.

"I don't know what else you wanted me to do!" she yells. "I planted those photos for you. I had them followed. Tipped the bloggers to write bad pieces. Nothing worked. Until last night. He's gone now. And you helped me, Brad. Because you still love me. And now we can be together."

"Here we go," Logan says, triple-checking that everything is recording.

"Except that now it's too fucking late," Brad says. "I told you to get him off the team months ago. *That's* what I asked of you. I wanted him gone before the season started. But getting him a girlfriend turned out to be the worst possible idea. How the fuck was that supposed to help me, when he was prancing around town with that pretty thing on his arm, pretending for the cameras that they were the next best thing?"

"Ha! I knew it!" Dipshit yells. I really don't remember his name, and at this point, I'm not going to try. "I knew they were fake!"

Both Katie and Brad look over to Dipshit in confusion. "Why are you still here?"

"Because!" He straightens himself up to feel important before answering Brad's question. "I was told Ainsley would be here. Is she meeting us?"

"No," Brad says point blank. "This is my hotel room. I don't know how you wound up here—how either of you did—but this insanity needs to stop. I never thought I'd say this, but I can't wait to be back in Milwaukee."

"I refuse," Dipshit says, crossing his arms and sitting at the desk in the room. "I was told that if I helped take down Linc that I'd get Ainsley back, and I'm not leaving until I do."

"Well, you're going to be waiting for a while," Brad says, walking toward his packed suitcase. "I knew going along with your plan was a bad idea."

"What do you mean, a bad idea?" Katie says. "It worked perfect! And you were excited to help. Because you still love me."

He laughs at her, and for just a second I feel bad for Katie. But just a second, because she just admitted to working with him to try to ruin my career. "I helped you because even though ruining Kincaid's career doesn't do anything for me now, he's still getting what he deserves. That suspension he got? He won't bounce back from it. But that's why I helped. For shits and giggles."

"But—" Katie looks like she's going to cry. Or kill him. One of the two with her. "But what about what you told me at the beginning of the season? Doesn't that mean anything?"

"Nope," Brad says without a care in the world. "We started this so I wouldn't get traded. That he'd get kicked off the team and I'd get my spot back when I returned from injury. But that happened a little too late, Katie. So in my opinion, our deal is null and void. We're not getting back together. Not now. Not ever. Now, you two can do whatever the fuck you want to do here. I have a plane to catch."

There's a silence in the room next to us. It lasts maybe five seconds, but when it breaks, it nearly shatters the glass windows. Because the screech that Katie lets out as she runs over to Brad, jumps on his back, and starts punching him is loud enough to wake the entire floor.

"Holy shit," Ainsley says in awe.

"Holy shit, she swore! She swore!" Quinn starts jumping up and down. "Best. Day. Ever."

I'm speechless. I can't believe what I'm seeing. Katie punches Brad while latched on his back, Dipshit hiding behind the bed to not get caught in the crossfire. And in this room, I overhear Maeve on the phone.

"Yes, I'd like to report a disturbance in Room 418. It sounds like a boxing match up here...yes...thank you."

While I'd love to keep watching, I only have one thing on my mind right now.

"Did you get it, Logan?"

He turns to me, taking his glasses off as he flashes me a smile. "Every single word."

guide to love rule #11

Everything happens for a reason.

38
ainsley

THERE WAS A TIME NOT TOO LONG AGO THAT I WAS SITTING AT THIS exact table at The Joint. My family was surrounding me. We'd just finished helping Quinn and Porter take care of their problem.

And I'd never felt more alone in my life.

Oh, how fast things can change.

Now here we are, two weeks later, gathered around the same table. I have Linc next to me, his arm around me, because the man doesn't go too long without touching me in some way. My head is on his shoulder as we take in our siblings and their conversations, just basking in the lightness of the night.

Because today was the day we were waiting for all week with bated breath.

Linc was reinstated. He was found to be at no fault, in not only the eyes of the Fury, but in the courts.

"To Ainsley and Linc!" Simon raises his glass. "And to the last Banks family shenanigan!"

"I'll drink to that," Logan says. "I've committed too many close-call crimes for this family."

Maeve kisses his cheek. "And we love you for it."

"They were pretty fun, though," Stella says. "I don't love

what we all had to go through for them to happen, but at least we made the payoff fun."

"And satisfying," I say. "Everyone got what was coming to them."

And in Linc's case, it was more than we could've hoped for.

Once security came up to the room, and saw the room looking like an eighties rock band just trashed it, Katie clawing at Brad, and Jonathan hiding in a corner, the three were detained for vandalism and destruction of property. Not going to lie, all of that was icing on the cake, considering we got everything we wanted and more from their videoed confessions.

A link was magically emailed to every important person in the Fury organization the next day. And for giggles, a few links were sent to some league officials. You know, in case they wanted to know that one of their marquee players was actively trying to sabotage another player's career.

They did. And Brad Rockwell was suspended for the rest of the season. And according to Linc, his contract was up at the end of the year. And no one wants a toxic teammate that tries to destroy the career of another guy on the same team.

Too bad. So sad.

As for Linc and the Fury, they were quick to release a statement clearing him of any wrongdoing. They said that upon further review, and getting more evidence into the situation, that Linc was not in breach of his contract, and that the incident in question was an accident. They did suspend him for a game, which he didn't fight in the least. He actually suggested it to make sure that it didn't seem like they were being too lenient on him. Also, all pending court cases against him have been dropped.

Oh, yeah, Jonathan dropped his lawsuit. No idea why, but maybe it had something to do with Logan also emailing the link of the hotel debacle to human resources of the hospital. And pointing out the day that he followed me to my car.

Maybe. I'm not sure though.

He also put in his two weeks' notice.

Oh no. I'm devastated…

As for Katie, at first we thought she went into hiding. After she was released by hotel security, she went dark. Literally. Deleted all of her social media, both work and personal. We tried to call her cell phone on a blocked number just to see what was going to happen, but it said the number was disconnected. At first, I hoped that she was somewhere getting help. Because yes, she was crazy. And she tried to ruin my and Linc's life. But at the end of the day, mental health is important, and if she needed help, I hoped she was somewhere getting it.

That is until last night when she created a new social media handle, and started posting multiple part stories about how Brad loved her and airing all their dirty laundry. We didn't want to watch it. The woman ruined our lives in the name of this man's "love." But when she started talking about how she'd sneak out of the man's house because his wife was coming home, we couldn't turn it off. Luckily, we haven't got to the part of the series where Linc and I come in. But once it happens, Simon, Logan, and the Fury media team have lawyers ready for cease and desists orders.

But until then, we're going to sit back and let her burn everything to the ground.

"This feels like the end of an era," Stella says as she leans into Emmett. "No more shenanigans. We're all together and happy. Our lives are going to be so boring now."

"I think boring is needed," Maeve says as Logan puts his arm around her chair. "But, can we all save the date for the last weekend in February?"

Everyone mumbles questions, and I look over to Linc. "Any plans?"

He shakes his head. "We'll have won the championship by then. So I'm down for whatever."

I hope they do. They lost last week. And honestly, all the cards were stacked against them. Linc was out for his suspension. Maddox tweaked his ankle and sat out the second half. Everything was just going against them.

But now they're refocused, Linc is back next week, and Maddox apparently "slapped some tape on it and it's good to go." Whatever that means. All I know is that I can't wait for my first championship game. Because I know they're going to be there. I can feel it.

"So if everyone is free the last weekend in February," Maeve continues, "we'd like to invite you all to Jamaica. It's about time we actually said our vows in front of family and friends."

A chorus of "hell yeahs" and applause are all that can be heard as we run to hug Maeve and Logan.

"Oh, and no one needs to worry about flights," Logan announces. "Because why have a private jet if you can't fly your family to an island for a week?"

More cheering erupts as Linc looks at me. "Have I said thank you?"

"For what?"

"For bringing me into this family."

For any other person, this could be chalked up as a joke about having a brother-in-law who owns a private jet. But knowing Linc how I do, that smile, with that thank you, means more.

Our family is big and loud and in each other's business. The exact opposite of anything Linc knew to be true after his childhood. We could've scared him off. He could've told me "thanks, but no thanks." But he didn't. If anything, he's fitting in with us like he was always meant to be here.

"You're welcome," I say. But before I can say anything else, Simon slaps Linc on the back.

"You motherfuckers played pool without me a few weeks ago, and I believe it's time for my challenge."

The guys laugh and all stand up, but not before giving each of their women a kiss before they leave.

"I need to use the restroom," Charlie says as she stands from the table. "Anyone else?"

We all shake our head as our future sister-in-law grabs her purse and heads toward the back. Which gives us a chance to just watch our men walk to the pool tables.

"Do you know, for the first time in our lives, we're all, at the same time, in not only relationships, but healthy ones?" Quinn says.

"Damn, you're right."

"I'm still never getting over you swearing," Stella says. "It's like a whole new Ainsley!"

I shrug. "I pick and choose when I do."

I don't tell them that I mostly use the words in the bedroom. Because now that I know I can yell "Holy shit!" when Linc eats me out? It's a much better experience.

"Quinn's right," Maeve continues. "We're all happy. In solid relationships. Have men who love us and who get along with each other. I mean, look at them."

If you didn't know that these men were all randomly grouped together, you'd never know it. You have Linc and Porter talking about something that's making them both use a lot of hand gestures. If I had to guess, it's something college football related. And I'm going to stay with that guess, because I see Emmett inserting himself into the conversation. Then you have Logan and Simon, who are in the middle of something before Charlie summons Simon away. We watch as she whispers into his ear before he's throwing down the pool cue and quickly telling everyone goodbye.

Good for them.

"Did we really just get lucky?" Stella asks. "I hate to think all of our lives were based on luck."

"Maybe not luck, but they were based in moments," Maeve adds. "Heartbreak. Missed flights. Crazy people trying to fuck with us."

"So many crazies," I joke.

"But we're here," Maeve says, holding up her mostly empty glass, and we all follow. "To the Banks sisters, and to the men we love."

"God help them," Quinn adds.

We chuckle and take sips of our drinks just when the guys come back to the table. Except instead of chatting, or talking like they were when they left, they all have odd looks on their faces.

"What did you guys do?"

Maeve's question is valid as Logan answers. "What makes you think we did anything, love?"

"Because I have a child, so I know a guilty look. And all of you look like you just spilled Kool-Aid on a white carpet."

"Not necessarily," Emmett says. "But we do have a question for you four."

We share the same confused look before Stella speaks up. "And what's that?"

They look to Emmett, giving him an encouraging nod. "I know this was supposed to be a night out here, but we were wondering if we could all go to Logan and Maeve's house to play video games?"

I swallow my chuckle as all four of these men look at their corresponding sister with pleading in their eyes.

"I've never seen his setup before," Linc continues. "And the clout I'd get with the team? Endless."

"And! He has a new prototype," Porter says. "Also, how many nights do we have not only a baby sitter, but also a fill-in bartender? Not many."

"Obviously you ladies can come too," Logan adds. "Name the snacks and wine you want. I'll have it delivered to the house and it'll be there by the time we arrive."

The four of us look at each other, all doing our best to keep in the laughter we want to let out. And how can we say no? I know I can't. Not when Linc is giving me puppy dog eyes and I'm promised a night with my favorite people in the world.

"Ice cream," Maeve says, and we all nod in agreement. "Lots of ice cream."

"Done and done," Logan says. "You're the best."

The four of them start celebrating—actually high-fiving like they just pulled off the con of the century.

"They're ours, huh?" Quinn asks.

"They are," I say. "And we wouldn't have it any other way."

epilogue

Linc

"All right, boys, we need one more. Right now."

The situation isn't lost on any of us. We didn't need Bryce to remind us that it's now or never.

There's six seconds left in the biggest game of our careers. Sure, some of these guys have been to the big game before. Been on the biggest stage there is in professional football. But they're the first ones to tell you that what you did in the past doesn't mean anything in the present. It's what you do right now.

And boy, isn't that the story of my life.

"Okay, here's what we're gonna do," Bryce says as he calls out the play.

With every formation and every position he calls out in our code, it hits me that the ball's coming to me. While I shouldn't be surprised because of the season I've had, the gravity still hits me like a ton of bricks. I had a good game tonight. I haven't reached the end zone yet, but I'm close to a hundred yards receiving. But those yards aren't gonna mean shit if I don't catch this pass.

"Ready…break!"

We all clap our hands in the huddle before going to our formation. Miami's defense is lined up exactly the way we hoped for our final play of the game. We're seven yards from the end zone. A little too far to run, but not far enough that the defense can rule it out.

Now I just need to do what I've been doing all season. And that's score a fucking touchdown.

I close my eyes for just a second, doing my best to block out the noise. The noise of the stadium. The noise in my head. The voice of the little devil that likes to perk up every once in a while telling me that I don't deserve to be here. I have to calm them. This without a doubt is the biggest play of my life. And like hell if I'm gonna let intrusive thoughts or a raucous crowd get in the way of what I need to do.

Time is going to expire in the middle of this play. Sure, if we don't score—and if the defense doesn't force a turnover—we could go to overtime. We had to do it in the second round of the playoffs and we'll do it again. But nobody wants that. I sure as hell don't. I'm gonna catch this pass. And then celebrate the best season of my fucking life.

I look over to the ref, making sure I'm lined up correctly as Bryce starts calling out his cadence. I shake my fingers, antsy to run where I need to go, but doing everything I can to not jump off early. Bryce yells for the go and we're all off.

I run a few yards up, then fake left before cutting right to the corner of the end zone. I'm Bryce's first option as long as I'm open. Miami only put one defender on me. And while he's given me fits all game, I've been able to beat him more times than not. And like hell if I'm going to let him beat me now.

I turn exactly when I'm supposed to, the ball already zinging through the air from Bryce's hand. He leaves it up a little high, but not so far that I won't be able to jump and grab it. We talked about this in the locker room at halftime. I have the height advantage in this matchup. Bryce told me if we had this look where he was going to throw it, and he's putting it right on the money.

Jumping off the ground is the last thing I remember before everything starts turning into a haze. I'm in the air. My arms reach up to catch the ball. I feel the leather in my hands and secure it before glancing at my feet to make sure I'm fully in the end zone.

And then I fall to the ground. Ball in hand.

Touchdown.

Holy fucking shit we just won it all.

The next however many seconds are a fucking blur. Music is playing. Whistles are blowing. Fans are screaming. My teammates are jumping on me where I can't even get up.

Three in four, baby. Three in fucking four.

Emotion runs over me as one of my teammates, likely Wyatt, lifts me up off the ground. I feel tears pooling in my eyes as we celebrate together, confetti raining down on the field. I'm hugging everyone I see, all while I still have the ball in my hand. I hope nobody is coming to get this, because they're gonna have to pry it from my cold dead hands.

My teammates start jogging to the center of the field when I notice a camera capturing everything. I'd be remiss if I didn't turn to it and cross my heart like I've done after every touchdown this season.

Ainsley Mae...the reason I'm here. The love of my life. She says I saved her that night, but that's a lie. She saved me.

Would I even be here without her? Part of me wants to say I would, but honestly, I'm not sure. Even without her, Katie and Brad would still have been working against me. It might not have played out the exact way it did, but their plan was in motion long before a beautiful nurse ran into me one random day at a hospital. They wanted to destroy me long before I saw the woman I was supposed to spend the rest of my life with at a karaoke bar.

I don't know how this season would have turned out if she wouldn't have walked into my life—literally. But I do know that I'm standing here, part of the championship winning team, and it's because of her. She's the reason. She's *my* reason.

"Holy shit! We fucking won!" I nearly fall over when

Maddox jumps on my back, shaking the hell out of me. "You fucking did it bro! You're a fucking beast."

"Thanks, but we were able to get that last drive because of the defense. You guys played your asses off tonight."

We share a hug before stepping away and slapping each other on the pads. "Tonight's celebration is going to be fucking epic! I have a feeling I'm going to remember it for the rest of my life!"

I can only laugh as we start making our way to the center of the field, confetti still coming down from the roof of the dome we're playing at in Las Vegas.

"Celebrating this kind of win in Vegas, it's the stuff guys dream about," I say.

Maddox slaps my pads again. "Hell yeah it is. You're coming, right?"

I nod. "Wouldn't miss it for the world."

And that's true. I might be bringing Ainsley, because besides my teammates, there's no one else I want to celebrate with than her. And while having a private celebration does sound good, we have plenty of time for that. There's only one night that you win it all and get to celebrate with the brothers around you that got the job done.

When everything came out of what Brad and Katie were doing, every single one of my teammates came to my defense. Each one made sure to tell the media in every interview they were doing how toxic Brad was as a teammate and how our locker room got better when I entered. Every one of them had my back. Pre and post sabotage.

But more than that, they've been my friends, my confidants, my brothers. So hell yeah, we're gonna celebrate. And if Maddox has his way, I'm guessing it's gonna be at some fucking karaoke bar in Las Vegas.

The next few minutes are a scramble as we're given our championship hats and are escorted onto the field. I don't know how the hell they built a stage in five minutes, but it's there and we're ushered toward it. I know I'm supposed to follow the pack, but I also know that family and loved ones of the winning team come onto the field to celebrate, and I'm not taking another step until I have Ainsley in my arms.

I do my best to search through the crowd, which is nothing but excited chaos. Part of me wonders if I'll be able to find her in the sea of people. But when I see her running toward me, wearing the jersey I got her all those months ago, I realize that I'd be able to find her anywhere.

"Aah!" she yells, launching herself into my arms. She wraps her arms and legs around me, squeezing me as tight as she can.

"You did it." she whispers. "I'm so proud of you."

Hearing those words and hearing that sentiment makes the tears come back.

It's been a long time since I've heard that I made someone proud. I know when my grandmother was alive, even when I made it hard as hell on her, she was proud of me. She might not have loved every decision I made. And God knows she would've beat my ass for some of the shit I did after she passed away. But at the end of the day, she was proud.

I take a second and close my eyes, burying my head into Ainsley's shoulder. I don't know if I believe in the afterlife, but I'm choosing to right now. Because that belief lets me hope that my parents are looking down on me, smiling with pride in their eyes. I hope that they're proud of the man I've become.

And while they aren't here with me physically, this woman is. The one who always knew I could be a better man. Who sees my work and knows what I've done to get here.

"I love you Ainsley Mae. Thank you for believing in me," I say, meeting her lips with a kiss. I wish I could deepen it, but I make myself release, and I'm glad I do. Because the look in her eye and the smile on her face… this is what I wouldn't remember when I think back to this night.

"I love you too, Linc Kincaid. Forever."

I smile and give her one more kiss on the forehead. "Promise?"

She gives me the best smile and a slight nod. "Cross my heart."

Thank you so much for reading Good Girl's Guide to Love. I hope you loved Linc and Ainsley just as much as I did! Of course, I couldn't end it here. There need to be one more chapter. Because we have to see how Linc is going to ask Ainsley to marry him. Check it out in the bonus scene!

Made with Flodesk

acknowledgments

I always cry at the end of a series. I did it with the Fury and also with Rolling Hills.

But when I tell you that I SOBBED when I wrote the final Banks sisters chapter, I don't think I'm doing what I did justice. I'm talking full on ugly tears. Think the Grey's Anatomy GIF with Sandra Oh saying "SOMEONE SEDATE ME!"

That was me.

I love these sisters, and this family, with my whole heart. I've never in my entire author career had as much fun writing books than I did with the Guide to Love series. There was a part of me in each of these sisters that was so personal, and it warmed my heart when readers have said they've related as well. And that's what you want as an author.

But I also know when it's time to say goodbye. They'll always have a voice in my brain, but I also know when it's time to move on to a new chapter. And what a chapter it will be.

Because I'm going back to my sports roots. And I can't WAIT to tell everyone what I have planned.

Now, to the thank yous…

Once again, the biggest thank you for this book has to be the staff at Panera and my magic booth(s). I'm convinced now that I can't write anywhere else, so thank you to the lovely staff, my awesome booth, the Unlimited Sip Club, and numerous Cinnamon Crunch Bagels. Y'all are the real MVPs.

To my parents. As always, you're my biggest cheerleaders even if you still have no idea what I'm doing.

Amanda, who would have thought when we met nine years ago that one day we'd be here together? Thank you for keeping my life in order. Thank you for reminding me to drink water. And thank you for being my best friend. I promise I won't fire you this week.

Kelly, you've been with me on this book journey since day one. Not only are you an amazing alpha reader, but you are an amazing friend.

Valentine, thank you for everything you, your mom, and the VPR team have done for me. Thanks for talking me off the ledge more times than I can count.

To my author tribe, you make this business fun and not so lonely. Thank you to Janice for being my writing buddy every morning. To my work wife Bella for the constant cheerleading. And Julia, you keep me sane most days. Thank you for talking me off many ledges.

Kiezha, thank you for correcting my bad grammar habits and being an amazing editor. Michele, thank you for dotting the Is and crossing the Ts.

Corinne, I'm here because of you. If you wouldn't have given me a chance I wouldn't have started writing. You forever changed my life.

Last but not least: Readers. I love you all. Whether this was your first book by me, or you've been here since Reformation, I'm truly thankful for all of you. The way you've loved the Banks sisters has given me a joy I didn't know there could be. There are so many amazing authors you could be reading. I'm humbled that you chose me.

about the author

Known for her witty sense of humor, Chelle Sloan is a former sports editor who after completing her Master's degree in journalism, decided to become a romance author. You know, because that's the normal path to writing happily ever afters.

An Ohio native, she's fiercely loyal to Cleveland sports, is the owner of way too many — yet not enough — tumblers and will be a New Kids on the Block fan until the day she dies. She does her best writing at Panera in her magic booth. When she's not writing, she's trying to learn to bake, fixing up her condo (badly and by watching YouTube videos), or falling in love with a book.

As for her own happily every after? Maybe one day...

Stay up to date with all things Chelle & join the VIP Squad!